P9-EFI-720

The
ORDER

ALSO BY DANIEL SILVA

The New Girl

The Other Woman

House of Spies

The Black Widow

The English Spy

The Heist

The English Girl

The Fallen Angel

Portrait of a Spy

The Rembrandt Affair

The Defector

Moscow Rules

The Secret Servant

The Messenger

Prince of Fire

A Death in Vienna

The Confessor

The English Assassin

The Kill Artist

The Marching Season

The Mark of the Assassin

The Unlikely Spy

DANIEL Silva

A NOVEL

The ORDER

HARPER

An Imprint of HarperCollins*Publishers*

HarperCollins books may be purchased for educational, business, or sales promotional use. For information, please email the Special Markets Department at SPsales@harpercollins.com.

FIRST EDITION

Library of Congress Cataloging-in-Publication Data has been applied for.

ISBN 978-0-06-283484-3
ISBN 978-0-06-283531-4 (International Edition)

20 21 22 23 24 LSC 10 9 8 7 6 5 4 3 2 1

As always, for my wife, Jamie, and my children, Lily and Nicholas

*When Pilate saw that he was accomplishing nothing,
but rather that a riot was starting, he took water and
washed his hands in front of the crowd, saying, "I am
innocent of this man's blood; see to that yourselves." And
all the people answered, "His blood shall be on us and our
children!"*

—MATTHEW 27:24–25

*Every misfortune that subsequently befell the Jews—
from the destruction of Jerusalem to Auschwitz—
carried an echo of that invented blood pact from the
trial.*

—ANN WROE, *PONTIUS PILATE*

*You have to be willingly ignorant of the past not to know
where all this leads.*

—PAUL KRUGMAN, THE *NEW YORK TIMES*

VATICAN CITY

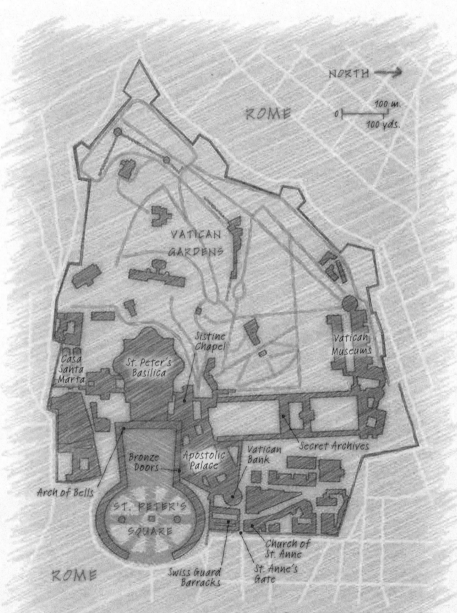

NORTH →

ROME

0   100 m.
    100 yds.

VATICAN
GARDENS

Vatican
Museums

Sistine
Chapel

Casa
Santa
Marta

St. Peter's
Basilica

Secret Archives

Vatican
Bank

Bronze
Doors

Apostolic
Palace

Arch of Bells

ST. PETER'S
SQUARE

Church of
St. Anne

St. Anne's
Gate

Swiss Guard
Barracks

ROME

His Holiness Pope Paul VII was introduced in *The Confessor*, the third book of the Gabriel Allon series. Subsequently, he appeared in *The Messenger* and *The Fallen Angel*. Born Pietro Lucchesi, he is the former Patriarch of Venice and the direct successor of Pope John Paul II. In my fictitious version of the Vatican, the papacies of Joseph Ratzinger and Jorge Mario Bergoglio, the supreme pontiffs Benedict XVI and Francis, did not occur.

PART ONE

INTERREGNUM

1

ROME

THE CALL ARRIVED AT 11:42 p.m. Luigi Donati hesitated before answering. The number displayed on the screen of his *telefonino* belonged to Albanese. There was only one reason why he would ring at such an hour.

"Where are you, Excellency?"

"Outside the walls."

"Ah, yes. It's a Thursday, isn't it?"

"Is there a problem?"

"Better not to say too much on the phone. One never knows who might be listening."

The night into which Donati stepped was damp and cold. He was dressed in a black clerical suit and Roman collar, not the fuchsia-trimmed cassock and simar he wore around the office, which was how men of his ecclesiastical rank referred to the Apostolic Palace. An archbishop, Donati served as private secretary to His Holiness Pope Paul VII. Tall and lean, with rich dark hair and movie-idol features, he had recently celebrated his sixty-third birthday. Age had done nothing to diminish his good looks. *Vanity Fair* magazine had recently christened him "Luscious Luigi." The article had caused him no end of embarrassment inside the backbiting world of the Curia. Still, given Donati's well-deserved reputation for ruthlessness, no one had dared to mention it to his face. No one but the Holy Father, who had teased him mercilessly.

Better not to say too much on the phone . . .

Donati had been preparing himself for this moment for a year or more, ever since the first mild heart attack, which he had concealed from the rest of the world and even much of the Curia. But why tonight of all nights?

The street was oddly quiet. Deathly quiet, thought Donati suddenly. It was a palazzo-lined avenue just off the Via Veneto, the sort of place a priest rarely set foot—especially a priest educated and trained by the Society of Jesus, the intellectually rigorous and sometimes rebellious order to which Donati belonged. His official Vatican car, with its SCV license plates, waited curbside. The driver was from the Corpo della Gendarmeria, the Vatican's 130-member police force. He headed westward across Rome at an unhurried pace.

He doesn't know . . .

On his mobile phone Donati scanned the websites of the leading Italian newspapers. They were in the dark. So were their colleagues in London and New York.

"Turn on the radio, Gianni."

"Music, Excellency?"

"News, please."

It was more drivel from Saviano, another rant about how Arab and African immigrants were destroying the country, as if the Italians weren't more than capable of making a fine mess of things themselves. Saviano had been badgering the Vatican for months about a private audience with the Holy Father. Donati, with no small amount of pleasure, had refused to grant it.

"That's quite enough, Gianni."

The radio went blessedly silent. Donati peered out the window of the luxury German-made sedan. It was no way for a Soldier of Christ to travel. He supposed this would be his final journey across Rome by chauffeured limousine. For nearly two decades he had served as something like the chief of staff of the Roman Catholic Church. It had been a tumultuous time—a terrorist attack on St. Peter's, a scandal involving antiquities and the Vatican Museums, the scourge of priestly sexual abuse— and yet Donati had relished every minute of it. Now, in the blink of an eye, it was over. He was once again a mere priest. He had never felt more alone.

The car crossed the Tiber and turned onto the Via della Conciliazione, the broad boulevard Mussolini had carved through Rome's slums. The floodlit dome of the basilica, restored to its original glory, loomed in the distance. They followed the curve of Bernini's Colonnade to St. Anne's Gate, where a Swiss Guard waved them onto the territory of the city-state. He was dressed in his night uniform: a blue tunic with a white schoolboy collar, knee-length socks, a black beret, a cape against the evening chill. His eyes were dry, his face untroubled.

He doesn't know . . .

The car moved slowly up the Via Sant'Anna—past the barracks

of the Swiss Guard, the church of St. Anne, the Vatican print-ing offices, and the Vatican Bank—before coming to a stop next to an archway leading to the San Damaso Courtyard. Donati crossed the cobbles on foot, boarded the most important lift in all of Christendom, and ascended to the third floor of the Apostolic Palace. He hurried along the loggia, a wall of glass on one side, a fresco on the other. A left turn brought him to the papal apartments.

Another Swiss Guard, this one in full dress uniform, stood straight as a ramrod outside the door. Donati walked past him without a word and went inside. Thursday, he was thinking. Why did it have to be a Thursday?

EIGHTEEN YEARS, THOUGHT DONATI AS he surveyed the Holy Father's private study, and nothing had changed. Only the tele-phone. Donati had finally managed to convince the Holy Father to replace Wojtyla's ancient rotary contraption with a modern multiline device. Otherwise, the room was exactly the way the Pole had left it. The same austere wooden desk. The same beige chair. The same worn Oriental rug. The same golden clock and crucifix. Even the blotter and pen set had belonged to Wojtyla the Great. For all the early promise of his papacy—the promise of a kinder, less repressive Church—Pietro Lucchesi had never fully escaped the long shadow of his predecessor.

Donati, by some instinct, marked the time on his wristwatch. It was 12:07 a.m. The Holy Father had retired to the study that evening at half past eight for ninety minutes of reading and writing. Ordinarily, Donati remained at his master's side or just down the hall in his office. But because it was a Thursday, the one night of the week he had to himself, he had stayed only until nine o'clock.

Do me a favor before you leave, Luigi . . .

Lucchesi had asked Donati to open the heavy curtains covering the study's window. It was the same window from which the Holy Father prayed the Angelus each Sunday at noon. Donati had complied with his master's wishes. He had even opened the shutters so His Holiness could gaze upon St. Peter's Square while he slaved over his curial paperwork. Now the curtains were tightly drawn. Donati moved them aside. The shutters were closed, too.

The desk was tidy, not Lucchesi's usual clutter. There was a cup of tea, half empty, a spoon resting on the saucer, that had not been there when Donati departed. Several documents in manila folders were stacked neatly beneath the old retractable lamp. A report from the Archdiocese of Philadelphia regarding the financial fallout of the abuse scandal. Remarks for next Wednesday's General Audience. The first draft of a homily for a forthcoming papal visit to Brazil. Notes for an encyclical on the subject of immigration that was sure to rile Saviano and his fellow travelers in the Italian far right.

One item, however, was missing.

You'll see that he gets it, won't you, Luigi?

Donati checked the wastebasket. It was empty. Not so much as a scrap of paper.

"Looking for something, Excellency?"

Donati glanced up and saw Cardinal Domenico Albanese eyeing him from the doorway. Albanese was a Calabrian by birth and by profession a creature of the Curia. He held several senior positions in the Holy See, including president of the

Pontifical Council for Interreligious Dialogue, and archivist and librarian of the Holy Roman Church. None of that, however, explained his presence in the papal apartments at seven minutes past midnight. Domenico Albanese was the camerlengo. It was his responsibility alone to issue the formal declaration that the throne of St. Peter was vacant.

"Where is he?" asked Donati.

"In the kingdom of heaven," intoned the cardinal.

"And the body?"

Had Albanese not heard the sacred calling, he might have moved slabs of marble for his living or hurled carcasses in a Calabrian abattoir. Donati followed him along a brief corridor, into the bedroom. Three more cardinals waited in the half-light: Marcel Gaubert, José Maria Navarro, and Angelo Francona. Gaubert was the secretary of state, effectively the prime minister and chief diplomat of the world's smallest country. Navarro was prefect of the Congregation for the Doctrine of the Faith, guardian of Catholic orthodoxy, defender against heresy. Francona, the oldest of the three, was the dean of the College of Cardinals. As such, he would preside over the next conclave.

It was Navarro, a Spaniard of noble stock, who addressed Donati first. Though he had lived and worked in Rome for nearly a quarter century, he still spoke Italian with a pronounced Castilian accent. "Luigi, I know how painful this must be for you. We were his faithful servants, but you were the one he loved the most."

Cardinal Gaubert, a thin Parisian with a feline face, nodded profoundly at the Spaniard's curial bromide, as did the three laymen standing in the shadow at the edge of the room: Dr.

Octavio Gallo, the Holy Father's personal physician; Lorenzo Vitale, chief of the Corpo della Gendarmeria; and Colonel Alois Metzler, commandant of the Pontifical Swiss Guard. Donati, it seemed, was the last to arrive. It was he, the private secretary, who should have summoned the senior princes of the Church to the bedside of the dead pope, not the camerlengo. Suddenly, he was racked by guilt.

But when Donati looked down at the figure stretched upon the bed, his guilt gave way to overwhelming grief. Lucchesi was still wearing his white soutane, though his slippers had been removed and his zucchetto was nowhere to be seen. Someone had placed the hands upon the chest. They were clutching his rosary. The eyes were closed, the jaw slack, but there was no evidence of pain on his face, nothing to suggest he had suffered. Indeed, Donati would not have been surprised if His Holiness woke suddenly and inquired about his evening.

He was still wearing his white soutane . . .

Donati had been the keeper of the Holy Father's schedule from the first day of his pontificate. The evening routine rarely varied. Dinner from seven to eight thirty. Paperwork in the study from eight thirty until ten, followed by fifteen minutes of prayer and reflection in his private chapel. Typically, he was in bed by half past ten, usually with an English detective novel, his guilty pleasure. *Devices and Desires* by P. D. James lay on the bedside table beneath his reading glasses. Donati opened it to the page marked.

Forty-five minutes later Rickards was back at the scene of the murder . . .

Donati closed the book. The supreme pontiff, he reckoned,

had been dead for nearly two hours, perhaps longer. Calmly, he asked, "Who found him? Not one of the household nuns, I hope."

"It was me," replied Cardinal Albanese.

"Where was he?"

"His Holiness departed this life from the chapel. I discovered him a few minutes after ten. As for the exact time of his passing . . ." The Calabrian shrugged his heavy shoulders. "I cannot say, Excellency."

"Why wasn't I contacted immediately?"

"I searched for you everywhere."

"You should have called my mobile."

"I did. Several times, in fact. There was no answer."

The camerlengo, thought Donati, was being untruthful. "And what were you doing in the chapel, Eminence?"

"This is beginning to sound like an inquisition." Albanese's eyes moved briefly to Cardinal Navarro before settling once more on Donati. "His Holiness asked me to pray with him. I accepted his invitation."

"He phoned you directly?"

"In my apartment," said the camerlengo with a nod.

"At what time?"

Albanese lifted his eyes to the ceiling, as though trying to recall a minor detail that had slipped his mind. "Nine fifteen. Perhaps nine twenty. He asked me to come a few minutes after ten. When I arrived . . ."

Donati looked down at the man stretched lifeless upon the bed. "And how did he get here?"

"I carried him."

"Alone?"

"His Holiness bore the weight of the Church on his shoulders," said Albanese, "but in death he was light as a feather. Because I could not reach you, I summoned the secretary of state, who in turn rang Cardinals Navarro and Francona. I then called Dottore Gallo, who made the pronouncement. Death by a massive heart attack. His second, was it not? Or was it his third?"

Donati looked at the papal physician. "At what time did you make the declaration, Dottore Gallo?"

"Eleven ten, Excellency."

Cardinal Albanese cleared his throat gently. "I've made a slight adjustment to the time line in my official statement. If it is your wish, Luigi, I can say that you were the one who found him."

"That won't be necessary."

Donati dropped to his knees next to the bed. In life, the Holy Father had been elfin. Death had diminished him further. Donati remembered the day the conclave unexpectedly chose Lucchesi, the Patriarch of Venice, to be the two hundred and sixty-fifth supreme pontiff of the Roman Catholic Church. In the Room of Tears he had chosen the smallest of the three ready-made cassocks. Even so, he had seemed like a small boy wearing his father's shirt. As he stepped onto the balcony of St. Peter's, his head was barely visible above the balustrade. The *vaticanisti* christened him Pietro the Improbable. Church hardliners had referred to him derisively as Pope Accidental.

After a moment Donati felt a hand on his shoulder. It was like lead. Therefore, it had to be Albanese's.

"The ring, Excellency."

It was once the responsibility of the camerlengo to destroy

the dead pope's Ring of the Fisherman in the presence of the College of Cardinals. But like the three taps to the papal forehead with a silver hammer, the practice had been done away with. Lucchesi's ring, which he seldom wore, would merely be scored with two deep cuts in the sign of the cross. Other traditions, however, remained in place, such as the immediate locking and sealing of the papal apartments. Even Donati, Lucchesi's only private secretary, would be barred from entering once the body was removed.

Still on his knees, Donati opened the drawer of the bedside table and grasped the heavy golden ring. He surrendered it to Cardinal Albanese, who placed it in a velvet pouch. Solemnly, he declared, "Sede vacante."

The throne of St. Peter was now empty. The Apostolic Constitution dictated that Cardinal Albanese would serve as temporary caretaker of the Roman Catholic Church during the interregnum, which ended with the election of a new pope. Donati, a mere titular archbishop, would have no say in the matter. In fact, now that his master was gone, he was without portfolio or power, answerable only to the camerlengo.

"When do you intend to release the statement?" asked Donati.

"I was waiting for you to arrive."

"Might I review it?"

"Time is of the essence. If we delay any longer . . ."

"Of course, Eminence." Donati placed his hand atop Lucchesi's. It was already cold. "I'd like to have a moment alone with him."

"A moment," said the camerlengo.

The room slowly emptied. Cardinal Albanese was the last to leave.

"Tell me something, Domenico."

The camerlengo paused in the doorway. "Excellency?"

"Who closed the curtains in the study?"

"The curtains?"

"They were open when I left at nine. The shutters, too."

"I closed them, Excellency. I didn't want anyone in the square to see lights burning in the apartments so late."

"Yes, of course. That was wise of you, Domenico."

The camerlengo went out, leaving the door open. Alone with his master, Donati fought back tears. There would be time for grieving later. He leaned close to Lucchesi's ear and gently squeezed the cold hand. "Speak to me, old friend," he whispered. "Tell me what really happened here tonight."

2

JERUSALEM—VENICE

IT WAS CHIARA WHO SECRETLY informed the prime minister that her husband was in desperate need of a holiday. Since reluctantly settling into the executive suite of King Saul Boulevard, he had scarcely granted himself even an afternoon off, only a few days of working convalescence after the bombing in Paris that had fractured two vertebrae in his lower back. Still, it was not something to be undertaken lightly. Gabriel required secure communications and, more important, heavy security. So, too, did Chiara and the twins. Irene and Raphael would soon celebrate their fourth birthday. The threat against the Allon family was so immense they had never once set foot outside the State of Israel.

But where would they go? Exotic travel to a distant destination was not an option. They would have to remain reasonably close to Israel so Gabriel, in the all-too-likely event of a national emergency, could be back at King Saul Boulevard in a matter of hours. There was no South African safari in their future, no trip to Australia or the Galapagos. It was probably for the best; Gabriel had a troubled relationship with wild animals. Besides, the last thing Chiara wanted was to exhaust him with yet another long flight. Now that he was the director-general of the Office, he was constantly shuttling to Washington to consult with his American partners at Langley. What he needed most was rest.

Then again, recreation did not come naturally to him. He was a man of enormous talent but few hobbies. He did not ski or snorkel, and he had never once wielded a golf club or a tennis racket except as a weapon. Beaches bored him unless they were cold and windblown. He enjoyed sailing, especially in the challenging waters off the west of England, or strapping a rucksack to his back and pounding across a barren moorland. Even Chiara, a retired Office field operative, was incapable of matching his breakneck pace for more than a mile or two. The children would surely wilt.

The trick would be to find something for Gabriel to *do* while they were on holiday, a small project that might occupy him for a few hours each morning until the children were awake and dressed and ready to begin their day. And what if this project could be carried out in a city where he was already comfortable? The city where he had studied the craft of art restoration and served his apprenticeship? The city where he and Chiara had met and fallen in love? She was a native of this city, and her father served as chief rabbi to its dwindling community of Jews. Furthermore, her mother had been pestering her about bringing the children for a visit. It would be perfect, she thought. The proverbial two birds with one stone.

But when? August was out of the question. It was far too hot and humid, and the city would be submerged beneath a sea of package tourists, the selfie-snapping hordes who followed snarling guides around the city for an hour or two before gulping down an overpriced cappuccino at Caffè Florian and returning to their cruise ships. But if they waited until, say, November, the weather would be cool and clear and they would have the *sestiere* largely to themselves. It would give them a chance to ponder their future without the distraction of the Office or daily life in Israel. Gabriel had informed the prime minister that he would serve only a single term. It was not too early to begin thinking about how they were going to spend the rest of their lives and where they were going to raise their children. Neither of them was getting any younger, Gabriel especially.

She did not inform him of her plans, as it would only invite a lengthy oration concerning all the reasons why the State of Israel would collapse if he took so much as a single day off from work. Instead, she conspired with Uzi Navot, the deputy director, to select the dates. Housekeeping, the Office division that acquired and managed safe properties, saw to the accommodations. The local police and intelligence services, with whom Gabriel was very close, agreed to handle the security.

All that remained was the project to keep Gabriel busy. In late October, Chiara rang Francesco Tiepolo, owner of the region's most prominent restoration firm.

"I have just the thing. I'll e-mail a photo."

Three weeks later, after a particularly contentious meeting

of Israel's fractious Cabinet, Gabriel returned home to find the Allon family's bags packed.

"You're leaving me?"

"No," said Chiara. "We're going on vacation. All of us."

"I can't possibly—"

"It's taken care of, darling."

"Does Uzi know?"

Chiara nodded. "And so does the prime minister."

"Where are we going? And for how long?"

She answered.

"What will I do with myself for two weeks?"

Chiara handed him the photograph.

"There's no way I can possibly finish it."

"You'll do as much as you can."

"And let someone else touch my work?"

"It won't be the end of the world."

"You never know, Chiara. It just might be."

THE APARTMENT OCCUPIED the *piano nobile* of a crumbling old palazzo in Cannaregio, the northernmost of Venice's six traditional *sestieri*. It had a grand salon, a large kitchen filled with modern appliances, and a terrace overlooking the Rio della Misericordia. In one of the four bedrooms, Housekeeping had established a secure link to King Saul Boulevard, complete with a tentlike structure—in the jargon of the Office, it was known as a chuppah—that allowed Gabriel to speak on the phone without fear of electronic eavesdropping. Carabinieri officers in plain clothes kept watch outside on the Fondamenta dei Ormesini.

With their consent, Gabriel carried a 9mm Beretta pistol. So did Chiara, who was a much better shot than he.

A few paces along the embankment was an iron bridge—the only one in Venice—and on the opposite side of the canal was a broad square called the Campo di Ghetto Nuovo. There was a museum, a bookstore, and the offices of the Jewish community. The Casa Israelitica di Riposo, a rest home for the elderly, occupied the northern flank. Next to it was a stark bas-relief memorial to the Jews of Venice who, in December 1943, were rounded up, interned in concentration camps, and later murdered at Auschwitz. Two heavily armed carabinieri kept watch over the memorial from a fortified kiosk. Of the two hundred and fifty thousand people who still made the sinking islands of Venice their home, only the Jews required round-the-clock police protection.

The apartment buildings lining the *campo* were the tallest in Venice, for in the Middle Ages their occupants had been forbidden by the Church to reside anywhere else in the city. On the uppermost floors of several of the buildings were small synagogues, now meticulously restored, that had once served the communities of Ashkenazi and Sephardic Jews who dwelled beneath. The ghetto's two functioning synagogues were located just to the south of the *campo*. Both were clandestine; there was nothing in their outward appearance to suggest they were Jewish houses of worship. The Spanish Synagogue had been founded by Chiara's ancestors in 1580. Unheated, it was open from Passover to the High Holidays of Rosh Hashanah and Yom Kippur. The Levantine Synagogue, located across a tiny square, served the community in winter.

Rabbi Jacob Zolli and his wife, Alessia, lived around the

corner from the Levantine Synagogue, in a narrow little house overlooking a secluded *corte*. The Allon family dined there on Monday evening, a few hours after their arrival in Venice. Gabriel managed to check his phone only four times.

"I hope there isn't a problem," said Rabbi Zolli.

"The usual," murmured Gabriel.

"I'm relieved."

"Don't be."

The rabbi laughed quietly. His gaze moved approvingly around the table, settling briefly on his two grandchildren, his wife, and finally his daughter. Candlelight shone in her eyes. They were the color of caramel and flecked with gold.

"Chiara has never looked more radiant. You've obviously made her very happy."

"Have I really?"

"There were definitely bumps along the road." The rabbi's tone was admonitory. "But I assure you, she thinks she's the luckiest person in the world."

"I'm afraid that honor belongs to me."

"Rumor has it she deceived you about your travel plans."

Gabriel frowned. "Surely there's a prohibition against that sort of thing in the Torah."

"I can't think of one."

"It was probably for the best," admitted Gabriel. "I doubt I would have agreed otherwise."

"I'm pleased you were finally able to bring the children to Venice. But I'm afraid you've come at a difficult time." Rabbi Zolli lowered his voice. "Saviano and his friends on the far right have awakened dark forces in Europe."

Giuseppe Saviano was Italy's new prime minister. He was

xenophobic, intolerant, distrustful of the free press, and had little patience for niceties such as parliamentary democracy or the rule of law. Neither did his close friend Jörg Kaufmann, the fledgling neofascist who now served as chancellor of Austria. In France it was widely assumed that Cécile Leclerc, leader of the Popular Front, would be the next occupant of the Élysée Palace. Germany's National Democrats, led by a former neo-Nazi skinhead named Axel Brünner, were expected to finish second in January's general election. Everywhere, it seemed, the extreme right was ascendant.

Its rise in Western Europe had been fueled by globalization, economic uncertainty, and the continent's rapidly changing demographics. Muslims now accounted for five percent of Europe's population. A growing number of native Europeans regarded Islam as an existential threat to their religious and cultural identity. Their anger and resentment, once restrained or hidden from public view, now coursed through the veins of the Internet like a virus. Attacks on Muslims had risen sharply. So, too, had physical assaults and acts of vandalism directed against Jews. Indeed, anti-Semitism in Europe had reached a level not seen since World War II.

"Our cemetery on the Lido was vandalized again last week," said Rabbi Zolli. "Gravestones overturned, swastikas . . . the usual. My congregants are frightened. I try to comfort them, but I'm frightened, too. Anti-immigrant politicians like Saviano have shaken the bottle and removed the cork. Their adherents complain about the refugees from the Middle East and Africa, but we are the ones they despise the most. It is the longest hatred. Here in Italy it is no longer frowned upon to be an anti-Semite. One can wear one's contempt for us quite openly now. And the results have been entirely predictable."

"The storm will pass," said Gabriel with little conviction.

"Your grandparents probably said the same thing. So did the Jews of Venice. Your mother managed to walk out of Auschwitz alive. The Jews of Venice weren't so fortunate." Rabbi Zolli shook his head. "I've seen this movie before, Gabriel. I know how it ends. Never forget, the unimaginable can happen. But let's not spoil the evening with unpleasant talk. I want to enjoy the company of my grandchildren."

Next morning Gabriel woke early and spent a few hours beneath the shelter of the chuppah talking to his senior staff at King Saul Boulevard. Afterward, he hired a motorboat and took Chiara and the children on a tour of the city and the lagoon islands. It was far too cold to swim on the Lido, but the children removed their shoes and chased gulls and terns along the beach. On the way back to Cannaregio, they stopped at the church of San Sebastiano in Dorsoduro to see Veronese's *Virgin and Child in Glory with Saints*, which Gabriel had restored during Chiara's pregnancy. Later, as the autumn light faded in the Campo di Ghetto Nuovo, the children joined in a noisy game of tag while Gabriel and Chiara looked on from a wooden bench outside the Casa Israelitica di Riposo.

"This might be my favorite bench in the world," said Chiara. "It's where you were sitting the day you came to your senses and begged me to take you back. Do you remember, Gabriel? It was after the attack on the Vatican."

"I'm not sure which was worse. The rocket-propelled grenades and the suicide bombers or the way you treated me."

"You deserved it, you dolt. I should have never agreed to see you again."

"And now our children are playing in the *campo*," said Gabriel.

Chiara glanced at the carabinieri post. "Watched over by men with guns."

The next day, Wednesday, Gabriel slipped from the apartment after his morning phone calls and with a varnished wooden case beneath his arm walked to the church of the Madonna dell'Orto. The nave was in semidarkness, and scaffolding concealed the double-framed pointed arches of the side aisles. The church had no transept, but in the rear was a five-sided apse that contained the grave of Jacopo Robusti, better known as Tintoretto. It was there that Gabriel found Francesco Tiepolo. He was an enormous, bearlike man with a tangled gray-and-black beard. As usual, he was dressed in a flowing white tunic with a scarf knotted rakishly around his neck.

He embraced Gabriel tightly. "I always knew you would come back."

"I'm on holiday, Francesco. Let's not get carried away."

Tiepolo waved his hand as though he were trying to scare away the pigeons in the Piazza di San Marco. "Today you're on holiday, but one day you'll die in Venice." He looked down at the grave. "I suppose we'll have to bury you somewhere other than a church, won't we?"

Tintoretto produced ten paintings for the church between 1552 and 1569, including *Presentation of the Virgin Mary in the Temple*, which hung on the right side of the nave. A massive canvas measuring 480 by 429 centimeters, it was among his masterworks. The first phase of the restoration, the removal of the discolored varnish, had been completed. All that remained was the inpainting, the retouching of those portions of the canvas lost to time and stress. It would be a monumental task. Gabriel reckoned it would take a single restorer a year, if not longer.

"What poor soul removed the varnish? Antonio Politi, I hope."

"It was Paulina, the new girl. She was hoping to observe you while you worked."

"I assume you disabused her of that notion."

"In no uncertain terms. She said you could have any part of the painting you wanted, except for the Virgin."

Gabriel lifted his gaze toward the upper reaches of the towering canvas. Miriam, the three-year-old daughter of Joachim and Anne, Jews from Nazareth, was hesitantly climbing the fifteen steps of the Temple of Jerusalem toward the high priest. A few steps below reclined a woman robed in brown silk. She was holding a young child, a boy or girl, it was impossible to tell.

"Her," said Gabriel. "And the child."

"Are you sure? They need a great deal of work."

Gabriel smiled sadly, his eyes on the canvas. "It's the least I can do for them."

HE REMAINED IN THE CHURCH until two o'clock, longer than he had intended. That evening he and Chiara left the children with their grandparents and dined alone in a restaurant on the other side of the Grand Canal in San Polo. The next day, Thursday, he took the children on a gondola ride in the morning and worked on the Tintoretto from midday until five, when Tiepolo locked the church's doors for the night.

Chiara decided to prepare dinner at the apartment. Afterward, Gabriel supervised the nightly running battle known as bath time before retreating to the shelter of the chuppah to deal with a minor crisis at home. It was nearly one by the time he crawled into bed. Chiara was reading a novel, oblivious to the television, which was muted. On the screen was a live shot of St. Peter's Basilica. Gabriel raised the volume and learned that an old friend had died.

3

CANNAREGIO, VENICE

Later that morning the body of His Holiness Pope Paul VII was moved to the Sala Clementina on the second floor of the Apostolic Palace. It remained there until early the following afternoon, when it was transferred in solemn procession to St. Peter's Basilica for two days of public viewing. Four Swiss Guards stood watch around the dead pontiff, halberds at the ready. The Vatican press corps made much of the fact that Archbishop Luigi Donati, the Holy Father's closest aide and confidant, rarely left his master's side.

Church tradition dictated that the funeral and burial of the pope occur four to six days after his death. Cardinal Camerlengo Domenico Albanese announced that it would take place the following Tuesday and that the conclave would convene ten days after that. The *vaticanisti* were predicting a hard-fought and divisive contest between reformers and conservatives. The smart money was on Cardinal José Maria Navarro, who had used his position as the Church's doctrinal gatekeeper to build a power base within the College of Cardinals that rivaled even the dead pope's.

In Venice, where Pietro Lucchesi had reigned as patriarch, the mayor declared three days of mourning. The bells of the city were silent, and a moderately attended prayer service was held in St. Mark's Basilica. Otherwise, life went on as normal. A minor *acqua alta* flooded a portion of Santa Croce; a colossal cruise ship plowed into a wharf on the Giudecca Canal. In the bars where locals gathered for coffee or a glass of brandy against the autumn chill, one rarely heard the dead pontiff's name. Cynical by nature, few Venetians bothered to attend Mass on a regular basis, and fewer still lived their lives in accordance with the teachings of the men from the Vatican. The churches of Venice, the most beautiful in all of Christendom, were places where foreign tourists went to gawk at Renaissance art.

Gabriel, however, followed the events in Rome with more than a passing interest. On the morning of the pope's funeral, he arrived at the church early and worked without interruption until twelve fifteen, when he heard the hollow echo of footfalls in the nave. He raised his magnifying visor and cautiously parted the tarpaulin shroud that covered his platform. General Cesare Ferrari, commander of the carabinieri's Division for the Defense of Cultural Patrimony, better known as the Art Squad, returned his gaze without expression.

Uninvited, the general stepped behind the shroud and contemplated the enormous canvas, which was awash in the searing white light of two halogen lamps. "One of his better ones, don't you think?"

"He was under enormous pressure to prove himself. Veronese had been publicly recognized as the successor of Titian and the finest painter in Venice. Poor Tintoretto was no longer receiving the sort of commissions he once did."

"This was his parish church."

"You don't say."

"He lived around the corner on the Fondamenta di Mori." The general swept aside the tarpaulin and went into the nave. "There used to be a Bellini in this church. *Madonna with Child*. It was stolen in 1993. The Art Squad has been looking for it ever since." He peered at Gabriel over his shoulder. "You haven't seen it, have you?"

Gabriel smiled. Shortly before becoming chief of the Office, he had recovered the most sought-after stolen painting in the world, Caravaggio's *Nativity with St. Francis and St. Lawrence*. He had made certain that the Art Squad received all the credit. It was for that reason, among others, that General Ferrari had agreed to provide round-the-clock security for Gabriel and his family during their Venetian holiday.

"You're supposed to be relaxing," said the general.

Gabriel lowered his magnifying visor. "I am."

"Any problems?"

"For inexplicable reasons, I'm having a bit of trouble recreating the color of this woman's garment."

"I was referring to your security."

"It seems my return to Venice has gone unnoticed."

"Not entirely." The general glanced at his wristwatch. "I don't suppose I could convince you to take a break for lunch?"

"I never eat lunch when I'm working."

"Yes, I know." The general switched off the halogen lamps. "I remember."

TIEPOLO HAD GIVEN GABRIEL A key to the church. Watched by the commander of the Art Squad, he engaged the alarm and locked the door. Together they walked to a bar a few doors down from Tintoretto's old house. The papal funeral played on the television behind the counter.

"In case you were wondering," said the general, "Archbishop Donati wanted you to attend."

"Then why wasn't I invited?"

"The camerlengo wouldn't hear of it."

"Albanese?"

The general nodded. "Apparently, he was never comfortable with the closeness of your relationship with Donati. Or with the Holy Father, for that matter."

"It's probably better I'm not there. I would have only been a distraction."

The general frowned. "They should have seated you in a place of honor. After all, were it not for you, the Holy Father would have died in the terrorist attack on the Vatican."

The barman, a skinny twentysomething in a black T-shirt, delivered two coffees. The general added sugar to his. The hand that stirred it was missing two fingers. He had lost them to a letter bomb when he was the commander of the Camorra-infested

Naples division of the carabinieri. The explosion had taken his right eye as well. The ocular prosthesis, with its immobile pupil, had left the general with a cold, unyielding gaze. Even Gabriel tended to avoid it. It was like staring into the eye of an all-seeing God.

At present, the eye was aimed toward the television, where the camera was panning slowly across a rogues' gallery of politicians, monarchs, and assorted global celebrities. Eventually, it settled on Giuseppe Saviano.

"At least he didn't wear his armband," murmured the general.

"You're not an admirer?"

"Saviano is a passionate defender of the Art Squad's budget. As a result, we get on quite well."

"Fascists love cultural patrimony."

"He considers himself a populist, not a fascist."

"That's a relief."

Ferrari's brief smile had no influence over his prosthetic eye. "The rise of a man like Saviano was inevitable. Our people have lost faith with fanciful notions like liberal democracy, the European Union, and the Western alliance. And why not? Between globalization and automation, most young Italians can't start a proper career. If they want a well-paying job, they have to go to Britain. And if they stay here . . ." The general glanced at the young man behind the bar. "They serve coffee to tourists." He lowered his voice. "Or Israeli intelligence officers."

"Saviano isn't going to change any of that."

"Probably not. But in the meantime, he projects strength and confidence."

"How about competence?"

"As long as he keeps the immigrants out, his supporters don't care if he can't put two words together."

"What if there's a crisis? A real crisis. Not one that's invented by a right-wing website."

"Like what?"

"It could be another financial crisis that wipes out the banking system." Gabriel paused. "Or something much worse."

"What could be worse than my life's savings going up in smoke?"

"How about a global pandemic? A novel strain of influenza for which we humans have no natural defense."

"A plague?"

"Don't laugh, Cesare. It's only a matter of time."

"And where will this plague of yours come from?"

"It will make the jump from animals to humans in a place where sanitary conditions leave something to be desired. A Chinese wet market, for example. It will start slowly, a cluster of local cases. But because we are so interconnected, it will spread around the globe like wildfire. Chinese tourists will bring it to Western Europe in the early stages of the outbreak, even before the virus has been identified. Within a few weeks, half of Italy's population will be infected, perhaps more. What happens then, Cesare?"

"You tell me."

"The entire country will have to be quarantined to prevent further spread. Hospitals will be so overwhelmed they'll be forced to turn away everyone but the youngest and the healthiest. Hundreds will die every day, perhaps thousands. The military will have to resort to mass cremation to prevent further spread. It will be—"

"A holocaust."

Gabriel nodded slowly. "And how do you suppose an incompetent subliterate like Saviano will react under those conditions? Will he listen to medical experts, or will he think he knows better? Will he tell his people the truth, or will he promise that a vaccine and lifesaving treatments are just around the corner?"

"He'll blame the Chinese and the immigrants and emerge stronger than ever." Ferrari looked at Gabriel seriously. "Is there something you know that you're not telling me?"

"Anyone with half a brain knows we're long overdue for something on the scale of the Great Influenza of 1918. I've told my prime minister that of all the threats facing Israel, a pandemic is by far the worst."

"I'm thankful that my only responsibility is to find stolen paintings." The general watched as the television camera panned across a sea of red vestments. "There sits the next pontiff."

"They say it's going to be Cardinal Navarro."

"That's the rumor."

"Do you have any insight?"

General Ferrari answered as though addressing a roomful of reporters. "The carabinieri make no effort to monitor the papal succession process. Nor do the other agencies of Italian security and intelligence."

"Spare me."

The general laughed quietly. "And what about you?"

"The identity of the next pope is of no concern to the State of Israel."

"It is now."

"What are you talking about?"

"I'll let *him* explain." General Ferrari nodded toward the television, where the camera had found Archbishop Luigi Donati, private secretary to His Holiness Pope Paul VII. "He was wondering whether you might have a spare moment or two to speak to him."

"Why didn't he just call me?"

"It's not something he wanted to discuss on the phone."

"Did he tell you what it was?"

The general shook his head. "Only that it was a matter of the utmost importance. He was hoping you were free for lunch tomorrow."

"Where?"

"Rome."

Gabriel made no reply.

"It's an hour away by plane. You'll be back in Venice in time for dinner."

"Will I?"

"Judging by the archbishop's tone of voice, I rather doubt it. He's expecting you at one o'clock at Piperno. He says you're familiar with it."

"It rings a distant bell."

"He'd like you to come alone. And don't worry about your wife and children. I'll take very good care of them during your absence."

"Absence?" It was not the word Gabriel would have chosen to describe a daylong excursion to the Eternal City.

The general was staring at the television again. "Look at those princes of the Church, all robed in red."

"The color symbolizes the blood of Christ."

Ferrari's good eye blinked with surprise. "How on earth did you know that?"

"I've spent the better part of my life restoring Christian art. It's safe to assume I know more about the history and teachings of the Church than most Catholics."

"Including me." The general's gaze returned to the screen. "Who do you suppose it will be?"

"They say Navarro is already ordering new furniture for the *appartamento*."

"Yes," said the general, nodding thoughtfully. "That's what they say."

4

MURANO, VENICE

P LEASE TELL ME YOU'RE JOKING."

"Trust me, it wasn't my idea."

"Do you know how much time and effort it took to arrange this trip? I had to meet with the prime minister, for heaven's sake."

"And for that," said Gabriel solemnly, "I am deeply and eternally sorry."

They were seated at the back of a small restaurant in Murano. Gabriel had waited until they had finished their entrées before telling Chiara of his plans to travel to Rome in the morning. Admittedly, his motives were selfish. The restaurant, which specialized in fish, was among his favorites in Venice.

"It's just one day, Chiara."

"Even you don't believe that."

"No, but it was worth a try."

Chiara raised a wineglass toward her lips. The last of her pinot grigio burned with the pale fire of reflected candlelight. "Why weren't you invited to the funeral?"

"Apparently, Cardinal Albanese couldn't find a spare seat for me in the whole of St. Peter's Square."

"He was the one who found the body, wasn't he?"

"In the private chapel," said Gabriel.

"Do you really think it happened that way?"

"Are you suggesting the Vatican Press Office might have issued an inaccurate *bollettino*?"

"You and Luigi collaborated on quite a few misleading statements over the years."

"But our motives were always pure."

Chiara placed her wineglass on the bone-white tablecloth and rotated it slowly. "Why do you suppose he wants to see you?"

"It can't be good."

"What did General Ferrari say?"

"As little as possible."

"How unlike him."

"He might have mentioned that it had something to do with the selection of the next supreme pontiff of the Roman Catholic Church."

The wineglass went still. "The conclave?"

"He didn't go into specifics."

Gabriel nudged his phone to life and checked the time. He had been forced at long last to part company with his beloved BlackBerry Key2. His new device was an Israeli-made Solaris, customized to his unique specifications. Larger and heavier than a typical smartphone, it had been built to withstand remote attack from the world's most sophisticated hackers, including the American NSA and Israel's Unit 8200. All of Gabriel's senior officers carried one, as did Chiara. It was her second. Raphael had tossed her first Solaris from the terrace of their apartment in Jerusalem. For all its inviolability, the device had not been designed to survive a fall of three floors and a collision with a limestone walkway.

"It's late," he said. "We should rescue your parents."

"We don't have to rush. They love having the children around. If it were up to them, we would never leave Venice."

"King Saul Boulevard might notice my absence."

"The prime minister, too." She was silent for a moment. "I must admit, I'm not looking forward to going home. I've enjoyed having you to myself."

"I only have two years left on my term."

"Two years and one month. But who's counting?"

"Has it been terrible?"

She made a face. "I never wanted to play the role of the complaining wife. You know the type, don't you, Gabriel? They're so annoying, those women."

"We always knew it would be difficult."

"Yes," she said vaguely.

"If you need help . . ."

"Help?"

"An extra pair of hands around the house."

She frowned. "I can manage quite well on my own, thank you. I just miss you, that's all."

"Two years will go by in the blink of an eye."

"And you promise you won't let them talk you into a second term?"

"Not a chance."

Her face brightened. "So how do you plan to spend your retirement?"

"You make it sound as though I should start looking for an assisted-living facility."

"You are getting on in years, darling." She patted the back of his hand. It didn't make him feel any younger. "Well?" she asked.

"I plan to devote my final years on this earth to making you happy."

"So you'll do anything I want?"

He regarded her carefully. "Within reason, of course."

She cast her eyes downward and picked at a loose thread in the tablecloth. "I had coffee with Francesco yesterday."

"He didn't mention it."

"I asked him not to."

"That explains it. And what did you talk about?"

"The future."

"What does he have in mind?"

"A partnership."

"Francesco and me?"

Chiara made no reply.

"*You?*"

She nodded. "He wants me to come to work for him. And when he retires in a few years . . ."

"What?"

"Tiepolo Restoration will be mine."

Gabriel recalled the words Tiepolo had spoken while standing over the tomb of Tintoretto. *Today you're on holiday, but one day you'll die in Venice* . . . He doubted this scheme had been hatched over coffee yesterday.

"A nice Jewish girl from the ghetto will be caring for the churches and *scuole* of Venice? Is that what you're saying?"

"Rather remarkable, isn't it?"

"And what will I do?"

"I suppose you can spend your days wandering the streets of Venice."

"Or?"

She smiled beautifully. "You can work for me."

This time it was Gabriel who looked down. His phone was aglow with an incoming message from King Saul Boulevard. He turned the device over. "It might be controversial, Chiara."

"Working for me?"

"Leaving Israel the minute my term is over."

"Do you intend to run for a seat in the Knesset?"

He rolled his eyes.

"Write a book about your exploits?"

"I'll leave that chore to someone else."

"So?"

He made no reply.

"If you stay in Israel, you'll be within easy reach of the Office. And if there's a crisis, they'll drag you back in to right the ship, just like they did to Ari."

"Ari wanted back in. I'm different."

"Are you really? Sometimes I'm not so sure about that. In fact, you're getting more like him every day."

"What about the children?" he asked.

"They adore Venice."

"School?"

"Believe it or not, we have several very fine ones."

"They'll turn into Italians."

She frowned. "A pity, that."

Gabriel exhaled slowly. "Have you seen Francesco's books?"

"I'll knock them into shape."

"The summers here are dreadful."

"We'll go to the mountains or sail the Adriatic. It's been years since you've sailed, darling."

Gabriel had run out of objections. In truth, he thought it was a marvelous idea. If nothing else, it would keep Chiara occupied during the final two years of his term.

"Do we have a deal?" she asked.

"I believe we do, provided we come to terms on my compensation package, which will be exorbitant."

He signaled the waiter for the check. Chiara was pulling at the loose thread in the tablecloth again.

"There's one thing that's bothering me," she said.

"About uprooting the children and moving to Venice?"

"The Vatican *bollettino*. Luigi always remained by Lucchesi's side late into the evening. And when Lucchesi went to the chapel to pray and meditate before bed, Luigi always went with him."

"True."

"So why was Cardinal Albanese the one who found the body?"

"I suppose we'll never know." Gabriel paused. "Unless I have lunch with Luigi in Rome tomorrow."

"You can go on one condition."

"What's that?"

"Take me with you."

"What about the children?"

"My parents can look after them."

"And who's going to look after your parents?"

"The carabinieri, of course."

"But—"

"Don't make me ask twice, Gabriel. I really hate playing the role of the complaining wife. They're so annoying, those women."

5

VENICE—ROME

NEXT MORNING THEY DROPPED THE children at the Zolli house after breakfast and hurried over to Santa Lucia in time to make the eight o'clock train to Rome. As the rolling plains of central Italy slid past their window, Gabriel read the newspapers and exchanged a few routine e-mails and texts with King Saul Boulevard. Chiara leafed through a thick stack of home design magazines and catalogs, licking the tip of her index finger with each turn of the page.

Occasionally, when the combination of shadows and light was favorable, Gabriel caught sight of their reflection in the glass. He had to admit, they were an attractive couple, he in his fashionable dark suit and white dress shirt, Chiara in her black leggings and leather jacket. Despite the pressure and long hours of his job—and his many injuries and brushes with death—Gabriel judged he had held up rather well. Yes, the lines around his jade-colored eyes were a bit deeper, but he was still trim as a cyclist, and he had retained all his hair. It was short and dark but very gray at the temples. It had changed color almost overnight, not long after the first assassination he carried out at the behest of the Office. The operation had taken place in the autumn of 1972, in the city where they would soon be arriving.

As they were approaching Florence, Chiara thrust a catalog beneath his nose and asked his opinion of the couch and coffee table displayed on the open page. His indifferent response earned him a glance of mild rebuke. It seemed Chiara had already begun scouring the real estate listings for their new home, adding still more evidence to support his theory that a return to Venice had been in the works for some time. For now, she had narrowed her search to two properties, one in Cannaregio and a second in San Polo, overlooking the Grand Canal. Both would substantially diminish the small fortune Gabriel had accumulated through his labors as a restorer, and both would require Chiara to commute to Tiepolo's offices in San Marco. The San Polo apartment was much closer, a few stops by vaporetto. It was also twice the price.

"If we sell Narkiss Street . . ."

"We're not selling it," said Gabriel.

"The San Polo apartment has an incredible room with high ceilings where you can build a proper studio."

"Which means I can supplement the starvation wages I'll make working for you by taking private commissions."

"Exactly."

Gabriel's phone pinged with the tone reserved for urgent messages from King Saul Boulevard.

Chiara watched uneasily as he read it. "Are we going home?"

"Not yet."

"What is it?"

"A car bombing in the Potsdamer Platz in Berlin."

"Casualties?"

"Probably. But there's no confirmation yet."

"Who did it?"

"The Islamic State is claiming responsibility."

"Do they have the capability to carry out a bombing in Western Europe?"

"If you'd asked me that question yesterday, I would have told you no."

Gabriel followed the updates from Berlin until the train pulled into Roma Termini. Outside, the sky was cerulean blue and cloudless. They walked through canyons of terra-cotta and sienna, keeping to the side streets and alleyways where watchers were easier to spot. While dawdling in the Piazza Navona, they agreed they were not being followed.

Ristorante Piperno was a short distance to the south, in a quiet *campo* near the Tiber. Chiara entered first and was shown by a dazzled white-jacketed waiter to a prized table near the window. Gabriel, who arrived three minutes later, sat outside in the warm autumnal sunlight. He could see Chiara's thumbs working furiously over the keypad of her phone. He drew his own device from the breast pocket of his suit jacket and typed, Something wrong?

Chiara's reply arrived a few seconds later. Your son just broke my mother's favorite vase.

I'm sure it was the vase's fault, not his.

Your lunch date is here.

Gabriel watched a worn-out Fiat sedan creeping hesitatingly over the cobbles of the tiny *campo*. It had ordinary Roman registration, not the special SCV plates reserved for cars from the Vatican. A tall, handsome cleric emerged from the backseat. His black cassock and simar were trimmed in amaranth red, the plumage of an archbishop. His arrival at Ristorante Piperno provoked only slightly less tumult than Chiara's.

"Forgive me," said Luigi Donati as he sat down opposite Gabriel. "I never should have agreed to speak to that reporter from *Vanity Fair*. I can't go anywhere in Rome these days without being recognized."

"Why did you do the interview?"

"She made it clear she was going to write the article with or without my cooperation."

"And you fell for it?"

"She promised it would be a serious profile of the man who helped to guide the Church through troubled waters. It didn't turn out as promised."

"I assume you're referring to the part about your physical appearance."

"Don't tell me you actually read it."

"Every word."

Donati frowned. "I must say, the Holy Father rather liked it. He thought it made the Church seem cool. His exact word, by the way. My rivals in the Curia didn't agree." He abruptly changed the subject. "I'm sorry about interrupting your holiday. I hope Chiara wasn't angry."

"Quite the opposite."

"Are you telling me the truth?"

"Have I ever misled you?"

"Do you really want me to answer that?" Donati smiled. It was an effort.

"How are you holding up?" asked Gabriel.

"I'm mourning the loss of my master and adjusting to my reduced circumstances and status loss."

"Where are you staying?"

"The Jesuit Curia. It's just down the street from the Vatican on the Borgo Santo Spirito. My rooms aren't as nice as my apartment in the Apostolic Palace, but they're quite comfortable."

"Have they found something for you to do?"

"I'm going to be teaching canon law at the Gregoriana. I'm also designing a course on the Church's troubled history with the Jews." He paused. "Perhaps someday I can convince you to deliver a guest lecture."

"Can you imagine?"

"I can, actually. The relationship between our two faiths has never been better, and it is because of your personal friendship with Pietro Lucchesi."

"I sent you a text the night he died," said Gabriel.

"It meant the world to me."

"Why didn't you respond?"

"For the same reason I didn't challenge Cardinal Albanese when he refused to allow you to attend the funeral. I needed your help on a sensitive matter, and I didn't want to cast any unnecessary light on the closeness of our relationship."

"And the sensitive matter?"

"It concerns the death of the Holy Father. There were certain . . . irregularities."

"Beginning with the identity of the person who discovered the body."

"You noticed that?"

"Actually, it was Chiara."

"She's a smart woman."

"Why did Cardinal Albanese find the body? Why wasn't it you, Luigi?"

Donati looked down at his menu. "Perhaps we should order something to start. How about the fried artichoke leaves and zucchini flowers? And the *filetti di baccalà*. The Holy Father always swore they were the best in Rome."

6

RISTORANTE PIPERNO, ROME

THE MAÎTRE D' INSISTED ON sending over a bottle of complimentary wine. It was something special, he promised, a fine white from a small producer in Abruzzo. He was certain His Excellency would find it more than satisfactory. Donati, with considerable ceremony, declared it divine. Then, when they were alone again, he described for Gabriel the final hours of the papacy of Pope Paul VII. The Holy Father and his private secretary had shared a meal—a last supper, said Donati gravely—in the dining room of the papal apartments. Donati had taken only a bit of consommé. Afterward, the two men had adjourned to the study, where Donati, at the Holy Father's request, had opened the curtains and the shutters of the window overlooking St. Peter's Square. It was the penultimate act of service he would perform for his master, at least while His Holiness was still alive.

"And the final act?" asked Gabriel.

"I laid out the Holy Father's nightly dose of medication."

"What was he taking?"

Donati recited the names of three prescription drugs, all for the treatment of a failing heart.

"You managed to conceal it quite well," said Gabriel.

"We're rather good at that around here."

"I seem to recall a brief stay in the Gemelli Clinic a few months ago for a severe chest cold."

"It was a heart attack. His second."

"Who knew?"

"Dottore Gallo, of course. And Cardinal Gaubert, the secretary of state."

"Why so much secrecy?"

"Because if the rest of the Curia had known about Lucchesi's physical decline, his papacy would have been effectively over. He had much work to do in the time he had left."

"What sort of work?"

"He was considering calling a third Vatican council to address the many profound issues facing the Church. The conservative wing is still coming to terms with Vatican II, which was completed more than a half century ago. A third council would have been divisive, to put it mildly."

"What happened after you gave Lucchesi his medicine?"

"I went downstairs, where my car and driver were waiting. It was nine o'clock, give or take a few minutes."

"Where did you go?"

Donati reached for his wineglass. "You know, you really should try some of this. It's quite good."

The arrival of the antipasti granted Donati a second reprieve. While plucking the first leaf from the fried Roman artichoke, he asked with contrived carelessness, "You remember Veronica Marchese, don't you?"

"Luigi . . ."

"What?"

"Bless me, Father, for I have sinned."

"It's not like that."

"Isn't it?"

Dr. Veronica Marchese was the director of the Museo Nazionale Etrusco and Italy's foremost authority on Etruscan civilization and antiquities. During the 1980s, while working on an archaeological dig near the Umbrian village of Monte Cucco, she fell in love with a fallen priest, a Jesuit, a fervent advocate of liberation theology, who had lost his faith while serving as a missionary in the Morazán Province of El Salvador. The affair ended abruptly when the fallen priest returned to the Church to serve as the private secretary to the Patriarch of Venice. Heartbroken, Veronica married Carlo Marchese, a wealthy Roman businessman from a noble family with close ties to the Vatican. Marchese had died after falling from the viewing gallery atop the dome of St. Peter's Basilica. Gabriel had been standing next to Carlo when he toppled over the protective barrier. Two hundred feet below, Donati had prayed over his broken body.

"How long has this been going on?" asked Gabriel.

"I've always loved that song," replied Donati archly.

"Answer the question."

"Nothing is *going on*. But I've been having dinner with her on a regular basis for a year or so."

"Or so?"

"Maybe it's more like two years."

"I assume you two don't dine in public."

"No," answered Donati. "Only in Veronica's home."

Gabriel and Chiara had attended a party there once. It was an art-and-antiquity-filled palazzo near the Villa Borghese. "How often?" he asked.

"Barring a work emergency, every Thursday evening."

"The first rule of illicit behavior is to avoid a pattern."

"There is nothing *illicit* about Veronica and me having dinner together. The discipline of celibacy does not forbid all contact with women. I simply can't marry her or—"

"Are you allowed to be in love with her?"

"Strictly speaking, yes."

Gabriel stared at Donati with reproach. "Why willingly place yourself in such close proximity to temptation?"

"Veronica says I do it for the same reason I used to climb mountains, to see whether I can maintain my footing. To see whether God will reach down and catch me if I fall."

"I assume she's discreet."

"Have you ever met anyone more discreet than Veronica Marchese?"

"And what about your colleagues at the Vatican?" asked Gabriel. "Did anyone know?"

"It is a small place filled with sexually repressed men who love nothing more than to exchange a good piece of gossip."

"Which is why you find it suspicious that a man with a failing heart died on the one night of the week you weren't in the Apostolic Palace."

Donati said nothing.

"Surely there's more than that."

"Yes," said Donati as he plucked another leaf from the artichoke. "Much more."

7

RISTORANTE PIPERNO, ROME

THERE WAS, FOR A START, the phone call from Cardinal Albanese. It arrived nearly two hours after the camerlengo said he had found the Holy Father dead in the private chapel. Albanese claimed to have called Donati several times without receiving an answer. Donati had checked his phone. There were no missed calls.

"Sounds like an open-and-shut case. Next?"

The condition of the papal study, answered Donati. Shutters and curtains closed. A half-drunk cup of tea on the desk. One item missing.

"What was it?"

"A letter. A *personal* letter. Not official."

"Lucchesi was the recipient?"

"The author."

"And the contents of the letter?"

"His Holiness refused to tell me."

Gabriel was not sure the archbishop was being entirely truthful. "I assume the letter was written in longhand?"

"The Vicar of Christ doesn't use a word processor."

"To whom was it addressed?"

"An old friend."

Donati then described the scene he encountered when Cardinal Albanese led him into the papal bedroom. Gabriel pictured the tableau as though it were rendered in oil on canvas by the hand of Caravaggio. The body of a dead pontiff stretched upon the bed, watched over by a trio of senior prelates. At the right side of the canvas, scarcely visible in the shadows, were three trusted laymen: the pope's personal physician, the chief of the Vatican's small police force, and the commandant of the Pontifical Swiss Guard. Gabriel had never met Dr. Gallo, but he knew Lorenzo Vitale, and liked him. Alois Metzler was another story.

Gabriel's private Caravaggio dissolved, as though washed away by solvent. Donati was recounting Albanese's explanation of having found, and then moved, the corpse.

"Frankly, it's the one part of his story that's plausible. My master was quite diminutive, and Albanese has the body of an ox." Donati was silent for a moment. "Of course, there is at least one other explanation."

"What's that?"

"That His Holiness never made it to the chapel. That he died at his desk in the study while drinking his tea. It was gone when I came out of the bedroom. The tea, that is. Someone removed the cup and saucer while I was praying over Lucchesi's body."

"I don't suppose it underwent a postmortem examination."

"The Vicar of Christ—"

"Was it embalmed?"

"I'm afraid so. Wojtyla's body turned quite gray while it was on display in the basilica. And then there was Pius XII." Donati winced. "A disaster, that. Albanese said he didn't want to take any chances. Or perhaps he was just covering his tracks. After all, if a body is embalmed, it would make it much harder to find any trace of poison."

"You really need to stop watching those forensic shows on television, Luigi."

"I don't *own* a television."

Gabriel allowed a moment to pass. "As I recall, there are no security cameras in the loggia outside the private apartments."

"If there were cameras, the apartments wouldn't be private, would they?"

"But there must have been a Swiss Guard on duty."

"Always."

"So he would have seen anyone entering the apartments?"

"Presumably."

"Did you ask him?"

"I never had the chance."

"Did you express your concerns to Lorenzo Vitale?"

"And what would Lorenzo have done? Investigate the death of a pope as a possible homicide?" Donati's smile was charitable. "Given your experience at the Vatican, I'm surprised you would even ask a question like that. Besides, Albanese never would have allowed it. He had his story, and he was sticking to it. He found the Holy Father in the private chapel a few minutes after ten o'clock and carried him without assistance to the bedroom. There, in the presence of three of the Church's most powerful cardinals, he set in motion the chain of events that led to a declaration that the throne of St. Peter was empty. All while I was having a late supper with a woman I once loved. If I challenge Albanese, he'll destroy me. And Veronica, too."

"What about a leak to a trusted reporter? There are several thousand camped out in St. Peter's Square."

"This matter is far too serious to be entrusted to a journalist. It needs to be handled by someone skillful and ruthless enough to find out what really happened. And quickly."

"Someone like me?"

Donati made no reply.

"I'm on holiday," protested Gabriel. "And I'm supposed to be back in Tel Aviv in a week."

"Leaving you just enough time to find out who killed the Holy Father before the beginning of the conclave. For all intents and purposes, it's already begun. Most of the men who will choose the next pope are holed up at the Casa Santa Marta." The Domus Sanctae Marthae, or Casa Santa Marta, was the five-story clerical guesthouse at the southern edge of the city-state. "I can assure you those red-hatted princes aren't talking about the sporting news over dinner each night. It is imperative we find out who was behind the murder of my master before they file into the Sistine Chapel and the doors are locked behind them."

"With all due respect, Luigi, you have absolutely no proof Lucchesi was murdered."

"I haven't told you everything I know."

"Now might be a good time."

"The missing letter was addressed to you." Donati paused. "Now ask me about the Swiss Guard who was on duty outside the papal apartments that night."

"Where is he?"

"He left the Vatican a few hours after the Holy Father's death. No one's seen him since."

8

RISTORANTE PIPERNO, ROME

GABRIEL WAS MOMENTARILY DISTRACTED BY the man who wandered into the *campo* as the waiters were clearing away the first course. He wore dark glasses and a hat and carried a nylon rucksack over one square shoulder. Gabriel reckoned he was of northern European stock, German or Austrian, perhaps a Scandinavian. He paused a few meters from their table as if to take his bearings—long enough for Gabriel to calculate the length of time it would take to draw the Beretta lodged against the small of his back. He drew his phone instead and snapped the man's photograph as he was leaving the square.

"Let's start with the letter." Gabriel returned the phone to his breast pocket. "But why don't we skip the part where you claim not to know why Lucchesi was writing it."

"I don't," Donati insisted. "But if I were to guess, it concerned something he found in the Secret Archives."

L'Archivio Segreto Vaticano, the Vatican Secret Archives, was the central repository for papal documents related to matters of both religion and state. Located near the Vatican Library in the Belvedere Palace, it contained an estimated fifty-three miles of shelf space, much of it in fortified underground bunkers. Among its many treasures was *Decet Romanum Pontificem*, Pope Leo X's 1521 papal bull ordering the excommunication of a troublesome German priest and theologian named Martin Luther. It was also the final resting place of much of the Church's dirtiest laundry. Early in Lucchesi's papacy, Gabriel had worked with Donati and the Holy Father to release diplomatic and other documents related to Pope Pius XII's conduct during World War II, when six million Jews were systematically murdered, often by Roman Catholics, with scarcely a word of protest from the Holy See.

"The Archives are regarded as the personal property of the papacy," Donati continued. "Which means a pope is allowed to see anything he wants. The same is not true for his private secretary. In fact, I wasn't always allowed to know the nature of the documents he was reviewing."

"Where did he do his reading?"

"Sometimes the *prefetto* would bring documents to the papal apartments. But if they were too fragile or sensitive, the Holy Father would review them in a special room inside the Archives, with the *prefetto* standing just outside the door. Perhaps you've heard of him. His name is—"

"Cardinal Domenico Albanese."

Donati nodded.

"So Albanese was aware of every document that passed through the Holy Father's hands?"

"Not necessarily." An unrepentant smoker, Donati removed a cigarette from an elegant gold case and tapped it against the cover before lighting it with a matching gold lighter. "As you might recall, His Holiness developed serious sleeping problems late in his papacy. He was always in bed at the same time each evening, about half past ten, but he rarely stayed there long. On occasion he was known to visit the Secret Archives for a bit of nocturnal reading."

"How did he get documents in the middle of the night?"

"He had a secret source." Donati's eye was caught by something over Gabriel's shoulder. "My God, is that—"

"Yes, it is."

"Why doesn't she join us?"

"She's busy."

"Watching your back?"

"And yours." Gabriel asked about the missing Swiss Guard.

"His name is Niklaus Janson. He recently completed his required two-year term of service, but at my request he agreed to remain for an additional year."

"You liked him?"

"I trusted him, which is far more important."

"Were there any black marks on his record?"

"Two missed curfews."

"When was the last violation?"

"A week before the Holy Father's death. He claimed he was out with a friend and lost track of the time. Metzler gave him the traditional punishment."

"What's that?"

"Scrubbing the rust off breastplates or chopping up old uniforms on the execution block in the courtyard of the barracks. The Guards call it the Scheitstock."

"When did you realize he was missing?"

"Two days after the Holy Father's death, I noticed that Niklaus wasn't one of the Guards chosen to stand watch over the body while it was on display in the basilica. I asked Alois Metzler why he had been excluded and was told, much to my surprise, that he was missing."

"How did Metzler explain his absence?"

"He said Niklaus was grief-stricken over the death of His Holiness. Frankly, he didn't seem terribly concerned. Neither did the camerlengo, for that matter." Donati tapped his cigarette irritably against the rim of the ashtray. "After all, he had a globally televised funeral to plan."

"What else do you know about Janson?"

"His comrades used to call him Saint Niklaus. He told me once that he briefly considered a vocation. He joined the Guard after completing his service in the Swiss Army. They still have compulsory service up there, you know."

"Where's he from?"

"A little village near Fribourg. It's a Catholic canton. There's a woman there, a girlfriend, perhaps his fiancée. Her name is Stefani Hoffmann. Metzler contacted her the day after the Holy Father's death. As far as I can tell, that was the extent of his efforts to determine Niklaus's whereabouts." Donati paused. "Perhaps you might be more effective."

"At what?"

"Finding Niklaus Janson, of course. I wouldn't think it would be too difficult for a man in your position. Surely you have certain capabilities at your disposal."

"I do. But I can't use them to find a missing Swiss Guard."

"Why ever not? Niklaus knows what happened that night. I'm sure of it."

Gabriel was not yet convinced that anything at all had happened that night, other than that an old man with a weakened heart, a man whom Gabriel loved and admired, had died while praying in his private chapel. Still, he had to admit there were enough troubling circumstances to warrant further investigation, beginning with the whereabouts of Niklaus Janson. Gabriel would try to find him, if only to put Donati's mind at ease. And his own mind, as well.

"Do you know the number for Janson's mobile?" he asked.

"I'm afraid not."

"Do they have a computer network over there in the Swiss Guard barracks, or are they still using parchment?"

"They went digital a couple of years ago."

"Big mistake," said Gabriel. "Parchment is much more secure."

"Is it your intention to hack into the computer network of the Pontifical Swiss Guard?"

"With your blessing, of course."

"I'll withhold it, if you don't mind."

"How jesuitical of you."

Donati smiled but said nothing.

"Go back to the Curia and keep your head down for a couple of days. I'll contact you when I have something."

"Actually, I was wondering whether you and Chiara might be free tonight."

"We were planning to go back to Venice."

"Is there any chance I can convince you to stay? I thought we might have dinner at a little place near the Villa Borghese."

"Will anyone be joining us?"

"An old friend."

"Yours or mine?"

"As a matter of fact, both."

Gabriel hesitated. "I'm not sure that's a good idea, Luigi. I haven't seen her since—"

"She was the one who suggested it. I believe you remember the address. Drinks are at eight o'clock."

9

CAFFÈ GRECO, ROME

WHAT DO YOU THINK?" ASKED Chiara.

"I definitely think I could get used to living here again."

They were seated in the elegant front room of Caffè Greco. Beneath their small round table were several glossy shopping bags, the plunder of a costly late-afternoon excursion along the Via Condotti. They had traveled from Venice to Rome without a change of clothing. They both needed something appropriate to wear for dinner at Veronica Marchese's palazzo.

"I was talking about—"

Gabriel gently cut her off. "I know what you were talking about."

"Well?"

"All of it can be explained rather easily."

Chiara was clearly unconvinced. "Let's start with the phone call."

"Let's."

"Why did Albanese wait so long to contact Donati?"

"Because the Holy Father's death was Albanese's moment in the spotlight, and he didn't want Donati interfering or second-guessing his decisions."

"His overinflated ego got the better of him?"

"Nearly everyone in a position of power suffers from one."

"Everyone but you, of course."

"That goes without saying."

"But why did Albanese take it upon himself to move the body? And why did he close the curtains and the shutters in the study?"

"For the exact reasons he said he did."

"And the teacup?"

Gabriel shrugged. "One of the household nuns probably took it."

"Did they take the letter off Lucchesi's desk, too?"

"The letter," admitted Gabriel, "is harder to explain."

"Almost as hard as the missing Swiss Guard." A waiter arrived with two coffees and a creamy Roman fruit tart. Fork in hand, Chiara hesitated. "I've already gained at least five pounds on this trip."

"I hadn't noticed."

She shot him an envious glance. "You haven't gained an ounce. You never do."

"I have the Tintoretto to thank for that."

Chiara nudged the tart closer to Gabriel. "You eat it."

"You're the one who ordered it."

Chiara dislodged a slice of strawberry from the bed of cream. "How long do you think it will take Unit 8200 to find Janson's phone number?"

"Given the insecurity of the Vatican network, I'd say about five minutes flat. Once they get it, it won't take them long to pinpoint his location." Gabriel inched the tart closer to Chiara. "And then we can go back to Venice and resume our holiday."

"What if the phone is powered off or lying on the bottom of the Tiber?" Chiara lowered her voice. "Or what if they've already killed him?"

"Janson?"

"Yes, of course."

"And who are *they*?"

"The same men who murdered the pope."

Gabriel frowned. "We're not there yet, Chiara."

"We passed *there* a long time ago, darling." Chiara sliced off a piece of the tart and pierced it through the cream and crust. "I have to admit I'm looking forward to dinner tonight."

"I wish I could say the same."

"What are you worried about?"

"An awkward pause in the conversation."

"You know, Gabriel, you didn't actually *kill* Carlo Marchese."

"I didn't exactly prevent him from falling over that barrier, either."

"Perhaps Veronica won't bring it up."

"I certainly don't intend to."

Chiara smiled and looked around the room. "What do you suppose normal people do on holiday?"

"We *are* normal people, Chiara. We just have interesting friends."

"With interesting problems."

Gabriel plunged his fork into the tart. "That, too."

THERE WAS AN OLD OFFICE safe flat at the top of the Spanish Steps, not far from the church of the Trinità dei Monti. House-keeping hadn't had time to stock the pantry. It was no matter; Gabriel wasn't anticipating a long stay.

In the bedroom they unpacked the shopping bags. Gabriel had acquired his evening wardrobe swiftly, with a single stop at Giorgio Armani. Chiara had been more discriminating in her conquest. A strapless black cocktail dress from Max Mara, a car-length coat from Burberry, a pair of stylish black pumps from Salvatore Ferragamo. Now Gabriel surprised her with a strand of pearls from Mikimoto.

Beaming, she asked, "What are these for?"

"You're the wife of the director-general of the Israeli intelligence service and the mother of two young children. It's the least I can do."

"Have you forgotten about the apartment on the Grand Canal?" Chiara placed the strand of pearls around her neck. She looked radiant. "What do you think?"

"I think I'm the luckiest man in the world." The cocktail dress was laid out on the bed. "Is that a negligee?"

"Don't start with me."

"Where do you intend to conceal your weapon?"

"I wasn't planning to bring one." She pushed him toward the door. "Go away."

He went into the sitting room. From its tiny terrace he could see the Spanish Steps descending sedately toward the piazza and, in the distance, the floodlit dome of the basilica floating above the Vatican. All at once he heard a voice. It was the voice of Carlo Marchese.

What is this, Allon?

Judgment, Carlo.

His body had split open on impact, like a melon. What Gabriel remembered most, however, was the blood on Donati's cassock. He wondered how the archbishop had explained Carlo's death to Veronica. It promised to be an interesting evening.

He went inside. From the next room he could hear Chiara singing softly to herself as she dressed, one of those silly Italian pop songs she so adored. Better the sound of Chiara's voice, he thought, than Carlo Marchese's. As always, it filled him with a sense of contentment. His journey was nearing its end. Chiara and the children were his reward for somehow having survived. Still, Leah was never far from his thoughts. She was watching him now from the shadows at the corner of the room, burned and broken, her scarred hands clutching a lifeless child— Gabriel's private pietà. *Do you love this girl?* Yes, he thought. He loved everything about her. The way she licked her finger when she turned the page of a magazine. The way she swung her handbag when she walked along the Via Condotti. The way she sang to herself when she thought no one was listening.

He switched on the television. It was tuned to the BBC. Remarkably, there had been no fatalities in the Berlin bombing, though twelve people had been wounded, four critically. Axel Brünner of the far-right National Democratic Party was blaming the attack on the pro-immigration policies of Germany's centrist chancellor. Neo-Nazis and other assorted right-wing extremists were gathering for a torchlight rally in the city of Leipzig. The Bundespolizei were bracing for a night of violence.

Gabriel changed the channel to CNN. The network's premier foreign affairs correspondent was broadcasting live from St. Peter's Square. Like her competitors, she was unaware of the fact that a letter addressed to the director-general of the Israeli secret intelligence service had mysteriously vanished from the pope's study the night of his death. Nor did she know that the Swiss Guard who had been standing watch outside the papal apartments was missing, too. If Niklaus Janson's phone was powered on and broadcasting a signal, the cyberwarriors at Unit 8200 would find it, perhaps before the night was out.

Gabriel switched off the television as Chiara came into the sitting room. He took his time with his appraisal—the pearls, the strapless black dress, the pumps. She was a masterpiece.

"Well?" she asked at last.

"You look . . ." He faltered.

"Like a mother of two who's gained eight pounds?"

"I thought you said five."

"I just stepped on the bathroom scale." She gestured toward the bedroom door. "It's all yours."

Gabriel quickly showered and dressed. Downstairs, they climbed into the back of a waiting embassy car. As they raced up the Via Veneto, his phone pulsed with an incoming message from King Saul Boulevard.

"What is it?"

"The Unit just breached the outer wall of the Swiss Guard's computer network. They're searching the database for Janson's personnel file and contact information."

"What if they've deleted it already?"

"Who?"

"The same men who murdered the pope, of course."

"We're not there yet, Chiara."

"Not yet," she agreed. "But we will be soon."

10

CASA SANTA MARTA

U NDER NORMAL CIRCUMSTANCES, SWISS GUARDS did not stand watch outside the Casa Santa Marta. But at eight fifteen that same evening, there were two. The clerical guesthouse was now occupied by several dozen princes of the Church, mainly from the distant corners of the realm. On the eve of the conclave, the remaining cardinal-electors would join them. After that, no one but the Casa Santa Marta's staff—nuns from the Daughters of St. Vincent de Paul—would be allowed to enter. For now, a select few, including Bishop Hans Richter, superior general of the Order of St. Helena, were free to come and go as they pleased. With Cardinal Domenico Albanese firmly in control of the machinery of the city-state, Bishop Richter's long exile was finally over.

One of the Swiss Guards held open the glass door, and Richter, his right hand raised in blessing, went inside. The gleaming white lobby echoed with a multilingual din. The 225 members of the College of Cardinals had spent the afternoon discussing the Church's future. Now they were partaking of white wine and canapés in the lobby before sitting down to supper in the Casa Santa Marta's simple dining room. The Apostolic Constitution dictated that only the 116 cardinals under the age of eighty would be allowed to take part in the conclave. The elderly cardinals emeriti made their preferences known during informal gatherings such as these, which was where the real pre-conclave horse trading took place.

Richter discreetly acknowledged the greetings of a pair of well-known traditionalists and endured the icy stare of Cardinal Kevin Brady, the liberal lion from Los Angeles who saw a pope each time he looked in the mirror. Brady was conspiring with tiny Duarte of Manila, the great hope of the developing world. Cardinal Navarro was brimming with confidence, as though the papacy was already his. It was obvious that Gaubert, who was scheming with Villiers of Lyon, did not plan to go down without a fight.

Only Bishop Hans Richter knew that none of them stood a chance. The next pope was at that moment standing near the reception desk, an afterthought in a room filled with towering egos and boundless ambition. He had been given his red hat by none other than Pietro Lucchesi, who had been deceived into believing he was a moderate, which he most definitely was not. Fifty million euros, discreetly deposited in bank accounts around the world, including twelve at the Vatican Bank, had all but guaranteed his election by the conclave. Securing the vast sum of money required to purchase the papacy had been the easiest part of the operation. Unlike the rest of the Church, which was on the verge of financial collapse, the Order of St. Helena was awash with cash.

Cardinal Domenico Albanese was whispering something into the ear of Angelo Francona, the dean of the College of Cardinals. Spotting Richter, he beckoned with a thick, furry hand. Francona, a leading liberal, immediately turned on his heel and fled.

"Did I do something to give offense?" asked Richter in flawless curial Italian.

"You offend by your very existence, Excellency." Albanese took Richter by the arm. "Perhaps we should speak in my room."

"Don't tell me you've actually moved in."

Albanese grimaced. As *prefetto* of the Secret Archives, he was entitled to a luxurious apartment above the Lapidary Gallery of the Vatican Museums. "I'm simply using my room here as an office until the start of the conclave."

"With any luck," said Richter quietly, "you won't have to stay long."

"The media are predicting a titanic struggle between the reformers and the reactionaries."

"Are they?"

"Seven ballots seems to be the general consensus."

A blue-habited nun offered Richter a glass of wine. Declining, he followed Albanese to the elevators. He could almost feel the eyes of the room boring holes in his back as they waited for a carriage to arrive. When one finally appeared, Albanese pressed the call button for the fourth floor. Mercifully, the doors closed before loquacious Lopes of Rio de Janeiro could squeeze inside.

Bishop Richter made several unnecessary adjustments to his purple-trimmed cassock as the carriage slowly rose. Handmade by an exclusive tailor in Zurich, it fit him to perfection. At seventy-four, he remained an imposing physical specimen, tall and square-shouldered, with iron-gray hair and an unbendable countenance to match.

He looked at Cardinal Albanese's reflection in the elevator doors. "What's on the menu this evening, Eminence?"

"Whatever they serve us will be overcooked." Albanese smiled gracelessly. Even in his red-trimmed cassock, he looked like the hired help. "Consider yourself lucky you don't have to actually take part in the conclave."

In the nomenclature of the Roman Catholic Church, the Order of St. Helena was a personal prelature—in effect, a global diocese without borders. As superior general of the Order, Richter held the rank of bishop. Nevertheless, he was among the most powerful men in the Roman Catholic Church. Several dozen cardinals, all secret members of the Order, were obliged to obey his every command, including Cardinal Domenico Albanese.

The elevator doors opened. Albanese led Bishop Richter along an empty corridor. The room they entered was in darkness. Albanese found the light switch.

Richter surveyed his surroundings. "I see you've assigned yourself one of the suites."

"The rooms were assigned by lottery, Excellency."

"Lucky you."

Bishop Richter held out his right hand, the wrist cocked slightly. Albanese dropped to his knees and placed his lips against the ring on Richter's third finger. It was identical in size to the

Ring of the Fisherman that Albanese had recently removed from the papal apartments.

"I swear to you, Bishop Richter, my eternal obedience."

Richter withdrew his hand, resisting the urge to reach for the small bottle of sanitizer in his pocket. Richter was a germophobe. Albanese always struck him as a carrier.

He moved to the window and parted the gauzy curtain. The suite was on the north side of the guesthouse, overlooking the Piazza Santa Marta and the facade of the basilica. The dome was aglow with floodlights. The wounds from the Islamic terrorist attack had healed nicely. If only the same could be said for the Holy Mother Church. She was a shadow of her former self, barely breathing, close to death.

Bishop Hans Richter had appointed himself her savior. He had been prepared to wait out Lucchesi's disastrous papacy before putting his plan into action. But His Holiness had given Richter no choice but to take matters into his own hands. It was Lucchesi who had erred, Richter assured himself, not he. Besides, God had been knocking on Lucchesi's door for some time. To Richter's way of thinking, he had merely given Pope Accidental an early start on the inevitable process of canonization.

Richter's thoughts were interrupted by a thunderous flush of the commode. When Albanese emerged, he was wiping his big hands on a towel—like a ditchdigger, thought Richter. And to think he actually regarded himself as a potential pope, the one Richter would choose to be his puppet pontiff. He was no intellectual giant, Albanese, but he had played the curial insider's game well enough to secure two critical papal appointments. As camerlengo, Albanese had shepherded Lucchesi's body from the papal apartments to his tomb beneath St. Peter's with no hint of scandal. He had also placed in Richter's hands copies of several sin-filled personnel files from the Vatican Secret Archives that had proven invaluable during the preparations for the conclave. For his reward, Albanese would soon be the secretary of state, the second most powerful position in the Holy See.

He dried his pitted face and then tossed the towel over the back of a chair. "With all due respect, Excellency, do you think it was wise to come here this evening?"

"Are you forgetting that many of those cardinals downstairs are now wealthy men because of me?"

"All the more reason you should keep a low profile until the conclave is over. I can only imagine what the likes of Francona and Kevin Brady are saying right now."

"Francona and Brady are the least of our problems."

The simple wooden armchair into which Albanese lowered himself groaned beneath his weight. "Is there any sign of the Janson boy?"

Richter shook his head.

"He was obviously distraught that night. It's possible he took his own life."

"We should be so lucky."

"Surely you don't mean that, Excellency. If Janson committed suicide, his soul would be in grave peril."

"It already is."

"As is mine," said Albanese quietly.

Richter placed a hand on the camerlengo's thick shoulder. "I granted you absolution for your actions, Domenico. Your soul is in a state of grace."

"And yours, Excellency?"

Richter removed his hand. "I sleep well at night knowing that in a few days' time, the Church will be in our control. I will allow no one to stand in our way. And that includes a pretty little peasant boy from Canton Fribourg."

"Then I suggest you find him, Excellency. The sooner the better."

Bishop Richter smiled coldly. "Is that the type of incisive and analytical thinking you intend to bring to the Secretariat of State?"

Albanese suffered the rebuke from his superior general in silence.

"Rest assured," said Bishop Richter, "the Order is using all of its considerable resources to find Janson. Unfortunately, we are no longer the only ones looking for him. It appears Archbishop Donati has joined the search."

"If we can't find Janson, what hope does Donati have?"

"Donati has something much better than hope."

"What's that?"

Bishop Richter gazed at the dome of the basilica. "Gabriel Allon."

11

VIA SARDEGNA, ROME

THE PALAZZO WAS OFTEN MISTAKEN for an embassy or a government ministry, for it was surrounded by a formidable steel fence and watched over by an array of outward-aimed security cameras. A Baroque fountain splashed in the forecourt, but the two-thousand-year-old Roman statue of Pluto that had once adorned the entrance hall was absent. In its place stood Dr. Veronica Marchese, director of Italy's National Etruscan Museum. She wore a stunning black pantsuit and a thick band of gold at her throat. Her dark hair was swept straight back and held in place by a clasp at the nape of her neck. A pair of cat's-eye spectacles gave her a faintly academic air.

Smiling, she kissed Chiara on both cheeks. She offered Gabriel only her hand, guardedly. "Director Allon. I'm so pleased you were able to come. I'm only sorry we didn't do this a long time ago."

The ice broken, she led them along a gallery hung with Italian Old Master paintings, all of museum quality. The works were but a small portion of her late husband's collection.

"As you can see, I've made a few changes since your last visit."

"Spring cleaning?" asked Gabriel.

She laughed. "Something like that."

The exquisite Greek and Roman statuary that once had lined the gallery was gone. Carlo Marchese's business empire, nearly all of it illegitimate, had included a brisk international trade in looted antiquities. One of his main partners had been Hezbollah, which supplied Carlo with a steady stream of inventory from Lebanon, Syria, and Iraq. In return, Carlo filled Hezbollah's coffers with hard currency, which it used to purchase weapons and fund terrorism. Gabriel had taken down the network. Then, after making a remarkable archaeological discovery one hundred and sixty-seven feet beneath the surface of the Temple Mount, he had taken down Carlo.

"A few months after my husband's death," Veronica Marchese explained, "I quietly disposed of his personal collection. I gave the Etruscan pieces to my museum, which is where they belonged in the first place. Most are still in storage, but I've placed a few on public display. Needless to say, the placards make no mention of their provenance."

"And the rest?"

"Your friend General Ferrari was good enough to take it off my hands. He was very discreet, which is unusual for him. The general likes good publicity." She looked at Gabriel with genuine gratitude. "I suppose I have you to thank for that. If it had become public that my husband controlled the global trade in looted antiquities, my career would have been destroyed."

"We all have our secrets."

"Yes," she said distantly. "I suppose we do."

Veronica Marchese's other secret waited in her formal drawing room, dressed in a cassock and a simar. Music played softly in the background. It was Mendelssohn's Piano Trio no. 1 in D Minor. The key of repressed passion.

Donati opened a bottle of prosecco and poured four glasses.

"You're rather good at that for a priest," said Gabriel.

"I'm an archbishop, remember?"

Donati carried one of the glasses to the brocade-covered chair in which Veronica had settled. A trained observer of human behavior, Gabriel knew an intimate gesture when he saw one. Donati was clearly comfortable in Veronica's drawing room. Were it not for the cassock and simar, a stranger might have presumed he was the man of the palazzo.

He sat down in the chair next to her, and an awkward silence ensued. Like an uninvited dinner guest, the past had intruded. For his part, Gabriel was thinking about his last encounter with Veronica Marchese. They were in the Sistine Chapel, just the two of them, standing before Michelangelo's *Last Judgment*. Veronica was describing for Gabriel the life that awaited Donati when the Ring of the Fisherman was removed from Pietro Lucchesi's finger for the last time. A teaching position at a pontifical university, a retirement home for aging priests. *So lonely. So terribly sad and lonely* . . . It occurred to Gabriel that Veronica, widowed and available, might have other plans.

At length, she complimented Chiara on her dress and pearls. Then she asked about the children and about Venice before lamenting the condition into which Rome, once the center of the civilized world, had fallen. These days, it was a national obsession. Eighty percent of the city's streets were riddled with unrepaired potholes, making driving, even walking, a perilous undertaking. Children carried toilet paper in their bookbags because the school bathrooms had none. Rome's buses ran perpetually behind schedule, if at all. An escalator at a busy subway stop had recently amputated the foot of a tourist. And then, said Veronica, there were the overflowing dumpsters and mounds of uncollected rubbish. The most popular website in the city was Roma Fa Schifo, "Rome Is Gross."

"And who is to blame for this deplorable state of affairs? A few years ago, Rome's chief prosecutor discovered that the Mafia had gained control of the municipal government and was steadily draining the city's finances. A Mafia-owned company was awarded the contract to collect the garbage. The company didn't bother to collect garbage, of course, because doing so would cost money and reduce its profit margin. The same was true of street repairs. Why bother to repair a pothole? Repairing potholes costs money." Veronica shook her head slowly. "The Mafia is Italy's curse." Then, with a glance at Gabriel, she added, "Mine, too."

"It will all be better now that Saviano is prime minister."

Veronica made a face. "Have we learned nothing from the past?"

"Apparently not."

She sighed. "He visited the museum not long ago. He was perfectly charming, as most demagogues are. It's easy to see why he appeals to Italians who don't live in palazzos near the Via Veneto." She placed her hand briefly on Donati's arm. "Or behind the walls of the Vatican. Saviano hated the Holy Father for his defense of immigrants and his warnings about the dangers posed by the rise of the far right. He saw it as a direct challenge orchestrated by the Holy Father's leftist private secretary."

"Was it?" asked Gabriel.

Donati sipped his wine thoughtfully before answering. "The Church remained silent the last time the extreme right seized power in Italy and Germany. In fact, powerful elements within the Curia supported the rise of fascism and National Socialism. They saw Mussolini and Hitler as a bulwark against bolshevism, which was openly hostile to Catholicism. The Holy Father and I resolved that this time we would not make the same mistake."

"And now," said Veronica Marchese, "the Holy Father is dead, and a Swiss Guard is missing." She looked at Gabriel. "Luigi tells me you've agreed to find him."

Gabriel frowned at Donati, who was suddenly brushing lint from the front of his spotless cassock.

"Did I speak out of turn?" asked Veronica.

"No. The archbishop did."

"Don't be angry with him. Life in the gilded cage of the Apostolic Palace can be very isolating. The archbishop often seeks my advice on temporal matters. As you know, I'm rather well connected in Roman political and social circles. A woman in my position hears all sorts of things."

"Such as?"

"Rumors," she replied.

"What kind of rumors?"

"About a handsome young Swiss Guard who was spotted at a gay nightclub with a curial priest. When I told the archbishop, he warned me that unproven allegations can do irreparable harm to a person's reputation, and advised me not to traffic in them."

"The archbishop would know," remarked Gabriel. "But one wonders why he didn't mention any of this at lunch this afternoon."

"Perhaps he didn't think it was relevant."

"Or perhaps he thought it would make me reluctant to help him if I thought I was going to get involved in a Vatican sex scandal."

Gabriel's phone pulsed against his heart. It was a message from King Saul Boulevard.

"Something wrong?" asked Donati.

"It appears as though Janson's file was deleted from the Swiss Guard's computer network a few hours after the Holy Father's death." Gabriel exchanged a glance with Chiara, who was suppressing a smile. "My colleagues at Unit 8200 are now searching the system's backup."

"Will they find anything?"

"Computer files are a bit like sin, Excellency."

"How so?"

"They can be absolved, but they never really go away."

THEY HAD DINNER ON THE palazzo's magnificent rooftop terrace, beneath gas heaters that burned the chill from the night air. It was a traditional Roman meal, spinach ravioli topped with butter and sage, followed by roasted veal and fresh vegetables. The conversation flowed as easily as the three bottles of vintage Brunello that Veronica unearthed from Carlo's cellar. Donati seemed perfectly at ease in his black clerical armor, with Veronica at his right hand and the lights of Rome glowing softly behind him. It might have been broken and filthy and hopelessly corrupt, but viewed from Veronica Marchese's terrace, with the air clear and crisp and scented with the aroma of cooking, Gabriel thought it was the most beautiful city in the world.

Carlo's name was never spoken over dinner, and there was no hint of the violence and scandal that bound them. Donati speculated on the outcome of the conclave but avoided the subject of Lucchesi's death. Mainly, he seemed to hang on Veronica's every word. The affection between them was painfully obvious. Donati was walking along the edge of an Alpine crevasse. For now, at least, God was watching over him.

Only Gabriel's phone served as a reminder of why they had gathered that night. Shortly after ten o'clock it shivered with an update from Tel Aviv. The cybersleuths at Unit 8200 had retrieved Niklaus Janson's original application to join the Swiss Guard. The next update came at half past ten, when the Unit found his complete service file. It was written in Swiss German, the official language of the Guard. It contained a reference to the two missed curfews, but there was nothing about a sexual relationship with a curial priest.

"What about his phone number? It has to be there. The guards are always on call."

"Patience, Excellency."

The wait for the next message was only ten minutes. "They found an old contact file, one that included an entry for Lance Corporal Niklaus Janson. It has a phone number and two e-mail addresses, a Vatican account and a personal account at Gmail."

"What now?" asked Donati.

"We find out where the phone is and whether Niklaus Janson is still in possession of it."

"And then?"

"We call him."

12

ROME–FLORENCE

DONATI WAS AWAKENED BY THE tolling of church bells. Slowly, he opened his eyes. Daylight rimmed the edges of the tightly drawn shade. He had overslept. He placed a hand to his brow. His head was heavy with Carlo Marchese's wine. His heart was heavy, too. He didn't dare dwell on the reason why.

He sat up and eased his feet to the cold parquet floor. It took a moment for the room to come into focus. A writing desk piled with books and papers, a simple wardrobe, a wooden prie-dieu. Above it, faintly visible in the gloom, was the crucifix, heavy and oaken, given to him by his master a few days after the conclave. It had hung in Donati's apartment in the Apostolic Palace. Now it hung here, in his room at the Jesuit Curia. How different it was from Veronica's lavish palazzo. It was the room of a poor man, he thought. The room of a priest.

The prie-dieu beckoned. Rising, Donati pulled on his dressing gown and crossed the room. He opened his breviary to the appropriate page and on his knees recited the first words of lauds, the morning prayer.

God, come to my assistance. Lord, make haste to help me . . .

Behind him on his bedside table his phone purred. Ignoring it, he read that morning's selection of psalms and hymns, along with a brief passage from Revelation.

And I saw another angel ascending from the rising of the sun . . .

Only when Donati had repeated the final line of the closing prayer did he rise and retrieve the phone. The message that awaited him was composed in colloquial Italian. The wording was ambiguous and full of misdirection and double meaning. Nevertheless, the instructions were clear. Had Donati not known better, he would have assumed the author was a creature of the Roman Curia. He was not.

And I saw another angel ascending from the rising of the sun . . .

Donati tossed the phone onto his unmade bed and quickly shaved and showered. Wrapped in a towel, he opened the doors of his wardrobe. Hanging from the rod were several cassocks and clerical suits, along with his choir dress. His civilian wardrobe was limited to a single sport jacket with elbow patches, two pairs of tan chinos, two white dress shirts, two crewneck pullovers, and a pair of suede loafers.

He dressed in one of the outfits and packed the spare in his overnight bag. Next he added a change of undergarments, toiletries, a stole, an alb, a cincture, and his traveling Mass kit. The mobile phone he slipped into his jacket pocket.

The corridor outside his rooms was empty. He heard the faint tinkle of glass and cutlery and earthenware emanating from the communal dining hall and, from the chapel, sonorous male voices at prayer. Unnoticed by his Jesuit brethren, he hurried downstairs and went into the autumn morning.

An E-Class Mercedes sedan waited in the Borgo Santo Spirito. Gabriel was behind the wheel; Chiara, in the passenger seat. When Donati slid into the back, the car shot forward. Several pedestrians, including a curial priest whom Donati knew in passing, scurried for cover.

"Is there a problem?" he asked.

Gabriel glanced into the rearview mirror. "I'll know in a few minutes."

The car swerved to the right, narrowly missing a flock of gray-habited nuns, and raced across the Tiber.

Donati fastened his safety belt and closed his eyes.

God, come to my assistance. Lord, make haste to help me . . .

THEY SPED NORTH ALONG THE Lungotevere to the Piazza del Popolo, then south to Piazza Venezia. Even by Rome's lofty standards, it was a hair-raising ride. Donati, a veteran of countless papal motorcades, marveled at the skill with which his old friend handled the powerful German-made car, and at the apparent calm with which Chiara occasionally offered directions or advice. Their route was indirect and full of sudden stops and abrupt turns, all designed to reveal the presence of motorized surveillance. In a city like Rome, where scooters were a common form of transport, it was a daunting task. Donati tried to be of help, but in time he gave up and watched the graffiti-spattered buildings and mountain ranges of uncollected garbage flashing past his window. Veronica was right. Rome was beautiful, but it was gross.

By the time they reached Ostiense, a chaotic working-class quarter in Municipio VIII, Gabriel appeared satisfied they were not being followed. He made his way to the A90, Rome's orbital motorway, and headed north to the E35 Autostrada, a toll road stretching the length of Italy to the Swiss border.

Donati eased his grip on the armrest. "Do you mind telling me where we're going?"

Gabriel pointed toward a blue-and-white sign at the side of the road.

Donati permitted himself a brief smile. It had been a long time since he had been to Florence.

UNIT 8200 HAD LOCATED THE phone on the Florence cellular grid shortly before five that morning. It was north of the Arno in San Marco, the quarter of the city where the Medici, the banking dynasty that transformed Florence into the artistic and intellectual heart of Europe, had stabled their menagerie of giraffes, elephants, and lions. Thus far, the Unit had been unable to penetrate the device and gain control of its operating system. It was merely monitoring the phone's approximate position using geolocation techniques.

"In layman's language, please?" asked Donati.

"Once we're inside a phone, we can listen to the owner's calls, read his e-mail and text messages, and monitor his browsing on the Internet. We can even take photographs and videos with the camera and use the microphone as a listening device."

"It's as though you're God."

"Not quite, but we certainly have the power to peer into someone's soul. We can learn their darkest fears and their deepest desires." Gabriel gave a rueful shake of his head. "The telecommunications industry and their friends in Silicon Valley promised us a brave new world of convenience, all at our fingertips. They told us not to worry, our secrets would be safe. None of it was true. They intentionally lied to us. They stole our privacy. And in the process, they've ruined everything."

"Everything?"

"Newspapers, movies, books, music . . . everything."

"I never knew you were such a Luddite."

"I'm an art restorer who specializes in Italian Old Masters. I'm a charter member of the club."

"And yet you carry a mobile phone."

"A very special mobile phone. Even my friends at the American NSA can't crack it."

Donati held up a Nokia 9 Android. "And mine?"

"I'd feel much better if you threw it out the window."

"My life is on this phone."

"Therein lies the problem, Excellency."

At Gabriel's request, Donati surrendered his phone to Chiara. After switching off the power, she removed the SIM card and the battery and placed both in her handbag. The soulless chassis she returned to Donati.

"I feel better already."

They stopped for coffee at an Autogrill near Orvieto and reached the outskirts of Florence a few minutes after noon. The Zona Traffico Limitato signs were flashing red. Gabriel left the

Mercedes in a public car park near the Basilica di Santa Croce, and together they set out toward San Marco.

According to the blue light on Gabriel's phone, Janson's device was just west of the San Marco Museum, probably on the Via San Gallo. Unit 8200 had cautioned that the geolocation plot was accurate only to about forty meters, which meant the phone could also be on the Via Santa Reparata or the Via della Ruote. All three streets were lined with small discount hotels and hostels. Gabriel counted at least fourteen such establishments where Niklaus Janson might have found lodging.

The exact spot upon which the blue dot rested corresponded to the address of a hotel appropriately called the Piccolo. Directly across the street was a restaurant where Gabriel lunched in the manner of a man for whom time was of no consequence. Donati, his phone reassembled and operational, dined on the Via Santa Reparata; Chiara, around the corner on the Villa della Ruote.

Gabriel and Chiara each had a copy of Janson's official Swiss Guard photograph on their phones. It showed a serious young man with short hair and small dark eyes set within an angular face. Trustworthy, thought Gabriel, but by no means a saint. Janson's file listed his height as the metric equivalent of about six feet. His weight was seventy-five kilograms, or one hundred and sixty-five pounds.

By three fifteen they had seen no sign of him. Chiara moved to the restaurant opposite the Hotel Piccolo; Donati, to the Villa della Ruote. On the Via Santa Reparata, Gabriel spent much of the time staring at his phone, exhorting the winking blue light into movement. At five o'clock, twelve hours after its initial discovery, its position was unchanged. Despairing, Gabriel conjured an image of an unplugged smartphone expiring slowly in an abandoned room littered with empty takeaway cartons.

A text message from Chiara lifted his spirits. I'm now fifteen pounds overweight. Maybe we should just call the number.

What if he was involved?

I thought you said we weren't there yet.

We aren't. But we're getting closer by the minute.

At half past five they changed positions a second time. Gabriel went to a restaurant on the Villa della Ruote. He took a table on the street and picked at a plate of spaghetti pomodoro without appetite.

"If it's not to your liking," said the waiter, "I can bring you something else."

Gabriel ordered a double espresso, his fifth of the afternoon, and with a slightly trembling hand reached for his phone. There was another message from Chiara.

Twenty pounds. I'm begging you, please call him.

Gabriel was sorely tempted. Instead, he watched the tourists trudging back to their hotels after a long day sampling the delights of Florence. There were four hotels along the street. The inappropriately named Grand Hotel Medici was adjacent to the restaurant, directly in Gabriel's line of sight.

He checked the time on his phone. It was six fifteen. Then he checked the position of the light on the geolocation graph and detected what appeared to be the faintest trace of a wobble. Thirty additional seconds of rigorous observation confirmed his suspicion. The light was definitely moving.

Because of the forty-meter margin for error, Gabriel quickly informed both Chiara and Donati of his findings. Donati replied that he saw no sign of Janson on the Via San Gallo, and a few seconds later Chiara reported the same from her outpost on the Via Santa Reparata. Gabriel replied to neither message, for he was scrutinizing the man who had just emerged from the Grand Hotel Medici.

Late twenties, short hair, about six feet, maybe a hundred and seventy pounds. He scanned the street in both directions, then headed to the right, past the restaurant. Gabriel dealt two crisp banknotes onto the table, counted slowly to ten, and rose. Trustworthy, he was thinking. But by no means a saint.

13

FLORENCE

CHIARA AND DONATI WAITED ON the Via Ricasoli, buffeted by the outbound flow of patrons from the Galleria dell'Accademia. Without warning, she threw her arms around Donati's neck and drew him close.

"Is this really necessary?"

"We don't want him to see your face. At least not yet."

She held Donati tightly as Niklaus Janson sliced through the crowds and passed them without a glance. Gabriel came along the street a moment later.

"Is there something you two would like to tell me?"

Donati freed himself and deliberately straightened his jacket. "Shall I call him now?"

"First we follow him. Then we call."

"Why wait?"

"Because we need to know whether anyone else is following him."

"What happens if you see someone?"

"Let's hope it doesn't come to that."

Gabriel and Donati set off along the street, trailed by Chiara. Before them was the Campanile di Giotto. Janson melted into the sea of tourists in the Piazza del Duomo and disappeared from view. When Gabriel finally spotted him again, the Swiss Guard was leaning against the octagonal baptistry, the mobile phone in his right hand. After a moment his thumb began tapping at the screen.

"What do you suppose he's doing?" asked Donati.

"Looks as though he's sending a text."

"To whom?"

"Good question."

Janson slipped the phone into the back pocket of his jeans and, rotating slowly, scanned the crowded square. His gaze swept directly across Gabriel and Donati. His face registered no sign of recognition.

"He's looking for someone," said Donati.

"It could be the person who just sent him the text."

"Or?"

"Maybe he's afraid someone is following him."

"Someone *is* following him."

At length, Janson left the piazza and set out along a shopping street called the Via Martelli. This time it was Chiara who followed in his wake. After about a hundred meters he turned into a slender alleyway. It brought him to yet another church square, the Piazza di San Lorenzo. The unfinished facade of the basilica loomed over the eastern flank. It was the color of sandstone and looked like a giant wall of exposed brick. Janson, after briefly consulting his phone, climbed the five steps and went inside.

On the western flank of the piazza was a parade of clothing vendors that catered to tourists. On the northern side was a gelateria. Chiara and Donati joined the queue at the counter. Gabriel crossed the square and entered the basilica. Janson stood before the tomb of Cosimo de Medici, thumbs working over the screen of his phone, seemingly oblivious to the florid-faced Englishwoman who was addressing a tour group as though they were hard of hearing.

The Swiss Guard sent a final text and went into the square, where he paused once again to survey his surroundings. Clearly, he was expecting someone. The person at the other end of the text messages, reckoned Gabriel. The person who had led him first to the Piazza del Duomo and then the Basilica di San Lorenzo.

Janson's gaze alighted briefly on Gabriel. Then he left the piazza along the Borgo San Lorenzo. No one in the square or the surrounding shops or restaurants appeared to follow him.

Gabriel walked over to the gelateria, where Donati and Chiara were balanced atop tall stools at a zinc-topped table. They hadn't touched their orders.

"Can we make contact with him now?" asked Donati.

"Not yet."

"Why not?"

"Because they're here, Excellency."

"Who?"

Gabriel turned without answering and set off after Niklaus

Janson. A moment later Chiara and Donati tossed their uneaten gelato into a rubbish bin and set off after Gabriel.

JANSON PASSED THROUGH the Piazza del Duomo a second time, all but confirming Gabriel's suspicion that the Swiss Guard was being guided by a hidden hand. Somewhere in Florence, he thought, someone was waiting for him.

Janson went next to the Piazza della Repubblica and from there made his way to the Ponte Vecchio. It had once been home to blacksmiths, tanners, and butchers. But in the late sixteenth century, after Florentines complained about the blood and the stench, the bridge became the domain of the city's jewelers and goldsmiths. Vasari designed a private corridor above the shops on the eastern side of the bridge for the Medici clan, thus enabling them to cross the river without having to mingle with their subjects.

The Medici were long gone, but the jewelers and goldsmiths remained. Janson made his way past the luminous shop windows before pausing mid-span beneath the arches of Vasari's Corridor to gaze down at the sluggish black waters of the Arno. Gabriel waited on the opposite side of the bridge. Between them flowed a steady stream of tourists.

Gabriel glanced to his left and saw Chiara and Donati approaching through the crowds. With a small movement of his head, he instructed them to join him. They stood side by side along the balustrade, Gabriel and Chiara facing Niklaus Janson, Donati facing the river.

"Well?" he asked.

Gabriel watched Janson for another moment. His back was turned toward the center of the span. Nevertheless, it was obvious that he was typing something on his phone again. Gabriel wanted to know the identity of the person, man or woman, with whom Janson was in contact. But it had gone on long enough.

"Go ahead, Luigi. Call him."

Donati drew his Nokia. Janson's number was already loaded into his contacts. With a touch of the screen, he dialed. A few seconds passed. Then Niklaus Janson hesitantly raised the phone to his ear.

14

PONTE VECCHIO, FLORENCE

G OOD EVENING, NIKLAUS. DO YOU recognize my voice?"
Donati tapped the speaker icon on the touchscreen of the
Nokia in time for Gabriel to hear Janson's startled reply.

"Excellency?"

"Yes."

"Where are you?"

"I was wondering the same about you."

There was no response from the young man on the opposite
side of the bridge.

"I need to speak to you, Niklaus."

"About what?"

"The night the Holy Father died."

Once again there was no answer.

"Are you still there, Niklaus?"

"Yes, Excellency."

"Tell me where you are. It's urgent I see you at once."

"I'm in Switzerland."

"It's not like you to lie to an archbishop."

"I'm not lying."

"You're not in Switzerland. You're standing in the middle of the Ponte Vecchio in Florence."

"How do you know that?"

"Because I'm standing behind you."

Janson wheeled round, the phone to his ear. "I don't see you."

Donati turned as well, slowly.

"Excellency? Is that you?"

"Yes, Niklaus."

"Who's the man standing next to you?"

"A friend."

"He's been following me."

"He was acting on my behalf."

"I was afraid he was going to kill me."

"Why would anyone want to kill you?"

"Forgive me, Excellency," he whispered.

"For what?"

"Grant me absolution."

"I have to hear your confession first."

He looked to his left. "There isn't time, Excellency."

Janson lowered the phone and started horizontally across the bridge. In the center of the span he stopped abruptly and spread his arms wide. The first shot struck him in the left shoulder, spinning him like a top. The second punched a hole through his chest and dropped him penitentially to his knees. There, with his arms now hanging limply at his sides, he received a third shot. It struck him above the right eye and sheared away a large portion of his skull.

On the ancient bridge the shots sounded like cannon fire. Instantly, a maelstrom of panic erupted. Gabriel spotted the assassin briefly as he fled the bridge to the south. Then, turning, he saw Chiara and Donati kneeling over Niklaus Janson. The final shot had driven him backward, with his legs trapped beneath him. Despite the terrible wound to his head, he was still alive, still conscious. Gabriel crouched over him. He was whispering something.

His phone was lying on the paving stones, its screen shattered. Gabriel slipped the device into his coat pocket, along with the nylon billfold he plucked from the back pocket of Janson's jeans. Donati was praying softly, the thumb of his right hand resting near the entrance wound in Janson's forehead. With two small movements, one vertical, the other horizontal, he absolved the Swiss Guard of his sins.

By then an anguished crowd had gathered around them. Gabriel heard expressions of shock and horror in a dozen different languages and, in the distance, the scream of approaching sirens. Rising, he pulled Chiara to her feet, then Donati. As they stepped away from the body, the crowd surged forward. Calmly, they walked north, into the flashing blue light of the first Polizia di Stato unit.

"What just happened?" asked Donati.

"I'm not sure," said Gabriel. "But we'll know in a minute."

AT THE FOOT OF THE Ponte Vecchio, they joined the exodus of frightened tourists fleeing through the archways of the Vasari

Corridor. When they reached the entrance of the Uffizi Gallery, Gabriel dug Janson's phone from his pocket. It was an iPhone, unlocked, eighty-four percent charged. His darkest fears, his deepest desires, his very soul, all at Gabriel's fingertips.

"Let's hope I was the only one who saw you take it," said Donati reproachfully. "*And* his wallet."

"You were. But try not to look so guilty."

"I just fled the scene of a murder. What on earth do I have to feel guilty about?"

Gabriel pressed the HOME button. Several applications were open, including a stream of text messages. He scrolled to the top of the exchange. There was no name, only a number. Written in English, the first text had arrived at 4:47 p.m. the previous afternoon.

Please tell me where you are, Niklaus . . .

"We've got him."

"Who?" asked Donati.

"The person who was sending text messages to Janson while we were following him."

Donati peered over Gabriel's right shoulder, Chiara over his left, their faces lit by the glow of the iPhone. All at once the light was extinguished. Gabriel pressed the HOME button again, but there was no response. The phone had not drifted off to sleep. It had shut down entirely.

Gabriel squeezed the power button and waited for the ubiquitous white apple to appear on the screen.

Nothing.

The phone was as dead as its owner.

"Perhaps you touched something by mistake," suggested Donati.

"Are you referring to the magic icon that instantly blows up the operating system and shreds the memory?" Gabriel looked up from the darkened screen. "It was erased remotely so we couldn't see what was on it."

"By whom?"

"The same men who deleted his personnel file from the Swiss Guard computer network." Gabriel looked at Chiara. "The same men who murdered the Holy Father."

"Do you believe me now?" asked Donati.

"Ten minutes ago, I had my doubts. Not anymore." Gabriel stared at the Ponte Vecchio. It was ablaze with flashing blue lights. "Were you able to make out what he was whispering before he died?"

"He was speaking in Aramaic. *Eli, Eli, lama sabachthani?* It means—"

"My God, my God, why have you forsaken me?"

Donati nodded slowly. "They were the last words Jesus cried out before dying on the cross."

"Why would he say such a thing?"

"Maybe the other guards were right," said Donati. "Maybe Niklaus was a saint after all."

15

VENICE—FRIBOURG, SWIZTERLAND

THEY RETURNED TO VENICE, COLLECTED two sleeping children from a house in the ancient ghetto, and carried them across the city's only iron bridge to an apartment on the Rio della Misericordia. There they passed a largely sleepless night, Donati in the spare room. At breakfast the following morning he could scarcely take his eyes off Raphael, who bore a striking resemblance to his famous father. The child had even been cursed with Gabriel's unnaturally green eyes. Irene looked like Gabriel's mother, never more so than when she was annoyed with him.

"It will only be a day or two," he assured her.

"That's what you always say, Abba."

They said their goodbyes downstairs on the Fondamenta dei Ormesini. Chiara's final kiss was decorous. "Do try not to get yourself killed," she whispered into Gabriel's ear. "Your children need you. And so do I."

Gabriel and Donati settled into the aft seating compartment of a waiting *motoscafo* and skimmed across the gray-green waters of the lagoon to Marco Polo Airport. In the crowded concourse, passengers were gathered beneath the television monitors. Another bomb had exploded in Germany. This time the target was a market in the northern city of Hamburg. A claim of responsibility had appeared on social media, along with a professionally edited video from the purported mastermind. In perfect colloquial German, his face concealed behind an Arab headdress, he promised the bombings would continue until the black flag of the Islamic State flew over the Bundestag. Having suffered two terrorist attacks in just forty-eight hours, Germany was now on high alert.

The bombing immediately snarled air travel across Europe, but somehow the late-morning Alitalia flight to Geneva departed on time. Despite the increased security at Switzerland's second-busiest airport, Gabriel and Donati cleared passport control with no delay. Transport had left a BMW sedan in the short-term car park, with the key taped beneath the front bumper. In the glove box, wrapped in a protective cloth, was a 9mm Beretta.

"It must be nice," remarked Donati. "I always have to pick up my gun at the counter."

"Membership has its privileges."

Gabriel followed the airport exit ramp to the E62 and headed northwest along the shore of the lake. Donati took note of the fact he was driving without the aid of a navigation device.

"Come to Switzerland often?"

"You might say that."

"They say it's going to be another bad year for snow."

"The state of Switzerland's winter tourism industry is the least of my concerns."

"You don't ski?"

"Do I look like a skier to you?"

"I never saw the point of it." Donati pondered the mountain peaks rising above the opposite shore of the lake. "Any fool can slide down a mountain, but it takes someone of character and discipline to walk up one."

"I prefer to walk along the sea."

"It's rising, you know. Apparently, Venice will soon be uninhabitable."

"At least it will discourage the tourists."

Gabriel switched on the radio in time to catch the hourly newscast on SFR 1. The death toll in Hamburg stood at four, with another twenty-five wounded, several critically. There was no mention of a Swiss citizen having been murdered the previous evening on the Ponte Vecchio in Florence.

"What are the Polizia di Stato waiting for?" asked Donati.

"If I had to guess, they're giving the Vatican a chance to get its story straight."

"Good luck with that."

The last item on the newscast concerned a report by the Episcopal Conference of Switzerland detailing a sharp increase in the number of new sexual abuse cases.

Donati sighed. "I wish they would talk about something uplifting. The bombing in Hamburg, for example."

"Did you know the report was coming?"

Donati nodded. "The Holy Father and I reviewed the first draft a few weeks before his death."

"How is it possible there are still *new* cases of abuse?"

"Because we apologized and asked for forgiveness, but we never addressed the root causes of the problem. And the Church has deservedly paid a terrible price. Here in Switzerland, Roman Catholicism is on life support. Baptisms, church weddings, and Mass attendance have all fallen to extinction levels."

"And if you had it to do over again?"

"Despite what my enemies used to say about me, I was not the pope. Pietro Lucchesi was. And he was an innately cautious man." Donati paused. "Too cautious, in my opinion."

"And if you were the one with the Ring of the Fisherman on his finger?"

Donati laughed.

"What's so funny?"

"The very idea is preposterous."

"Humor me."

Donati considered his answer carefully. "I'd start by reforming the priesthood. It's not enough merely to weed out the pedophiles. We must create a new and dynamic global community of Catholic religious if the Church is to survive and flourish."

"Does that mean you would admit women into the priesthood?"

"You said it, not me."

"How about married priests?"

"Now we're sailing into treacherous waters, my friend."

"Other faiths allow their clergy to marry."

"And I respect those faiths. The question is, can I as a Roman

Catholic priest love and cherish a wife and children while at the same time serving the Lord and tending to the spiritual needs of my flock?"

"What's the answer?"

"No," said Donati. "I cannot."

A sign warned they were approaching the lakeside resort town of Vevey. Gabriel turned onto the E27 and followed it north to Fribourg. It was a bilingual city, but the streets bore French names. The rue du Pont-Muré stretched for about a hundred meters through the elegant Old Town, above which soared the spire of the cathedral. Gabriel parked the car in the Place des Ormeaux and took a table at Café des Arcades. Alone, Donati crossed the street to Café du Gothard.

It was a formal, old-fashioned restaurant, with a dark wooden floor and heavy iron fixtures overhead. At that hour, the twilight between lunch and dinner, only one other table was occupied, by an English couple who looked as though they had just declared a fragile truce after a long and calamitous battle. The maître d' showed Donati to a table near the window. He dialed Gabriel's number and then laid his Nokia facedown on the tabletop. Several minutes elapsed before Stefani Hoffmann appeared. She placed a menu before him and with considerable effort smiled.

"Something to drink?"

16

CAFÉ DU GOTHARD, FRIBOURG

S HE TUCKED A LOOSE STRAND of blond hair behind her ear
and peered at Donati over the top of an order pad. Her eyes
were the color of an Alpine lake in summer. The rest of her face
matched their beauty. The cheekbones were broad, the jawline
was sharp, the chin was narrow with a slight indentation.

She had addressed Donati in French. He responded in the
same language. "A glass of wine, please."

With the tip of her pen she pointed toward the section of
the menu devoted to the café's selection of wines. They were
mainly French and Swiss. Donati chose a Chasselas.

"Something to eat?"

"Just the wine for now, thank you."

She walked over to the bar and checked her phone while a
black-shirted colleague poured the wine. The glass sat atop her

tray for a moment or two before she finally delivered it to Donati's table.

"You're not from Fribourg," she observed.

"How could you possibly tell?"

"Italy?"

"Rome."

Her expression was unchanged. "What brings you to dull Fribourg?"

"Business."

"What business are you in?"

Donati hesitated. He had never found a satisfactory way to admit what he did for his living. "I suppose I'm in the business of salvation."

Her eyes narrowed. "You're a clergyman?"

"A priest," said Donati.

"You don't look much like a priest." Her eyes flashed over him provocatively. "Especially in those clothes."

He wondered whether she addressed all her customers in so forward a manner. "Actually, I'm an archbishop."

"Where's your archdiocese?" She was obviously familiar with the lexicon of Catholicism.

"A remote corner of North Africa that was once part of the Roman Empire. There are very few Christians there any longer, let alone Catholics."

"A titular see?"

"Exactly."

"What do you really do?"

"I'm about to begin teaching at the Pontifical Gregorian University in Rome."

"You're a Jesuit?"

"I'm afraid so."

"And before the Gregoriana?"

Donati lowered his voice. "I served as the private secretary to His Holiness Pope Paul the Seventh."

A shadow seemed to fall across her face. "What are you doing in Fribourg?" she asked again.

"I came to see you."

"Why?"

"I need to talk to you about Niklaus."

"Where is he?"

"You don't know?"

"No."

"When was the last time you heard from him?"

"It was the morning of the pope's funeral. He wouldn't tell me where he was."

"Why not?"

"He said he didn't want them to know."

"Who?"

She started to answer, but stopped. "Have you seen him?" she asked.

"Yes, Stefani. I'm afraid I have."

"When?"

"Last night," said Donati. "On the Ponte Vecchio in Florence."

FROM HIS OBSERVATION POST AT Café des Arcades, Gabriel listened as Donati quietly told Stefani Hoffmann that Niklaus Janson was dead. He was glad it was his old friend on the other side of the street and not him. If Donati always labored over how to acknowledge his occupation, Gabriel likewise struggled over how to tell a woman that a loved one—a son, a brother, a father, a fiancé—had been murdered in cold blood.

She didn't believe Donati at first, which was to be expected. His response, that he had no motive to lie about such a thing, did little to dilute her skepticism. The Vatican, she shot back, lied all the time.

"I don't work for the Vatican," answered Donati. "Not anymore."

He then suggested they speak somewhere private. Stefani Hoffmann said the restaurant closed at ten, and that her boss would kill her if she left him in the lurch.

"Your boss will understand."

"What do I say to him about Niklaus?"

"Absolutely nothing."

"My car is in the Place des Ormeaux. Wait for me there."

Donati went into the street and lifted the phone to his ear. "Were you able to hear all that?"

"She knows," answered Gabriel. "The question is, how much?"

Donati slipped the phone into his pocket without killing the connection. Stefani Hoffmann emerged from the restaurant a few minutes later, a scarf around her neck. Her car was a worn-out Volvo. Donati lowered himself into the passenger seat as Gabriel slid behind the wheel of the BMW. Through his earpiece he heard the click of Donati's safety belt, followed an instant later by a wail of anguish from Stefani Hoffmann.

"Is Niklaus really dead?"

"I saw it happen."

"Why didn't you stop it?"

"There was nothing to be done."

Stefani Hoffmann reversed out of the parking space and

turned onto the rue du Pont-Muré. Ten seconds later, Gabriel did the same. As they left the Old Town on the Route des Alpes, Donati asked why Niklaus Janson had fled the Vatican the night of the Holy Father's death. Her response was scarcely audible.

"He was afraid."

"Afraid of what?"

"That they were going to kill him."

"Who, Stefani?"

For a long moment there was only the rattle of the Volvo's engine, followed a moment later by the sound of Stefani Hoffmann screaming. Gabriel lowered the volume on his phone. He was glad it was his old friend sitting next to her and not him.

17

RECHTHALTEN, SWITZERLAND

As they approached the hamlet of St. Ursen, Stefani Hoffmann became aware of the fact they were being followed.

"It's only an associate of mine," explained Donati.

"Since when do priests have *associates*?"

"He's the man who helped me find Niklaus in Florence."

"I thought you said you came to Fribourg alone."

"I said no such thing."

"Is this associate of yours a priest, too?"

"No."

"Vatican intelligence?"

Donati was tempted to inform Stefani Hoffmann that there was no department of the Holy See known as *Vatican intelligence*; that it was a canard invented by Catholicism's enemies; that the real intelligence-gathering apparatus of the Vatican was the Universal Church itself, with its global network of parishes, schools, universities, hospitals, charitable organizations, and nuncios in capitals around the world. He spared her this discourse, at least for the moment. Still, he was curious why she would ask such a question. It could wait, he decided, until his *associate* had joined them.

The next village was Rechthalten. Donati recognized the name. It was the village where Niklaus Janson had been born and raised. Its inhabitants were overwhelmingly Roman Catholic. Most were employed in what government statisticians referred to as the primary sector of the economy, a polite way of saying they worked the land. A handful, like Stefani Hoffmann, commuted each day to Fribourg. She had moved out of the family home about a year ago, she said, and was living alone in a cottage at the far eastern edge of the town.

It was shaped like an A, with a small sun deck on the upper floor. She turned into the unpaved drive and switched off the engine. Gabriel arrived a few seconds later. In German he introduced himself as Heinrich Kiever. It was the name on the false German passport he had displayed earlier that afternoon at Geneva Airport.

"Are you sure you're not a priest?" Stefani Hoffmann accepted his outstretched hand. "You look more like a priest than the archbishop."

She led them inside the cottage. The ground floor had been converted into an artist's studio. Stefani Hoffmann, Donati remembered suddenly, was a painter. Her latest work was propped on an easel in the center of the room. The man she knew as Heinrich Kiever stood before it, a hand to his chin, his head tilted slightly to one side.

"This is quite good."

"Do you paint?"

"Only the occasional watercolor while on holiday."

Stefani Hoffmann was clearly dubious. She removed her coat and scarf and looked at Donati as tears fell from her blue eyes. "Something to drink?"

HER BREAKFAST DISHES WERE STILL on the table in her tiny kitchen. She cleared them away and filled the electric kettle with bottled water. As she spooned coffee into the French press, she apologized for the chaotic state of the cottage, and for its modesty. It was all she could afford, she lamented, on her salary from the restaurant and the small amount of money she earned through the sale of her paintings.

"We're not all rich private bankers, you know."

She addressed them in German. Not the dialect of Swiss German spoken in the village, but proper High German, the language of her Alemannic brethren to the north. She had learned to speak it in school, she explained, beginning at the age of six. Niklaus Janson had been a classmate. He was an awkward boy, skinny, shy, bespectacled, but at seventeen he was somehow magically transformed into an object of striking beauty. The first time they made love, he insisted on removing his crucifix. Afterward, he confessed to Father Erich, the village priest.

"He was a very religious boy, Niklaus. It was one of the things I liked about him. He said he never mentioned my name in the confessional, but Father Erich gave me quite a look when I took communion the next Sunday."

After completing their secondary education at the local *Kan-*

tonsschule, Stefani studied art at the University of Fribourg, and Niklaus, whose father was a carpenter, enlisted in the Swiss Army. At the conclusion of his service, he returned to Rechthalten and started looking for work. It was Father Erich who suggested he join the Swiss Guard, which was undermanned at the time and desperately looking for recruits. Stefani Hoffmann was vehemently opposed to the idea.

"Why?" asked Donati.

"I was afraid I was going to lose him."

"To what?"

"The Church."

"You thought he might become a priest?"

"He talked about it all the time, even after he got out of the military."

He was subjected to no background check or formal interview. Father Erich's affirmation that Niklaus was a practicing Catholic of good moral character was all it took. On the night before he left for Rome, he gave Stefani an engagement ring with a small diamond. She was wearing it a few months later when she attended the solemn ceremony, held in the San Damaso Courtyard, where Niklaus swore to lay down his life to defend the Vatican and the Holy Father. He was exceedingly proud of his dress uniform and red-plumed medieval-style helmet, but Stefani thought he looked rather silly, a toy soldier in the world's smallest army. After the ceremony he took his parents to meet His Holiness. Stefani was not allowed to come.

"Only wives and mothers could meet the Holy Father. The Guard doesn't like girlfriends."

She saw Niklaus every couple of months, but they did their best to keep up their relationship with daily video calls and text messages. The work of the Swiss Guard was grueling and, most of the time, terribly dull. Niklaus used to recite the rosary while standing his three-hour shifts, his feet pointing outward at sixty-degree angles, as per Swiss Guard regulations. He spent most of his free time in the Swiss Quarter, the Guard's enclave near St. Anne's Gate. Like most Swiss, he thought Rome was a filthy mess.

Within a year of joining the Guard, he was working inside the Apostolic Palace. There he observed the comings and goings of the most senior princes of the Church—Gaubert, the secretary of state; Albanese, keeper of the Secret Archives; Navarro, keeper of the faith itself. But the Vatican official Niklaus admired most did not wear a red hat. He was the Holy Father's private secretary, Archbishop Luigi Donati.

"He used to say that if the Church had any sense, it would make you the next pope."

She managed a smile, which faded as she described Niklaus's downward spiral into depression and drinking. Somehow Donati had missed the signs of Niklaus's emotional turmoil. One priest, however, had noticed. A priest who worked in a relatively insignificant department of the Roman Curia, something to do with establishing a dialogue between the Church and nonbelievers.

"Could it have been the Pontifical Council for Culture?" probed Donati gently.

"Yes, that's it."

"And the priest's name?"

"Father Markus Graf."

Donati gave his associate a look that made it clear the priest in question was pure trouble. Stefani Hoffmann, while pouring boiling water into the French press, explained why.

"He's a member of a reactionary order. Secretive, too."

"The Order of St. Helena," said Donati, more for Gabriel's benefit than Stefani Hoffmann's.

"Do you know him?"

Donati revealed a flash of his old arrogance. "Father Graf and I move in rather different circles."

"I met him once. He's slippery as an eel. But quite charismatic. Seductive, even. Niklaus was quite taken with him. The Guard has its own chaplain, but Niklaus chose Father Graf as his confessor and spiritual guide. They also began spending a great deal of time together socially."

"Socially?"

"Father Graf had a car. He used to take Niklaus to the mountains around Rome so he wouldn't be homesick. The Apennines aren't exactly the Alps, but Niklaus enjoyed getting out of the city."

"He was reprimanded twice for curfew violations."

"I'm sure it had something to do with Father Graf."

"Was there anything more to their relationship?"

"Are you asking whether Niklaus and Father Graf were lovers?"

"I suppose I am."

"The thought crossed my mind. Especially after the way he acted the last time I went to Rome."

"What happened?"

"He refused to have sex with me."

"Did he give you a reason?"

"Father Graf had instructed him not to engage in sexual intercourse outside of marriage."

"And how did you react?"

"I said we should get married right away. Niklaus agreed, but on one condition."

"He said you had to become a lay member of the Order of St. Helena."

"Yes."

"I assume Niklaus was already a member."

"He swore his oath of obedience to Bishop Richter at the Order's palazzo on the Janiculum Hill. He said Bishop Richter had reservations about certain aspects of my character but had agreed to allow me to join."

"How did Bishop Richter know about you?"

"Father Erich. He's a member of the Order, too."

"What did you do?"

"I threw my engagement ring into the Tiber and returned to Switzerland."

"Do you recall the date?"

"How could I forget? It was the ninth of October." She poured three cups of coffee and placed one before the man she knew as Heinrich Kiever. "Doesn't he have any questions for me?"

"Herr Kiever is a man of few words."

"Just like Niklaus." She sat down at the table. "After I refused to join the Order, he cut off all communication. Tuesday was the first time I'd spoken to him in weeks."

"And you're sure it was the morning of the Holy Father's funeral?"

She nodded. "He sounded awful. For a moment, I didn't think it was him. When I asked what was wrong, he just cried."

"What did you do then?"

"I asked him again."

"And?"

She raised her coffee to her lips. "He told me everything."

18

RECHTHALTEN, SWITZERLAND

NIKLAUS HAD ALREADY PULLED TWO shifts that day. Arch of Bells in the morning, Bronze Doors in the afternoon. When he arrived at the papal apartments at nine p.m., his legs were shaking with fatigue. The first person he saw was the Holy Father's private secretary. He was on his way out.

"Did he know where I was going?"

"Dinner with a friend. Outside the walls."

"Did he know the friend's name?"

"A rich woman who lived near the Villa Borghese. Her husband died in a fall from the dome of the basilica. Niklaus said you were there when it happened."

"Where did he hear a thing like that?"

"Where do you think?"

"Father Graf?"

She nodded. She was holding her mug of coffee with both hands. A nimbus of steam swirled about her flawless face.

"What happened after I left?"

"Cardinal Albanese arrived around nine thirty."

"The cardinal told me he didn't arrive until ten."

"That was his *second* visit," said Stefani Hoffmann. "Not the first."

Cardinal Albanese had not told Donati about an earlier visit to the *appartamento*. Nor had he included it in the official Vatican time line. That single inconsistency, were it ever to become public, would be enough to plunge the Church into scandal.

"Did Albanese tell Niklaus why he was there?"

"No. But he was carrying an attaché case with the coat of arms of the Archives on the side."

"How long did he stay?"

"Only a few minutes."

"Did he have the attaché case when he left?"

She nodded.

"And when he came back at ten o'clock?"

"He told Niklaus that the Holy Father had invited him to pray in the private chapel."

"Who arrived next?"

"Three cardinals. Navarro, Gaubert, and Francona."

"The time?"

"Ten fifteen."

"When did Dottore Gallo arrive?"

"Eleven o'clock. Colonel Metzler and a Vatican cop showed up a few minutes after that." She lowered her voice. "Then you, Archbishop Donati. You were the last."

"Did Niklaus know what was happening inside?"

"He had a pretty good idea, but he wasn't certain until the ambulance attendants arrived with the gurney."

A few minutes after they entered the apartment, she continued, Metzler came out. He confirmed the obvious. The Holy Father was dead. He warned Niklaus that he was never to speak of what he had witnessed that evening. Not to his comrades in the Guard, not to his friends and family, and certainly not to the media. Then he ordered Niklaus to remain on duty until the Holy Father's body was removed and the apartment sealed. The camerlengo performed the ritual at half past two.

"Did Cardinal Albanese remove anything from the apartment when he left?"

"One item. He said he wanted something to help him remember the saintliness of the Holy Father. Something he had touched."

"What was it?"

"A book."

Donati's heart banged against his rib cage. "What kind of book?"

"An English murder mystery." Stefani Hoffmann shook her head. "Can you imagine that?"

BY THE TIME NIKLAUS LEFT the Apostolic Palace, the Press Office had announced the Holy Father's death. St. Peter's Square was ablaze with the spectral light of the television crews, and in the cloisters and courtyards of the Vatican, nuns and priests were gathered in small groups, praying, weeping. Niklaus was weeping, too. Alone in his room in the barracks, he changed into civilian clothing and tossed a few things into his duffel bag. He slipped out of the Vatican around five thirty that morning.

"Why did he go to Florence instead of coming home to Switzerland?"

"He was afraid they would find him."

"The Guard?"

"The Order."

"And you had no other contact other than the single phone call? No texts or e-mails?"

"Only the package. It arrived the day after I spoke to him."

"What was it?"

"A dreadful devotional painting of Jesus in the Garden of Gethsemane. I can't imagine why he would send me such a thing."

"Was there anything else in the package?"

"Niklaus's rosary." She paused, then added, "And a letter."

"A letter?"

She nodded.

"To whom was it addressed?"

"Me. Who else?"

"What did it say?"

"He apologized for joining the Order of St. Helena and breaking off our engagement. He said it was a terrible mistake. He said they were evil. Especially Bishop Richter."

"May I read it?"

"No," she said. "Some parts are too private."

Donati let it go. For now. "Colonel Metzler told me he spoke to you."

"He called me the day after the Holy Father died. He said Niklaus had left the barracks without authorization. He asked whether I'd spoken to him. I told him I hadn't, which was true at the time."

"Was Metzler the only person who contacted you?"

"No. I heard from someone else the next day."

"Who?"

"Herr Bauer. The man from Vatican intelligence."

There it was again, thought Donati. *Vatican intelligence* . . .

"Did Herr Bauer show you any identification?"

She shook her head.

"Did he say what division of Vatican intelligence he worked for?"

"Papal security."

"First name?"

"Maximillian."

"Swiss?"

"German. Probably from Bavaria, judging by the accent."

"He phoned you?"

"No. He showed up at the restaurant unannounced, like you and Herr Kiever."

"What did he want?"

"The same thing Metzler wanted. Where was Niklaus?"

"And when you told him you didn't know?"

"I'm not sure he believed me."

"Describe him, please."

It was Gabriel who had posed the question. Stefani Hoffmann lifted her eyes to the ceiling.

"Tall, well dressed, late forties, maybe early fifties."

With his expression, Gabriel made it clear her answer was a disappointment. "Come now, Stefani. You can do better than that. You're an artist, after all."

"I'm a contemporary painter who reveres Rothko and Pollock. Portraits aren't my specialty."

"But surely you could produce one in a pinch."

"Not a good one. And not from memory."

"Perhaps I can be of help."

"How?"

"Bring me your sketchpad and a box of acrylic pencils, and I'll show you."

THEY WORKED WITHOUT PAUSE FOR the better part of the next hour, side by side at the kitchen table, with Donati watching anxiously over their shoulders. As Gabriel suspected, Stefani Hoffmann's memory of the man she knew as Maximillian Bauer was far sharper than even she had imagined. All it took were the right sort of questions posed by an expert draftsman and student of human anatomy—a gifted restorer who could mimic the brushstrokes of Bellini and Titian and Tintoretto, a healer who had repaired the tattered face of Mary and the pierced hand of Christ.

It was a noble face she described. High cheekbones, a slender nose, a refined chin, a thin mouth that did not smile easily, all crowned by a shock of gray-blond hair. He was a worthy opponent, thought Gabriel. A man not to be trifled with. A man who never lost at games of chance.

"So much for the occasional watercolor on holiday," said Stefani Hoffmann. "You're obviously a professional. But I'm afraid the eyes are all wrong."

"I drew the eyes the way you described them."

"Not quite."

She took the pad and on a blank page sketched a pair of humorless eyes set deeply beneath the ledge of a prominent brow. Gabriel then sketched the rest of the face around them.

"That's him. That's the man who came to see me."

Gabriel looked over his shoulder at Donati. "Do you recognize him?"

"I'm afraid not."

Stefani Hoffmann took the sketch from Gabriel and deepened the lines around the mouth. "Now it's perfect," she said. "But what are you going to do with it?"

"I'm going to find out who he really is."

She looked up from the sketchpad. "But who are *you*?"

"I'm an associate of the archbishop."

"Are you a priest?"

"No," said Gabriel. "I'm a professional."

WHICH LEFT ONLY THE LETTER. The letter in which Niklaus Janson had described the Order of St. Helena as evil. Three times Donati asked to see it. Three times Stefani Hoffmann refused. The letter was of an intensely personal nature, written by an emotionally distressed man whom she had known since childhood. A man who had been publicly murdered on the most famous bridge in Italy. She would not show such a letter to her closest friend and confidante, she insisted, let alone a Roman Catholic archbishop.

"In that case," said Donati, "might I at least see the picture?"

"Jesus in the Garden of Gethsemane? You don't get enough of that sort of thing at the Vatican?"

"I have my reasons."

It was propped against the wall behind Stefani Hoffmann's chair, still entombed in a shallow cardboard box. Donati checked the waybill. It was from a DHS Express near Roma Termini. Niklaus must have shipped it before boarding the train to Florence.

Donati removed the picture from the box and freed it from its cocoon of bubble wrap. It was about fourteen inches by twelve. The illustration itself was a rather shopworn depiction of Jesus on the night before his torture and execution at the hands of the Romans. The frame, museum glass, and matting were of high quality.

"Bishop Richter gave it to him the day he swore his oath of allegiance to the Order," explained Stefani Hoffmann. "If you turn it over, you'll see the Order's coat of arms."

Donati was still staring at the image of Jesus.

"Don't tell me you actually like it."

"It's not exactly Michelangelo," he admitted. "But it's nearly identical to a picture that hung in my parents' bedroom in the little house in Umbria where I was raised."

Donati did not tell Stefani Hoffmann that after his mother's death he found several thousand euros hidden inside the picture. His mother, justifiably, had distrusted Italian banks.

He turned over the picture. The Order of St. Helena's coat of arms was embossed on the back of the matting, which was held in place by four metal brackets. One of the clasps, however, was loose.

Donati removed the other three and attempted to pry away the matting. Failing, he turned over the frame and allowed the weight of the glass panel to do the task for him.

It landed on the tabletop without shattering. Donati separated the matting from the picture and found a cream-colored envelope, also of high quality. It, too, was decorated with a coat of arms.

The private papal armorial of His Holiness Pope Paul VII.

Donati lifted the flap. Inside were three sheets of rich stationery, almost like fine linen. He read the first lines. Then he returned the letter to the envelope and pushed it across the table toward Gabriel.

"Forgive me," he said. "I believe this belongs to you."

19

LES ARMURES, GENEVA

IT WAS APPROACHING NINE O'CLOCK by the time Gabriel and Donati arrived in Geneva, too late to make the last flight to Rome. They checked into adjacent rooms at a small hotel near the St. Pierre Cathedral and then walked to Les Armures, a wood-paneled restaurant in the Old Town. After placing his order, Gabriel rang a friend who worked for the NDB, Switzerland's small but capable foreign intelligence and internal security service. The friend, whose name was Christoph Bittel, was the head of the counterterrorism division. He answered guardedly. Gabriel had a long and distinguished track record in Switzerland. Bittel was still cleaning up the mess from his last visit.

"Where are you?"

Gabriel answered truthfully.

"I'd order the veal cutlet if I were you."

"I just did."

"How long have you been in the country?"

"A few hours."

"I don't suppose you arrived on a valid passport?"

"Define valid."

Bittel sighed before inquiring as to the reason for Gabriel's call.

"I'd like you to place a Swiss citizen under protective surveillance."

"How unusual. What's the Swiss citizen's name?"

Gabriel told him, then recited her address and place of work.

"Is she an ISIS terrorist? A Russian assassin?"

"No, Bittel. She's a painter."

"Anyone in particular you're worried about?"

"I'll send you a composite. But whatever you do, don't give the job to that kid who watched my back in Bern a couple of years ago."

"He's one of my best men."

"He's also a former Swiss Guard."

"Does this have something to do with Florence?"

"Why do you ask?"

"The Polizia di Stato just released the name of the victim in that shooting last night. He was a Swiss Guard. Come to think of it, he was from Rechthalten, too."

Gabriel killed the connection and checked the website of *Corriere della Sera*, Italy's premier newspaper. Donati went straight to the Twitter feed of the Vatican Press Office. There was a brief *bollettino*, five minutes old. It expressed the Holy See's shock and sorrow over the senseless and random act of gun violence that had claimed the life of Lance Corporal Niklaus Janson of the Pontifical Swiss Guard. It made no mention of the fact that Janson was on duty outside the papal apartments the night of the Holy Father's death. Nor did it explain why he was in Florence while his comrades were working overtime in preparation for the conclave.

"It's a masterpiece of curial doublespeak," said Donati. "On its face, the statement is entirely accurate. But the lies of omission are glaring. Clearly, Cardinal Albanese has no intention of allowing Niklaus's murder to delay the opening of the conclave."

"Perhaps we can convince him to see the error of his ways."

"With what? A tawdry tale of sex and secretive religious orders, told by a woman who was bitter over the dissolution of her engagement to a handsome young Swiss Guard?"

"You don't believe her story?"

"I believe every word of it. But that doesn't change the fact that it's pure hearsay, or that every element can be denied."

"Except for this." Gabriel displayed the envelope. The high-quality cream-colored envelope embossed with the private papal armorial of His Holiness Pope Paul VII. "Do you really expect me to believe you didn't know what was in this letter?"

"I didn't."

Gabriel removed the three sheets of stationery from the envelope. The letter had been composed in pale blue ink. The salutation was informal. First name only. *Dear Gabriel* . . . There were no preliminaries or pleasantries.

While researching in the Vatican Secret Archives, I came upon a most remarkable book . . .

The book, he continued, had been given to him by a member of the Archives staff, without the knowledge of the *prefetto*. It was stored in what was known as the *collezione*, a secret archive within the Secret Archives, located on the lower level of the Manuscript Depository. The material in the *collezione* was highly sensitive. Some of the books and files were political and administrative in nature. Others were doctrinal. None were referenced in the one thousand directories and catalogues housed in the Index Room. Indeed, nowhere within the Archives was there a written inventory of the material. The knowledge was passed down through the centuries verbally, *prefetto* to *prefetto*.

The letter did not identify the book in question, only that it had been suppressed by the Church during the Middle Ages and had circulated secretly until the Renaissance, when it was finally hunted out of existence. The copy contained in the Secret Archives was thought to be the last. The Holy Father had concluded it was authentic and accurate in its depiction of an important historical event. It was his intention to place the book in Gabriel's hands at the earliest possible date. Gabriel would be free to do with it as he pleased. His Holiness asked only that he treat the material with the utmost sensitivity. The book would ignite a global sensation. Its unveiling would have to be carefully managed. Otherwise, the Holy Father warned, it would be dismissed as a hoax.

The letter was unfinished. The final sentence was a fragment, the last word incomplete. *Archi* . . . Gabriel reckoned the Holy Father had been interrupted midsentence by the appearance of his killer. Donati did not disagree. His prime suspect was Cardinal Camerlengo Domenico Albanese, *prefetto* of the Vatican

Secret Archives. Gabriel politely informed Donati that he was mistaken.

"Then why did Albanese lie to me about his earlier visit to the *appartamento*?"

"I'm not saying he wasn't involved in the Holy Father's murder. But he wasn't the actual killer. He was only the bagman." Gabriel held up the letter. "Can we stipulate that the existence of this letter in Stefani Hoffmann's home is proof that Niklaus Janson did not tell her everything that happened that night?"

"So stipulated."

Gabriel lowered the letter. "When Albanese arrived at nine thirty, the Holy Father was already dead. That's when he removed the book from the papal study. He came back to the papal apartments at ten o'clock and carried the Holy Father's body from the study into the bedroom."

"But why didn't he remove the letter when he removed the book?"

"Because it wasn't there. It was in Niklaus Janson's pocket. He removed it before Albanese arrived the first time."

"Why?"

"If I had to guess, Niklaus was feeling guilty about letting the murderer into the papal apartments. After the killer left, he went inside to investigate. That was when he found the Holy Father dead and an unfinished letter lying on the desk blotter."

"Why would Niklaus Janson have let a murderer into the papal apartments? He loved the Holy Father."

"That's the easy part. The killer was someone he knew. Someone he trusted." Gabriel paused. "Someone he was sworn to obey."

Donati made no reply.

"Did Veronica tell you that Janson and Father Graf were involved in a sexual relationship?"

Donati hesitated, then nodded.

"Why didn't you tell me?"

"Because I didn't think it was true." He paused. "Until tonight."

"Who are they, Luigi?"

"The Order of St. Helena?"

"Yes."

"They're trouble," said Donati. "Pure, unadulterated, undiluted, irredeemable trouble."

20

LES ARMURES, GENEVA

T HEN AGAIN, DONATI ADDED, the Order of St. Helena had been trouble from the beginning—the year of our Lord 1928, the midpoint between the end of the first world war and the beginning of the second, a time of great social and political upheaval and uncertainty over the future. In the southern German state of Bavaria, an obscure priest named Father Ulrich Schiller came to believe that only Roman Catholicism, in partnership with monarchs and political leaders from the extreme right, could save Europe from the godless Bolsheviks. He established his first seminary in the town of Bergen in Upper Bavaria and quietly recruited a network of like-minded political leaders and businessmen that stretched westward to Spain and Portugal and eastward to the doorstep of the Soviet Union. The lay membership of the Order soon dwarfed its priestly cast and was the true source of its power and influence. The names were kept secret. Inside the Order, only Father Schiller had access to the directory.

"It was a leather-bound ledger," said Donati. "Quite beautiful, apparently. Father Schiller entered the names himself, along with the secret contact information. Each member was assigned a number and swore an oath, not to the Church but to the Order. It was all very political and quasi-military. The Order wasn't terribly concerned with doctrine during those early years. They saw themselves first and foremost as holy warriors, prepared to do battle with the enemies of Christ and Roman Catholicism."

"What was the origin of the name?"

"Father Schiller made a pilgrimage to Jerusalem in the early twenties. He prayed for hours on end in the Garden of Gethsemane and the Church of the Holy Sepulchre. It's built on the site where Helena, the mother of Constantine, was said to have found the exact spot where Jesus was crucified and buried."

"Yes, I know," said Gabriel. "I happen to live not far from there."

"Forgive me," replied Donati.

Father Schiller, he continued, was obsessed with the Crucifixion. He flogged himself daily, and during the holy season of Lent, he pierced his palms with a nail and slept wearing a crown of thorns. His devotion to the memory of Christ's suffering and death went hand in hand with his hatred of Jews, whom he viewed as the murderers of God.

"We're not talking about doctrinal anti-Judaism. Father

Schiller was a rabid anti-Semite. Even during the earliest years of the Zionist movement, he was alarmed by the prospect of Jews controlling the sacred Christian sites of Jerusalem."

It was only natural, Donati resumed, that a man such as Father Schiller would find common cause with the Austrian corporal who seized power in Germany in 1933. Father Schiller was not an ordinary member of the Nazi party; he wore a coveted golden party badge. In his 1936 book *The Doctrine of National Socialism,* he argued that Adolf Hitler and the Nazis offered the surest path to a Christian Europe. Hitler read the book and admired it greatly. He kept a copy at his mountain retreat in the Obersalzberg near Berchtesgaden. During a contentious meeting with the archbishop of Munich, he cited Father Schiller's book as proof that Catholics and Nazis could work together to defend Germany against the Bolsheviks and the Jews.

"Hitler once remarked to Father Schiller that when it came to the Jews, he was merely carrying out the same policy the Church had adopted fifteen hundred years earlier. Father Schiller did not dispute Hitler's interpretation of Catholic history."

"Do I have to ask how the Order conducted itself during the war?"

"I'm afraid it remained loyal to Hitler even after it became clear he was determined to murder every last Jew in Europe. Priests from the Order traveled with SS Einsatzgruppen units in the Baltics and the Ukraine and granted the murderers absolution each night when the killing was done. French members of the Order sided with Vichy, and in Italy they supported Mussolini to the bitter end. The Order also had ties to the clerical

fascists in Slovakia and Croatia. The conduct of those two re-
gimes is an indelible stain on the history of the Church."

"And when the war was over?"

"A new war began. A global contest between the West and
the godless Soviet Union. Father Schiller and the Order were
suddenly very much in vogue."

With the tacit approval of Pope Pius XII, Schiller helped
dozens of fugitive German and Croatian war criminals escape to South America, which the Order regarded as the next
battlefield in the war between Christianity and communism.
Funded by the Vatican, it established a network of seminaries
and schools throughout Latin America and recruited thousands
of new lay members—mainly wealthy landowners, soldiers, and
secret policemen. During the dirty wars of the 1970s and 1980s,
the Order once again sided with the murderers rather than the
victims.

"In 1987, the year of Father Schiller's death, the Order was at
the zenith of its power. It had at least fifty thousand lay members, a thousand ordained priests, and another thousand dioce-
san clergy who were members of something called the Priestly
Society of the Order of St. Helena. When Lucchesi and I moved
into the Apostolic Palace, they were among the most influential
forces within the Church."

"What did you do?"

"We clipped their wings."

"How did they react?"

"Exactly as you would expect. Bishop Hans Richter loathed
my master. Almost as much as he loathes me."

"Is Richter German?"

"Austrian, actually. So is Father Graf. He's Bishop Richter's private secretary, acolyte, and personal bodyguard. He carries a gun whenever the bishop is in public. I'm told he knows how to use it."

"I'll keep that in mind." Gabriel showed Donati the photograph he snapped when they were lunching at Piperno in Rome.

"That's him. He must have followed me from the Jesuit Curia."

"Where might I find him?"

"You're not to go anywhere near him. Or Bishop Richter."

"Hypothetically," said Gabriel.

"Richter divides his time between his palazzo on the Janiculum Hill and the Order's headquarters in the village of Menzingen in Canton Zug. The Order relocated there in the 1980s. In case you're wondering, the bishop does not travel commercially. The Order of St. Helena is extraordinarily wealthy. He has a private jet at his disposal twenty-four hours a day."

"Who owns it?"

"A secret benefactor. The man behind the curtain. At least that's the rumor." Donati took up the Holy Father's letter. "I only wish my master had told you the name of the book."

"Are you familiar with the *collezione*?"

Donati nodded slowly.

"Would you be able to find it?"

"That would require gaining access to the Manuscript Depository, no easy feat. After all, they're called the Secret Archives for a reason." Donati looked at the composite sketch of the man who had questioned Stefani Hoffmann. "You know, Gabriel, you really should consider taking up painting for a living."

"Is he a member of the Order?"

"If he is, he isn't a priest."

"How can you be sure?"

"Because the Order would never send one of their priests to question someone like Stefani Hoffmann."

"Who would they send?"

"A professional."

21

ROME—OBERSALZBERG, BAVARIA

AT FIVE O'CLOCK THE FOLLOWING morning, Bishop Hans Richter was awakened by a gentle knock at his door. A moment later a youthful seminarian entered the room bearing a tray of coffee and a stack of newspapers. The boy placed the tray at the edge of the bed and, receiving no additional instructions, withdrew.

Richter sat up and poured a cup of coffee from the ornate silver decanter. After adding sugar and steamed milk, he reached for the newspapers. His spirits sank as he opened *La Repubblica*. The news from Florence was splashed across the front page. It was obvious the vague statement issued by the Sala Stampa had not played well—especially with Alessandro Ricci, the paper's star investigative reporter and author of a best-selling book about the Order. Ricci saw evidence of a conspiracy. Then again, he usually did. Still, there was no denying that Niklaus Janson's death was a disaster, one with the potential to threaten Richter's ambitions at the coming conclave.

He turned to the papers from Germany. They were filled with stories and photographs from the market bombing in Hamburg. The embattled German chancellor had ordered anti-terrorist police to stand guard outside all major rail stations, airports, government buildings, and foreign embassies. Even so, Germany's interior minister had predicted that another attack was likely, probably within the coming days. A new opinion poll showed a sudden surge in support for Axel Brünner and his anti-immigrant National Democrats. Brünner and the chancellor were now locked in a statistical dead heat.

Richter set aside the newspapers and rose from his canopied Biedermeier bed. His apartment was three thousand square meters, larger than any of the Vatican lodgings occupied by the most senior princes of the Church. The rest of the room's luxurious furnishings—the chest of drawers, the armoire, the writing desk, the occasional tables and framed mirrors—were resplendent Biedermeier antiques as well. The paintings were all Italian and Dutch Old Masters, including works by Titian, Veronese, Rembrandt, Van Eyck, and Van der Weyden. They were but a small portion of the Order's massive collection, most of which had been acquired for investment purposes. The collection was hidden in a vault beneath the Paradeplatz in downtown Zurich, along with much of Bishop Richter's vast personal fortune.

He entered his luxurious bathroom complex. It featured a shower with four heads, a large Jacuzzi, a steam room, a sauna, and a built-in audiovisual system. To the accompaniment of

Bach's Brandenburg Concertos, he bathed and shaved and moved his bowels. Afterward, he dressed not in his usual magenta-trimmed cassock but in a tailored business suit. Then he pulled on an overcoat and a scarf and headed downstairs.

Father Graf was waiting outside in the forecourt next to an elegant Mercedes-Maybach limousine. He was a trim, athletic priest of forty-two, with an angular face, neatly combed blond hair, and bright blue eyes. Like Bishop Richter, he was of noble Austrian descent. Indeed, the blood that flowed through both their veins was midnight blue. He, too, was dressed in business rather than clerical attire. He looked up from his mobile phone as Richter approached and in German bade him a pleasant morning.

The rear door of the Maybach was open. Richter slid into the backseat. Father Graf joined him. The car passed through the Order's formidable stone-and-steel security gate and turned into the street. The umbrella pines were silhouettes in the first sienna light of dawn. Richter thought it was almost beautiful.

Father Graf was staring at his phone again.

"Anything interesting in the news this morning?" asked Richter.

"The Polizia di Stato released the identity of the young man who was shot to death in Florence."

"Anyone we know?"

The priest looked up. "Do you know what would have happened if Niklaus had crossed that bridge?"

"He would have given Pope Accidental's letter to Gabriel Allon." Richter paused. "All the more reason why you should have removed it from the papal study."

"It was Albanese's job. Not mine."

Richter frowned. "He is a cardinal and a member of the Order, Markus. Try to show him at least a modicum of respect."

"If it wasn't for the Church, he'd be a bricklayer."

Richter examined his reflection in the vanity mirror. "The bricklayer's *bollettino* has bought us some valuable breathing room. But it is only a matter of time before the press find out where Niklaus was working the night of the Holy Father's death, and that he was a member of the Order."

"In six days, it won't matter."

"Six days is an eternity. Especially for a man like Gabriel Allon."

"At the moment, I'm more worried about our old friend Alessandro Ricci."

"As am I. His sources inside the Curia are impeccable. You can be sure our enemies are talking to him."

"Perhaps I should have a word with him, too."

"Not yet, Markus. But in the meantime, keep an eye on him." Richter looked out his window and frowned. "My God, this city really is atrocious."

"It will be different after we take power, Excellency."

Indeed, thought Bishop Richter. Much different.

THE ORDER'S GULFSTREAM G550 WAS waiting on the tarmac outside Signature Flight Support at Ciampino Airport. It delivered Bishop Richter and Father Graf to Salzburg, where they boarded an executive helicopter for the short flight across the German border. Andreas Estermann, a former German intelligence officer who served as the Order's chief of security

and operations, waited on the helipad of the compound outside Berchtesgaden, his gray-blond hair twisting in the wash of
the rotors. He pressed his lips to the ring on Bishop Richter's
proffered right hand, then gestured toward a waiting Mercedes
sedan.

"We should hurry, Excellency. I'm afraid you're the last to
arrive."

The car bore them smoothly up the private valley to the chalet, a modern citadel of stone and glass set against the base of
the towering mountains. A dozen other vehicles lined the drive,
watched over by a small battalion of armed security men. All
wore black ski jackets emblazoned with the logo of the Wolf
Group, a Munich-based conglomerate.

Estermann escorted Bishop Richter and Father Graf inside
and up a flight of stairs. To the left was an anteroom filled with
aides and dark-suited security men. Bishop Richter handed Father Graf his overcoat and followed Estermann into the great
hall.

It was sixty feet by fifty, with a single enormous window gazing northward across the Obersalzberg. The walls were hung
with Gobelin tapestries and several oil paintings, including what
appeared to be *Venus and Amor* by Bordone. A bust of Richard
Wagner frowned at Richter from its perch atop a plinth. The
longcase clock, which was crowned by a heraldic Roman-style
eagle, read nine o'clock. Richter, as usual, had arrived precisely
on time.

He surveyed the others with a jaundiced eye. They were,
without exception, an unappetizing lot, scoundrels and grifters,
each and every one. But they were also a necessary evil, a means
to an end. The laborites and secular social democrats were the

cause of Europe's calamitous plight. Only these creatures were prepared to undertake the hard work necessary to undo the damage of seventy-five years of postwar liberal twaddle.

There was, for example, Axel Brünner. His fancy suit and rimless spectacles could not conceal the fact that he was a former skinhead and street brawler whose only claim to fame was a distant blood relationship to the infamous Nazi who had rounded up the Jews of Paris. He was chatting with Cécile Leclerc, his comely counterpart from France, who had inherited her anti-immigrant party from her father, a moron from Marseilles.

Richter felt a warm blast of coffee-scented breath and, turning, found himself shaking the oily paw of the Italian prime minister, Giuseppe Saviano. The next hand he grasped was attached to Peter van der Meer, the platinum-haired, putty-skinned Catholic from Amsterdam who had promised to rid his country of all Muslims by 2025, an admirable if entirely unattainable goal. Jörg Kaufmann, the camera-ready Austrian chancellor, greeted Bishop Richter like an old friend, which he was. Richter had presided over Kaufmann's baptism and First Communion, along with his recent wedding to Austria's most famous fashion model, a union Richter approved with considerable misgivings.

Presiding over this menagerie was Jonas Wolf. He wore a heavy roll-neck sweater and flannel dress trousers. His silver mane of hair was swept back from his face, which was dominated by a bird-of-prey nose. It was a face to be stamped on a coin, thought Richter. Perhaps one day, when the Muslim invaders had been cast out and the Roman Catholic Church was once again ascendant, it would be.

At five minutes past nine, Wolf took his place at the head of the conference table, which had been placed near the soaring window. Andreas Estermann had been assigned the seat at Wolf's right hand; Bishop Richter, at his left. At the German's request, Richter led the assemblage in a recitation of the Lord's Prayer.

"And may you grant us the strength and determination to complete our sacred mission," intoned Richter in conclusion. "We do this in your name, through our Lord Jesus Christ, who lives and reigns with you in the unity of the Holy Spirit, one God, for ever and ever."

"Amen," came the response along the table.

Jonas Wolf opened a leather folder. The conference was now in session.

THE MOUNTAIN PEAKS WERE RECEDING into darkness when Wolf finally gaveled the session to a close. A fire was lit, cocktails served. Richter, who drank only room-temperature mineral water, somehow became entangled with Cécile Leclerc, who insisted on addressing him in her impenetrable French-accented German. Richter managed to decipher every fourth or fifth word, which was a blessing. Like her father, Cécile was no intellectual. Somehow she had managed to acquire a law degree from an elite Paris institution of learning. Still, one could easily picture her behind the counter of a Provençal *boucherie* with a bloody apron around her ample waist.

Therefore, Richter was relieved when Jonas Wolf, perhaps sensing his discomfort, cut in like a dancer on a ballroom floor and asked whether they might have a word in private. Followed by Andreas Estermann, they walked through the unpopulated rooms of the chalet to Wolf's chapel. It was the size of a typical parish church. The walls were hung with German and Dutch Old Master paintings. Above the altar was a magnificent *Crucifixion* by Lucas Cranach the Elder.

Wolf genuflected and then rose unsteadily to his feet. "All in all, a productive session, don't you think, Excellency?"

"I must admit, I was a bit distracted by Van der Meer's hair."

Wolf nodded sympathetically. "I've spoken to him about it. He insists it's part of his branding."

"Branding?"

"It's a modern word used to describe one's image on social media." Wolf gestured toward Estermann. "Andreas is our expert on that sort of thing. He's convinced Van der Meer's hair is a political asset."

"He looks like Kim Novak in *Vertigo*. And that ridiculous comb-over! How on earth does he maneuver it all into place?"

"Apparently, it takes a great deal of time and effort. He buys hair spray by the case. He's the only man in Holland who doesn't go outside when it rains."

"It conveys a sense of vanity and deep insecurity. Our candidates must be above reproach."

"They can't all be as polished as Jörg Kaufmann. Brünner has his problems, too. Fortunately, the bombings in Berlin and Hamburg have given his campaign a badly needed boost."

"The new polls are encouraging. But can he win?"

"If there is another attack," said Wolf, "his victory will be all but assured."

He sat down in the first pew. Richter joined him. There followed a companionable silence. Richter might have despaired of the rabble upstairs, but Jonas Wolf he truly admired. Wolf was one of the few men who had been a member of the Order longer than Richter. He was its most prominent layman, a co-superior general in everything but name. For more than a decade, he and Richter had been engaged in a clandestine crusade to transform Western Europe and the Church of Rome. Sometimes even they were astounded by the speed with which they had succeeded. Italy and Austria were already theirs. Now the German Federal Chancellery was within their grasp, as was the Apostolic Palace. The seizure of power was nearly complete. Lesser men would serve as their public standard-bearers, but it would be Jonas Wolf and Bishop Hans Richter of the Order of St. Helena who would be whispering in their ears. They saw themselves in apocalyptic terms. Western civilization was dying. Only they could save it.

Andreas Estermann was the third member of their holy trinity. He was the Project's irreplaceable man. Estermann dispersed the money, worked with the local parties to hone their platforms and recruit presentable candidates, and oversaw a network of operatives drawn from Western European intelligence services and police forces. In a computer-filled warehouse outside Munich, he had established an information warfare unit that flooded social media daily with false or misleading stories about the threat posed by Muslim immigrants. Estermann's cyber unit also possessed the ability to hack phones and crack computer networks, a capability that had produced mountains of invaluable compromising material.

At present, Estermann was pacing silently along the right side of the nave. Bishop Richter could see that something was troubling him. It was Jonas Wolf who explained. The previous evening, Archbishop Donati and Gabriel Allon had traveled to Canton Fribourg, where they had met with Stefani Hoffmann.

"I thought she told you she didn't know anything."

"I had the distinct impression she wasn't telling the truth," answered Estermann.

"Was the Janson boy in possession of the letter when he was killed?"

"Our friends in the Polizia di Stato say not. Which means it's probably in the hands of Archbishop Donati."

Bishop Richter exhaled heavily. "Will no one rid me of this meddlesome priest?"

"I would advise against it," said Estermann. "Donati's death would undoubtedly delay the start of the conclave."

"Then perhaps we should kill his friend instead."

Estermann stopped pacing. "Easier said than done."

"Where are they now?"

"Back in Rome."

"Doing what?"

"We're good, Bishop Richter. But not that good."

"May I offer you a piece of advice?"

"Of course, Excellency."

"Get better. And quickly."

22

ROME

THE MAIN ENTRANCE OF THE Vatican Secret Archives was
located on the northern side of the Belvedere Courtyard.
Only accredited historians and researchers were granted access, and only after a thorough vetting, presided over by none
other than the *prefetto*, Cardinal Domenico Albanese. Visitors were not permitted to venture beyond the *sala di studio*, a
reading room furnished with two long rows of ancient wooden
desks, recently upgraded with electrical outlets for laptop computers. With rare exceptions, only members of the staff went
down to the Manuscript Depository, which was reached via a
cramped lift in the Index Room. Even Donati had never been
there. Try as he might, he could fathom no set of circumstances, no reasonable-sounding cover story, that would allow

him to wander the Depository unaccompanied, let alone with the director-general of Israel's secret intelligence service at his side.

It was for that reason Gabriel and Donati went straight to the Israeli Embassy after their return to Rome. There they descended to a secure communications room known as the Holy of Holies, where Gabriel conducted a conference call with Uzi Navot and Yuval Gershon, the director of Unit 8200. Navot was appalled by the operation Gabriel had in mind. Gershon, however, could not believe his good fortune. Having cracked the data network of the Pontifical Swiss Guard, he was now being asked to seize control of the power supply and security system of the Vatican Secret Archives. For a cyberwarrior, it was a dream assignment.

"Can it be done?" asked Gabriel.

"You're joking, right?"

"How long will it take?"

"Forty-eight hours, to be on the safe side."

"I can give you twenty-four. But twelve would be better."

It was dusk when Gabriel and Donati finally slipped from the Israeli compound in the back of an embassy car. After dropping Donati at the Jesuit Curia, the driver took Gabriel to the safe flat near the top of the Spanish Steps. Exhausted, he crawled into the unmade bed and plunged into a dreamless sleep. His phone woke him at seven the next morning. It was Yuval Gershon.

"I'd feel better if we did a few dry runs, but we're ready when you are."

Gabriel showered and dressed, then walked through the cold

Roman morning to the Borgo Santo Spirito. Donati met him at the entrance of the Jesuit Curia and escorted him upstairs to his rooms.

It was half past eight.

"You can't possibly be serious."

"Would you prefer to dress as a nun?"

Gabriel looked at the clothing laid out on the bed: a clerical suit, a black shirt with a Roman collar. He had utilized many disguises during his long career, but never had he concealed himself beneath the mantle of a priest.

"Who am I supposed to be?"

Donati handed him a Vatican pass.

"Father Franco Benedetti?"

"It has a certain flair, don't you think?"

"That's because it's a Jewish name."

"So is Donati."

Gabriel frowned at the photograph. "I look nothing like him."

"Consider yourself lucky. But don't worry, the Swiss Guards probably won't even bother to check it."

Gabriel did not disagree. While restoring Caravaggio's *Deposition of Christ* for the Vatican Museums, he had been issued a pass that granted him access to the conservation labs. The Swiss Guard at St. Anne's Gate had rarely given it more than a cursory glance before waving him onto the territory of the city-state. Most members of Rome's large religious community seldom bothered to display their credentials. Annona, the name of the Vatican supermarket, worked like a secret password.

Gabriel held the clerical suit against his body.

"Stefani Hoffmann was right," said Donati. "You really do look like a priest."

"Let's hope no one asks for my blessing."

Donati waved his hand dismissively. "There's nothing to it."

Gabriel went into the bathroom and changed. When he emerged, Donati straightened the Roman collar.

"How do you feel?"

Gabriel slipped a Beretta into the waistband of his trousers at the small of his back. "Much better."

Donati grabbed his briefcase on the way out the door and led Gabriel downstairs to the street. They walked to Bernini's Colonnade, then turned to the right. The Piazza Papa Pio XII was jammed with satellite trucks and reporters, including a correspondent from French television who pressed Donati for a comment on the approaching conclave. She relented when the archbishop shot her a curial glare.

"Very impressive," said Gabriel, sotto voce.

"I have something of a reputation."

They passed beneath the Passetto, the elevated escape route last utilized by Pope Clement VII in 1527 during the Sack of Rome, and walked along the pink facade of the Swiss Guard barracks. A halberdier in a simple blue uniform stood watch at St. Anne's Gate. Donati crossed the invisible border without slowing. Waving Father Benedetti's pass, Gabriel did the same. Together they headed up the Via Sant'Anna toward the Apostolic Palace.

"Do you suppose that nice Swiss boy is watching us?"

"Like a hawk," murmured Donati.

"How long before he tells Metzler you're back in town?"

"If I had to guess, he already has."

CARDINAL DOMENICO ALBANESE, PREFECT OF the Vatican Secret Archives and camerlengo of the Holy Roman Church, was sampling the global television coverage of the pending conclave when the power suddenly failed in his apartment above the Lapidary Gallery. It was not an altogether unusual occurrence. The Vatican received most of its electricity from Rome's notoriously fickle grid. Consequently, the denizens of the Curia spent much of their time in the dark, which surely would not have come as a surprise to their critics.

Most curial cardinals scarcely noticed the periodic outages. Domenico Albanese, however, was the ruler of a climate-controlled empire of secrets, much of it underground. Electricity was necessary for the smooth administration of his realm. Because it was a Sunday, the Archives were officially closed, thus reducing the likelihood of a priceless Vatican treasure walking out the door. Still, Albanese preferred to err on the side of caution.

He lifted the receiver of the phone on his desk and dialed the Archives' control room. There was no answer. In fact, there was no sound at all. Albanese rattled the switch. Only then did he realize there was no dial tone. It appeared the Vatican's phone system was down as well.

He was still dressed in his nightclothes. Fortunately, he lived above the store. A private corridor overlooking the Belvedere Courtyard delivered him to the upper level of the Secret Archives. There was not a light burning anywhere. In the control room a pair of security guards sat staring at a wall of darkened video monitors. The entire network appeared frozen.

"Why haven't you switched over to auxiliary power?" asked Albanese.

"It's not functioning, Eminence."

"Is there anyone inside the Archives?"

"The *sala di studio* and the Index Rooms are empty. So is the Manuscript Depository."

"Go downstairs and have a look, just to be sure."

"Right away, Eminence."

Satisfied his kingdom was safe from danger, Albanese returned to his apartment and drew his morning bath, unaware of the two men walking along the Via Sant'Anna, past the entrance of the Vatican Bank. One of the men had a gun concealed beneath his ill-fitting clerical suit and an unusually large mobile phone pressed to his ear. Highly secure, it was connected to an operations room in north Tel Aviv, where a team of the world's most formidable hackers awaited his next command. Needless to say, Albanese's realm was far from secure. Indeed, at that moment, it was in mortal peril.

BEFORE REACHING THE ENTRANCE TO the Belvedere Courtyard, Gabriel and Donati turned to the right and wound their way through the business quarter of Vatican City to a seldom-used service door at the base of the antiquity-filled Chiaramonti Museum. It was adjacent to a complex of industrial air conditioners that controlled the climate in the Manuscript Depository, which lay several meters beneath their feet.

Gabriel stared directly into the lens of the security camera. "Can you see me?"

"Nice outfit," said Yuval Gershon.

"Just open the door."

The deadbolt thumped. Donati pulled the latch and led Gabriel into a small foyer. Directly before them was a second door and another security camera. Gabriel gave the signal, and Yuval Gershon opened the door remotely.

Beyond it was a stairwell. Four flights down, Gabriel and Donati arrived at another door. It was the first level of the Manuscript Depository. Four additional flights brought them to the second level and yet another door. A buzzer groaned, a deadbolt snapped. Donati seized the latch, and together they went inside.

23

VATICAN SECRET ARCHIVES

THE DARKNESS WAS IMPENETRABLE. GABRIEL switched on his phone's unusually bright flashlight and was somewhat disappointed by what he saw. At first glance, the Manuscript Depository looked like the underground level of an ordinary university library. There were even trolleys piled with books. He illuminated the spine of one of the volumes. It was a collection of wartime diplomatic documents and cables from the Secretariat of State.

"Next time," promised Donati.

An empty aisle stretched before them, lined on both sides with gunmetal-gray shelves. Gabriel and Donati followed it to an intersection and turned to the right. After about thirty meters, a woven wire mesh storage enclosure blocked their path.

Gabriel played the beam of his flashlight around the interior.

The books resting on the metal shelves were very old. Some were the size of a typical monograph. Others were smaller and covered in cracked leather. None looked as though they had been produced by anything other than a human hand.

"I think we've come to the right place."

They were now at the westernmost edge of the Depository, directly beneath the Cortile della Pigna. Donati led Gabriel past a row of enclosures to an unmarked metal door, pale green, watched over by a security camera. There was no sign or placard to indicate the sort of material stored in the chamber behind it. The professional-grade locks looked newly installed. There was one for the deadbolt and a second for the latch. Both appeared to be five-pin mechanisms.

Gabriel handed his phone to Donati. Then he drew a thin metal tool from the pocket of his borrowed clerical suit and inserted it into the mechanism for the deadbolt.

"Is there anything you *can't* do?" asked Donati.

"I can't pick this lock if you don't stop talking."

"How long will it take?"

"That depends on how many more questions you intend to ask."

Donati aimed the beam of the flashlight at the lock. Gabriel worked the tool gently inside the mechanism, testing for resistance, listening for the drop of a pin.

"Don't bother," said a voice calmly. "You won't find what you're looking for."

Gabriel turned. In the darkness he could see nothing. Donati aimed the phone's flashlight into the void. It illuminated a man in a cassock. No, thought Gabriel. Not a cassock. A robe.

The man moved forward, soundlessly, on sandaled feet. He was identical to Gabriel in height and build, about five eight, no more than a hundred and sixty pounds. His hair was black and curly, his skin was dark. He had an ancient face, like an icon come to life.

He took another step forward. His left hand was heavily bandaged. So was his right. It was clutching a manila envelope.

"Who are you?" asked Donati.

His face registered no change in expression. "You don't know me? I'm Father Joshua, Excellency."

He spoke fluent Italian, the language of the Vatican, but it was obviously not his native tongue. His name seemed to mean nothing to Donati.

He lifted his eyes to the ceiling. "You mustn't stay long. Cardinal Albanese instructed the security guards to search the Depository. They're on their way."

"How do you know?"

He lowered his gaze toward the pale-green door. "I'm afraid the book is gone, Excellency."

"Do you know what it was?"

"This will tell you everything you need to know." The priest handed Donati the envelope. The flap was sealed with clear packing tape. "Don't open it until you're outside the walls of the Vatican."

"What is it?" asked Donati.

The priest lifted his eyes toward the ceiling again. "It's time for you to leave, Excellency. They're coming."

ONLY THEN WAS GABRIEL ABLE to hear the voices. He seized his phone from Donati and extinguished the light. The darkness was absolute.

"Follow me," whispered Father Joshua. "I know the way."

They walked in a single file, the priest leading, Gabriel behind Donati. They made a right turn, then a left, and a moment later they were back at the door through which they had entered the Depository. It opened to Father Joshua's touch. He raised a hand in farewell and then melted once more into the gloom.

They entered the stairwell and climbed the eight flights of steps. Gabriel's phone had lost its connection to Unit 8200. When he redialed, Yuval Gershon answered instantly.

"I was getting worried."

"Can you see us?"

"I can now."

Gershon unlocked the last two doors simultaneously. Outside, the sharp Roman sunlight dazzled their eyes. Donati slipped the envelope into his briefcase and reset the combination locks.

"Maybe I should carry that," said Gabriel as they set off toward the Via Sant'Anna.

"I outrank you, Father Benedetti."

"That's true, Excellency. But I'm the one with the gun."

IT WAS AT THAT INSTANT the lights flickered to life in Cardinal Domenico Albanese's apartment. Dripping wet, he lifted the receiver of his internal Vatican phone and heard the pleasing pulse of a dial tone. The duty officer in the Archives control room answered on the first ring. Yes, he said, the power had been restored. The computer network was in the process of rebooting, and the security cameras and automatic doors were once again functioning normally.

"Is there any evidence of an intrusion?"

"None, Eminence."

Relieved, Albanese placed the receiver gently in its cradle and took a moment to ponder the view from the window of his private study. It lacked the grandeur of the vista from the papal apartments—he could not see St. Peter's Square or even the dome of the basilica—but it allowed him to monitor the comings and goings at St. Anne's Gate.

At present, the Via Sant'Anna was deserted except for a tall archbishop and a smallish priest in a slightly ill-fitting clerical suit. They were headed toward the gate at a parade-ground clip. The priest's hands were empty, but in the right hand of the archbishop was a fine leather briefcase. Albanese recognized it. Indeed, he had often expressed admiration for the bag. He recognized the archbishop as well.

But who was the priest? Albanese had but one suspect. He reached for his phone and made one final call.

A DEVOUT CATHOLIC WHO ATTENDED Mass daily, Colonel Alois Metzler, commandant of the Pontifical Swiss Guard, did his best to avoid the office on Sundays. But because it was the Sunday before the start of a conclave, a most sacred undertaking that would be watched by billions around the world, he was at his desk in the Swiss Guard barracks when Cardinal Albanese telephoned. The camerlengo was molto agitato. In frenetic Italian, which Metzler spoke fluently if reluctantly, he explained that Archbishop Luigi Donati and his friend Gabriel Allon had just broken into the Secret Archives and were at that moment headed toward St. Anne's Gate. Under no circumstances, shouted the cardinal, were they to be allowed to leave the territory of Vatican City.

If the truth be told, Metzler was in no mood to tangle with the likes of Donati and his friend from Israel, whom Metzler had seen in action on more than one occasion. But because the throne of St. Peter was empty, he had no choice but to obey a direct order from the camerlengo.

Rising, he hurried through the barracks to the lobby, where a duty officer sat behind a half-moon desk, his eyes on a bank of video monitors. In one, Metzler saw Donati marching toward St. Anne's Gate, a priest at his side.

"Good God," Metzler murmured.

The *priest* was Allon.

Through the open door of the barracks, Metzler saw a young halberdier standing in the Via Sant'Anna, hands clasped behind his back. He shouted at the sentry to block the gate, but it was too late. Donati and Allon strode across the invisible border in a black blur and were gone.

Metzler hastened after them. They were now walking swiftly through the crowds of tourists along the Via di Porta Angelica. Metzler called Donati's name. The archbishop stopped and turned. Allon kept walking.

Donati's smile was disarming. "What is it, Colonel Metzler?"

"Cardinal Albanese believes you just entered the Secret Archives without authorization."

"And how would I have done that? The Archives are closed today."

"The cardinal believes you had help from your friend."

"Father Benedetti?"

"I saw him in the monitor, Excellency. I know who that was."

"You were mistaken, Colonel Metzler. And so was Cardinal Albanese. Now if you will excuse me, I'm late for an appointment."

Donati turned without another word and set off toward St. Peter's Square. Metzler addressed his back.

"Your Vatican pass is no longer valid, Excellency. From now on, you stop at the Permissions Desk like everyone else."

Donati raised a hand in affirmation and kept walking. Metzler returned to his office and immediately rang Albanese.

The camerlengo was molto agitato.

GABRIEL WAS WAITING FOR DONATI near the end of the Colonnade. Together they returned to the Jesuit Curia. Upstairs in his rooms, Donati drew the envelope from his briefcase and pried open the flap. Inside, between two protective sheets of clear film, was a single page of handwritten text. The left edge of the page was clean and straight, but the right was tattered and frayed. The characters were Roman. The language was Latin.

Donati's hands shook as he read it.

EVANGELIUM SECUNDUM PILATI . . .

The Gospel according to Pontius Pilate.

PART TWO

ECCE HOMO

24

JESUIT CURIA, ROME

EVEN HIS FIRST NAME WAS lost to the mists of time—the name his mother and father had called him the day he was presented to the gods and a golden amulet, a *bulla*, was hung round his tiny neck to ward off evil spirits. Later in life he would have answered to his cognomen, the third name of a Roman citizen, a hereditary label used to distinguish one branch of a family from the others. His had three syllables, not two, and sounded nothing like the version that would follow him down through the ages and into infamy.

The year of his birth is not known, nor the place. One school of thought held that he was from Roman-ruled Spain—perhaps Tarragona on the Catalonian coast or Seville, where even today, near the Plaza de Arguelles, there stands an elaborate Andalusian palace known as the Casa de Pilatos. Another theory, prevalent in the Middle Ages, imagined he was the illegitimate child of a German king called Tyrus and a concubine named Pila. As the legend goes, Pila did not know the name of the man who impregnated her, so she combined her father's name with her own and called the boy Pilatus.

His most likely place of birth, however, was Rome. His ancestors were probably Samnites, a warlike tribe who inhabited the craggy hills south of the city. His second name, Pontius, suggested he was a descendant of the Pontii, a clan that produced several important Roman military figures. His cognomen, Pilatus, meant "skilled with a javelin." It was possible Pontius Pilate, through his military exploits, earned the name himself. The more plausible explanation is that he was the son of a knight and a member of the equestrian order, the second tier of Roman nobility, falling just beneath the senatorial class.

If so, he would have enjoyed a comfortable Roman upbringing. The family home would have had an atrium, a colonnaded garden, running water, and a private bath. A second dwelling, a villa, would have overlooked the sea. He would have traveled the streets of Rome not on foot but held aloft in a litter by slaves. Unlike most children at the dawn of the first millennium, he would have never known hunger. He would have wanted for nothing.

His education would have been rigorous—several hours of instruction each day in reading, writing, mathematics, and, when he was older, the finer points of critical thinking and debate, skills that would serve him well later in life. He would have honed his physique with regular weight lifting and then recovered from his efforts with a trip to the baths. For entertainment he would have reveled in the blood-soaked spectacles of the games. It was unlikely he ever saw the Flavian Amphitheatre, the great circular colosseum built in the low valley between the Caelian, Esquiline, and Palatine hills. The project was funded with spoils from the Temple in Jerusalem, which he knew intimately. He would not witness its destruction in 70 C.E., though surely he must have known its days were numbered.

The new and restive province of Judea was some fourteen hundred miles from Rome, a journey of three weeks or more by sea. Pontius Pilate, after serving several years as a junior officer in the Roman army, arrived there in 26 C.E. It was not a coveted post; Syria to the north and Egypt to the southeast were far more important. But what Judea lacked in stature it more than made up for in potential trouble. Its native population considered themselves chosen by their God and superior to their pagan, polytheist occupiers. Jerusalem, their holy city, was the only place in the Empire where local inhabitants did not have to prostrate themselves before an image of the emperor. Pilate, if he was to succeed, would have to handle them with care.

He had no doubt seen these people in Rome. They were the bearded, circumcised inhabitants of Regio XIV, a crowded quarter on the west side of the Tiber that would one day become known as Trastevere. There were perhaps four and a half million of them spread throughout the Empire. They had thrived under Roman rule, taking advantage of the freedom of commerce and movement the Empire afforded them. Everywhere they settled they were wealthy and much admired as a God-fearing people who loved their children, respected human life, and looked after the poor, the sick, the widowed, and the orphaned. Julius Caesar spoke highly of them and granted them important rights of association, which allowed them to worship their God instead of Rome's.

But those who lived in the ancestral homeland of Judea, Samaria, and the Galilee were a less cosmopolitan lot. Violently anti-Roman, they were riven with sects, perhaps as many as twenty-four, including the puritanical Essenes, who did not recognize the authority of the Temple. A massive complex atop Mount Moriah in Jerusalem, it was controlled by Sadducee aristocrats who profited through their association with the occupation and worked closely with the Roman prefect to assure stability.

Pilate was only the fifth to serve in the post. His headquarters were in Caesarea, a Roman enclave of gleaming white marble on the Mediterranean coast. There was a curving promenade by the sea where he could stroll when the weather was fine, and Roman temples where he made sacrifices to his gods, not theirs. Pilate, if he were so inclined, might well have imagined he had never left home.

It was not his task to remake the inhabitants of the province— they would one day become known as Jews—in Rome's image. Pilate was a collector of taxes, a facilitator of trade, and a writer of endless reports to Emperor Tiberius, which he sealed with wax and marked with the signet ring he wore on the last finger of his left hand. Rome, by and large, did not involve itself in every facet of culture and society in the lands it occupied. Its laws hibernated during periods of tranquillity and awoke only when there was a threat to order.

Troublemakers typically received a warning. And if they foolishly persisted, they were dealt with swiftly and brutally. Pilate's immediate predecessor, Valerius Gratus, once dispatched two hundred Jews simultaneously with Rome's preferred method of execution: death on the cross. After a revolt in 4 B.C.E., two thousand were crucified outside Jerusalem. So powerful was their faith in their one God, they went to the cross without fear.

As prefect, Pilate was Judea's chief magistrate, its judge and jury. Even so, the Jews handled much of the province's civil administration and law enforcement through the Sanhedrin, the rabbinical tribunal that convened daily—except for religious festivals and the Sabbath—in the Hall of Hewn Stones on the north side of the Temple complex. Pilate was under orders from Emperor Tiberius to grant the Jews wide latitude in running their own affairs, especially when it came to matters of their religion. He was to remain in the background whenever possible, the hidden hand, Rome's invisible man.

But Pilate, quick-tempered and vindictive, soon developed a reputation for savagery, theft, endless executions, and needless provocations. There was, for example, his decision to affix military standards bearing the emperor's likeness to the walls of the Antonia Fortress, which overlooked the Temple itself. Predictably, the Jews reacted with fury. Several thousand surrounded Pilate's palace in Caesarea, where a weeklong standoff ensued. When the Jews made it clear that they were prepared to die if their demands were not met, Pilate relented and the standards were removed.

And then there was Pilate's admittedly impressive aqueduct, which he financed, at least in part, with sacred money, *corban*, stolen from the Temple treasury. Once again he was confronted by a large crowd, this time at the Great Pavement, the elevated platform outside Herod's Citadel, which served as Pilate's Jerusalem headquarters. Sprawled impassively atop his curule chair,

Pilate silently endured their abuse for a time before ordering his soldiers to unsheathe their swords. Some of the unarmed Jews were hacked to pieces. Others were trampled in the melee.

Lastly, there were the gold-plated shields dedicated to Tiberius that he hung in his Jerusalem apartments. The Jews demanded the shields be removed. And when Pilate refused, they dispatched a letter of protest to none other than the emperor himself. It reached Tiberius while he was on holiday in Capri, or so claimed the philosopher Philo. Seething with rage over his prefect's needless blunder, Tiberius ordered Pilate to remove the shields without delay.

He went to Jerusalem as seldom as possible, usually to oversee security during Jewish festivals. Passover, the celebration of the Jews' deliverance from bondage in Egypt, was rife with both religious and political implications. Hundreds of thousands of Jews from across the Empire—in some cases, entire villages—descended on the city. The streets were jammed with pilgrims and perhaps a quarter-million bleating sheep awaiting ritual slaughter. Lurking in the shadows were the Sicarii, cloaked Jewish zealots who killed Roman soldiers with their distinctive daggers and then disappeared into the crowds.

At the center of this pandemonium was the Temple. Roman soldiers kept watch on the celebrations from their garrison at the Antonia; Pilate, from his splendid private chambers in Herod's Citadel. Any hint of unrest—a challenge to Roman rule or to the collaborative Temple authorities—would have been dealt with ruthlessly, lest the situation spin out of control. One spark, one agitator, and Jerusalem might erupt.

It was into this volatile city—perhaps in the year 33 c.e., or perhaps as early as 27 or as late as 36—that there came a

Galilean, a healer, a worker of miracles, a preacher of parables who warned that the kingdom of heaven was at hand. He arrived, as prophesied, astride an ass. It is possible Pilate already knew of this Galilean and that he witnessed his tumultuous entrance into Jerusalem. There were many such messianic figures in first-century Judea, men who called themselves the "anointed one" and promised to rebuild David's kingdom. Pilate viewed these preachers as a direct threat to Roman rule and extinguished them without mercy. Invariably, their adherents suffered the same fate.

Historians disagree on the nature of the incident that led to the Galilean's earthly demise. Most concur that a crime was committed—perhaps a physical attack on the currency traders in the Royal Portico, perhaps a verbal tirade against the Temple elite. It is possible Roman soldiers witnessed the disturbance and took the Galilean into custody straightaway. But tradition holds that he was arrested by a joint Roman-Jewish force on the Mount of Olives after sharing a final Pesach meal with his disciples.

What happened next is still less clear. Even the traditional accounts are riddled with contradictions. They suggest that sometime after midnight, the Galilean was brought to the house of the high priest, Joseph ben Caiaphas, where he was subjected to a brutal interrogation by a portion of the Sanhedrin. Contemporary historians, however, have cast doubt on this version of the story. After all, it was both Passover and the eve of the Sabbath, and Jerusalem was bursting at the seams with Jews from around the known world. Caiaphas, having put in a long day at the Temple, is unlikely to have welcomed the late-night intrusion. Moreover, the trial as described—it was purportedly conducted outside in the courtyard by the light of a bonfire—was strictly forbidden by the Laws of Moses and therefore could not have taken place.

One way or another, the Galilean ended up in the hands of Pontius Pilate, the Roman prefect and chief magistrate of the province. Tradition holds that he presided over a public tribunal, but no official record of such a proceeding survives. One central fact, however, is indisputable. The Galilean was put to death by crucifixion, the Roman method of execution reserved solely for insurrectionists, probably just outside the city walls, where his punishment would serve as a warning. Pilate might have witnessed the man's suffering from his chambers in Herod's Citadel. But in all likelihood, given his fearsome reputation, the entire episode was quickly forgotten, swept away by some new problem. Pilate, after all, was a busy man.

But then again, the prefect may well have carried a memory of the man long after ordering his execution, especially during the final years of his rule in Judea, as followers of the Galilean, who was called Jesus of Nazareth, took the first halting steps toward creating a new faith. Traumatized by what they had witnessed, they comforted each other with accounts of the Galilean's ministry, accounts that would eventually be written down in books, evangelizing pamphlets known as gospels, which circulated among communities of early believers. And it was there that Archbishop Luigi Donati, in his rooms at the Jesuit Curia on the Borgo Santo Spirito in Rome, picked up the thread of the story.

25

JESUIT CURIA, ROME

MARK, NOT MATTHEW, WAS THE first. It was written in colloquial koine Greek sometime between 66 and 75 C.E., more than thirty years after the death of Jesus, an eternity in the ancient world. The gospel circulated anonymously for several decades before Church Fathers ascribed it to a companion of the apostle Peter, a conclusion rejected by most contemporary biblical scholars, who contend the author's identity is not known.

His audience was a community of gentile Christians living in Rome, directly under the thumb of the emperor. It is unlikely he spoke the language of Jesus or his disciples, and he probably possessed only passing familiarity with the geography and customs of the land in which the story was set. By the time he took up his pen, nearly all of the firsthand witnesses had died off or been killed. For his source material he drew upon an oral tradition and perhaps a few written fragments. In the fifteenth chapter, a blameless and benevolent Pilate is portrayed as having bowed to the demands of a Jewish crowd to sentence Jesus to death. The earliest versions of Mark concluded abruptly with the discovery of Jesus' empty tomb, an ending many early Christians considered anticlimactic and unsatisfying. Later versions of Mark had two alternative endings. In the so-called Longer Ending, a resurrected Jesus appears in different forms to his disciples.

"Mark's original author did not compose the alternative ending," explained Donati. "It was probably written hundreds of years after his death. In fact, the fourth-century Codex Vaticanus, the oldest known copy of the New Testament, contains the original empty tomb ending."

The Gospel of Matthew, Donati continued, was composed next, probably between 80 and 90 c.e., but perhaps as late as 110, long after the cataclysmic First Roman-Jewish War and the destruction of the Temple. Matthew's audience was a community of Jewish Christians living in Roman-occupied Syria. He drew heavily from Mark, borrowing six hundred verses. But scholars believe Matthew expanded on the work of his predecessor with the help of the Q source, a theoretical collection of the sayings of Jesus. His work reflects the sharp divide between Jewish Christians who accepted Jesus as the messiah and Jews who did not. The depiction of Jesus' appearance before Pilate is similar to Mark's, with one critical addition.

"Pilate, the ruthless Roman prefect, washes his hands in front of the Jewish crowd gathered on the Great Pavement and declares himself innocent of Christ's blood. To which the crowd replies, 'His blood shall be on us and our children.' It is the most consequential line of dialogue ever composed. Two thousand years of persecution and slaughter of Jews at the hands of Christians can be traced back to those nine terrible words."

"Why were they written?" asked Gabriel.

"As a Roman Catholic prelate and a man of great personal faith, I believe the Gospels were divinely inspired. That said, they were composed by human beings long after the events took place and were based on stories of Jesus' life and ministry told by his earliest followers. If there was indeed a tribunal of some sort, Pilate undoubtedly spoke very few, if any, of the words the Gospel writers put in his mouth. The same would be true, of course, of the Jewish crowd, if there was one. *Let his blood be upon us and our children?* Did they really shout such an awkward and outlandish line? And with a single voice? Where were the followers of Jesus who came to Jerusalem with him from the Galilee? Where were the dissenters?" Donati shook his head. "That passage was a mistake. A sacred mistake, but a mistake nonetheless."

"But was it an innocent mistake?"

"A professor of mine at the Gregoriana used to refer to it as the longest lie. Privately, of course. Had he done so openly, he would have been dragged before the Congregation of the Doctrine of the Faith and defrocked."

"Is the scene in Matthew's Gospel a lie?"

"The author of Matthew would tell you that he wrote the story as he had heard it himself and as he believed it to be. That said, there is no doubt that his Gospel, like Mark's, shifted the blame for Jesus' death from the Romans to the Jews."

"Why?"

"Because within a few short years of the Crucifixion, the Jesus movement was in grave danger of being reabsorbed by Judaism. If there was a future, it lay with the gentiles living under Roman rule. The evangelists and the Church Fathers had to make the new faith acceptable to the Empire. There was nothing they could do to change the fact that Jesus died a Roman death at the hands of Roman troops. But if they could suggest that the Jews had forced Pilate's hand . . ."

"Problem solved."

Donati nodded. "And I'm afraid it gets worse in the later Gospels. Luke suggests it was the Jews rather than the Romans who nailed Jesus to the cross. John makes the accusation straight out. It is inconceivable to me that Jews would crucify one of their own. They might well have stoned Jesus for blasphemy. But the cross? Not a chance."

"Then why was the passage included in the Christian canon?"

"It is important to remember that the Gospels were never intended to be factual records. They were theology, not history. They were evangelizing documents that laid the foundation of a new faith, a faith that by the end of the first century was in sharp conflict with the one from which it had sprung. Three centuries later, when the bishops of the early Church convened the Synod of Hippo, there were many different gospels and other texts circulating among the Christian communities of North Africa and the Eastern Mediterranean. The bishops canonized only four, knowing full well they contained numerous discrepancies and inconsistencies. For example, all the canonical Gospels give a slightly different account of the three days leading up to Jesus' execution."

"Did the bishops also know they were planting the seeds for two thousand years of Jewish suffering?"

"A fair question."

"What's the answer?"

"By the end of the fourth century, the die had been cast. The refusal of the Jews to accept Jesus as their savior was regarded as a mortal threat to the early Church. How could Jesus be the one true path to salvation if the very people who heard his message with their own ears clung to their faith? Early Christian theologians wrestled with the question of whether the Jews should even be allowed to exist. St. John Chrysostom of Antioch preached that synagogues were whorehouses and dens of thieves, that Jews were no better than pigs and goats, that they had grown fat from having too much to eat, that they should be marked for slaughter. Not surprisingly, there were numerous attacks on the Jews of Antioch, and their synagogue was destroyed. In 414 the Jews of Alexandria were wiped out. Regrettably, it was only the beginning."

Still dressed in his borrowed clerical suit, Gabriel went to the window and, parting the blinds, peered into the Borgo Santo Spirito. Donati was seated at his writing desk. Before him, still in its sheath of protective plastic, was the page from the book.

EVANGELIUM SECUNDUM PILATI . . .

"For the record," said Donati after a moment, "the Nicene Creed, which was written at the First Council of Nicaea, states unequivocally that Jesus suffered under Pontius Pilate. Furthermore, the Church declared in *Nostra Aetate* in 1965 that the Jews as a people are not collectively responsible for the death of Jesus. And twenty-three years after that, Pope Wojtyla issued

'We Remember,' his statement on the Church and the Holocaust."

"I remember it, too. It went to great pains to suggest that two thousand years of Church teaching that Jews were the murderers of God had absolutely nothing to do with the Nazis and the Final Solution. It was a whitewash, Excellency. It was curial word salad."

"Which is why my master stood at the bimah in the Great Synagogue of Rome and begged the Jews for forgiveness." Donati paused. "You remember that, too, don't you? You were there, if I recall."

Gabriel took down a copy of the Bible from Donati's bookcase and opened it to the twenty-seventh chapter of Matthew. "What about this?" He pointed out the relevant passage. "Am I personally guilty of the murder of God, or are the writers of the four Gospels guilty of the most vicious slander in history?"

"The Church has declared that you are not."

"And I thank the Church for belatedly making that clear." Gabriel tapped the page with this fingertip. "But the book still says I am."

"Scripture cannot be changed."

"The Codex Vaticanus would suggest otherwise." Gabriel returned the Bible to its place on the shelf and resumed his study of the street. "And the other gospels? The ones bishops rejected at the Synod of Hippo?"

"They were deemed apocryphal. For the most part, they were literary elaborations on the four canonical Gospels. Ancient fan fiction, if you will. There were books like the Infancy Gospel of Thomas that focused on the early life of Jesus. There were Gnostic gospels, Jewish Christian gospels, the Gospel of Mary, even the Gospel of Judas. There was also a significant body of Passion apocrypha, stories devoted to Jesus' suffering and death. One was called the Gospel of Peter. Peter didn't write it, of course. It was pseudepigrapha, or falsely inscribed. The same was true of the Gospel of Nicodemus. That book is better known as the *Acta Pilati*."

Gabriel turned away from the window. "The Acts of Pilate?"

Donati nodded. "Nicodemus was a member of the Sanhedrin who lived on a great estate outside Jerusalem. He was said to have been a secret disciple of Jesus and a confidant of Pilate. He's depicted in Caravaggio's *Deposition of Christ*, the figure in the sienna-colored garment grasping Jesus' legs. Caravaggio gave him Michelangelo's face, by the way."

"Really?" asked Gabriel archly. "I never knew."

Donati ignored the remark. "Dating the Acts of Pilate is difficult, but most scholars agree it was probably written in the late fourth century. It purports to contain material composed by Pilate himself while he was in Jerusalem. It was quite popular here in Italy in the fifteenth and sixteenth centuries. In fact, it was printed twenty-eight times during that period." Donati held up his phone. "To read it now, all you need is one of these."

"Were there other Pilate books?"

"Several."

"Such as?"

"The Memoirs of Pilate, the Martyrdom of Pilate, and the Report of Pilate, to name a few. The Handing Over of Pilate describes his appearance before Emperor Tiberius after he was recalled to Rome. Never mind that Tiberius was dead by the time Pilate arrived. There was also the Letter of Pilate to Claudius, the Letter of Pilate to Herod, the Letter of Herod to Pilate, the

Letter of Tiberius to Pilate . . ." Donati's voice trailed off. "You get the point."

"What about the Gospel of Pilate?"

"I am unfamiliar with an apocryphal piece of Christian writing by that name."

"Are any of the other books considered credible?"

"No," said Donati. "They're all forgeries. And they all attempt to exonerate Pilate for Jesus' death while at the same time implicating the Jews."

"Just like the canonical Gospels." The bells of St. Peter's Basilica tolled midday. "What do you suppose is going on behind the walls of the Vatican?"

"If I had to guess, Cardinal Albanese is desperately searching for Father Joshua. I fear what will happen if he finds him. As camerlengo, Albanese has enormous authority. Practically speaking, the Order of St. Helena is running the Roman Catholic Church. The question is, do they intend to relinquish their power? Or do they have a plan to keep it?"

"We still can't prove that the Order killed Lucchesi."

"Not yet. But we have five days to find the evidence." Donati paused. "And the Gospel of Pilate, of course."

"Where do we start?"

"Father Robert Jordan."

"Who is he?"

"My professor from the Gregoriana."

"Is he still in Rome?"

Donati shook his head. "He entered a monastery a few years ago. He doesn't use a phone or e-mail. We'll have to drive up there, but there's no guarantee he'll see us. He's quite brilliant. And difficult, I'm afraid."

"Where's the monastery?"

"A small town of considerable religious importance on the slopes of Monte Subasio in Umbria. I'm sure you've heard of it. In fact, I believe you and Chiara used to live not far from there."

Gabriel permitted himself a brief smile. It had been a long time since he had been to Assisi.

26

ROME—ASSISI

TRANSPORT REQUIRED A MINIMUM OF four hours to acquire an untraceable car, so Gabriel, after changing into his own clothing, walked to a Hertz outlet near the Vatican walls and rented an Opel Corsa hatchback. He was followed there inexpertly by a man on a motorcycle. Black trousers, black shoes, a black nylon coat, a black helmet with a tinted visor. The same motorcyclist followed Gabriel back to the Jesuit Curia, where he collected Donati.

"That's him," said Donati, peering into the sideview mirror. "That's definitely Father Graf."

"I think I'll pull over and have a quiet word with him."

"Perhaps you should just lose him instead."

He put up a good fight, especially in the traffic-clogged streets of central Rome, but by the time they reached the Autostrada,

Gabriel was confident they were not being followed. The afternoon had turned cloudy and cold. So had Gabriel's mood. He leaned his head against the window, a hand balanced atop the wheel.

"Was it something I said?" asked Donati at last.

"What's that?"

"You haven't uttered a word in ten minutes."

"I was enjoying the remarkable beauty of the Italian countryside."

"Try again," said Donati.

"I was thinking about my mother. And about the number tattooed on her arm. And about the candles that burned day and night in the little house where I grew up in Israel. They were for my grandparents, who were gassed upon arrival at Auschwitz and fed into the fires of the crematoria. They had no other grave but those candles. They were ashes on the wind." Gabriel was silent for a moment. "That's what I was thinking about, Luigi. I was thinking about how differently the history of the Jews might have unfolded if the Church hadn't declared war on us in the Gospels."

"Your characterization is unfair."

"Do you know how many Jews there should be in the world? Two hundred million. We could be more numerous than the populations of Germany and France combined. But we were wiped out time and time again, culminating with the pogrom to end all pogroms." Quietly, Gabriel added, "All because of those nine words."

"It must be said that throughout the Middle Ages, the Church intervened on countless occasions to protect the Jews of Europe."

"Why did they need protecting in the first place?" Gabriel answered his own question. "They needed protection because of what the Church was teaching. And it also must be said, Excellency, that long after Jews were emancipated in Western Europe, they remained ghettoized in the city controlled by the papacy. Where did the Nazis get the idea of making the Jews wear the Star of David? They had to look no further than Rome."

"One has to distinguish between religious anti-Judaism and racial anti-Semitism."

"That is a distinction without a difference. Jews were resented because they were shopkeepers and moneylenders. And do you know *why* they were shopkeepers and moneylenders? Because for more than a millennium, they were forbidden to do anything else. And yet even now, after the horrors of the Holocaust, after all the films and books and memorials and attempts to change hearts and minds, the longest hatred endures. Germany admits it cannot protect its Jewish citizens from harm. French Jews are moving to Israel in record numbers to escape anti-Semitism. In America neo-Nazis march openly while Jews are being shot and killed in their synagogues. What is the source of this irrational hatred? Could it be that for nearly two thousand years the Church taught that the Jews were collectively guilty of deicide, that we were the very murderers of God?"

"Yes," admitted Donati. "But what shall we do about it?"

"Find the Gospel of Pilate."

South of Orvieto they turned off the Autostrada and headed into the rolling hills and thick forests of Donati's native Umbria. By the time they reached Perugia, the sun had burned a hole in the clouds. To the east, at the base of Monte Subasio, glowed the distinctive red marble of Assisi.

"There's the Abbey of St. Peter." Donati pointed out the bell tower at the northern end of the city. "It's inhabited by a small group of monks from the Cassinese Congregation. They live according to the Rule of Saint Benedict. *Ora et labora*: pray and work."

"Sounds a bit like the job description of the chief of the Office."

Donati laughed. "The monks support a number of local organizations, including a hospital and an orphanage. They agreed to give Father Jordan lodging in the abbey when he retired from the Gregoriana."

"Why Assisi?"

"After working for forty years as a Jesuit academic and writer, he longed for a more contemplative existence. But you can be sure he finds time to research and write. He's one of the world's foremost authorities on the apocryphal gospels."

"What happens if he won't see us?"

"I'm sure you'll think of something," remarked Donati.

Gabriel left the Opel in a car park outside the city walls and followed Donati through the archway of the Porta San Pietro. The abbey was a few paces along a shadowed street, behind walls of red stone. The outer door was locked. Donati rang the bell. There was no answer.

He checked the time. "Midafternoon prayers. Let's take a walk."

They set out along the street against a flow of outward-bound package tourists, Gabriel in dark trousers and a leather coat, Donati in his magenta-trimmed cassock. He attracted no more than passing interest. The Abbey of St. Peter was not the only monastery or convent in Assisi. It was a city of religious.

It became Christian, explained Donati, just two hundred

years after the Crucifixion. St. Francis was born in Assisi at the end of the twelfth century. Known for his lavish clothing and circle of rich friends, he encountered a beggar one afternoon in the marketplace and was so moved he gave the man everything he had in his pockets. Within a few years he was living as a beggar himself. He cared for lepers in a lazar house, worked as a lowly kitchen servant in a monastery, and in 1209 founded a religious order that required its members to embrace a life of total and complete poverty.

"Francis is one of the Church's most beloved saints, but he didn't invent the notion of caring for the poor. It was ingrained in Christianity from the beginning. And now, two millennia later, thousands of Roman Catholics around the world are doing the same thing, every hour of every day. I think that's worth preserving, don't you?"

"I once told Lucchesi that I would never want to live in a world without the Roman Catholic Church."

"Did you? He never mentioned it." They arrived at the basilica. "Shall we go inside and see the paintings?"

"Next time," quipped Gabriel.

It was three fifteen. They retraced their steps to the abbey, and once again Donati rang the bell. A moment passed before a male voice answered. He spoke Italian with a distinct British accent.

"Good afternoon. May I help you?"

"I'm here to see Father Jordan."

"I'm afraid he doesn't accept visitors."

"I believe he'll make an exception in my case."

"Your name?"

"Archbishop Luigi Donati." He released the call button and gave Gabriel a sidelong glance. "Membership has its privileges."

The lock snapped open. A hairless, black-habited Benedictine waited in the shadows of an internal courtyard. "Forgive me, Excellency. I wish someone had told us you were coming." He extended a soft, pale hand. "I'm Simon, by the way. Follow me, please."

They entered the church of San Pietro through a side door, crossed the nave, and emerged into another internal court. The next door gave onto the abbey itself. The monk conveyed them to a modestly furnished common room overlooking a green garden. Actually, thought Gabriel, it was more like a small farm. Surrounded by a high wall, it was invisible to the outside world.

The Benedictine asked them to make themselves comfortable and then withdrew. Ten minutes elapsed before he finally returned. He was alone.

"I'm sorry, Excellency. But Father Jordan is praying now and wishes not to be disturbed."

Donati opened his briefcase and removed the manila envelope. "Show him this."

"But—"

"Now, Don Simon."

Gabriel smiled as the monk fled the room. "It seems your reputation precedes you."

"I doubt Father Jordan will be so easily impressed."

Another fifteen minutes passed before the British monk returned. This time he was accompanied by a small, dark man with a weathered face and a shock of unkempt white hair. Father Robert Jordan was wearing an ordinary cassock rather than the black habit of the Benedictines. In his right hand was the envelope.

"I came here to get away from Rome. Now it seems Rome

has come to me." Father Jordan's gaze settled on Gabriel. "Mr. Allon, I presume."

Gabriel said nothing.

Father Jordan removed the page from the envelope and held it up to the afternoon light streaming through the window. "It's paper, not vellum. It looks to be from the fifteenth or sixteenth century."

"I'll have to take your word for it," replied Donati.

Father Jordan lowered the page. "I've been searching for this for more than thirty years. Where on earth did you find it?"

"It was given to me by a priest who works in the Secret Archives."

"Does the priest have a name?"

"Father Joshua."

"Are you sure?"

"Why?"

"Because I'm quite certain I know everyone who works in the Archives, and I've never heard of anyone by that name." Father Jordan looked down at the page again. "Where's the rest of it?"

"It was removed from the papal study the night of the Holy Father's death."

"By whom?"

"Cardinal Albanese."

Father Jordan looked up sharply. "Before or after His Holiness died?"

Donati hesitated, then said, "It was after."

"Dear God," whispered Father Jordan. "I was afraid you were going to say that."

27

ABBEY OF ST. PETER, ASSISI

THE MONK RETURNED WITH AN earthenware carafe of water, a loaf of coarse bread from the monastery's bakery, and a bowl of olive oil produced by an abbey-supported cooperative. Father Jordan explained that he had worked there the previous summer, repairing the damage done to his body by a lifetime of teaching and study. It was obvious he had spent a great deal of time in the out-of-doors of late; his sunbaked face was the color of terra-cotta. His Italian was animated, flawless. Indeed, were it not for his name and his American-accented English, Gabriel would have assumed that Robert Jordan had lived his entire life in the hills and valleys of Umbria.

In truth, he had been raised in the comfortable Boston suburb of Brookline. A brilliant Jesuit academic, he served on the faculties at Fordham and Georgetown before coming to the

Pontifical Gregorian University, where he taught history and theology. His private research, however, focused on the apocryphal gospels. Of particular interest to Father Jordan were the Passion apocrypha, especially the gospels and letters focusing on Pontius Pilate. They were, he said, depressing reading, for they seemed to have but one purpose—to acquit Pilate of the death of Jesus and place the blame squarely on the heads of the Jews and their descendants. Father Jordan believed that, intentionally or not, the Gospel writers had erred in their depiction of the trial and execution of Jesus, an error compounded by the inflammatory teachings of Church Fathers from Origen to Augustine.

In the mid-1980s, he learned he was not alone. Without the knowledge of the Jesuit superior general or his chancellor at the Gregoriana, he joined the Jesus Task Force, a group of Christian scholars who attempted to create an accurate portrait of the historical Jesus. The group published its findings in a controversial book. It argued that Jesus was an itinerant sage and faith healer who neither walked on water nor miraculously fed the multitudes with five loaves of bread and two fish. He was put to death by the Romans as a public nuisance—not for challenging the authority of the Temple elite—and did not rise bodily from the dead. The concept of the Resurrection, the task force concluded, was based on visions and dreams experienced by Jesus' closest followers, a view first put forward in 1835 by the theologian David Friedrich Strauss, a German Protestant.

"When the book was published, my name didn't appear in the text. Even so, I was terrified my participation would become public. Late at night I waited for the dreaded knock at the door from the Holy Office of the Inquisition."

Donati reminded Father Jordan that the Holy Office was now known as the Congregation of the Doctrine of the Faith.

"A rose by any other name, Father Donati."

"I'm an archbishop, Robert."

Father Jordan smiled. His participation in the task force, he continued, did not shake his belief in the divinity of Jesus or the core tenets of Christianity. If anything, it strengthened his faith. He had never believed that everything in the New Testament—or in the Torah, for that matter—happened as described, and yet he believed with all his heart in the Bible's core truths. It was why he had come to Assisi, to be closer to God, to live his life the way Jesus had led his, unburdened by property or possessions.

He remained deeply troubled, however, by the Gospels' accounts of the Crucifixion, for they had led to countless deaths and untold suffering on the part of the Jewish people. Father Jordan had made it his life's work to find out what really happened that day in Jerusalem. He was convinced that somewhere there was a firsthand account. Not an apocryphal document but a genuine eyewitness report, written by an actual participant in the proceedings.

"Pontius Pilate?" asked Donati.

Father Jordan nodded. "I'm not alone in my belief that Pilate wrote about the Crucifixion. Tertullian, the very founder of Latin Christianity, the first theologian to use the word *Trinity*, was convinced that Pilate sent a detailed report to Emperor Tiberius. None other than Justin Martyr shared his opinion."

"With all due respect to Tertullian and Justin, they couldn't possibly have known whether that was true."

"I concur. In fact, I believe they were wrong on at least one key point."

"What's that?"

"Pilate didn't write about the Crucifixion until long after Tiberius was dead." Father Jordan looked down at the page. "But I'm afraid we're getting ahead of ourselves. To understand what happened, it's necessary to go back in time."

"How far?" asked Donati.

"Thirty-six C.E. Three years after the death of Jesus."

Which is where Father Robert Jordan, in the common room of the Abbey of St. Peter in the sacred city of Assisi, picked up the thread of the story.

28

ABBEY OF ST. PETER, ASSISI

IT WAS THE SAMARITANS WHO finally did Pilate in. They had a holy mountain of their own, Mount Gerizim, where it was said that Moses had placed the Ark of the Covenant after the arrival of the Jews in the Promised Land. Jewish rebels had dealt the Romans a humiliating defeat there eighty years earlier. Pilate, in one final act of brutality, evened the score. Untold numbers were massacred or crucified, but a few survived. They informed the Roman governor of Syria of Pilate's savagery, and the governor told Tiberius, who ordered Pilate to return to Rome at once. His decade-long reign as prefect of Judea was over.

He was given three months to put his affairs in order, say his goodbyes, and brief his successor. Some of his personal records he undoubtedly destroyed. But some he surely carried back to Rome, where Tiberius waited to pass judgment on his conduct.

It promised to be an unpleasant encounter. The best he could hope for was exile. The worst was death, either at the emperor's hand or his own. He was certainly in no hurry to get home.

By December of 36 C.E., he was finally ready to leave. A journey by sea was not possible, not in the dead of winter, the season of storms, so he traveled by Roman roads. Fortuna, however, was smiling on him. By the time he arrived, Tiberius was dead.

"It's possible Pilate appeared before Tiberius's successor," said Father Jordan. "But there's no record of it. Besides, the new emperor was probably too busy consolidating his own power to waste time on a disgraced prefect from a distant province. Perhaps you've heard of him. His name was Caligula."

It is at this point, Father Jordan continued, that Pontius Pilate vanishes from the pages of history and enters the realm of legend and myth. In addition to the fabricated accounts of the apocryphal gospels, countless stories and folktales circulated throughout Europe during the Middle Ages. According to the thirteenth-century *Golden Legend*, a compendium of stories about the lives of saints, Pilate was allowed to live out his days in relative peace as an exile in Gaul. The author of a popular fourteenth-century chivalric romance disagreed. Pilate, went the tale, was cast by his enemies into a deep well near Lausanne, where he spent twelve years alone in the darkness, weeping inconsolably.

Much of the lore depicted him as a deathless soul condemned to wander the countryside for all eternity, his hands soaked with the blood of Jesus. One legend claimed he was living atop a mountain near Lucerne. The story was so persistent that in the fourteenth century the mountain's name was changed to Pilatus. It was said that on Good Fridays, Pilate could be seen sitting atop the chair of judgment in the middle of a foul-smelling lake. Other times he was seen perched on a rock, writing. Richard Wagner scaled Pilatus in 1859 to have a look for himself. Nine years later, accompanied by a royal party, Queen Victoria did the same.

"I actually hiked up it once myself," confessed Donati.

"Did you see him?"

"No."

"That's because he was never there."

"Where was he?"

"Most of the Church Fathers believed he committed suicide not long after his return to Rome. But Origen, the early Church's first great theologian and philosopher, was convinced that Pilate had been allowed to live out the remainder of his life in peace. On this matter, at least, I side with Origen. That said, I suspect we might disagree over how Pilate spent his retirement."

"You believe he wrote?"

"No, Luigi. I *know* that Pontius Pilate wrote a detailed memoir of his tumultuous years as prefect of the Roman province of Judea, including his role in the most portentous execution in human history." Father Jordan tapped the plastic-covered page. "And it was used as the source material for the pseudepigraphic gospel that bears his name."

"Who was the real author?"

"If I were to hazard a guess, he was a highly educated Roman, fluent in Latin and Greek, with a deep knowledge of Jewish history and the Laws of Moses."

"Was he a gentile or a Jew?"

"Probably a gentile. But what's important is that he was a deeply committed Christian."

"Are you suggesting that Pilate became a Christian as well?"

"Pilate? Heavens no. That's apocryphal nonsense. I have no doubt he remained a pagan until his dying breath. The Gospel of Pilate is a work of history rather than faith. Unlike the authors of the canonical Gospels, Pilate had seen Jesus with his own eyes. He knew what he looked like, how he spoke. More important, he knew exactly why Jesus was put to death. After all, he was the one who sent him to the cross."

"Why did he write about it?" asked Gabriel.

"A good question, Mr. Allon. Why does any public servant or political figure write about his role in an important event?"

"To make money," quipped Gabriel.

"Not in the first century." Father Jordan smiled. "Besides, Pilate had no need of money. He had used his position as prefect to enrich himself."

"In that case," said Gabriel, "I suppose he would have wanted to tell his side of the story."

"Correct," said Father Jordan. "Remember, Pilate was only a few years older than Jesus. If he had lived for fifteen years after the Crucifixion, he would have known that the followers of the man he executed in Jerusalem were in the early stages of forming a new religion. Had he lived to the age of seventy, not unheard of in the first century, he would have been hard pressed not to notice the flourishing early Church in Rome itself."

"When do you think Pilate wrote his account?" asked Donati.

"That's impossible to know. But I believe the book that became known as the Gospel of Pilate was written at approximately the same time as Mark."

"Would the author of Mark have known of its existence?"

"Possibly. It's also possible that the author of the Gospel of Pilate knew of Mark's existence. But the more relevant question is, why was Mark canonized and the Gospel of Pilate ruthlessly suppressed?"

"And the answer?"

"Because the Gospel of Pilate offers a completely different account of Jesus' final days in Jerusalem, one that contradicts Church doctrine and dogma." Father Jordan paused. "Now ask the next obvious question, Luigi."

"If the Gospel of Pilate was suppressed and hunted out of existence by the Church, how do you know about it?"

"Ah, yes," said Father Jordan. "That's the truly interesting part of the story."

29

ABBEY OF ST. PETER, ASSISI

T O TELL THE STORY OF how he had learned of the existence of the Gospel of Pilate, Father Jordan first had to explain how the book was disseminated, and how it was suppressed. It was written for the first time, he said, in the same fashion as the canonical Gospels, on papyrus, though in Latin rather than Greek. He reckoned it was copied and recopied perhaps a hundred times in this fragile, unstable form and that it circulated among the Latin-literate portion of the early Church. Around the dawn of the second millennium it was produced in book form for the first time, almost certainly at a monastery on the Italian peninsula. Like the *Acta Pilati*, the Gospel of Pilate was read widely during the Renaissance.

"The *Acta* was translated into several languages and circulated throughout the Christian world. But the Gospel of Pilate was never translated out of its original Latin. Therefore, its readership was far more elite."

"For example?" asked Donati.

"Artists, intellectuals, noblemen, and the daring priest or monk who was willing to risk Rome's wrath."

Before Donati could pose his next question, his phone pinged with an incoming text message.

Father Jordan glared at him with reproach. "Those things aren't allowed in here."

"Forgive me, Robert, but I'm afraid I live in the real world." Donati read the message, expressionless. Then he switched off the phone and asked Father Jordan when the Gospel of Pilate was suppressed.

"Not until the thirteenth century, when Pope Gregory IX launched the Inquisition. He was more concerned about the threat to orthodoxy posed by the Cathars and Waldensians, but the Gospel of Pilate was high on his list of heresies. I found three references to the book in the files of the Inquisition. No one seems to have noticed them but me."

"I suppose His Holiness gave the job to the Dominicans."

"Who else?"

"Did they happen to keep any copies?"

"Trust me, I asked."

"And?"

Father Jordan laid his hand on the page. "In all likelihood, this is the last one. But at the time, I was convinced there had to be another copy out there somewhere, probably hidden away in the library or archives of a noble family. I wandered the length and breadth of Italy for years, knocking on the doors of crumbling old palazzi, sipping espresso and wine with faded counts and countesses, even the odd prince and principessa. And then, late one afternoon, in the leaky cellar of a once-grand palace in Trastevere, I found it."

"The book?"

"A letter," said Father Jordan. "It was written by a man called Tedeschi. He went into considerable detail about an interesting book he had just read, a book called the Gospel of Pilate. There were direct quotes, including a passage regarding the decision to execute a man named Jesus of Nazareth, a troublesome Galilean who had ignited a disturbance in the Royal Portico of the Temple during Passover."

"Did the family let you keep it?"

"I didn't bother to ask."

"Robert . . ."

Father Jordan gave a mischievous smile.

"Where is it now?"

"The letter? Somewhere safe, I assure you."

"I want it."

"You can't have it. Besides, I've told you everything you need to know. The Gospel of Pilate calls into question the New Testament's account of the seminal event in Christianity. For that reason, it is a most dangerous book."

The Benedictine appeared in the doorway.

"I'm afraid I have kitchen duty tonight," said Father Jordan.

"What's on the menu?"

"Stone soup, I believe."

Donati smiled. "My favorite."

"It's the specialty of the house. You're welcome to join us, if you like."

"Perhaps another time."

Father Jordan rose. "It was wonderful to see you again, Luigi. If you ever want to get away from it all, I'll put in a good word with the abbot."

"My world is out there, Robert."

Father Jordan smiled. "Spoken like a true liberation theologian."

DONATI WAITED UNTIL THEY WERE outside the walls of the abbey before switching on his phone. Several unread text messages flowed onto the screen. All were from the same person: Alessandro Ricci, the Vatican correspondent for *La Repubblica*.

"He's the one who texted me while we were talking to Father Jordan."

"About what?"

"He didn't say, but apparently it's urgent. We should probably hear what he has to say. Ricci knows more about the inner workings of the Church than any reporter in the world."

"Have you forgotten that I'm the director-general of the Israeli secret intelligence service?" Donati didn't answer. He was typing furiously on his phone. "He was lying, you know."

"Alessandro Ricci?" asked Donati absently.

"Father Jordan. He knows more about the Gospel of Pilate than he told us."

"You can tell when someone is lying?"

"Always."

"How do you go through life that way?"

"It isn't easy," said Gabriel.

"He was telling the truth about at least one thing."

"What's that?"

Donati looked up from his phone. "There's no one named Father Joshua who works at the Secret Archives."

30

VIA DELLA PAGLIA, ROME

ALESSANDRO RICCI LIVED AT THE quiet end of the Via della Paglia, in a small rose-colored apartment building. His name did not appear on the intercom panel. Ricci's work had earned him a long list of enemies, some of whom wanted him dead.

Donati pressed the correct button, and they were admitted at once. Ricci was waiting on the second-floor landing, dressed entirely in black. His fashionable spectacles were black, too. They were propped on his bald head, which was polished to a high gloss. His gaze was fixed not on the tall, handsome man wearing the cassock of an archbishop but on the leather-jacketed figure of medium height standing next to him.

"Dear God, it's you! The great Gabriel Allon, savior of *Il Papa*."

He drew them into the apartment. No one would have mistaken it for the home of anyone but a writer, and a divorced one at that. There wasn't a single flat surface that wasn't piled with books and papers. Ricci apologized for the clutter. He had spent much of the day on the BBC, where his elegantly accented English was much in demand. He had to be back at the Vatican in two hours for an appearance on CNN. He hadn't much time to talk.

"Too bad," he added with a glance at Gabriel. "I have a few questions I'd like to ask you."

Ricci cleared a couple of chairs and immediately dug a crumpled pack of Marlboros from the breast pocket of his jacket. Donati in turn produced his elegant gold cigarette case. There followed the familiar rituals of the tobacco addicted—the stroke of a lighter, the offer of a flame, a moment or two of small talk. Ricci expressed his condolences over the death of Lucchesi. Donati asked about Ricci's mother, who had been unwell.

"The letter from the Holy Father meant the world to her, Excellency."

"It didn't stop you from writing a rather nasty piece about how much money the Vatican was spending renovating the apartments of certain curial cardinals."

"Did I make any mistakes?"

"Not one."

The conversation turned to the coming conclave. Ricci mined Donati for a nugget of gold, something he might reveal to his American audience later that evening. It didn't need to be earth-shattering, he said. A juicy piece of curial gossip would suffice. Donati failed to oblige him. He claimed he had been too busy putting his affairs in order to give much thought to the selection of Lucchesi's successor. At this, Ricci smiled. It was the smile of a reporter who knew something.

"Is that why you went to Florence last Thursday to find the missing Swiss Guard?"

Donati didn't bother with a denial. "How did you know?"

"The Polizia have pictures of you on the Ponte Vecchio." Ricci looked at Gabriel. "You, too."

"Why haven't they tried to contact me?" asked Donati.

"The Vatican asked them not to. And for some reason, the Polizia agreed to keep you out of it."

Donati stabbed out his cigarette. "What else do you know?"

"I know that you were having dinner with Veronica Marchese the night the Holy Father died."

"Wherever did you hear a thing like that?"

"Come on, Archbishop Donati. You know I can't divulge—"

"Where?" asked Donati evenly.

"A source close to the camerlengo."

"That means it came directly from Albanese."

The reporter said nothing, all but confirming Donati's suspicions. "Why haven't you reported the story?" he asked.

"I've written it, but I wanted to give you a chance to comment before I push the button."

"Respond to what exactly?"

"Why were you having dinner with the wife of a dead mobster the night the Holy Father died? And why were you standing a few meters from Niklaus Janson when he was assassinated on the Ponte Vecchio?"

"I'm afraid I can't help you, Alessandro."

"Then let me help *you*, Excellency."

Cautiously, Donati asked, "How?"

"Tell me what really happened that night in the Apostolic Palace, and I'll make sure no one ever finds out where you were."

"Are you blackmailing me?"

"I wouldn't dream of it."

"An old man died in his bed," said Donati after a moment. "That's all that happened."

"Lucchesi was murdered. And you know it. That's why you came here tonight."

Donati was slow in rising. "You should be aware of the fact that you're being used."

"I'm a reporter, I'm used to it."

Donati beckoned Gabriel with a nod.

"Before you leave," said Ricci, "there's one more thing you need to know. A couple of hours ago, I told a global television audience that I thought Cardinal José Maria Navarro would be the next supreme pontiff of the Roman Catholic Church."

"A daring choice on your part."

"I was being untruthful, Excellency."

"I'm sure it wasn't the first time." Donati immediately regretted his words. "Forgive me, Alessandro. It's been a long day. Don't bother to get up. We'll see ourselves out."

"Aren't you going to ask me the name of the next pope, Excellency?"

"You can't possibly—"

"It's Cardinal Franz von Emmerich, the archbishop of Vienna."

Donati frowned. "Emmerich? He's not on anyone's list."

"He's on the only list that matters."

"Whose is that?"

"The one in Bishop Hans Richter's pocket."

"He's planning to steal the papacy? Is that what you're saying?"

Ricci nodded.

"How?"

"With money, Excellency. How else? Money makes the world go round. The Order of St. Helena, too."

31

VIA DELLA PAGLIA, TRASTEVERE

ALESSANDRO RICCI BEGAN BY REMINDING Donati that during the final year of the Wojtyla papacy, he had published a best-selling book on the Order of St. Helena that, the state of his apartment notwithstanding, had made him a wealthy man. Not hedge-fund wealthy, he hastened to add, but enough money to look after his mother and a brother who had never worked a day in his life. The Pole had not liked the book. Neither had Bishop Hans Richter, who had agreed to be interviewed for the project. It was the last time he would ever submit to questioning by a journalist.

Donati granted himself the luxury of a smile at Bishop Richter's expense. "You *were* rather unkind to him."

"You read it?"

Donati deliberately removed another cigarette from his case. "Go on."

The book, explained Ricci, shone a harsh light on the Order's close relationship with Hitler and the Nazis during World War II. It also explored the Order's finances. It was not always so wealthy. Indeed, during the depression of the 1930s, the Order's founder, Father Ulrich Schiller, was forced to wander Europe, hat in hand, seeking donations from wealthy patrons. But as the continent drifted toward war, Father Schiller developed a far more lucrative method of filling his coffers. He extorted cash and valuables from wealthy Jews in exchange for promises of protection.

"One of Father Schiller's victims lived here in Trastevere. He owned several factories up north. In exchange for false baptismal records for himself and his family, he gave the Order several hundred thousand lire in cash, along with numerous Italian Old Master paintings and a collection of rare books."

"Do you happen to remember his name?" asked Gabriel.

"Why do you ask?" replied Ricci, displaying the sharp ear of a seasoned journalist.

"I'm just curious, that's all. Stories about art intrigue me."

"It's all in my book."

"You wouldn't have a copy lying around, would you?"

Ricci inclined his head toward a wall of books. "It's called *The Order.*"

"Catchy." Gabriel wandered over to the shelves and craned his neck sideways.

"Second shelf, near the end."

Gabriel took down the book and reclaimed his seat.

"Chapter four," said Ricci. "Or maybe it's five."

"Which is it?"

"Five. Definitely five."

Gabriel leafed through the pages of the book while its author resumed his lecture on the finances of the Order of St. Helena. By the end of the war, he said, it had burned through its cash reserves. Its fortunes changed with the outbreak of the Cold War, when Pope Pius XII, an anti-Communist crusader, showered Father Schiller and his right-wing priests with money. Pope John XXIII put the Order on a tight budget. But by the early 1980s it was not only financially independent, it was fabulously rich. Alessandro Ricci had not been able to pinpoint the source of the Order's financial turnaround—at least not to the satisfaction of his risk-averse publisher, who feared a lawsuit. But Ricci was now confident he knew the identity of the Order's main benefactor. He was a reclusive German billionaire named Jonas Wolf.

"Wolf is a traditionalist Catholic who celebrates the Tridentine Latin Mass daily in his private chapel. He's also the owner of a German conglomerate known as the Wolf Group. The company is opaque, to put it mildly. But in my opinion, it's nothing more than the Order of St. Helena Incorporated. Jonas Wolf is the one who supplied the money to buy the papacy."

"And you're sure it's Emmerich?" asked Donati.

"I've got it cold. By next Saturday evening at the latest, Franz von Emmerich will be standing on the balcony of St. Peter's dressed in white. The real pope, however, will be Bishop Hans Richter." Ricci shook his head with disgust. "It seems the

Church hasn't changed so much, after all. Remind me, Excellency. How much did Rodrigo Borgia give Sforza to secure the papacy in 1492?"

"If memory serves, it was four mule-loads of silver."

"That's a pittance compared to what Wolf and Richter paid."

Donati closed his eyes and squeezed the bridge of his nose. "How much did it cost him?"

"The rich Italians didn't come cheap. The poorer prelates from the Third World fetched a few hundred thousand each. Most were more than happy to take the Order's money. But a few were blackmailed into accepting it."

"How?"

"As *prefetto* of the Secret Archives, Cardinal Albanese had access to a great deal of dirt, most of it sexual in nature. I'm told Bishop Richter used it quite ruthlessly."

"How were the bribes paid?"

"The Order considers them donations, Excellency. Not bribes. Which means it's all perfectly permissible as far as the Church is concerned. In fact, it happens all the time. Do you remember that American cardinal who got caught up in the sexual abuse scandal? He was spreading money around the Curia like chicken feed in a bid to save his career. It wasn't his personal money, of course. It was donated by the parishioners of his archdiocese."

"Who's your source?" asked Donati. "And don't try to hide behind some gallant front of journalistic integrity."

"Let's just say that my source has firsthand knowledge of Richter's scheming."

"He was offered a payment?"

Ricci nodded.

"Did he show you any proof?"

"The offer was made verbally."

"Which explains why you haven't gone to print."

"Print? You're dating yourself, Excellency."

"I work for the oldest institution on the planet." Donati crushed out his cigarette as though he were vowing never to smoke again. "And now you think I'm going to tell you everything I know so you can write your story and throw the conclave into turmoil?"

"If I don't report what I know, Bishop Richter and his friend Jonas Wolf will be in control of the Church. Is that what you want?"

"Are you even a practicing Catholic?"

"I haven't been to Mass in twenty years."

"Then please spare me the sanctimony." Donati reached for his cigarette case but stopped. "Give me until Thursday night."

"It won't hold that long. I have to publish by tomorrow at the latest."

"If you do, you'll be making the biggest mistake of your career."

Ricci glanced at his watch. "I have to get back to the Vatican for my appearance on CNN. Are you sure you don't have anything for me?"

"The Holy Spirit will determine the identity of the next Roman pontiff."

"Hardly." Ricci turned to Gabriel, who had yet to look up from the book. "Did you find what you were looking for, Mr. Allon?"

"Yes," said Gabriel. "I believe I have." He held up the book. "Is there any chance I can keep this?"

"I'm afraid it's my last copy. But it's still in print."

"Lucky you." Gabriel returned the book to Ricci. "I have a feeling it's going to be a bestseller again."

32

TRASTEVERE, ROME

FOR A LONG TIME AFTER leaving Alessandro Ricci's apartment, Gabriel and Donati wandered the streets of Trastevere—Regio XIV, as Pilate would have known it—seemingly without direction or destination. Donati's mood was as black as his cassock. This was the Luigi Donati, thought Gabriel, who had made so many enemies inside the Roman Curia. The pope's ruthless son of a bitch, a hard man in black with a whip and a chair. But he was also a man of enormous faith who, like Gabriel, was cursed with an unyielding sense of right and wrong. He was not afraid to get his hands dirty. Nor did he often turn the other cheek. In fact, given the opportunity, he usually preferred to return the favor.

A rectangular piazza opened before them. On one side was

a gelateria. On the other was the church of Santa Maria della Scala. Despite the lateness of the hour, the doors were open. Several young Romans, men and women in their twenties, were sitting on the steps, smiling, laughing. They seemed to temporarily lift Donati's spirits.

"There's something I need to do."

They entered the church. The nave was ablaze with candlelight and filled with perhaps a hundred more young Catholics, most of whom were engaged in animated discussions. Two folk singers were strumming guitars at the foot of the altar, and in the side aisles a half-dozen priests were sitting on folding chairs, offering spiritual guidance and hearing confessions.

Donati surveyed the scene with obvious approval. "It's a program Lucchesi and I created a few years ago. Once or twice a week, we open one of the historic churches and offer young people a place to spend an hour or two free from the distractions of the outside world. As you can see, there aren't a lot of rules. Light a candle, say a prayer, find a new friend. Someone who's interested in more than posting pictures of themselves on social media. That said, we don't discourage them from sharing their experiences online if the spirit moves them." He lowered his voice. "Even the Church has to adapt."

"It's extraordinary."

"We're not quite as dead as our critics like to think. This is my Church in action. This is the Church of the future." Donati gestured toward an empty pew. "Make yourself comfortable. I won't be long."

"Where are you going?"

"When I lost Lucchesi, I lost my confessor."

Donati went to the side aisle and sat down before a startled young priest. Once the initial awkwardness of the encounter faded, the young priest adopted a serious expression as he listened to the former papal private secretary unburdening his soul. Gabriel could only wonder what transgressions his old friend might have committed while cloistered in the Apostolic Palace. He had always been somewhat envious of the Catholic sacrament of confession. It was far less cumbersome than the daylong ordeal of hunger and atonement that the Jews had inflicted upon themselves.

Donati was leaning forward, elbows on his knees. Gabriel gazed straight ahead, toward the small golden cross, the instrument of Roman brutality, atop the baldachin. The emperor Constantine claimed to have seen it in the sky above the Milvian Bridge, and he had made it the symbol of the new faith. For the Jews of medieval Europe, however, the cross had been something to fear. It had been emblazoned in red on the tunics of the Crusaders who massacred Gabriel's ancestors in the Rhineland on their way to Jerusalem. And it had hung round the necks of many of the murderers who fed millions into the flames at Treblinka, Sobibor, Chelmno, Belzec, Majdanek, and Birkenau, actions for which they received not a single word of rebuke from their spiritual leader in Rome.

His blood shall be on us and our children . . .

After accepting the young priest's absolution, Donati crossed the nave and knelt at Gabriel's side, head bowed in prayer. Eventually, he made the sign of the cross and, rising from his knees, sat down on the pew.

"I said one for you as well. I figured it couldn't hurt."

"It's good to know you still have a sense of humor."

"Trust me, it's hanging by a thread." Donati looked at the two folk singers. "What *is* that song they're playing?"

"You're asking me?"

Donati laughed quietly.

"You know," said Gabriel, "I'm supposed to be on holiday with my wife and children."

"You can always take a holiday."

"I can't, actually."

Donati made no reply.

"There *is* a relatively easy way out of this," said Gabriel. "Be the second source for Ricci's article. Tell him everything. Let it blow up in the press. There's no way the Order will go forward under those circumstances."

"You underestimate Bishop Richter." Donati cast his eyes around the nave. "And what about this? How will these young people feel about their Church then?"

"Better a temporary scandal than His Holiness Pope Emmerich."

"Perhaps. But it would deprive us of a valuable opportunity to make sure the next pope finishes the job my master started." Donati gave Gabriel a sideways glance. "You don't really believe that nonsense about the Holy Spirit choosing the pope, do you?"

"I don't even know what the Holy Spirit is."

"Don't worry, you're not alone."

"Do you have a candidate in mind?" asked Gabriel.

"My master and I gave red hats to several men who would make fine popes. All I need is access to the cardinal-electors before they enter the Sistine Chapel to cast their first vote."

"On Friday afternoon?"

Donati shook his head. "Friday is too late. It would have to be Thursday evening at the latest. That's when the cardinals are locked into the Casa Santa Marta."

"Won't they be sequestered?"

"In theory. But in reality, it's rather porous. That said, there's no guarantee the dean of the Sacred College will allow me to speak to them. Not unless I have ironclad, undeniable proof of the Order's conspiracy." Donati patted Gabriel's shoulder. "I wouldn't think that would be too difficult for a man in your position."

"That's exactly what you said about Niklaus Janson."

"Is it?" Donati smiled. "I'd also like you to bring me proof that the Order murdered my master. And the book, of course. We mustn't forget the Gospel of Pilate."

Gabriel stared at the golden cross atop the baldachin. "Don't worry, Excellency. We haven't."

33

ISRAELI EMBASSY, ROME

ABRIEL DROPPED DONATI AT THE Jesuit Curia, then headed to the Israeli Embassy. Downstairs, he locked the first page of the Gospel of Pilate in an Office safe and rang Yuval Gershon of Unit 8200 on a secure phone in the Holy of Holies. It was past midnight in Tel Aviv. Gershon was in bed.

"What now?" he asked warily.

"A German conglomerate called the Wolf Group."

"Anyone specific?"

"Herr Wolf."

"How deep?"

"Proctological."

Gershon exhaled into the mouthpiece of his phone. "And I thought it was going to be something unreasonable."

"I'll get to the unreasonable request in a minute."

"Are you looking for something in particular?"

Gabriel recited several keywords and names. One of the names was his own. Another was the name of the Roman military officer who had served as the prefect of Judea from approximately 26 C.E. to December of 36.

"*The* Pontius Pilate?" asked Gershon.

"How many Pontius Pilates do you know, Yuval?"

"I assume this has something to do with our visit to the Secret Archives."

Gabriel indicated it did. He also insinuated that while inside the Archives, he had been given the first page of a rather interesting document.

"By whom?"

"A priest named Father Joshua."

"That's strange."

"Why?"

"Because you and Archbishop Donati were the only ones in the Manuscript Depository."

"We spoke to him."

"If you say so. What else?"

"The Institute for Works of Religion, better known as the Vatican Bank. I just e-mailed you a list of names. I want to know whether any of them received large payments lately."

"Define large."

"Six figures or more."

"How many names are we talking about?"

"One hundred and sixteen."

Gershon swore softly. "Are you forgetting that I have pictures of you dressed as a priest?"

"I'll make it up to you, Yuval."

"Who are these guys?"

"The cardinals who will elect the next pope."

Gabriel killed the connection and dialed Yossi Gavish, the chief of the Office's analytical division. Born in Golder's Green, educated at Oxford, he still spoke Hebrew with a pronounced British accent.

"Father Gabriel, I presume?"

"Check your in-box, my son."

A moment passed. "It's lovely, boss. But who is he?"

"He's a lay member of something called the Order of St. Helena, but I have a feeling he might be one of us. Show it around the building, and send it to Berlin Station."

"Why Berlin?"

"He speaks German with a Bavarian accent."

"I was afraid you were going to say that."

Gabriel hung up the phone and placed one more call. Chiara answered, her voice heavy with sleep.

"Where are you?" she asked.

"Somewhere safe."

"When are you coming home?"

"Soon."

"What does that mean?"

"It means I have to find something first."

"Is it good?"

"Do you remember when Eli and I found the ruins of Solomon's Temple?"

"How could I forget?"

"This might be better."

"Is there anything I can do to help?"

"Close your eyes," said Gabriel. "Let me listen to you sleep."

GABRIEL SPENT THE NIGHT ON a cot inside the station and at half past seven the next morning rang General Cesare Ferrari. He informed the general that he needed to borrow the Art Squad's formidable laboratory to test a document. He did not say what the document was or where he had found it.

"Why do you need our labs? Yours are the best in the world."

"I don't have time to send it to Israel."

"What sort of tests are we talking about?"

"Analysis of the paper and ink. I'd also like you to establish the age."

"It's old, this document?"

"Several centuries," said Gabriel.

"You're sure it's paper and not vellum?"

"So I've been told."

"I have a staff meeting at the palazzo at half past ten." The palazzo was the Art Squad's elegant cream-colored headquarters in the Piazza di Sant'Ignazio. "If, however, you were to wander into the back room of Caffè Greco at nine fifteen, you might find me enjoying a cappuccino and a cornetto. And by the way," he said before ringing off, "I have something to show you as well."

Gabriel arrived a few minutes early. General Ferrari had the back room to himself. From his old leather briefcase he removed a manila folder, and from the folder eight large photographs, which he arrayed on the table. The last depicted Gabriel removing the wallet from Niklaus Janson's pocket.

"Since when does the commander of the Art Squad get to see surveillance photos from a murder investigation?"

"The chief of the Polizia wanted you to have a look at them. He was hoping you might be able to identify the assassin."

The general laid another photograph on the table. A man in a motorcycle helmet and leather jacket, right arm extended, a gun in his hand. A woman nearby had noticed the weapon and had opened her mouth to scream. Gabriel only wished he had seen it, too. Niklaus Janson might still be alive.

Gabriel examined the gunman's clothing. "I don't suppose you have one without the helmet."

"I'm afraid not." Ferrari returned the photographs to the manila folder. "Perhaps you should show me this document of yours."

It was locked inside a stainless-steel attaché case. Gabriel removed it and handed it wordlessly across the table. The general scrutinized it through the protective plastic cover.

"The Gospel of Pilate?" He looked up at Gabriel. "Where did you get this?"

"The Vatican Secret Archives."

"They *gave* it to you?"

"Not exactly."

"What does that mean?"

"It means Luigi and I broke into the Archives and took it."

General Ferrari looked down at the document again. "I assume this has something to do with the Holy Father's death."

"Murder," said Gabriel quietly.

General Ferrari's expression remained unchanged.

"You don't seem terribly surprised by the news, Cesare."

"I assumed that Archbishop Donati was suspicious about the

circumstances of the Holy Father's death when he asked me to make contact with you in Venice."

"Did he mention a missing Swiss Guard?"

"He might have. And a missing letter, too." The general held the page aloft. "Is this the document Lucchesi wanted you to see?"

Gabriel nodded.

"In that case, there's no need to test it. The Holy Father wouldn't have tried to give it to you if it wasn't genuine."

"I'd feel better if I knew when it was written and where the paper and ink came from."

The general raised it to the light of an overhead chandelier. "You're right, it's definitely paper."

"How old could it be?"

"The first mills in Italy were established in Fabriano in the late thirteenth century, and during the fifteenth century paper gradually replaced vellum in bookbinding. There were mills in Florence, Treviso, Milan, Bologna, Parma, and your beloved Venice. We should be able to determine if this was produced in one of them. But it's not something that can be done quickly."

"How long will it take?"

"To do the job right . . . several weeks."

"I'm going to need the results a bit sooner than that."

The general sighed.

"If it wasn't for you," said Gabriel, "I'd still be in Venice with my family."

"Me?" The general shook his head. "I was only the messenger. It was Pietro Lucchesi who summoned you." He glanced at the manila folder. "Those photos are yours to keep. A small souvenir of your brief visit to our country. Don't worry about the Polizia. I'll think of something to say to them. I always do."

With that, the general departed. Gabriel checked his phone and saw that he had received a text message from Christoph Bittel, his friend from the Swiss security service.

Call me as quickly as you can. It's important.

Gabriel dialed.

Bittel answered instantly. "For God's sake, what the hell took you so long?"

"Please tell me she's all right."

"Stefani Hoffmann? She's fine. I'm calling about the man in that sketch of yours."

"What about him?"

"It's not something we should discuss on the phone. How quickly can you get to Zurich?"

34

SISTINE CHAPEL

FROM INSIDE THE SISTINE CHAPEL came the unholy clamor of hammering. Cardinal Domenico Albanese climbed the two shallow steps and entered. A newly installed wooden ramp sloped toward the opening in the *transenna*, the marble screen that divided the chapel in two. Beyond it stretched a temporary wooden floor covered in pale tan carpeting. Twelve long tables stood along the edges of the chapel, two rows of three on each side, covered in tan baize, with pleated skirts of magenta.

In the center of the space stood a small ornate table with thin curved legs. For now, the table was empty. But on Friday afternoon, when the cardinal-electors processed into the chapel to begin the conclave, there would be a Bible open to the first page of the Gospel of Matthew. Each cardinal, including Albanese, would lay his hand on the Gospel and swear an oath of secrecy.

He would also swear not to conspire with "any group of people or individuals" who might wish to intervene in the election of the next Roman pontiff. To break such a sacred vow would be a grievous sin. A cardinal sin, thought Albanese.

The sound of hammering intruded on his reverie. The workmen were constructing a camera platform near the stoves. The first hour of the conclave—the opening procession, the singing of "Veni Creator Spiritus," the swearing of the oath—would be televised. After that, the master of pontifical liturgical celebrations would announce "Extra omnes," and the doors would be closed and locked from the outside.

Inside, a first ballot would be taken, if only to get a sense of the room. The Scrutineers and Revisers would perform their due diligence, checking and rechecking the count. If the pre-conclave hype was to be believed, Cardinal José Maria Navarro would emerge as the early front runner. The ballots would then be burned in the older of the two stoves. The second stove would simultaneously release a chemically enhanced plume of black smoke. And thus the faithful gathered in St. Peter's Square— and the unfaithful poised over their laptops in the press center— would learn that the Church of Rome was still without a pontiff.

Cardinal Navarro's lead would shrink on the second ballot. And on the third, a new name would emerge: Cardinal Franz von Emmerich, the archbishop of Vienna and a secret member of the Order of St. Helena. By the fifth ballot, Emmerich would be unstoppable. By the sixth, the papacy would be his. No, thought Albanese suddenly. The papacy would be the Order's.

They planned to waste little time in undoing the modest reforms put in place by Lucchesi and Donati. All power would be centralized in the Apostolic Palace. All dissent would be ruthlessly repressed. There would be no more talk of women in the priesthood or allowing priests to marry. Nor would there be any heartfelt encyclicals about climate change, the poor, the rights of workers and immigrants, and the dangers posed by the rise of the far right in Western Europe. Indeed, the new secretary of state would forge close ties between the Holy See and the authoritarian leaders of Italy, Germany, Austria, and France—all doctrinaire Catholics who would serve as a bulwark against secularism, democratic socialism, and, of course, Islam.

Albanese moved toward the altar. Behind it was Michelangelo's *Last Judgment*, with its swirling cyclone of souls rising toward heaven or falling into the depths of hell. It never failed to stir Albanese. It was the reason he had become a priest, the fear that he would suffer for all eternity in the emptiness of the underworld.

That fear, after lying dormant within Albanese for many years, had risen again. It was true that Bishop Richter had granted him absolution for his role in the murder of Pietro Lucchesi. But in his heart Albanese did not believe such a mortal sin could truly be forgiven. Granted, it was Father Graf who had done the deed. But Albanese had been an accessory before and after the fact. He had played his role flawlessly, with one exception. He had failed to find the letter—the letter Lucchesi was writing to Gabriel Allon about the book he had found in the Secret Archives. The only explanation was that the Janson boy had taken it. Father Graf had killed him as well. Two murders. Two black marks on Albanese's soul.

All the more reason why the conclave had to go precisely as planned. It was Albanese's job to make certain the cardinal-electors who had accepted the Order's money cast their ballots for Emmerich at the appropriate time. A sudden and decisive move toward the Austrian would raise suspicion of tampering. His support had to build gradually, ballot by ballot, so that nothing looked amiss. Once Emmerich was clad in white, the Order would face no threat of exposure. The Vatican was one of the world's last absolute monarchies, a divine dictatorship. There would be no investigation, no exhumation of the dead pontiff's body. It would almost be as though it had never happened.

Unless, thought Albanese, there was another unexpected development like the one that had occurred the previous morning at the Secret Archives. Gabriel Allon and Archbishop Donati had undoubtedly found something. What it was, Albanese could not say. He only knew that after leaving the Archives, Allon and Donati had traveled to Assisi, where they had met with a certain Father Robert Jordan, the Church's foremost expert on the apocryphal gospels. Afterward, they had returned to Rome, where they had met with one Alessandro Ricci, the world's foremost expert on the Order of St. Helena. It was hardly an encouraging sign.

"Truly magnificent, is it not?"

Albanese turned with a start.

"Forgive me," said Bishop Richter. "I didn't mean to disturb you."

Albanese addressed his superior general with a cool and distant formality. "Good morning, Excellency. What brings you to the Sistina?"

"I was told I might find the camerlengo here."

"Is there a problem?"

"Not at all. In fact, I have rather good news."

"What's that?"

Richter smiled. "Gabriel Allon just left Rome."

I T WAS HALF PAST FOUR when Gabriel arrived in Zurich. He rode in a taxi to the Paradeplatz, the St. Peter's Square of Swiss banking, and then walked along the stately Bahnhofstrasse to the northern tip of the Zürichsee. A BMW sedan drew alongside him on the General-Guisan-Quai. Behind the wheel was Christoph Bittel. Bald and bespectacled, he looked like just another gnome heading home to the lakeside suburbs after a long day spent tabulating the hidden riches of Arab sheikhs and Russian oligarchs.

Gabriel dropped into the passenger seat. "Where were we?"

"The man in the sketch." Bittel eased into the rush-hour traffic. "I'm sorry it took me so long to make the connection. It's been a few years since I've seen him."

"What's his name?"

"Estermann," said Bittel. "Andreas Estermann."

As GABRIEL SUSPECTED, ESTERMANN WAS a professional. For thirty years he had worked for the BfV, Germany's internal security service. Not surprisingly, the BfV maintained close links with its sister service in Switzerland, the NDB. Early in his career, Bittel had traveled to Cologne to brief his German counterparts on Soviet espionage activity in Bern and Geneva. Estermann was his contact.

"When the meeting was over, he invited me for a drink. Which was odd."

"Why?"

"Estermann doesn't touch alcohol."

"Does he have a problem?"

"He has lots of problems, but alcohol isn't one of them."

In the years that followed their first meeting, Bittel and Estermann bumped into each other from time to time, as practitioners of the secret trade are prone to do. Neither one of them was what you might describe as an action figure. They were not operatives, they were glorified policemen. They conducted investigations, wrote reports, and attended countless conferences where the primary challenge was keeping one's eyes open. They shared lunches and dinners whenever their paths crossed. Estermann often funneled intelligence to Bittel outside normal channels. Bittel reciprocated whenever possible, but always with the approval of the top floor. His superiors considered Estermann a valuable asset.

"And then the planes crashed into the World Trade Center, and everything changed. Especially Estermann."

"How so?"

"He had moved from counterintelligence to counterterrorism a couple of years before nine-eleven, just like me. He claimed he was on to the Hamburg Cell from the beginning. He swore he could have stopped the plot in its tracks if his superiors had allowed him to do his job properly."

"Was any of it true?"

"That he could have single-handedly prevented the worst terrorist attack in history?" Bittel shook his head. "Maybe Gabriel Allon could have done it. But not Andreas Estermann."

"How did he change?"

"He became incredibly bitter."

"At whom?"

"Muslims."

"Al-Qaeda?"

"Not just al-Qaeda. Estermann resented all Muslims, especially those who lived in Germany. He was unable to separate the hard-core jihadist from the poor Moroccan or Turk who came to Europe looking for a better life. It got worse after the attack on the Vatican. He lost all perspective. I found his company difficult to bear."

"But you maintained the relationship?"

"We're a small service. Estermann was a force multiplier." Bittel smiled. "Like you, Allon."

He turned into the car park of a marina along the western shore of the lake. At the end of the breakwater was a café. They sat outside in the blustery evening air. Bittel ordered two beers and replied to several text messages he had received during the drive from downtown Zurich.

"Sorry. We're a bit on edge at the moment."

"About what?"

"The bombings in Germany." Bittel peered at Gabriel over his phone. "You don't happen to know who's behind them, do you?"

"My analysts think we're dealing with a new network."

"Just what we needed."

The waitress appeared with their drinks. She was a raven-haired woman of perhaps twenty-five, very beautiful, an Iraqi, perhaps a refugee from Syria. When she placed the bottle of beer in front of Gabriel, he thanked her in Arabic. A brief exchange of pleasantries followed. Then, smiling, the woman withdrew.

"What were you talking about?" asked Bittel.

"She was wondering why we were sitting out here by the lake instead of inside where it's warm."

"What did you tell her?"

"That we were intelligence officers who didn't like to speak in insecure rooms."

Bittel made a face and drank some of his beer. "It's a good thing Estermann didn't see you talking to her like that. He doesn't approve of being civil to Muslim immigrants. Nor does he approve of speaking their language."

"How does he feel about Jews?"

Bittel picked at the label of his beer bottle.

"Go ahead, Bittel. It won't hurt my feelings."

"He's a bit of an anti-Semite."

"What a shocker."

"It tends to go hand in hand."

"What's that?"

"Islamophobia and anti-Semitism."

"Did you and Estermann ever discuss religion?"

"Endlessly. Especially after the attack on the Vatican. He's a devout Catholic."

"And you?"

"I'm from Nidwalden. I was raised in a Catholic home, I married a Catholic girl in a ceremony officiated by the Church, and all three of our children were baptized."

"But?"

"I haven't been to Mass since the sexual abuse scandal broke."

"Do you follow the teachings of the Vatican?"

"Why should I follow them if they don't?"

"I assume Estermann disagreed with you."

Bittel nodded. "He's a lay member of an extremely conservative order based here in Switzerland."

"The Order of St. Helena."

Bittel's eyes narrowed. "How did you know?"

Gabriel demurred. "I assume Estermann wanted you to join."

"He was like an evangelist. He said I could be a secret member, that no one would know other than his bishop. He also said there were lots of people like us in the Order."

"Us?"

"Intelligence officers and security types. Prominent businessmen and politicians, too. He said joining the Order would do wonders for my post-NDB career."

"How did you handle it?"

"I told him I wasn't interested and changed the subject."

236

"When was the last time you spoke to him?"

"It's been five years, at least. Probably more like six."

"What was the occasion?"

"Estermann's retirement from the BfV. He wanted to give me his new contact information. Apparently, he struck gold. He's working for a big German firm based in Munich."

"The Wolf Group?"

"How did—"

"Lucky guess," said Gabriel.

"Estermann told me to call him when I was ready to leave the NDB. There's a Wolf Group office here in Zurich. He said he would make it worth my while."

"You don't happen to have his cell number, do you?"

"Sure. Why?"

"I'd like you to take him up on his offer. Tell him you're going to be in Munich on Wednesday evening. Tell him you want to talk about your future."

"But I can't possibly go to Munich on Wednesday."

"He doesn't need to know that."

"What do you have in mind?"

"Drinks. Somewhere quiet."

"I told you, he doesn't drink. He's a Diet Coke man. Always a Diet Coke." Bittel tapped the tabletop thoughtfully. "There's a place in the Beethovenplatz called Café Adagio. Very chic. Discreet, too. The question is, what's going to happen when he gets there?"

"I'm going to ask him a few questions."

"About what?"

"The Order of St. Helena."

"Why are you interested in the Order?"

"They murdered a friend of mine."

"Who's the friend?"

"His Holiness Pope Paul the Seventh."

Bittel's expression betrayed no sentiment, least of all surprise. "Now I know why you wanted me to keep an eye on the Hoffmann woman."

"Send the message, Bittel."

His thumbs hovered over his phone. "Do you know what will happen if I'm linked to this in any way?"

"The Office will lose a valuable partner. And I'll lose a friend."

"I'm not sure I want to be your friend, Allon. They all seem to end up dead." Bittel typed the message and tapped SEND. Five long minutes elapsed before his phone pinged with a response. "You're on. Six o'clock Wednesday evening at Café Adagio. Estermann's looking forward to it."

Gabriel gazed at the black waters of the lake. "That makes two of us."

36

MUNICH

EXCEPT FOR A FEW DAYS in September 1972, Munich had never mattered much to the Office. Nevertheless, if only for sentimental reasons, Housekeeping maintained a large walled villa in the bohemian quarter of Schwabing, not far from the Englischer Garten. Eli Lavon arrived there at ten fifteen the following morning. Gloomily, he surveyed the heavy antique furnishings in the formal drawing room.

"I can't believe we're back here again." He looked at Gabriel and frowned. "You're supposed to be on holiday."

"Yes, I know."

"What happened?"

"A death in the family."

"My condolences."

Lavon tossed his overnight bag carelessly onto a couch. He had wispy, unkempt hair and a bland, forgettable face that even the most gifted portrait artist would have struggled to capture in oil on canvas. He appeared to be one of life's downtrodden. In truth, he was a natural predator who could follow a highly trained intelligence officer or hardened terrorist down any street in the world without attracting a flicker of interest. He was now the chief of the Office division known as Neviot. Its operatives included surveillance artists, pickpockets, thieves, and those who specialized in planting hidden cameras and listening devices behind locked doors.

"I saw an interesting photo of you the other day. You were dressed as a priest and walking into the Vatican Secret Archives with your friend Luigi Donati. I was only sorry I couldn't join you." Lavon smiled. "Find anything interesting?"

"You might say that."

Lavon raised a tiny hand. "Do tell."

"We should probably wait until the others arrive."

"They're on their way. *All* of them." Lavon's lighter flared. "I assume this has something to do with the unfortunate passing of His Holiness Pope Paul the Seventh."

Gabriel nodded.

"I take it His Holiness did not die of natural causes."

"No," said Gabriel. "He did not."

"Do we have a suspect?"

"A Catholic order based in Canton Zug."

Lavon stared at Gabriel through a cloud of smoke. "The Order of St. Helena?"

"You've heard of them?"

"Unfortunately, I dealt with the Order in a previous life."

During a lengthy hiatus from the Office, Lavon had run a small investigative agency in Vienna called Wartime Claims and Inquiries. Operating on a shoestring budget, he had tracked down millions of dollars' worth of looted Holocaust assets. He left Vienna after a bomb destroyed his office and killed two of his employees, both young women. The perpetrator, a former SS officer named Erich Radek, had died in an Israeli prison cell. Gabriel was the one who put him there.

"It was a case involving a Viennese family named Feldman," explained Lavon. "The patriarch was Samuel Feldman, a well-to-do exporter of high-quality textiles. In the autumn of 1937, as storm clouds were gathering over Austria, two priests from the Order came calling on Feldman at his apartment in the First District. One of the priests was the Order's founder, Father Ulrich Schiller."

"And what did Father Schiller want from Samuel Feldman?"

"Money. What else?"

"What was he offering in return?"

"Baptismal certificates. Feldman was desperate, so he gave Father Schiller a substantial sum of cash and other valuables, including several paintings."

"And when the Nazis rolled into Vienna in March 1938?"

"Father Schiller and the promised baptismal certificates were nowhere to be found. Feldman and most of his family were deported to the Lublin district of Poland, where they were murdered by Einsatzgruppen. One child survived the war in hiding in Vienna, a daughter named Isabel. She came to me after the Swiss banking scandal broke and told me the story."

"What did you do?"

"I made an appointment to see Bishop Hans Richter, the superior general of the Order of St. Helena. We met at its medieval priory in Menzingen. A nasty piece of work, the bishop. There were moments when I had to remind myself that I was actually speaking to a Roman Catholic cleric. Needless to say, I left empty-handed."

"Did you let it drop?"

"Me? Of course not. And within a year, I found four other cases of the Order soliciting donations from Jews in exchange for promises of protection. Bishop Richter wouldn't see me again, so I turned over my material to an Italian investigative reporter named Alessandro Ricci. He found a few more cases, including a wealthy Roman Jew who gave the Order several paintings and valuable rare books in 1938. I'm afraid his name escapes me."

"Emanuele Giordano."

Lavon eyed Gabriel over the ember of his cigarette. "How is it possible you know that name?"

"I met with Alessandro Ricci last night in Rome. He told me the Order of St. Helena is planning to steal the conclave and elect one of their members the next pope."

"Knowing the Order, I'm sure it involves money."

"It does."

"Is that why they killed the pope?"

"No," said Gabriel. "They killed him because he wanted to give me a book."

"What kind of book?"

"Do you remember when we found the ruins of Solomon's Temple?"

Lavon absently rubbed his chest. "How could I forget?"

Gabriel smiled. "This is better."

THE OFFICE, LIKE THE Roman Catholic Church, was guided by ancient doctrine and dogma. Sacred and inviolable, it dictated that members of a large operational team travel to their destination by different routes. The exigencies of the situation, however, required all eight members of the team to journey to Munich on the same El Al flight. Nevertheless, they staggered their arrival at the safe house, if only to avoid attracting unwanted attention from the neighbors.

The first to arrive was Yossi Gavish, the tweedy, British-born head of Research. He was followed by Mordecai and Oded, a pair of all-purpose field hands, and a kid named Ilan who knew how to make the computers work. Next came Yaakov Rossman and Dina Sarid. Yaakov was the head of Special Ops. Dina was a human database of Palestinian and Islamic terrorism who possessed an uncanny knack for spotting connections others missed. Both spoke fluent German.

Mikhail Abramov wandered in around noon. Tall and lanky, with pale bloodless skin and eyes like glacial ice, he had immigrated to Israel from Russia as a teenager and joined the Sayeret Matkal, the IDF's elite special operations unit. Often described as Gabriel without a conscience, he had personally assassinated several top terror masterminds from Hamas and Palestinian Islamic Jihad. He now carried out similar assignments on behalf of the Office, though his extraordinary talents were not limited to the gun. A year earlier he had led a team into Tehran and stolen Iran's entire nuclear archives.

He was accompanied by Natalie Mizrahi, who also happened to be his wife. Born and educated in France, fluent in the Algerian dialect of Arabic, she had traded a promising medical career for the dangerous life of an undercover Office field agent. Her first assignment took her to Raqqa, the capital of the short-lived caliphate of the Islamic State, where she penetrated ISIS's external terrorism network. Were it not for Gabriel and Mikhail, the operation would have been her last.

Like the other members of the team, Natalie had only the vaguest idea why she had been ordered to Munich. Now, in the half-light of the formal drawing room, she listened intently as Gabriel told the team the story of a well-deserved family vacation that was not to be. Summoned to Rome by Archbishop Luigi Donati, he had learned that Pope Paul VII, a man who had done much to undo the Catholic Church's terrible legacy of anti-Semitism, had died under mysterious circumstances. Though skeptical that the Holy Father had been murdered, Gabriel had nonetheless agreed to use the resources of the Office to undertake an informal investigation. It led him to Florence, where he witnessed the brutal killing of a missing Swiss Guard, and then to a cottage outside Fribourg, where an unfinished letter fell from a framed picture of Jesus in the Garden of Gethsemane.

The letter concerned a book His Holiness had discovered in the Vatican Secret Archives. A book purportedly based on the memoirs of the Roman prefect of Judea who sentenced Jesus to death by crucifixion. A book that contradicted the accounts of Jesus' death contained in the canonical Gospels, accounts that were the seedbed of two thousand years of sometimes murderous anti-Semitism.

The book was missing, but the men who took it were hiding in plain sight. They were members of a reactionary and secretive Catholic order founded in southern Germany by a priest who found much to admire in the politics of the European far right, especially National Socialism. The spiritual descendants of this priest, whose name was Ulrich Schiller, planned to steal the approaching papal conclave and elect one of their own as the next supreme pontiff of the Roman Catholic Church. As chief of the Office, Gabriel had determined that such a development would not be in the interests of the State of Israel or Europe's 1.5 million Jews. Therefore, it was his intention to help his friend Luigi Donati steal the conclave back.

To do so required undeniable proof of the Order's plot. Time was of the essence. Gabriel needed the information no later than Thursday night, the eve of the conclave. Fortunately, he had identified two important lay members involved in the conspiracy. One was a reclusive German industrialist named Jonas Wolf. The other was a former BfV officer named Andreas Estermann.

Estermann would be arriving at Café Adagio on the Beethovenplatz at six p.m. Wednesday. He would be expecting a Swiss intelligence officer named Christoph Bittel. He would find the Office instead. Immediately following his abduction, he would be brought to the Munich safe house for questioning. Gabriel decreed that the interrogation would not be a fishing expedition. Estermann would merely sign his name to a statement the team had already prepared, a bill of particulars detailing the Order's plot to steal the conclave. A retired professional, he would not break easily. Leverage would be required. The team would have to find that, too. All in a span of just thirty hours.

They lodged not a word of protest and posed not a single question. Instead, they opened their laptops, established secure links to Tel Aviv, and went to work. Two hours later, as a gentle snow whitened the lawns of the Englischer Garten, they fired their first shot.

37

MUNICH

THE E-MAIL THAT LANDED ON Andreas Estermann's phone a
few seconds later appeared to have been sent by Christoph
Bittel. In truth, it had been dispatched by a twenty-two-year-
old MIT-educated hacker from Unit 8200 in Tel Aviv. It sat
on Estermann's device for nearly twenty minutes, long enough
for Gabriel to fear the worst. Finally, Estermann opened it and
clicked on the attachment, a decade-old photograph of a Swiss-
German gathering of spies in Bern. In doing so, he unleashed
a sophisticated malware attack that instantly seized control of
the phone's operating system. Within minutes, it was export-
ing a year's worth of e-mails, text messages, GPS data, tele-
phone metadata, and Internet browsing history, all without
Estermann's knowledge. The Unit bounced the material se-
curely from Tel Aviv to the safe house, along with a live feed

from the phone's microphone and camera. Even Estermann's calendar entries, past and future, were theirs to peruse at will. On Wednesday evening he had a single appointment: drinks at Café Adagio, six o'clock.

Estermann's contacts contained the private mobile numbers of Bishop Hans Richter and his private secretary, Father Markus Graf. Both succumbed to malware attacks launched by Unit 8200, as did Cardinal Camerlengo Domenico Albanese and Cardinal Archbishop Franz von Emmerich of Vienna, the man whom the Order had selected to be the next pope.

Elsewhere in Estermann's contacts the team found evidence of the Order's astonishing reach. It was as if an electronic version of Father Schiller's leather-bound ledger had fallen into their laps. There were private phone numbers and e-mail addresses for Austrian chancellor Jörg Kaufmann, Italian prime minister Giuseppe Saviano, Cécile Leclerc of France's Popular Front, Peter van der Meer of the Dutch Freedom Party, and, of course, Axel Brünner of Germany's far-right National Democrats. Analysis of the phone's metadata revealed that Estermann and Brünner had spoken five times during the past week alone, a period that coincided with Brünner's sudden surge in German public opinion polls.

Fortunately for the team, Estermann conducted much of his personal and professional correspondence via text message. For sensitive communications he used a service that promised end-to-end encryption and complete privacy, a promise Unit 8200 had long ago rendered empty. Not only was the team able to see his current texts in real time, they were able to review his deleted messages as well.

Gabriel's name featured prominently in several exchanges, as did Luigi Donati's. Indeed, Donati had appeared on the Order's early-warning system within hours of the Holy Father's death. The Order had been aware of Gabriel's arrival in Rome and of his presence in Florence. It had learned of his visit to Switzerland from Father Erich, the village priest from Rechthalten. The phone betrayed that Estermann had visited Switzerland as well. GPS data confirmed he spent forty-nine minutes in Café du Gothard in Fribourg on the Saturday after the Holy Father's death. Afterward, he had driven to Bonn, where he switched off the phone for a period of two hours and fifty-seven minutes.

If there was a bright spot, it was the cleanliness of Estermann's personal life. The team found no evidence of a mistress or fondness for pornography. Estermann's consumption of news was broad but tilted decidedly to the right. Several of the German websites he visited daily trafficked in false and misleading stories that inflamed public opinion against Muslim immigrants and the political left. Otherwise, he had no nasty browsing habits.

But no man is perfect, and few are without at least one weakness. Estermann's, it turned out, was money. Analysis of his encrypted text messages revealed that he was in regular contact with a certain Herr Hassler, owner of a private bank in the principality of Liechtenstein. Analysis of Herr Hassler's records, conducted without his consent, revealed the existence of an account in Estermann's name. The team had found numerous such accounts spread throughout the world, but the one in tiny Liechtenstein was different.

"Estermann's wife, Johanna, is the beneficiary," said Dina Sarid.

"What's the current balance?" asked Gabriel.

"Just north of a million and a half."

"When was it opened?"

"About three months ago. He's made sixteen deposits. Each one was one hundred thousand euros exactly. If you ask me, he's skimming from the payments he's making to the cardinals."

"What about the Vatican Bank?"

"The accounts of twelve of the cardinal-electors have received large wire transfers in the last six weeks. Four were over a million. The rest were around eight hundred thousand. All of them can be traced back to Estermann."

But the ultimate source of the money was the secretive Munich-based conglomerate that Alessandro Ricci had described as the Order of St. Helena Inc. Eli Lavon, the team's most experienced financial investigator, took it upon himself to penetrate the company's defenses. They were formidable, which came as no surprise. After all, he had matched wits with the Order once before. Twenty years ago, he had been at a distinct disadvantage. Now he had Unit 8200 in his corner, and he had Jonas Wolf.

The German businessman proved to be as elusive as the company that bore his name, beginning with the basics of his biography. As far as Lavon could tell, Wolf had been born *some*where in Germany, *some*time during the war. He had been educated at Heidelberg University—of that, Lavon was certain—and had earned a PhD in applied mathematics. He acquired his first company, a small chemical firm, in 1970 with money borrowed from a friend. Within ten years he had expanded into shipping, manufacturing, and construction. And by the mid-1980s he was an extraordinarily wealthy man.

He purchased a graceful old town house in the Maxvorstadt

district of Munich and a valley high in the Obersalzberg, northeast of Berchtesgaden. It was his intention to create a baronial refuge for his family and their descendants. But when his wife and two sons were killed in a private plane crash in 1988, Wolf's mountain redoubt became his prison. Once or twice a week, weather permitting, he traveled to Wolf Group's headquarters in north Munich by helicopter. But for the most part he remained in the Obersalzberg, surrounded by his small army of bodyguards. He had not granted an interview in more than twenty years. Not since the release of an unauthorized biography that accused him of arranging the plane crash that killed his family. Reporters who tried to pry open the locked rooms of his past faced financial ruin or, in the case of a meddlesome British investigative journalist, physical violence. Wolf's involvement in the reporter's death—she was killed by a hit-and-run driver while cycling through the countryside near Devon—was much rumored but never proven.

To Eli Lavon, the story of Jonas Wolf's spectacular rise sounded too good to be true. There was, for a start, the loan Wolf had received to purchase his first company. Lavon had a hunch, based on hard-won experience, that Wolf's lender had been a Canton Zug–based concern known as the Order of St. Helena. Furthermore, Lavon was of the opinion—again, it was merely well-informed conjecture—that the Wolf Group was far larger than advertised.

Because it was an entirely private company, one that had never received a single loan from a single German bank, Lavon's options for traditional financial inquiry were limited. Estermann's phone, however, opened many doors within the firm's computer network that might otherwise have remained closed, even to the cybersleuths at Unit 8200. Shortly after eight o'clock that evening, they tunneled into Jonas Wolf's personal database and found the keys to the kingdom, a two-hundred-page document detailing the company's global holdings and the staggering income they generated.

"Two and a half billion in pure profit last year alone," announced Lavon. "And where do you think it all goes?"

That evening the team set aside its work long enough to share a traditional family meal. Mikhail Abramov and Natalie Mizrahi were absent, however, for they dined at Café Adagio in the Beethovenplatz. It was located in the basement level of a yellow building on the square's northwestern flank. By day it served bistro fare, but at night it was one of the neighborhood's most popular bars. Mikhail and Natalie pronounced the food mediocre but judged the likelihood of successfully abducting a patron to be quite high.

"Three stars on the Michelin scale," quipped Mikhail upon their return to the safe house. "If Estermann comes to Café Adagio alone, he leaves in the back of a van."

The team took delivery of the vehicle in question, a Mercedes transit van, at nine the following morning, along with two Audi A8 sedans, two BMW motor scooters, a set of false German registration plates, four Jericho .45-caliber pistols, an Uzi Pro compact submachine gun, and a 9mm Beretta with a walnut grip.

At which point the tension in the safe house seemed to rise by several notches. As was often the case, Gabriel's mood darkened as the zero hour drew near. Mikhail reminded him that a year earlier, in a warehouse in a drab commercial district of Tehran, a sixteen-member team had blowtorched its way into thirty-two safes and removed several hundred computer discs and millions of pages of documents. The team had then loaded the material into a cargo truck and driven it to the shore of the Caspian Sea, where a boat had been waiting. The operation had shocked the world and proved once again that the Office could strike at will, even in the capital of its most implacable foe.

"And how many Iranians did you have to kill in order to get out of the country alive?"

"Details, details," said Mikhail dismissively. "The point is, we can do this with our eyes closed."

"I'd rather you do it with your eyes open. It will substantially increase our chances of success."

By midday Gabriel had managed to convince himself that they were doomed to failure, that he would spend the rest of his life in a German prison cell for crimes too numerous to recall, an ignoble end to a career against which all others would be measured. Eli Lavon accurately diagnosed the source of Gabriel's despair, for he was suffering from the same malady. It was Munich, thought Lavon. And it was the book.

It was never far from their thoughts, especially Lavon's. There was not one member of the team whose life had not been altered by the longest hatred. Nearly all had lost relatives to the fires of the Holocaust. Some had been born only because one member of a family had found the will to survive. Like Isabel Feldman, the only surviving child of Samuel Feldman, who handed over a small fortune in cash and valuables to the Order of St. Helena in exchange for false baptismal certificates and false promises of protection.

Another such woman was Irene Frankel. Born in Berlin, she was deported to Auschwitz in the autumn of 1942. Her parents were gassed upon arrival, but Irene Frankel left Auschwitz on the Death March in January 1945. She arrived in the new State of Israel in 1948. There she met a man from Munich, a writer, an intellectual, who had escaped to Palestine before the war. In Germany his name had been Greenberg, but in Israel he had taken the name Allon. After marrying, they vowed to have six children, one for each million murdered, but a single child was all her womb could bear. She named the child Gabriel, the messenger of God, the interpreter of Daniel's visions.

At two o'clock they all realized it had been several minutes since anyone had seen him or heard his voice. A rapid search of the safe house revealed no trace of him, and a call to his phone received no answer. Unit 8200 confirmed the device was powered on and that it was moving through the Englischer Garten at a walking pace. Eli Lavon was confident he knew where it was headed. The child of Irene Frankel wanted to see where it had happened. Lavon couldn't blame him. He was suffering from the same malady.

38

MUNICH

IN JULY 1935, TWO AND a half years after electorally seizing control of Germany, Adolf Hitler formally declared Munich "the Capital of the Movement." The city's ties to National Socialism were undeniable. The Nazi Party was formed in Munich in the turbulent years after Germany's defeat in World War I. And it was in Munich, in the autumn of 1923, that Hitler led the abortive Beer Hall Putsch that resulted in his brief incarceration at Landsberg Prison. There he penned the first volume of *Mein Kampf*, the rambling manifesto in which he described Jews as germs that needed to be exterminated. During his first year as chancellor, the year in which he transformed Germany into a totalitarian dictatorship, the book sold more than a million copies.

Throughout the fifteen cataclysmic years of the Nazi era,

Hitler traveled to Munich frequently. He maintained a large, art-filled apartment at Prinzregentenplatz 16 and commissioned the construction of a personal office building overlooking the Königsplatz. Known as the Führerbau it contained living quarters for Hitler and his deputy, Rudolf Hess, and a cavernous central hall with twin stone staircases that led to a conference room. British prime minister Neville Chamberlain signed the Munich Agreement in the Führerbau on September 30, 1938. Upon his return to London, he predicted the accord would deliver "peace in our time." A year later the Wehrmacht invaded Poland, plunging the world into war and setting in motion the chain of events that would lead to the destruction of Europe's Jews.

Much of central Munich was leveled by a pair of devastating Allied bombing raids in April 1944, but somehow the Führerbau survived. Immediately after the war, the Allies used it as a storage facility for looted art. It was now the home of a respected school of music and theater, where pianists, cellists, violinists, and actors perfected their craft in rooms where murderers once walked. Bicycles lined the building's leaden facade, and at the foot of the main steps stood two bored-looking Munich police officers. Neither paid any heed to the man of medium height and build who paused to review a schedule of upcoming public recitals.

He continued past the Alte Pinakothek, Munich's world-class art museum, and then turned left onto the Hessstrasse. It was ten minutes before he caught his first glimpse of the modern tower rising above the Olympic Park. The old Olympic Village lay to the north, not far from the headquarters of BMW and a highly profitable German conglomerate known as the Wolf

Group. He found the Connollystrasse and followed it to the squat three-story apartment house at number 31.

The building had long ago been converted into student housing, but in early September 1972 it had been inhabited by members of Israel's Olympic team. At 4:30 a.m. on September 5, eight Palestinian terrorists dressed in tracksuits scaled an undefended fence. Carrying duffel bags filled with Kalashnikov rifles, Tokarev semiautomatic pistols, and Soviet-made hand grenades, they used a stolen key to unlock the door of apartment 1. Two Israelis, wrestling coach Moshe Weinberg and weight lifter Yossef Romano, were murdered during the first moments of the siege. Nine others were taken hostage.

For the remainder of that day, as a global television audience watched in horror, German authorities negotiated with two heavily disguised terrorists—one known as Issa, the other Tony—while across the street the Games continued. Finally, at ten p.m., the hostages were flown by helicopter to Fürstenfeldbruck Air Base, where German police had put in place an ill-conceived rescue operation. It ended with the death of all nine Israelis.

Within hours of the massacre, Israeli prime minister Golda Meir ordered a legendary Office agent named Ari Shamron to "send forth the boys." The operation was code-named Wrath of God, a phrase chosen by Shamron to give his undertaking the patina of divine sanction. One of the boys was a gifted young painter from the Bezalel Academy of Arts and Design named Gabriel Allon. Another was Eli Lavon, a promising biblical archaeologist. In the Hebrew-based lexicon of the team, Lavon was an *ayin*, a tracker. Gabriel was an *aleph*, an assassin. For three years they stalked their prey across Western Europe and the Middle East, killing at night and in broad daylight, living in fear that at any moment they might be arrested by local authorities and charged as murderers. In all, twelve men died at their hands. Gabriel personally killed six of the terrorists with a .22-caliber Beretta pistol. Whenever possible, he shot his victims eleven times, one for each Jew murdered at Munich. When finally he returned to Israel, his temples were gray. Lavon was left with numerous stress disorders, including a notoriously fickle stomach that troubled him to this day.

He crept up on Gabriel without a sound and joined him in front of Connollystrasse 31.

"I wouldn't do that again if I were you, Eli. You're lucky I didn't shoot you."

"I tried to make a bit of noise."

"Try harder next time."

Lavon looked up toward the balcony of apartment 1. "Come here often?"

"Actually, it's been a while."

"How long?"

"A hundred years," said Gabriel distantly.

"I come here every time I'm in Munich. And I always think the same thing."

"What's that, Eli?"

"Our Olympic team should never have been assigned to this building. It was too isolated. We expressed our concerns to the Germans a few weeks before the Games began, but they assured us our athletes would be safe. Unfortunately, they neglected to tell us that German intelligence had already received a tip from a Palestinian informant that the Israeli team had been targeted."

"It must have slipped their minds."

"Why didn't they warn us? Why didn't they take steps to protect our athletes?"

"You tell me."

"They didn't tell us," said Lavon, "because they didn't want anything to spoil their postwar coming-out party, least of all a threat against the descendants of the same people they had tried to exterminate just thirty years before. Remember, the German intelligence and security services were founded by men like Reinhard Gehlen. Men who had worked for Hitler and the Nazis. Men of the right who hated communism and Jews in equal measure. It's no wonder they were attracted to someone like Andreas Estermann." He turned to Gabriel. "Did you happen to notice the last job he held before his retirement?"

"Head of Department Two, the counterextremism division."

"So why is he spending so much time on the phone with the likes of Axel Brünner? And why does he have the private cell number of every far-right leader in Europe?" Lavon paused. "And why did he turn off his phone for three hours in Bonn the other night?"

"Maybe he has a girlfriend there."

"Estermann? He's a choirboy."

"A doctrinaire choirboy."

Lavon lifted his gaze once more toward the facade of the building. A light was burning in the window of apartment 1. "Do you ever imagine how differently our lives would have turned out if it hadn't happened?"

"Munich?"

"No," answered Lavon. "*All* of it. Two thousand years of hatred. We'd be as numerous as all the stars in the sky and the sand on the seashore, just as God promised Abraham. I'd be living in a grand apartment in the First District of Vienna, a leader in my field, a man of distinction. I'd spend my afternoons sipping coffee and eating strudel at Café Sacher, and my evenings listening to Mozart and Haydn. Occasionally, I'd visit an art gallery and see works by a famous Berlin painter named Gabriel Frankel, the son of Irene Frankel, the grandson of Viktor Frankel, perhaps the greatest German painter of the twentieth century. Who knows? Perhaps I might even be wealthy enough to purchase one or two of his works."

"I'm afraid life doesn't work that way, Eli."

"I suppose not. But would it be too much to ask for them to stop hating us? Why is anti-Semitism on the rise again in Europe? Why is it not safe to be a Jew in this country? Why has the shame of the Holocaust worn off? Why won't it ever end?"

"Nine words," said Gabriel.

A silence fell between them. It was Lavon who broke it.

"Where do you suppose it is?"

"The Gospel of Pilate?"

Lavon nodded.

"Up a chimney."

"How appropriate." Lavon's tone was uncharacteristically bitter. He started to light a cigarette but stopped himself. "It goes without saying that the Nazis were the ones who annihilated the Jews of Europe. But they could not have carried out the Final Solution unless Christianity had first plowed the soil. Hitler's willing executioners had been conditioned by centuries of Church teachings about the evils of the Jews. Austrian Catholics made up a disproportionate share of the death camp officers, and the survival rates for Jews were far lower in Catholic countries."

"But thousands of Catholics risked their lives to protect us."

"Indeed, they did. They chose to act on their own initiative rather than wait for encouragement from their pope. As a result, they saved their Church from the moral abyss." Lavon's eyes searched the old Olympic Village. "We should be getting back to the safe house. It will be dark soon."

"It already is," said Gabriel.

Lavon finally lit his cigarette. "Why do you suppose he switched off his phone for three hours the other night?"

"Estermann?"

Lavon nodded.

"I don't know," answered Gabriel. "But I intend to ask him."

"Maybe you should ask him about the Gospel of Pilate, too."

"Don't worry, Eli. I will."

WHEN GABRIEL AND LAVON RETURNED to the safe house, the members of the snatch team were gathered in the sitting room, dressed for an evening out at a trendy café in the Beethovenplatz. There was no outward sign of nerves other than the incessant tapping of Mikhail's forefinger against the arm of his chair. He was listening intently to the voice of Andreas Estermann, who was addressing the members of his senior staff about the need to increase security at all Wolf Group facilities, especially the chemical plants. It seemed Estermann had received a warning from an old contact at the BfV, a warning the team had overheard. The system, apparently, was blinking red.

By five fifteen it was blinking red inside the safe house as well. The members of the snatch team took their leave in the same manner they had arrived—intermittently, alone or in pairs, so as not to attract attention from the neighbors. By 5:45 they all had reached their fail-safe points.

Their quarry left Wolf Group headquarters seventeen minutes later. Gabriel watched his progress on an open laptop computer, a blinking blue light on a map of central Munich, courtesy of the compromised phone. It had already told Gabriel nearly everything he needed to know to prevent the Order of St. Helena from stealing the conclave. Still, there were one or two matters Andreas Estermann needed to clear up. If he had any sense, he would offer no resistance. Gabriel was in a dangerously bad mood. They were in Munich, after all. The Capital of the Movement. The city where murderers once walked.

39

BEETHOVENPLATZ, MUNICH

JUST NORTH OF MUNICH'S CENTRAL train station, the traffic came to an abrupt halt. It was another police checkpoint. There were several around the city, mainly near transportation hubs and in squares and markets where large numbers of pedestrians congregated. The entire country was on edge, bracing itself for the next attack. Even the BfV, Andreas Estermann's old service, was convinced another bombing was inevitable. Estermann was of a similar mind. Indeed, he had reason to believe the next attack would occur as early as tomorrow morning, probably in Cologne. If successful, the physical destruction and death toll would tear at the very soul of the country, touch an ancient nerve. It would be Germany's 9/11. Nothing would ever be the same.

Estermann checked the time on his iPhone, then swore

softly. Immediately, he pleaded with God for forgiveness. The strictures of the Order forbade all forms of profanity, not just those involving the Lord's name. Estermann did not smoke cigarettes or drink alcohol, and regular fasting and exercise helped to keep down his weight, despite a weakness for traditional German cooking. His wife, Johanna, was a member of the Order, too. So were their six children. The size of their family was unusual in modern Germany, where birth rates had fallen below replacement level.

Estermann again checked the time. *6:04 . . .* He dialed Christoph Bittel's number but received no answer. Then he dashed off a text message, explaining that he had left the office later than planned and was now stuck in traffic. Bittel replied instantly. It seemed he was running behind schedule as well, which was not like him. Bittel was usually as punctual as a Swiss timepiece.

At last, the traffic inched forward. Estermann saw the reason for the delay. The police were searching a delivery van outside the entrance of the station. The passengers, two young men, Arabs or Turks, lay spread-eagled on the pavement. Estermann took no small amount of pleasure in their predicament. When he was a boy growing up in Munich, he rarely saw a foreigner, especially one with brown or black skin. That changed in the 1980s, when the floodgates opened. Twelve million immigrants now resided in Germany, fifteen percent of the population. The overwhelming majority were Muslims. Unless present trends were reversed, native Germans would soon be a minority in their own land.

Estermann turned onto the Goethestrasse, a quiet street lined with elegant old apartment houses, and eased into an empty space along the curb at ten minutes past six. He lost three additional minutes purchasing a chit from the automatic dispenser and another two walking the rest of the way to Café Adagio. It was a dimly lit room with a few tables arranged around a platform where, later that evening, a trio of American jazz musicians would perform. Estermann did not care for jazz. Nor did he much like the clientele of Café Adagio. At a darkened table in the corner, two women—at least Estermann thought they were women—were kissing. A couple of tables away sat two men. One had a hard, pitted face. The other was thin as a reed. They looked like Eastern Europeans, maybe Jews. At least they weren't queers. Estermann hated queers even more than he hated Jews and Muslims.

Bittel was nowhere to be seen. Estermann sat down at a table as far from the other patrons as possible. At length, a tattooed girl with purple hair wandered over. She looked at Estermann for a moment as though waiting for him to utter the secret password.

"Diet Coke."

The waitress withdrew. Estermann checked his phone. Where the hell was Bittel? And why in God's name had he chosen a place like Café Adagio?

ANDREAS ESTERMANN'S DISCOMFORT WAS SO transparent that Gabriel waited ten additional minutes before informing the German that, owing to a work emergency, Christoph Bittel would not be able to meet for a drink as planned. Estermann's face, viewed through the camera lens of his compromised phone, twisted into a grimace. He sent a curt response, tossed a five-euro banknote onto the table, and stormed into the street.

265

Fuming, he pounded along the pavements of the Goethestrasse to his car, where his rising anger boiled over.

A man was sitting on the hood, his boots resting on the bumper, a girl between his legs. His pale skin was luminous in the lamplight. The girl was very dark, like an Arab. Her hands were resting on the man's thighs. Her mouth was on his.

Estermann would have only limited memory of what happened next. There was an exchange of words, followed by an exchange of blows. Estermann threw a single wild punch but was on the receiving end of several compact, carefully delivered elbows and knees.

Incapacitated, he crumpled to the pavement. From somewhere a van materialized. Estermann was hurled into the back like war dead. He felt a sharp pain in his neck, and instantly his vision began to swim. The last thing he remembered before losing consciousness was the face of the woman. She was an Arab, he was sure of it. Estermann hated Arabs. Almost as much as he hated Jews.

40

MUNICH

THERE IS NO SUCH THING, practitioners of the secret trade like to say, as a perfect covert operation. The best a careful planner can do is limit the chances of failure and exposure—or, worse still, of arrest and prosecution. Sometimes the planner willingly accepts a modicum of risk when lives are at stake or his cause is just. And sometimes he must resign himself to the fact that a small measure of serendipity, of providence, will determine whether his ship reaches port safely or smashes itself to pieces on the rocks.

Gabriel struck just such a bargain with the operational gods that evening in Munich. Yes, he had lured Andreas Estermann to Café Adagio for what he thought was a meeting with an old acquaintance. But it was Estermann, not Gabriel and his team, who had selected the place of his abduction. Fortunately, Estermann chose well. There was no traffic camera to record his disappearance, and no witness other than a dachshund in the window of an adjacent apartment building.

Ninety minutes later, after a brief stop in the countryside west of Munich for a change of license plates, the van returned to the safe house near the Englischer Garten. Bound and blindfolded, Andreas Estermann was transferred to a makeshift holding cell in the basement. Typically, Gabriel would have left him there for a day or two to ponder his fate while deprived of sight, sound, and sleep. Instead, at half past ten, he instructed Natalie to hasten Estermann's return to consciousness. She injected him with a mild stimulant along with a little something to take the edge off. Something to distort his sense of reality. Something to loosen his tongue.

Consequently, Estermann offered no resistance when Mordecai and Oded secured him to a metal chair outside the holding cell. On the opposite side of a table, flanked by Yaakov Rossman and Eli Lavon, sat Gabriel. Behind him was a tripod-mounted Solaris phone. Blindfolded, Estermann knew none of this. He only knew that he was in a great deal of trouble. The matter before him, however, was easily resolved. All that was required was his signature on a statement. A bill of particulars. Names and numbers.

At 10:34 p.m., Estermann's inquisitor spoke for the first time. The camera captured the expression on the portion of the German's face not concealed by the blindfold. Later, the video would be analyzed by the specialists at King Saul Boulevard. All were in agreement on one point. It was a look of profound relief.

THOUGH CURSED WITH A FLAWLESS memory, Gabriel sometimes found it hard to accurately recall his mother's face. Two
of her self-portraits hung in his bedroom in Jerusalem. Each
night before he drifted off to sleep, he saw her as she had seen
herself, a tormented figure rendered in the manner of the German Expressionists.

Like many young women who survived the Holocaust, she
struggled with the demands of caring for a child. She was prone
to melancholia and violent mood swings. She could not show
pleasure on festive occasions and did not partake of rich food or
drink. She wore a bandage always on her left arm, over the faded
numbers tattooed into her skin. *29395 . . .* She referred to them
as her mark of Jewish weakness. Her emblem of Jewish shame.

Painting, like motherhood, was an ordeal for her. Gabriel used
to sit on the floor at her feet, scribbling in his sketchpad, while
she labored at her easel. To distract herself, she used to tell stories
of her childhood in Berlin. She spoke to Gabriel in German, in
her thick Berlin accent. It was Gabriel's first language, and even
now it was the language of his dreams. His Italian, while fluent,
bore the faint but unmistakable trace of a foreigner's intonation.
But not his German. No matter where he traveled in the country,
no one ever assumed he was anything but a native speaker of the
language, one who had been raised in the center of Berlin.

Andreas Estermann clearly assumed that was the case as
well, which prompted his misplaced expression of relief. It faded
quickly once Gabriel explained why he had been taken into custody. Gabriel did not identify himself, though he implied he
was a secret member of the Order of St. Helena who had been

asked by Herr Wolf and Bishop Richter to investigate certain financial irregularities that had recently come to their attention. These irregularities concerned the existence of a bank account in the principality of Liechtenstein. Gabriel recited the current balance and the dates on which deposits had been made. Then he read aloud the text messages Estermann had exchanged with his private banker, Herr Hassler, lest Estermann entertain any thought of wriggling off the hook.

Next Gabriel turned his attention to the source of the money that Estermann had embezzled from the Order. It was money, he said, that was supposed to have been delivered to the cardinal-electors who had agreed to vote for the Order's candidate at the coming conclave. At the mention of the prelate's name, Estermann gave a start and then spoke for the first time. With a single objection, he confirmed both the existence of the plot and the name of the cardinal whom the Order had selected to be the next pope.

"How do you know it's Emmerich?"

"What do you mean?" asked Gabriel.

"Only a handful of us are aware of the conclave operation."

"I'm one of them."

"But I would know who you are."

"Why would you assume that?"

"I know the names of all the secret members of the Order."

"Obviously," said Gabriel, "that's not the case."

Receiving no further protest, Gabriel returned to the topic of the payments. It seemed several of the prelates had informed Cardinal Albanese that the agreed-upon sums of cash had not appeared in their accounts.

"But that's not possible! Father Graf told me last week that all the cardinals had received their money."

"Father Graf is working with me on this matter. He misled you at my request."

"Bastard."

"The Order forbids such language, Herr Estermann. Especially when it concerns a priest."

"Please don't tell Bishop Richter."

"Don't worry, it will be our little secret." Gabriel paused. "But only if you tell me what you did with the money you were supposed to deliver to the cardinal-electors."

"I wired it into their accounts, just as Herr Wolf and Bishop Richter instructed. I never stole a single euro."

"Why would the cardinals lie?"

"Isn't it obvious? They're trying to extort us into paying more money."

"What about the account in Liechtenstein?"

"It is an operational account."

"Why is your wife the beneficiary?"

Estermann was silent for a moment. "Do Herr Wolf and Bishop Richter know about the account?"

"Not yet," said Gabriel. "And if you do everything I tell you, they never will."

"What do you want?"

"I want you to call Herr Hassler first thing in the morning and tell him to wire that money to me."

"Yes, of course. What else?"

Gabriel told him.

"All forty-two names? We'll be here all night."

"Is there somewhere else you have to be?"

"My wife is expecting me for dinner."

"I'm afraid you missed dinner a long time ago."

"Can you at least remove the blindfold and these restraints?"

"The names, Herr Estermann. Now."

"Is there any particular order you want them?"

"How about alphabetically?"

"It would help if I had my phone."

"You're a professional. You don't need your phone."

Estermann tilted his head toward the ceiling and drew a breath. "Cardinal Azevedo."

"Tegucigalpa?"

"There's only one Azevedo in the College of Cardinals."

"How much did you pay him?"

"One million."

"Where's the money?"

"Bank of Panama."

"Next?"

Estermann cocked his head. "Ballantine of Philadelphia."

"How much?"

"One million."

"Where's the money?"

"The Vatican Bank."

"Next?"

THE LAST NAME ON ESTERMANN's list was Cardinal Péter Zikov, the archbishop of Esztergom-Budapest, one million euros, payable to his personal account at Banco Popolare Hungary. All totaled, 42 of the 116 cardinal-electors who would choose the successor to Pope Paul VII had received money in exchange for their votes. The total cost of the operation was slightly less than $50 million. Every penny of it had come from the coffers of the Wolf Group, the global conglomerate otherwise known as the Order of St. Helena Inc.

"And that's all of the names?" probed Gabriel. "You're sure you haven't left anyone out?"

Estermann shook his head vigorously. "The other eighteen cardinals who will vote for Emmerich are members of the Order. They received no payment beyond their monthly stipends." He paused. "And then there's Archbishop Donati, of course. Two million euros. I deposited the money after he and the Israeli broke into the Secret Archives."

Gabriel glanced at Eli Lavon. "And you're sure you didn't deposit that money in an account I don't know about?"

"No," said Estermann. "It's in Donati's personal account at the Vatican Bank."

Gabriel turned to a fresh page in his notebook, despite the fact he hadn't bothered to write down a single name or number. "Let's go through it one more time, shall we? Just to make certain we haven't missed anyone."

"Please," begged Estermann. "I have a terrible headache from the drugs you gave me."

Gabriel looked at Mordecai and Oded and in German instructed them to return Estermann to the holding cell. Upstairs in the drawing room, he and Lavon reviewed the recording on a laptop computer.

"That clerical suit you wore into the Secret Archives the

other day must have rubbed off on you. For a moment even I was convinced you were a member of the Order."

Gabriel advanced the recording and clicked PLAY.

Two million euros. I deposited the money after he and the Israeli broke into the Secret Archives . . .

Gabriel clicked PAUSE. "Rather clever on their part, don't you think?"

"They obviously don't intend to go down without a fight."

"Neither do I."

"What do you have in mind?"

"I'm going to have a word with him." Gabriel paused. "Face-to-face."

"You've got everything you need," said Lavon. "Let's get out of here before some nice German police officer knocks on the door and asks if we know anything about a missing senior executive from the Wolf Group."

"We can't release him until white smoke rises from the chimney of the Sistine Chapel."

"So we'll tape him to a tree somewhere in the Alps on our way down to Rome. With any luck, no one will find him until the glaciers melt."

Gabriel shook his head. "I want to know why he has the private phone number of every major far-right leader in Western Europe. And I want that book."

"It went up a chimney. You said so yourself."

"Just like my grandparents."

Gabriel turned without another word and headed downstairs to the cellar. There he instructed Mordecai and Oded to remove Estermann from the holding cell. Once again, the German offered no resistance as he was secured to the chair. At 12:42 a.m., the blindfold was removed. The camera of the Solaris phone captured the expression on Estermann's face. Later, at King Saul Boulevard, all were in agreement on one point. It was one of Gabriel's finest hours.

NATALIE GAVE ESTERMANN A HANDFUL of ibuprofen for his head and a plate of leftover Turkish takeaway. He swallowed the pain reliever tablets greedily but turned up his nose at the food. He likewise ignored the glass of Bordeaux she placed before him.

"She looks like an Arab," he said when she was gone.

"She's from France, actually. She and her parents had to immigrate to Israel to escape the anti-Semitism there."

"I hear it's very bad."

"Almost as bad as Germany."

"It's the immigrants who are causing problems, not ethnic Germans."

"Isn't it pretty to think so." Gabriel looked at the untouched wineglass. "Have some. You'll feel better."

"Alcohol is forbidden by the Order." Estermann frowned. "I would have thought you knew that." He looked down at his plate without enthusiasm. "I wonder if you might have any proper German food."

"That would be rather difficult, given the fact we are no longer in Germany."

Estermann adopted a superior smile. "I've lived in Munich most of my life. I know how it smells, how it sounds. If I had to guess, we're in the city center, rather close to the Englischer Garten."

"Eat your food, Estermann. You're going to need your strength."

He wrapped two pieces of grilled lamb in a *bazlama* flatbread and hesitantly took a first bite.

"That wasn't so bad, was it?"

"Where did you get it?"

"A little takeaway near the Hauptbahnhof."

"That's where all the Turks live, you know."

"In my experience that's generally the best place to get Turkish food."

Estermann ate one of the dolmades. "It's quite good, actually. Still, it's not what I would have chosen for my last meal."

"Why so glum, Estermann?"

"We both know how this is going to end."

"The ending," said Gabriel, "has yet to be written."

"And what must I do to survive this night?"

"Answer every question I ask."

"And if I don't?"

"I'll be tempted to waste a perfectly good bullet on you."

Estermann lowered his voice. "I have children, Allon."

"Six," said Gabriel. "A very Jewish number."

"Really? I never knew." Estermann looked at the glass of wine.

"Have some," said Gabriel. "You'll feel better."

"It's forbidden."

"Live a little, Estermann."

He reached for the wineglass. "I certainly hope so."

ANDREAS ESTERMANN'S STORY BEGAN, OF all places, with the Munich Massacre. His father had been a policeman, too. A real policeman, he added. Not the secret variety. In the early-morning hours of September 5, 1972, he was awakened with news that Palestinian guerrillas had kidnapped several Israeli athletes at the Olympic Village. He remained inside the command post during the daylong negotiations and witnessed the rescue attempt at Fürstenfeldbruck. Despite its failure, Estermann's father was awarded his department's highest commendation for his efforts that day. He tossed it in a drawer and never looked at it again.

"Why?"

"He thought it was a disaster."

"For whom?"

"Germany, of course."

"What about the innocent Israelis who were murdered that night?"

Estermann shrugged.

"I suppose your father thought they had it coming to them."

"I suppose he did."

"He was a supporter of the Palestinians?"

"Hardly."

His father, Estermann continued, was a member of the Order of St. Helena, as was their parish priest. Estermann joined when he was a student at Munich's Ludwig Maximillian University. Three years later, during a particularly chilly phase of the Cold War, he joined the BfV. By any objective measure, he had a fine career, the failure to disrupt the Hamburg Cell notwithstanding. In 2008 he left the counterterrorism division and took command of Department 2, which monitored neo-Nazis and other right-wing extremists.

"A bit like the fox guarding the henhouse, don't you think?"

"A bit," admitted Estermann with a wry smile.

He kept a close eye on the worst of the worst, he continued, and helped federal prosecutors put a few behind bars. But for the most part, he worked to advance the country's rightward drift by shielding extreme political parties and groups from scrutiny, especially when it came to the source of their funding. On the whole, his term as director of Department 2 had been wildly successful. The German far right exploded in size and influence during his tenure. He retired from the BfV in 2014, three years ahead of schedule, and the next day went to work as head of security for the Wolf Group.

"The Order of St. Helena Incorporated."

"You've obviously read Alessandro Ricci's book."

"Why did you leave the BfV early?"

"I'd done everything I could from the inside. Besides, by 2014 we were close to achieving our goals. Bishop Richter and Herr Wolf decided that the Project required my full attention."

"The Project?"

Estermann nodded.

"What was it?"

"A response to an incident that occurred at the Vatican in the autumn of 2006. You might remember it. In fact," said Estermann, "I believe you were there that day."

HE NEEDLESSLY REMINDED GABRIEL OF the horrific details. The attack had occurred a few minutes after noon, during a Wednesday General Audience in St. Peter's Square. Three suicide bombers, three shoulder-launch RPG-7s: a calculated insult to the Christian concept of the Trinity, which Islam regarded as polytheism, or *shirk*. More than seven hundred people were killed, making it the worst terrorist attack since 9/11. Among the dead were the commandant of the Swiss Guard, four curial cardinals, eight bishops, and three *monsignori*. The Holy Father would have died as well if Gabriel hadn't shielded his body from the falling debris.

"And what did Lucchesi and Donati do?" asked Estermann. "They called for dialogue and reconciliation."

"I assume the Order had a better idea."

"Islamic terrorists had just attacked the heart of Christendom. Their goal was to turn Western Europe into a colony of the caliphate. Let's just say that Bishop Richter and Jonas Wolf were in no mood to negotiate the terms of Christianity's surrender. In fact, when discussing their plan, they borrowed a famous phrase from the Jews."

"What was that?"

"Never again."

"How flattering," said Gabriel. "And the plan?"

"Radical Islam had declared war on the Church and Western civilization. If the Church and Western civilization could not summon the strength to fight back, the Order would do it for them."

It was Jonas Wolf, he continued, who chose to call the operation the Project. Bishop Richter had argued for something biblical, something with historical sweep and gravitas. But Wolf insisted on blandness over grandeur. He wanted a harmless-sounding word that could be used in an e-mail or a phone conversation without raising suspicion.

"And the nature of the Project?" asked Gabriel.

"It was to be a twenty-first-century version of the Reconquista."

"I assume your ambitions weren't limited to the Iberian Peninsula."

"No," said Estermann. "Our goal was to erase the Islamic presence from Western Europe and restore the Church to its proper place of ascendancy."

"How?"

"The same way our founder, Father Schiller, waged a successful war against communism."

"By throwing in your lot with fascists?"

"By supporting the election of traditionalist politicians in the predominantly Roman Catholic heartland of Western Europe." His words had the dryness of a policy paper. "Politicians who would take the difficult but necessary steps to reverse current demographic trends."

"What sort of steps?"

"Use your imagination."

"I'm trying. And all I can see are cattle cars and smokestacks."

"No one's talking about that."

"You're the one who used the word *erase*, Estermann. Not me."

"Do you know how many Muslim immigrants there are in Europe? In one generation, two at the most, Germany will be an Islamic country. France and the Netherlands, too. Can you imagine what life will be like for the Jews then?"

"Why don't you leave us out of it and explain to me how you're going to get rid of twenty-five million Muslims."

"By encouraging them to leave."

"And if they don't?"

"Deportations will be necessary."

"All of them?"

"Every last one."

"What's your role in this? Are you Adolf Eichmann or Heinrich Himmler?"

"I'm the chief of operations. I funnel the Order's money to our chosen political parties and run our intelligence and security service."

"I assume you have a cyber unit."

"A good one. Between the Order and the Russians, little of what your average Western European reads online these days is true."

"Are you working with them?"

"The Russians?" Estermann shook his head. "But more often than not, our interests align."

"The chancellor of Austria is quite fond of the Kremlin."

"Jörg Kaufmann? He's our rock star. Even the American president adores him, and he doesn't like anyone."

"What about Giuseppe Saviano?"

"Thanks to the Order, he came from nowhere to win the last election."

"Cécile Leclerc?"

"A real warrior. She told me that she intends to build a bridge between Marseilles and North Africa. Needless to say, the traffic will flow only one way."

"That leaves Axel Brünner."

"The bombings have given him a real boost in the polls."

"You wouldn't know anything about them, would you?"

"My old friends at BfV are convinced the cell is based in Hamburg. It's a real mess, Hamburg. Lots of radical mosques. Brünner will clean it up once he's in power."

Gabriel smiled. "Thanks to you, the only way Brünner will ever see the inside of the Federal Chancellery is if he gets a job as a janitor."

Estermann was silent.

"You were on the verge of getting everything you wanted. And yet you put it all at risk by murdering an old man with a bad heart. Why kill him? Why not simply wait for him to die?"

"That was the plan."

"What changed?"

"The old man found a book in the Secret Archives," said Estermann. "And then he tried to give it to you."

42

MUNICH

IT WAS IN EARLY OCTOBER, after the Holy Father's return from a long weekend at Castel Gandolfo, that the Order realized it had a problem. His health failing, perhaps sensing that the end was near, he had embarked on a review of the Vatican's most sensitive documents, especially those related to the early Church and the Gospels. Of particular interest to His Holiness were the apocryphal gospels, books the Church Fathers had excluded from the New Testament.

Cardinal Domenico Albanese, the *prefetto* of the Secret Archives, carefully curated the Holy Father's reading list, hiding material he did not want the pontiff to see. But quite by chance, while visiting the papal study with several other curial cardinals, he noticed a small book, several centuries old, bound in cracked red leather, lying on the table next to the Holy Father's desk. It was an apocryphal piece of early Christian writing that was supposed to be locked in the *collezione*. When Albanese asked the Holy Father how he had obtained the book, His Holiness replied that it had been given to him by a certain Father Joshua, a name Albanese did not recognize.

Alarmed, Albanese immediately informed his superior general, Bishop Hans Richter, who in turn contacted the Order's chief of security and intelligence, Andreas Estermann. Several weeks later, in mid-November, Estermann learned the Holy Father had begun work on a letter—a letter he intended to give to the man who had saved his life during the attack on the Vatican.

"And thus," said Estermann, "his fate was sealed."

"How did you know about the letter?"

"I planted a transmitter in the papal study years ago. I heard the Holy Father telling Donati that he was writing to you."

"But Lucchesi didn't tell Donati *why* he was writing to me."

"I heard the pope tell someone else. I was never able to determine who he was talking to. In fact, I couldn't hear the other person's voice."

"Why was the Order so worried about the prospect of Lucchesi giving me the book?"

"Let me count the ways."

"You were afraid it called into question the historical accuracy of the Gospels."

"Obviously."

"But you were also concerned about the book's provenance. It was given to the Order in 1938 by a wealthy Roman Jew named Emanuele Giordano, along with a large sum of cash and several works of art. Signore Giordano did not make this contribution out of the goodness of his heart. The Order was running quite an extortion racket in the thirties. It targeted wealthy Jews, who were promised protection and lifesaving baptismal certificates in exchange for cash and valuables. That money was the venture capital for the Wolf Group." Gabriel paused. "All of which I would have exposed if Lucchesi had placed the book in my hands."

"Not bad, Allon. I always heard you were good."

"How did the Gospel of Pilate end up in the Secret Archives?"

"Father Schiller turned it over to Pius the Twelfth in 1954. His Holiness should have burned it. He buried it in the Archives instead. If Father Joshua hadn't found it, Lucchesi would still be alive."

"How did Father Graf kill him?"

The question surprised Estermann. After a moment's hesitation he held up the first two fingers of his right hand and moved his thumb as though squeezing the plunger of a syringe.

"What was in it?"

"Fentanyl. Apparently, the old man put up quite a fight. Father Graf gave him the injection through his soutane and held his hand over his mouth as he was dying. One of the tasks of the camerlengo is to supervise the preparation of the Holy Father's body for burial. Albanese made certain no one noticed the small hole in his right thigh."

"I think I'll put a hole in Father Graf the next time I see him." Gabriel laid a photograph on the table. A man in a motorcycle helmet on the Ponte Vecchio in Florence, right arm extended, a gun in his hand. "He's a rather good shot."

"I trained him myself."

"Did Niklaus let him into the papal apartments the night of the murder?"

Estermann nodded.

"Did he know what Father Graf was planning to do?"

"Saint Niklaus?" Estermann shook his head. "He loved the Holy Father and Donati. Father Graf manipulated him into opening the door. I heard Niklaus go into the study a few minutes after Father Graf left. That's when he took the letter off the desk."

Gabriel placed it on the table, next to the photograph.

"Where did you find it?"

"It was in his pocket when he was killed."

"What does it say?"

"It says you'd better tell me what happened to the Gospel of Pilate after Albanese removed it from the study."

"He gave it to Bishop Richter."

"And what did Bishop Richter do with it?"

"He did what Father Schiller and Pius the Twelfth should have done a long time ago."

"He destroyed it?"

The German nodded.

Gabriel drew the Beretta from the small of his back. "How do you want the story to end?"

"I want to see my children again."

"Correct answer. Now let's try for two in a row." Gabriel leveled the Beretta at Estermann's head. "Where's the book?"

THERE WAS A HEATED QUARREL, but then no Office operation was complete without one. Yaakov Rossman appointed himself the spokesman for the opposition. The team, he argued, had already pulled off the near impossible. Hastily assembled in a city on high alert, it had succeeded in making a former German intelligence officer disappear without a trace. Under skillful interrogation, he had surrendered the information necessary to prevent the Catholic Church from falling into the hands of a malignant, reactionary order with ties to Europe's far right. What was more, the proverbial tree had fallen in the operational forest without a sound. It was better not to push their luck with a risky final gambit, said Yaakov. Better to put Estermann on ice and make a leisurely run for Munich Airport.

"I'm not leaving without that book," said Gabriel. "And Estermann is going to get it for me."

"What makes you think he'll agree to do it?"

"Because it's better than the alternative."

"What if he's lying?" asked Yaakov. "What if he's sending you on a wild-goose chase?"

"He isn't. Besides, his story is easily verifiable."

"How?"

"The phone."

The phone to which Gabriel was referring belonged to Father Markus Graf. Gabriel ordered Unit 8200, which had gained access to the device after acquiring its number, to check the GPS data stored in the operating system. Shortly after five a.m. Munich time, Yuval Gershon called back with the Unit's findings. The GPS data matched Estermann's story.

At which point all debate ended. There was, however, a minor problem of transport.

"If things go sideways up there," said Eli Lavon, "you won't be able to get back to Rome tonight."

"Not without a private plane," conceded Gabriel.

"Where are we going to get a plane?"

"I suppose we could just steal one."

"Could be messy."

"In that case," said Gabriel, "we'll borrow one instead."

MARTIN LANDESMANN, THE SWISS FINANCIER and philan-
thropist, famously slept only three hours a night. Therefore,
when he answered his phone at five fifteen, he sounded alert and
full of entrepreneurial vitality. Yes, he said, business was good.
Quite good, in fact. No, he replied with a mirthless laugh, he
was not selling nuclear components to the Iranians again. Because of Gabriel, all that was in Landesmann's past.

"And you?" he asked earnestly. "How's your business these
days?"

"International chaos is a growth industry."

"I'm always looking for investment opportunities."

"Financing isn't a problem, Martin. What I need is a plane."

"I'm taking the Boeing Business Jet to London later this
morning, but the Gulfstream is available."

"I suppose it will have to do."

"Where and when?"

Gabriel told him.

"Destination?"

"Tel Aviv, with a brief stopover at Ciampino in Rome."

"Where shall I send the bill?"

"Put it on my tab."

Gabriel rang off and called Donati in Rome.

"I was beginning to think I would never hear from you," he
said.

"Don't worry, I have everything you need."

"How bad is it?"

"Twelve on the Bishop Richter scale. But I'm afraid there's a complication involving someone close to the previous pope. I'd rather not discuss it over the phone."

"When will you be here?"

"I need to tie up one or two loose ends before I leave. And don't even think about setting foot outside the Jesuit Curia until I get there."

Gabriel killed the connection.

"Tell me something," asked Lavon. "What's it like to be you?"

"Exhausting."

"Why don't you sleep for a couple of hours while we pack up?"

"I'd love to. But I have one more question I'd like to ask our newest asset."

"What's that?"

Gabriel told him.

"That's two questions," said Lavon.

Smiling, Gabriel carried Estermann's phone downstairs. The German was drinking coffee at the interrogation table, watched over by Mikhail and Oded. He was unshaven, and his right cheek was bruised. With a razor and a bit of makeup, he would be as good as new.

Warily, he watched as Gabriel sat down in the chair opposite. "What is it now?"

"We're going to clean you up. Then we're going to take a drive."

"Where?"

Gabriel stared at Estermann blankly.

"There's no way you'll get past the guards at the checkpoint."

"I won't have to. You'll do it for me."

"It won't work."

"For your sake, it better. But before we leave, I'd like you to answer one more question." Gabriel placed Estermann's phone on the table. "Why did you go to Bonn after you spoke to Stefani Hoffmann? And why did you switch off your phone for two hours and fifty-seven minutes?"

"I didn't go to Bonn."

"Your phone says you did." Gabriel tapped the screen. "It says you left Café du Gothard at two thirty-four p.m. and that you reached the outskirts of Bonn around seven fifteen, which is rather good time, I must say. At that point, you switched off your phone. I want to know why."

"I told you, I didn't go to Bonn."

"Where did you go?"

The German hesitated. "I was in Grosshau. It's a little farming village a few miles to the west."

"What's in Grosshau?"

"A cottage in the woods."

"Who lives there?"

"A man named Hamid Fawzi."

"Who is he?"

"He's a creation of my cyber unit."

"Is he the reason bombs are going off in Germany?"

"No," said Estermann. "I am."

43

COLOGNE, GERMANY

GERHARDT SCHMIDT WAS NOT KNOWN for working long hours. Typically, he arrived at BfV headquarters in Cologne with a minute or two to spare before the ten a.m. senior staff meeting, and barring some emergency he was in the backseat of his official limousine no later than five. Most nights he stopped at one of the city's better watering holes for a drink. But only one. Everything in moderation, that was Schmidt's personal maxim. It would be chiseled on his tombstone.

The bombings in Berlin and Hamburg had proven detrimental to Schmidt's salubrious daily schedule. That morning he was at his desk at the ungodly hour of eight o'clock, a time when ordinarily he would still be in bed with coffee and the papers. Consequently, when his secure phone pulsed with an incoming call from Tel Aviv at eight fifteen, he was there to answer it.

He had been expecting to hear the voice of Gabriel Allon, the legendary director-general of the Israeli secret intelligence service. Instead, it was Uzi Navot, Allon's deputy, who bade Schmidt a pleasant morning in perfect German. Schmidt had a grudging respect for Allon, but Navot he loathed. For many years the Israeli had worked undercover in Europe, running networks and recruiting agents, including three who worked for the BfV.

Within a few seconds, however, Schmidt was deeply remorseful he had ever uttered an unkind word—indeed, that he had ever entertained a slanderous thought—about the man at the other end of the secure line. It seemed the Israelis, as was often the case, had tapped into a vein of magic intelligence, this time regarding the new cell wreaking havoc in Germany. Navot was predictably evasive about how he had acquired this intelligence. It was a mosaic, he claimed, a blend of human sources and electronic intercepts. Lives were at stake. The clock was ticking.

Whatever the source of the information, it was highly specific. It concerned a property in Grosshau, a tiny farming hamlet located on the edge of the dense German forest known as the Hürtgenwald. The property was owned by something called OSH Holdings, a Hamburg-based concern. There were two structures, a traditional German farmhouse and an outbuilding fashioned of corrugated metal. The farmhouse was largely unfurnished. In the outbuilding, however, was a ten-year-old Mitsubishi light-duty cargo truck loaded with two dozen drums of ammonium nitrate fertilizer, nitromethane, and Tovex, the makings of an ANNM bomb.

The truck was registered to a Hamid Fawzi, a refugee, originally from Damascus, who had settled in Frankfurt after Syria erupted into civil war. Or so claimed his social media pages, which were updated frequently. An engineer by training, Fawzi worked as an IT specialist for a German consulting firm, which was also owned by OSH Holdings. His wife, Asma, wore a full-face veil whenever she left their apartment. They had two children, a daughter named Salma and a boy named Mohammad.

According to Navot's intelligence, a single operative was scheduled to arrive at the property that morning at ten o'clock. He could not say whether it would be Hamid Fawzi. He was quite certain, however, about the target: the immensely popular Cologne Christmas market now under way at the historic cathedral.

Gerhardt Schmidt had a long list of questions he wanted to ask Navot, but there wasn't time for anything more than an expression of profound gratitude. After hanging up, he immediately rang the interior minister, who in turn rang the chancellor, along with Schmidt's counterpart at the Bundespolizei. The first officers arrived at the farmhouse at eight thirty. A few minutes after nine, they were joined by four teams from GSG 9, Germany's elite tactical and counterterrorism unit.

The officers made no attempt to enter the outbuilding, which was sealed with a heavy-duty lock. Instead, they concealed themselves in the surrounding woods and waited. At ten a.m. sharp, a Volkswagen Passat estate car came bumping up the property's rutted drive. The man behind the wheel wore dark glasses and a woolen watch cap. His hands were gloved.

He parked the Volkswagen outside the farmhouse and walked over to the outbuilding. The GSG 9 officers waited until he had opened the lock before emerging from the cover of the trees. Startled, the man reached inside his coat, apparently for a weapon, but wisely stopped when he saw the size of the force arrayed against him. This came as something of a surprise to the GSG 9 officers. They had been trained to expect jihadist terrorists to fight to the death.

The officers were surprised a second time when, after handcuffing the man, they removed his dark glasses and woolen cap. Blond and blue-eyed, he looked as though he had stepped off a Nazi propaganda poster. A rapid search found him to be in possession of a Glock 9mm pistol, three mobile phones, several thousand euros in cash, and an Austrian passport issued in the name Klaus Jäger. The Bundespolizei immediately contacted their brethren in Vienna, who knew Jäger well. He was a former Austrian police officer who had been relieved of duty for consorting with known neo-Nazis.

It was at this point, at half past ten, that the story broke on the website of *Die Welt*, Germany's most respected newspaper. Based on an anonymous source, it stated that the Bundespolizei, acting on intelligence developed by BfV chief Gerhardt Schmidt, had arrested one of the men responsible for the bombings in Berlin and Hamburg. He was not a member of the Islamic State, as previously suspected, but a known neo-Nazi with ties to Axel Brünner and the far-right National Democratic Party. The attacks, reported *Die Welt*, were part of a cynical plot to drive up Brünner's support before the general election.

Within minutes, Germany was thrown into political turmoil. Gerhardt Schmidt, however, was suddenly the most popular man in the country. After hanging up with the chancellor, he rang Uzi Navot in Tel Aviv.

"Mazel tov, Gerhardt. I just saw the news."

"I don't know how I'll ever repay you."

"I'm sure you'll think of something."

"There's only one problem," said Schmidt. "I need to know the name of your source."

"I'll never tell. But if I were you, I'd take a hard look at OSH Holdings. I suspect it will lead you to an interesting place."

"Where?"

"I wouldn't want to spoil the surprise."

"Did you and Allon know that Brünner and the far right were behind the bombings?"

"The far right?" Navot sounded incredulous. "Who could imagine such a thing?"

44

BAVARIA, GERMANY

THE SOURCE OF UZI NAVOT's remarkably accurate intelligence left Munich at 10:15 a.m. in the trunk of an Audi sedan. He remained there, bound and gagged, until the car reached the Bavarian village of Irschenberg, where he was placed in the backseat next to Gabriel. Together they listened to the breaking news on ARD as the car began the ascent toward the Obersalzberg.

"Something tells me the Brünner boomlet just ended." Gabriel looked down at Estermann's phone, which was vibrating. "Speak of the devil. That's the third time he's called."

"He probably thinks I'm behind the story you planted in *Die Welt*."

"Why would he think that?"

"The bombing operation was highly compartmentalized. I

was one of four people who knew the attacks were part of the Order's efforts to help him win the general election."

"Talk about fake news," remarked Gabriel.

"You're the one who engineered that story in *Die Welt*."

"But everything I told them was true."

In the front passenger seat, Eli Lavon laughed quietly before lighting a cigarette. Mikhail, who spoke only limited German, concentrated on his driving.

"I really wish your associate would put out that cigarette," protested Estermann. "And must the other one tap his fingers like that? It's very annoying."

"Would you rather he tap on you instead?"

"He did quite enough of that last night." Estermann worked his jaw from side to side. "Wolf is probably wondering why he hasn't heard from me."

"He will in an hour or so. Something tells me he'll be relieved to see you."

"I wouldn't be so sure about that."

"How many guards will be at the checkpoint?"

"I told you that already."

"Yes, I know. But tell me again."

"Two," said Estermann. "Both will be armed."

"Remind me what happens when someone arrives."

"The guards call Karl Weber, the chief of security. If the guests are expected, Weber allows the car to proceed. If they're not on the list, he checks in with Wolf. During the day, he's usually in his study. It's on the second floor of the chalet. The gospel is in the safe."

"What's the combination?"

"Eighty-seven, ninety-four, ninety-eight."

"Not exactly hard to remember, is it?"

"Wolf requested it."

"Sentimental reasons?"

"I wouldn't know. Herr Wolf is rather guarded when it comes to his personal life." Estermann pointed toward the Alps. "Beautiful, aren't they? There are no mountains like that in Israel."

"That's true," admitted Gabriel. "But there are no people like you, either."

These days, it is common practice for politicians of every ideological stripe to line their pockets by writing—or hiring someone to write—a book. Some are memoirs, others are clarion calls for action on issues near and dear to the politician's heart. Those copies that are not sold in bulk to supporters generally gather dust in warehouses or in the living rooms of journalists who are sent free copies by the publisher with the hope they might murmur something favorable on cable television or social media. The only winner in this charade is the politician, who typically pockets a large advance. He assures himself he deserves this money because of the enormous personal and financial sacrifice he has made by serving in government.

In the case of Adolf Hitler, the book that made him wealthy was written a decade before his rise to power. He used a portion of the royalties to purchase Haus Wachenfeld, a modest holiday chalet in the mountains above Berchtesgaden. He commissioned an ambitious renovation of the dwelling in 1935, based on a rough sketch he made on a board borrowed from Albert Speer, his minister of armaments and war production. The result was the Berghof, a residence Speer described as "most impractical for the reception of official visitors."

As Hitler's power and paranoia increased, so did the Nazi footprint in the Obersalzberg. Perched atop the summit of the Kehlstein was the Eagle's Nest, a chalet used by senior party officials for meetings and social occasions; and within walking distance of the Berghof was the lavish teahouse where Hitler whiled away afternoons with Eva Braun and Blondi, his beloved Alsatian. Several hundred RAF Lancaster bombers attacked the complex on April 25, 1945, inflicting heavy damage on the Berghof. The German government razed the teahouse in the 1950s, but the Eagle's Nest remains a popular tourist attraction to this day, as does the village of Berchtesgaden.

Andreas Estermann watched the snow falling on the tidy cobblestone streets. "It's the first storm of the season."

"Climate change," replied Gabriel.

"You don't really believe that nonsense, do you? It's a weather pattern, that's all."

"Perhaps you should read something other than *Der Stürmer* now and again."

Frowning, Estermann pointed out the postcard-perfect shops and cafés. "I think this is worth defending, don't you? Can you imagine what this town would look like with a minaret?"

"Or a synagogue?"

Estermann was impervious to Gabriel's irony. "There are no Jews down here in the Obersalzberg, Allon."

"Not anymore."

Gabriel glanced over his shoulder. Directly behind them was the second Audi sedan. Yaakov was driving, Yossi and Oded were in the back. Dina and Natalie were following in the Mercedes van. Gabriel dialed Natalie's number and told her to wait in the village.

"Why can't we come with you?"

"Because things might get ugly."

"Heaven knows we've never been in an ugly situation before."

"You can file a complaint with Personnel first thing tomorrow morning."

Gabriel killed the connection and instructed Mikhail to make a left turn at the end of the street. They sped along the banks of a granite-colored river, past small hotels and holiday cottages.

"We're less than three kilometers away," said Estermann.

"You *do* remember what will happen if you try to warn him?"

"You'll drop me down a deep hole."

Gabriel returned Estermann's phone. "Place the call in speaker mode."

Estermann dialed. The phone rang unanswered. "He's not picking up."

"I have a suggestion."

"What's that?"

"Call him again."

45

OBERSALZBERG, BAVARIA

JONAS WOLF WAS NOT A regular watcher of television. He regarded it as the true opiate of the masses and the source of the West's drift into hedonism, secularism, and moral relativism. On that morning, however, he had switched on the news in his comfortable study at eleven fifteen, expecting to see the first reports of a major terrorist attack at Cologne's historic cathedral. Instead, he had learned that a truck bomb had been discovered at a remote compound in western Germany and that a former Austrian police officer with known ties to the extreme right had been taken into custody. *Die Welt* had linked the man to the bombings in Berlin and Hamburg and, more ominously, to Axel Brünner and the National Democratic Party. The attacks were purportedly part of a ruthless operation by Brünner and the far right to inflame the German electorate on the eve of the general elections.

For now, at least, Wolf's name had not been mentioned in the coverage of the unfolding scandal. He doubted he would escape scrutiny for long. But how had the Bundespolizei learned of the compound in Grosshau in the first place? And how had the reporter at *Die Welt* tied the bombings to Brünner's campaign so quickly? Wolf had but one suspect.

Gabriel Allon . . .

It was for that reason Wolf did not answer the first call he received from Andreas Estermann's iPhone. Now was not the time, he thought, to be talking to an accomplice who was calling from a cellular device. But when Estermann rang a second time, Wolf lifted the receiver hesitantly to his ear.

Estermann's voice sounded an octave higher than normal. It was the voice, thought Wolf, of a man under obvious duress. It seemed a member of the Order who still worked for the BfV had warned Estermann that he and Wolf were about to be arrested in connection with the bombings. Estermann was approaching the estate with several of his men. He wanted Wolf to be downstairs when he arrived. He had already instructed Platinum Flight Services, the fixed-base operator at Salzburg Airport, to prepare one of the Gulfstreams for departure. A flight plan had been filed for Moscow. They would be airborne in less than an hour. Wolf was to bring his passport and as much cash as he could fit in a single briefcase.

"And the gospel, Herr Wolf. Whatever you do, don't leave it behind."

The connection went dead. Wolf replaced the receiver and

raised the volume of the television. A pack of reporters had cornered Brünner outside NDP headquarters in Berlin. His denials of involvement in the bombings had all the credibility of a murderer pleading his innocence while clutching a bloody knife in his hand.

Wolf muted the volume. Then he reached for the phone and rang Otto Kessler, the general manager of Platinum Flight Support. After an exchange of pleasantries, Wolf asked if his plane was ready for departure.

"Which plane, Herr Wolf?"

"A man from my company was supposed to have called you."

Kessler assured Wolf that no one had contacted him. "You won't have a problem getting a departure slot, though. There's only one other private aircraft leaving this afternoon."

"And who might that be?" asked Wolf indifferently.

"Martin Landesmann."

"*The* Martin Landesmann?"

"It's his plane, but I'm not sure he'll be on board. It was empty when it arrived."

"Where is it going?"

"Tel Aviv, with a brief stop in Rome."

Gabriel Allon . . .

"And what time is Landesmann scheduled to depart?" asked Wolf.

"Two o'clock, weather permitting. The snow is forecast to worsen later this afternoon. We've been told to expect a complete ground stop sometime around four."

Wolf rang off and immediately dialed Bishop Richter at the Order's palazzo on the Janiculum Hill in Rome. "I trust you've seen the news, Excellency."

"A troubling development," replied Richter with his typical understatement.

"I'm afraid it's about to get worse."

"How much worse?"

"Germany is lost. At least for now. But the papacy is still within our reach. You must do everything in your power to keep our friend from the Society of Jesus away from the cardinals."

"He has two million reasons to keep his mouth shut."

"Two million and one," said Wolf.

He hung up the phone and contemplated the river landscape hanging on the wall of his study. Painted by the Dutch Old Master Jan van Goyen, it had once belonged to a wealthy Viennese Jewish businessman named Samuel Feldman. Feldman had given it to Father Schiller, the founder of the Order, in exchange for a set of false baptismal certificates for himself and his family. Regrettably, the baptismal certificates had not arrived in time to prevent the deportation of Feldman and his kin to the Lublin district of German-occupied Poland, where they were murdered.

Concealed behind the landscape was Wolf's safe. He worked the tumbler—*87, 94, 98*—and opened the heavy stainless-steel door. Inside was two million euros in cash, fifty gold ingots, a seventy-year-old Luger pistol, and the last remaining copy of the Gospel of Pilate.

Wolf removed only the gospel. He laid the book on his desk and opened it to the Roman prefect's account of the arrest and execution of a Galilean troublemaker called Jesus of Nazareth. Ignoring the advice of Bishop Richter, Wolf had read the passage the night Father Graf brought the book from Rome. Much to his shame, he had read it many times since. Fortunately, his would be the last eyes to ever see it.

He carried the book to the window of his study. It overlooked the front of the chalet and the long road running the length of his private valley. In the distance, faintly visible through the falling snow, was the Untersberg, the mountain where Frederick Barbarossa had awaited his legendary call to rise and restore the glory of Germany. Wolf had heard the same call. The fatherland was lost. *At least for now* . . . But perhaps there was still a chance to save his Church.

The snow is forecast to worsen later this afternoon. We've been told to expect a complete ground stop sometime around four . . .

Wolf checked the time. Then he dialed Karl Weber, his security chief. As always, Weber answered on the first ring.

"Yes, Herr Wolf?"

"Andreas Estermann will be arriving any minute. He's expecting me to meet him outside in the drive, but I'm afraid there's been a change in plan."

MIKHAIL TURNED ONTO WOLF'S PRIVATE road and climbed steadily through a dense forest of spruce and birch. After a moment the trees broke and a valley opened before them, ringed on three sides by towering mountains. Clouds draped the highest peaks.

Estermann gave an involuntary start when Gabriel drew his Beretta.

"Don't worry, I'm not going to shoot you. Unless, of course, you give me the flimsiest of excuses."

"The guardhouse is on the left side of the road."

"Your point?"

"I'm seated on the passenger side. If there's an exchange of gunfire, I might be caught in the crossfire."

"Thus increasing my chances of survival."

Behind them, Yaakov flashed his headlamps.

"What's his problem?" asked Mikhail.

"I imagine he'd like to overtake us before we reach the checkpoint."

"What do you want me to do, boss?"

"Can you shoot and drive at the same time?"

"Is the pope Catholic?"

"There is no pope right now, Mikhail. That's why we're about to have a conclave."

The guardhouse appeared before them, veiled by snowfall. Two security men in black ski jackets stood in the middle of the road, each holding an HK MP5 submachine pistol. They didn't appear concerned by the two cars approaching at high speed. Nor did they give any indication that they were planning to move out of the way.

"Shall I run them over?" asked Mikhail.

"Why not?"

Mikhail lowered the two windows on the passenger side of the car and put his foot to the floor. The two security men retreated to the shelter of the guardhouse. One waved cordially as the cars passed.

"It looks as though your ruse worked, Allon. They're supposed to stop every car."

Mikhail raised the windows. To their left, across a snow-covered meadow, an Airbus executive helicopter stood on its pad with the sadness of an abandoned toy. Wolf's chalet appeared a moment later. A single figure stood in the drive. His black ski jacket was identical to the ones worn by the men at the checkpoint. His hands were empty.

"That's Weber," said Estermann. "He's got a nine-millimeter under his jacket."

"Is he right-handed or left?"

"What difference does it make?"

"It might determine whether he's still alive thirty seconds from now."

Estermann frowned. "I believe he's right-handed."

Mikhail braked to a halt and climbed out with the Uzi Pro in his hand. Behind them, Yaakov and Oded, both armed with Jericho pistols, leapt from the second car.

Gabriel waited until Weber had been relieved of his weapon before joining them. Calmly, he approached the German security man and addressed him in the Berlin accent of his mother.

"Herr Wolf was supposed to be waiting for us. It is urgent we leave for the airport at once."

"Herr Wolf asked me to show you inside."

"Where is he?"

"Upstairs," said Weber. "In the great hall."

46

OBERSALZBERG, BAVARIA

THE STAIRCASE WAS WIDE AND straight and covered by a bright red carpet. Weber led the way, hands in the air, Mikhail's Uzi Pro pointed at the small of his back. Gabriel was flanked by Eli Lavon and Estermann. The German appeared decidedly uneasy.

"Something bothering you, Estermann?"

"You'll see in a minute."

"Maybe you should tell me now. I'm not crazy about surprises."

"Herr Wolf usually doesn't entertain visitors in the great hall."

At the top of the stairs, Weber turned to the left and led them into an anteroom. He stopped outside a pair of ornate double doors. "This is as far as I'm allowed to go. Herr Wolf is waiting inside."

"Who else is in there?" asked Gabriel.

"Only Herr Wolf."

Gabriel leveled the Beretta at Weber's head. "You're sure about that?"

Weber nodded.

Gabriel aimed the Beretta toward one of the armchairs. "Have a seat."

"It's not permitted."

"It is now."

Weber sat down. Oded lowered himself into the chair opposite, the Jericho .45 on his knee.

Gabriel looked at Estermann. "What are you waiting for?"

Estermann opened the double doors and led them inside.

IT WAS A CAVERNOUS SPACE, about sixty feet by fifty. One wall was given over almost entirely to a panoramic window. The other three were hung with Gobelin tapestries and what appeared to be Old Master paintings. There was a monumental classicist china closet, an enormous clock crowned by an eagle, and a bust of Wagner that appeared to be the work of Arno Becker, the German architect and sculptor beloved by Hitler and the Nazi elite.

There were two seating areas, one near the window and another in front of the fireplace. Gabriel crossed the room and joined Jonas Wolf before the hearth. The heat of the fire was volcanic. Atop the embers lay a book. Only the leather cover remained.

"I suppose burning books comes naturally to someone like you."

Wolf was silent.

"You're not armed, are you, Wolf?"

"A pistol."

"Would you get it for me, please?"

Wolf reached beneath his cashmere blazer.

"Slowly," cautioned Gabriel.

Wolf produced the weapon. It was an old Luger.

"Do me a favor and toss it onto that chair over there."

Wolf did as he was told.

Gabriel looked at the blackened remains of the book. "Is that the Gospel of Pilate?"

"No, Allon. It *was* the gospel."

Gabriel placed the barrel of the Beretta against the nape of Wolf's neck. Somehow he managed not to pull the trigger. "Do you mind if I have a look at it?"

"Be my guest."

"Would you get it for me, please?"

Wolf made no movement.

Gabriel twisted the barrel of the Beretta. "Don't make me ask twice."

Wolf reached for the fireplace tools.

"No," said Gabriel.

Crouching, Wolf stretched a hand into the inferno. A foot to the backside was enough to send him headlong into the flames. By the time he managed to extricate himself, his mane of silver hair was a memory.

Gabriel feigned indifference to his cries of pain. "What did it say, Wolf?"

"I never read it," he gasped.

"I find that difficult to believe."

"It was heresy!"

"How did you know if you didn't read it?"

Gabriel walked over to one of the paintings, a reclining nude in the manner of Titian. Next to it was another nude, this one by Bordone, one of Titian's pupils. There was also a landscape by Spitzweg and Roman ruins by Panini. None of the paintings, however, was genuine. They were all twentieth-century copies.

"Who did your work for you?"

"A German art restorer named Gunther Haas."

"He's a hack."

"He charged me a small fortune."

"Did he know where these paintings hung during the war?"

"We never discussed it."

"I doubt Gunther would have cared much. He was always a bit of a Nazi."

Gabriel looked at Eli Lavon, who seemed to be locked in a staring contest with the Wagner bust. After a moment he placed a hand on the large wooden cabinet upon which it stood. "This is where the speakers for the projection system were hidden." He pointed toward the wall above. "And the screen was behind that tapestry. He could raise it when he wanted to show a film to his guests."

Gabriel sidestepped a long rectangular table and stood before the massive window. "And this could be lowered, right, Eli? Unfortunately, when he drew up the plans for the Berghof, he put the garage directly beneath the great room. When the wind was right, the stench of petrol was unbearable." Gabriel glanced over his shoulder at Wolf. "I'm sure you didn't make the same mistake."

"I have a separate garage," boasted Wolf.

"Where's the button for the window?"

"On the wall to the right."

Gabriel flipped the switch and the glass glided soundlessly into its pocket. Snow blew into the room. It was coming down harder now. He watched a plane rising slowly into the sky above Salzburg, then cast a discreet glance at his wristwatch.

"You should probably be on your way, Allon. That Gulfstream you borrowed from Martin Landesmann is scheduled to leave for Rome at two." Wolf conjured an arrogant smile. "It's a forty-minute drive to the airport at least."

"Actually, I was thinking about staying long enough to watch the Bundespolizei put you in handcuffs. The German far right will never recover from this, Wolf. It's over."

"That's what they said about us after the war. But now we're everywhere. The police, the intelligence and security services, the courts."

"But not the Reich Chancellery. And not the Apostolic Palace."

"I own that conclave."

"Not anymore." Gabriel turned away from the open window and surveyed the room. It was beginning to make him feel ill. "This must have taken a great deal of work."

"The furnishings were the most difficult part. Everything had to be custom-made based on old photographs. The room is exactly the way it was, with the exception of that table. There was usually a vase of flowers in the center. I use it to display cherished photographs."

They were framed in silver and precisely arranged. Wolf with his beautiful wife. Wolf with his two sons. Wolf at the tiller of a sailboat. Wolf cutting the ceremonial ribbon at a new factory. Wolf kissing the ring of Bishop Hans Richter, superior general of the poisonous Order of St. Helena.

One photograph was larger than the others, and its frame was more ornate. It was a photograph of Adolf Hitler sitting at the original table with a child, a boy of two or three, balanced on his knee. The retractable window was open. Hitler looked drawn and gray. The boy looked frightened. Only the man wearing the uniform of a senior SS officer appeared pleased. Smiling, he was standing with his arms akimbo and his head thrown back with obvious delight.

"I assume you recognize the Führer," said Wolf.

"I recognize the SS officer, too." Gabriel contemplated Wolf for a moment. "The resemblance is quite striking."

Gabriel returned the photograph to the table. Another plane was clawing its way skyward above Salzburg. He checked his wristwatch. It was approaching one o'clock. Time enough, he reckoned, for one last story.

47

OBERSALZBERG, BAVARIA

Eli Lavon recognized Wolf's father. He was Rudolf Fromm, a desk-murderer from Department IVB4 of the Reich Main Security Office, the division of the SS that carried out the Final Solution. Fromm was an Austrian by birth and a Roman Catholic by religion, as was his wife, Ingrid. They were both from Linz, the town along the Danube where Hitler was born. Wolf was their only child. His real name was Peter— Peter Wolfgang Fromm. The photograph was taken in 1945 during Hitler's last visit to the Berghof. Wolf's mother had been chatting off camera with Eva Braun when it was snapped. Exhausted, his hand trembling uncontrollably, Hitler had refused to pose for another.

A month after the visit, with the Red Army closing in on Berlin, Rudolf Fromm stripped off his SS uniform and went into hiding. He managed to evade capture and in 1948, with the help of a priest from the Order of St. Helena, made his way to Rome. There he acquired a Red Cross identification card and passage on a ship bound from Genoa to Buenos Aires. Fromm's son remained in Berlin with his mother until 1950, when she hanged herself in their squalid single-room apartment. Alone in the world, he was taken in by the same priest from the Order who had helped his father.

He entered the Order's seminary in Bergen and studied for the priesthood. At eighteen, however, he was visited by Father Schiller, who told him that God had other plans for the brilliant, handsome son of a Nazi war criminal. He left the seminary with a new name and entered Heidelberg University, where he studied mathematics. Father Schiller gave him the money to buy his first company in 1964, and within a few years he was one of the richest men in Germany, the very embodiment of the country's postwar economic miracle.

"How much money did Father Schiller give you?"

"I believe it was five million deutsche marks." Wolf hauled himself into one of the chairs next to the fire. "Or perhaps it was ten. To be honest, I can't remember. It was a long time ago."

"Did he tell you where the money came from? That the Order had extorted it from terrified Jews like Samuel Feldman in Vienna and Emanuele Giordano in Rome?" Gabriel was silent for a moment. "Now is the part when you tell me you've never heard of them."

"Why bother?"

"I suppose some of their money was used to help men like your father escape."

"Rather ironic, don't you think?" Wolf smiled. "My father

handled the Feldman case personally. One member of the family slipped through his net. A daughter, I believe. Many years after the war, she told her sad story to a private Jewish investigator in Vienna. His name escapes me."

"I believe it was Eli Lavon."

"Yes, that's it. He tried to extort money from Bishop Richter." Wolf laughed bitterly. "A fool's errand, if there ever was one. He got what he deserved, too."

"I take it you're referring to the bomb that destroyed his office in Vienna."

Wolf nodded. "Two members of his staff were killed. Both Jews, of course."

Gabriel looked at his old friend. He had never once seen him commit an act of violence. But he was certain that Eli Lavon, if handed a loaded gun, would have used it to kill Jonas Wolf.

The German was inspecting the burns on his right hand. "He was quite the tenacious character, this man Lavon. The stereotypical stiff-necked Jew. He spent several years trying to track down my father. He never found him, of course. He lived quite comfortably in Bariloche. I visited him every two or three years. Because our names were different, no one ever suspected we were related. He became quite devout in his old age. He was very contented."

"He had no regrets?"

"For what?" Wolf shook his head. "My father was proud of what he did."

"I suppose you were proud, too."

"Very," admitted Wolf.

Gabriel felt as though a knife had been thrust into his heart. He calmed himself before speaking again. "In my experience, most children of Nazi war criminals don't share the fanaticism of their fathers. Oh, they have no love for the Jews, but they don't dream of finishing the job their parents started."

"You obviously need to get out more, Allon. The dream is alive and well. It's not just some empty chant at a pro-Palestinian rally any longer. You have to be blind not to see where all this is leading."

"I see quite well, Wolf."

"But not even the great Gabriel Allon can stop it. There isn't a country in Western Europe where it's safe to be a Jew. You've also worn out your welcome in the United States, the other Jewish homeland. The white nationalists in America oppose immigration and the dilution of their political power, but the real focus of their hatred is the Jews. Just ask the fellow who shot up that synagogue in Pennsylvania. Or those fine young men who carried their torches through that college town in Virginia. Who do you think they were emulating, with their haircuts and their Nazi salutes?"

"There's no accounting for taste."

"Your Jewish sense of humor is perhaps your least endearing trait."

"Right now, it's the only thing preventing me from blowing your brains out." Gabriel returned to the seating area before the fire. Almost nothing remained of the book. He took up the poker and stirred the embers. "What did it say, Wolf?"

"Wouldn't you like to know."

Gabriel wheeled around and brought the heavy iron tool down with all his strength against Wolf's left elbow. The cracking of bone was audible.

Wolf writhed in agony. "Bastard!"

"Come on, Wolf. You can do better than that."

"I'm made of much sterner stuff than Estermann. You can beat me to a pulp with that thing, but I'll never tell you what was in that book."

"What are you so afraid of?"

"The Roman Catholic Church cannot be wrong. And it most certainly cannot be deliberately wrong."

"Because if the Church was wrong, your father would have been wrong, too. There would have been no religious justification for his actions. He would have been just another genocidal maniac."

Gabriel allowed the poker to fall from his grasp. He was suddenly exhausted. He wanted nothing more than to leave Germany and never come back again. He would be forced to leave without the Gospel of Pilate. But he resolved that he would not leave empty-handed.

He looked down at Wolf. The German was clutching his ruined elbow. "You might find this hard to believe, but things are about to get much worse for you."

"Is there no way we can reach some sort of accommodation?"

"Only if you give me the Gospel of Pilate."

"I burned it, Allon. It's gone."

"In that case, I suppose there's no deal to be made. You might, however, want to consider doing at least one good deed before they lock you up. Think of it as a mitzvah."

"What do you have in mind?"

"It wouldn't be right for me to suggest something. It has to come from the heart, Wolf."

Wolf closed his eyes in pain. "In my study you will find a rather fine river landscape, about forty by sixty centimeters. It was painted by a minor Dutch Old Master named—"

"Jan van Goyen."

Gabriel and Wolf both turned toward the sound of the voice. It belonged to Eli Lavon.

"How do you know that?" asked Wolf, astonished.

"A few years ago, a woman from Vienna told me a sad story."

"Are you—"

"Yes," said Lavon. "I am."

"Is she still alive?"

"I believe so."

"Then please give her the painting. Behind it you'll find my safe. Take as much cash and gold as you can carry. The combination is—"

Gabriel supplied it for him. "Eighty-seven, ninety-four, ninety-eight."

Wolf glared at Estermann. "Is there anything you *didn't* tell him?"

It was Gabriel who answered. "He didn't know why you chose such a peculiar combination. The only explanation is that it was your father's SS number. Eight, seven, nine, four, nine, eight. He must have joined in 1932, a few months before Hitler seized power."

"My father knew which way the wind was blowing."

"You must have been very proud of him."

"Perhaps you should be leaving, Allon." Wolf managed a hideous smile. "They say the storm is going to get much worse."

GABRIEL REMOVED THE PAINTING FROM its stretcher while Eli Lavon packed the bundles of banknotes and the gleaming gold ingots into one of Wolf's costly titanium suitcases. When the safe was cleaned out, he placed the Luger inside, along with the HK 9mm they had taken from Karl Weber.

"Too bad we can't squeeze Wolf and Estermann in there as well." Lavon closed the door and spun the tumbler. "What are we going to do with them?"

"I suppose we could take them to Israel."

"I'd rather walk to Israel than fly there with the likes of Jonas Wolf."

"I thought for a minute you were going to kill him."

"Me?" Lavon shook his head. "I've never been one for the rough stuff. But I did enjoy watching you hit him with that poker."

Gabriel's phone pulsed. It was Uzi Navot calling from King Saul Boulevard. "Are you planning to stay for dinner?" he asked.

Gabriel laughed in spite of himself. "Can this wait? We're a bit busy at the moment."

"I thought you should know that I just got a call from my new best friend, Gerhardt Schmidt. The Bundespolizei are on their way to arrest Wolf. You might want to vacate the premises before they arrive."

Gabriel killed the connection. "Time to go."

Lavon closed the lid of the suitcase and with Gabriel's help tipped it onto its wheels. "It's a good thing we're flying on a private plane. This thing must weigh seventy kilos at least."

Together they wheeled the suitcase into the next room. Estermann and Karl Weber were tending to Wolf's injuries, watched over by Mikhail and Oded. Yossi was inspecting one of the Gobelin tapestries. Yaakov was standing in front of the open window, listening to the distant wail of sirens.

"They're definitely getting louder," he said.

"That's because they're on their way here." Gabriel beckoned to Mikhail and Oded and started toward the door.

Wolf called out to him from across the room. "Who do you think it will be?"

Gabriel stopped. "What's that, Wolf?"

"The conclave. Who's going to be the next pope?"

"They say Navarro is already ordering new furniture for the *appartamento*."

"Yes," said Wolf, smiling. "That's what they say."

PART THREE

EXTRA OMNES

48

JESUIT CURIA, ROME

LUIGI DONATI WAS A MAN of many virtues and admirable traits, but patience was not one of them. He was by nature a pacer and a twirler of pens who did not suffer fools or even minor delays gladly. Rome tested him daily. So had life behind the walls of the Vatican, where nearly every encounter with the backbiting bureaucrats of the Curia had driven him to utter distraction. All conversations within the Apostolic Palace were coded and cautious and laden with ambition and fear of a misstep that could doom an otherwise promising career. One seldom said what one was really thinking, and one never, *never*, put it in writing. It was far too dangerous. The Curia did not reward boldness or creativity. Inertia was its sacred calling.

But at least Donati had never been bored. And with the exception of the six weeks he had spent in the Gemelli Clinic recovering from a bullet wound, he had never been powerless. At present, however, he was both. When combined with his aforementioned lack of forbearance, it was a lethal combination.

His old friend Gabriel Allon was to blame. In the three days since he had left Rome, Donati had heard from him only once, at 5:20 that morning. "I have everything you need," Gabriel had promised. Unfortunately, he neglected to tell Donati what it was he had discovered. Only that it was a twelve on the Bishop Richter scale—a rather clever pun, Donati had to admit—and that there was an additional complication involving someone close to the previous pope. A complication that could not be discussed over the phone.

For the subsequent eleven hours, Donati had heard not so much as a ping from his old friend. Hence, he had passed a thoroughly unpleasant day behind the walls of the Jesuit Curia. The news from Germany, while shocking, at least provided a distraction. Donati watched it with a few of his colleagues on the television in the common room. The German police had prevented a truck bombing targeting Cologne Cathedral. The purported terrorists were not from the Islamic State but a shadowy neo-Nazi organization with links to the far-right politician Axel Brünner. One member of the cell, an Austrian national, had been arrested, as had Brünner himself. At four thirty Germany's interior minister announced that two other men implicated in the scandal had been found dead at an estate in the Obersalzberg. Both had been killed by the same handgun in what appeared to be a case of murder-suicide. The murder victim was a former German intelligence officer named Andreas Estermann. The suicide was the reclusive billionaire Jonas Wolf.

"Dear God," whispered Donati.

Just then, his Nokia shivered with an incoming call. He tapped ANSWER and raised the device to his ear.

"Sorry," said Gabriel. "The traffic in this town is a nightmare."

"Have you seen the news from Germany?"

"Wonderful, isn't it?"

"Is that what you meant by tying up one or two loose ends?"

"You know what they say about idle hands."

"Please tell me you—"

"I didn't pull the trigger, if that's what you're asking."

Donati sighed. "Where are you?"

"Waiting for you to let me in."

GABRIEL STOOD IN THE ENTRANCE, framed by the doorway. The last three days had been unkind to his appearance. Truth be told, he looked like something the cat had dragged in. Donati led him upstairs to his rooms and chained the door. He checked the time. It was 4:39.

"You mentioned something about a twelve on the Bishop Richter scale. Perhaps you can be a bit more specific."

Gabriel delivered his briefing while peering through the blinds into the street. It was swift but thorough and only lightly redacted. It detailed the Order's plan to erase Islam from Western Europe, the circumstances surrounding the murder of His Holiness Pope Paul VII, and the macabre room in which Jonas Wolf, the son of a Nazi war criminal, burned the last copy of the Gospel of Pilate. Central to the Order's sweeping political ambitions was control of the papacy. Forty-two cardinal-electors had accepted money in exchange for their votes at the conclave. Another eighteen were secret members of the Order who planned to cast their ballots for Bishop Richter's proxy supreme pontiff: Cardinal Franz von Emmerich, the archbishop of Vienna.

"And the best part is that I have it all on video." Gabriel glanced over his shoulder. "Is that specific enough for you?"

"That's only sixty votes. They need seventy-eight to secure the papacy."

"They're counting on momentum to carry Emmerich over the top."

"Do you know the names of all forty-two cardinals?"

"I can list them alphabetically if you like. I also know how much each was paid and where the money was deposited." Gabriel released the blind and turned. "And I'm afraid it only gets worse."

He tapped the touchscreen of his phone. A moment later it emitted the sound of two men speaking German.

He has two million reasons to keep his mouth shut.

Two million and one . . .

He paused the recording.

"Bishop Richter and Jonas Wolf, I presume?"

Gabriel nodded.

"What are the two million reasons why I shouldn't tell the conclave what I know about the Order's plot?"

"It's the amount of money Wolf and Richter put in your account at the Vatican Bank."

"They want to make it appear as though I'm as corrupt as they are?"

"Obviously."

"And the *one*?"

"I'm still working on that."

Donati's eyes flashed with anger. "And to think they wasted two million dollars on such an obvious ploy."

"Perhaps you can put it to good use."

"Don't worry, I will."

Donati dialed Angelo Francona, dean of the College of Cardinals. There was no answer.

He checked the time again. It was 4:45.

"I suppose you should give me the names."

"Azevedo of Tegucigalpa," said Gabriel. "One million. Bank of Panama."

"Next?"

"Ballantine of Philadelphia. One million. Vatican Bank."

"Next?"

AT THAT SAME MOMENT, Cardinal Angelo Francona was standing like a sentinel near the reception desk of the Casa Santa Marta. Resting on the white marble floor at his feet was a large aluminum case filled with several dozen mobile phones, tablets, and notebook computers, all carefully labeled with the owners' names. For security reasons, the switchboard of the clerical guesthouse remained operative, but the phones, televisions, and radios had been removed from its 128 rooms and suites. Francona's *telefonino* was in the pocket of his cassock, silenced but still functioning. He planned to switch it off the instant the last cardinal walked through the door. At that point, the men who would select the next supreme Roman pontiff would effectively be cut off from the outside world.

At present, 112 of the 116 voting-eligible cardinals were safely beneath the Casa Santa Marta's roof. Several were milling about the lobby, including Navarro and Gaubert, the two leading contenders to succeed Lucchesi. At last check, Cardinal Camerlengo Domenico Albanese was upstairs in his suite. A migraine. Or so he claimed.

Francona felt a pre-conclave headache coming on as well. Only once before had he taken part in the election of a pope. It was the conclave that had shocked the Catholic world by choosing a diminutive, little-known patriarch from Venice to succeed Wojtyla the Great. Francona had been among the group of liberals who had tipped the conclave in Lucchesi's favor. Regrettably, Lucchesi's papacy would be remembered for the terrorist attack on the basilica and the sexual abuse scandal that had left the Church on the brink of moral and financial collapse.

Therefore, the conclave that would commence the following afternoon had to be utterly above reproach. Already a cloud was hanging over it. It had been placed there by the murder of that poor Swiss Guard in Florence. There was more to the story, Francona was sure of it. His task now was to preside over a scandal-free conclave, one that would produce a pontiff who could heal the Church's wounds, unite its factions, and lead it into the future. He wanted it over and done with as quickly as possible. Secretly, he feared it was spinning out of control and that anything could happen.

The double glass doors of the guesthouse opened, and Cardinal Franz von Emmerich, the doctrinaire archbishop of Vienna, flowed into the lobby as though propelled by a private conveyor belt. The suitcase he was towing was the size of a steamer trunk.

At the reception desk, he collected a room key from the nuns and then reluctantly surrendered his iPhone to Francona.

"I don't suppose I was lucky enough to be assigned to one of the suites."

"I'm afraid not, Cardinal Emmerich."

"In that case, I hope we reach a decision quickly."

The Austrian made for the elevators. Alone again, Francona checked his phone and was surprised to see he had three missed calls. All were from the same person. There were no messages, which was not his typical style.

Francona hesitated, forefinger floating above the touchscreen. It was unorthodox, but strictly speaking it was not a violation of the rules governing the conduct of the conclave, as laid out in *Universi Dominici Gregis.*

Francona dithered for another precious minute before finally dialing the number and lifting the phone to his ear. A few seconds later he closed his eyes. It was spinning out of control, he thought. Anything could happen. *Anything . . .*

THE CONVERSATION LASTED THREE MINUTES and forty-seven seconds. Donati was selective in what he revealed. Indeed, he focused only on the immediate matter at hand, which was the plot by the reactionary Order of St. Helena to seize the papacy and drag Western Europe into the dark ages of its fascist past.

"Emmerich?" Francona was incredulous. "But you and Lucchesi were the ones who gave him his red hat."

"In retrospect, a mistake."

"How many cardinal-electors are involved?"

Donati answered.

"Dear God! Can you prove any of it?"

"Twelve of the cardinals asked the Order to deposit the money in the Vatican Bank."

"You've been snooping through the accounts, have you?"

"The information was given to me."

"By your Israeli friend?"

"Angelo, please! We haven't time."

Francona sounded suddenly short of breath.

"Are you all right, Eminence?"

"The news comes as quite a shock, that's all."

"I'm sure it does. The question is, what are we going to do about it?"

There was a silence. At last, Francona said, "Give me the names of the cardinals. I'll discuss it with them privately."

"You are a good and decent man, Cardinal Francona." Donati paused. "Too decent for something like this."

"What are you suggesting?"

"Let *me* talk to the cardinals. All of them. At the same time."

"The Casa Santa Marta is closed to everyone but the cardinal-electors and the staff."

"I'm afraid you're going to make an exception. Otherwise, I'll have no choice but to seek a public forum."

"The media? You wouldn't dare."

"Watch me."

Donati could practically hear Francona trying to steel himself. "Give me a few minutes to think it over. I'll call you when I've made my decision."

Which is when the connection went dead, at 4:52 p.m. It was ten minutes past five when Donati's phone finally rang again.

"I've asked the cardinals to come to the chapel before dinner. Be sure to mind your manners. Remember, you're not the private secretary anymore. You'll be a titular archbishop in a roomful of red. They will be under no obligation to listen. In fact, I would expect a rather hostile reception."

"When?"

"I'll meet you in the Piazza Santa Marta at five twenty-five. If you are so much as a minute—"

"Wait!"

"What is it now, Luigi?"

"I no longer have a Vatican pass."

"Then I suppose you'll have to find some other way of getting past the Swiss Guards at the Arch of Bells."

Francona rang off without another word. Donati opened his contacts, scrolled to the letter M, and dialed. "Answer your phone," he whispered. "Answer your damn phone."

49

VILLA GIULIA, ROME

SINCE TAKING CONTROL OF ITALY'S Museo Nazionale Etrusco, Veronica Marchese had labored tirelessly to increase the museum's flagging attendance numbers. In a city such as Rome, it was no easy task. The sweating, backpacked hordes who flocked to the Colosseo and the Fontana di Trevi rarely found their way to the Villa Giulia, the elegant sixteenth-century palazzo on the northern fringes of the Borghese Gardens that housed the world's finest collection of Etruscan art and artifacts, including several notable pieces from the personal collection of the director's late husband. Carlo had posthumously contributed to the museum in other ways. A small portion of his ill-gotten fortune had financed a redesign of the museum's antiquated website. He had also paid for a costly global print advertising campaign and a splashy gala attended by numerous Italian sports and entertainment celebrities. The star of the evening, however, had been Archbishop Luigi Donati, the strikingly handsome papal private secretary and subject of a recent fawning profile in *Vanity Fair* magazine. Veronica had greeted him that night as though he were a stranger, and had pretended not to notice the impossibly pretty young women hanging on his every word.

If only they had seen the version of Luigi Donati who had wandered into an archaeological dig in Umbria one soft afternoon in the spring of 1992—the tall, bearded man in torn jeans, worn-out sandals, and a Georgetown University sweatshirt. He wore it often, the sweatshirt, for he owned little else, save for a collection of tattered paperbacks. They were piled on the bare floor next to the bed they shared in a little villa in the hills near Perugia. For a few glorious months, he was entirely hers. They forged a plan. He would leave the priesthood and become a civilian lawyer, a fighter of lost causes. They would marry, have many children. All that changed when he met Pietro Lucchesi. Heartbroken, Veronica gave herself to Carlo Marchese, and the tragedy was complete.

Carlo's fall from the dome of St. Peter's had allowed Veronica and Luigi to rekindle a small part of their relationship. Secretly, she had hoped that with Lucchesi's passing, she might reclaim the rest. She realized now it had been nothing more than a silly fantasy, one that was entirely unbecoming for a woman of her age and station in life. Fate and circumstances had conspired to keep them apart. They were doomed to dine politely each Thursday evening, like characters in a Victorian novel. They would grow old, but not together. So lonely, she thought. So terribly sad and lonely. But it was the punishment she deserved for losing her heart to a priest. Luigi had sworn a vow long before he wandered into that dig in Monte Cucco. The other woman in his life was the Bride of Christ, the Roman Catholic Church.

They had spoken only once since the night they had dinner with Gabriel Allon and his wife, Chiara. The conversation had taken place that morning, as Veronica was driving to work. Luigi had spoken with his usual curial opacity. Even so, his words had shocked her. Pietro Lucchesi had been murdered in the papal apartments. The reactionary Order of St. Helena was behind it. They were planning to seize control of the Church at the next conclave.

"Were you in Florence when—"

"Yes. And you were right. Janson was involved with Father Graf."

"Maybe next time you'll listen."

"Mea culpa. Mea maxima culpa."

"I don't suppose I'll see you this evening?"

"I'm afraid I have plans."

"Be careful, Archbishop Donati."

"And you as well, Signora Marchese."

As part of her campaign to drive up attendance at the museum, Veronica had extended its hours. The Museo Nazionale Etrusco was now open until eight p.m. But at five o'clock on a cold and dreary Thursday in December, its exhibition rooms were as silent as tombs. The administrative and curatorial staffs had left for the night, as had Veronica's secretary. She had only Maurizio Pollini for company—Schubert's Piano Sonata in C Minor, the sublime second movement. She and Luigi used to listen to it over and over again at the villa near Perugia.

At five fifteen she packed her bag and pulled on her overcoat.

She was meeting a friend for a drink on the Via Veneto. A girl-friend. The only kind of friend she had these days. Afterward, they were having dinner at an out-of-the-way osteria, the kind of place known only to Romans. They served *cacio e pepe* in the bowl in which it was prepared. Veronica intended to eat every delectable strand, then clean the inside of the bowl with a piece of crusty bread. If only Luigi were sitting at the opposite side of the table.

Downstairs, she paused in front of the Euphronios krater. The museum's star attraction, it was widely regarded as one of the most beautiful pieces of art ever created. Gabriel, she remembered, had thought otherwise.

You don't care for Greek vases?

I don't believe I said that.

It was no wonder Luigi liked him so much. They shared the same fatalistic sense of humor.

She bade the security guards a pleasant evening and, declining their offer of an escort, went into the chill evening. Her car was parked a few meters from the entrance in her reserved space, a flashy Mercedes convertible, metallic gray. One day she would manage to convince Luigi to actually get into it. She would drive him against his will to a little villa in the hills near Perugia. They would share a bottle of wine and listen to Schubert. Or perhaps Mendelssohn's Piano Trio no. 1 in D Minor. *The key of repressed passion* . . . It was lying just beneath the surface, dormant but not extinct, the terrible craving. A touch of her hand was all it would take. They would be young again. The same plan, thirty years delayed. Luigi would leave the priesthood, they would marry. But no children. Veronica was far too old, and she didn't want to share him with anyone. There would be a scandal, of course. Her name would be dragged through the mud. They would have no choice but to go into seclusion. A Caribbean island, perhaps. Thanks to Carlo, money was not an issue.

It was unbecoming, Veronica reminded herself as she unlocked the Mercedes with the remote. Still, there was no harm in merely *thinking* about it. Unless, of course, she became so distracted that she failed to notice the man walking toward her car. He was in his mid-thirties, with neat blond hair. Veronica relaxed when she saw the white square of a Roman collar beneath his chin.

"Signora Marchese?"

"Yes?" she replied automatically.

He drew a gun from beneath his coat and smiled beautifully. It was no wonder Niklaus Janson had fallen for him.

"What do you want?" she asked.

"I want you to drop your bag and your keys."

Veronica hesitated, then allowed the key and the bag to fall from her hand.

"Very good." Father Graf's smile vanished. "Now get in the car."

50

ST. PETER'S SQUARE

COLONEL ALOIS METZLER, COMMANDANT OF the Pontifical Swiss Guard, was waiting at the foot of the Egyptian obelisk when Gabriel and Donati arrived in St. Peter's Square. Having sprinted the length of the Borgo Santo Spirito, both were gasping for breath. Metzler, however, looked as though he were posing for his official portrait. He had brought along two plainclothes killers for protection. Having worked with the Swiss Guard on numerous occasions, including during a papal visit to Jerusalem, Gabriel knew that each man was carrying a Sig Sauer 226 9mm pistol. For that matter, so was Metzler.

He directed his hooded gaze toward Gabriel and smiled. "What happened, Father Allon? Did you renounce your vows?" He posed his next question to Donati. "Do you know what happened after you and your friend pulled that stunt at the Archives?"

"I suspect Albanese was a bit miffed."

"He told me that I would be relieved of duty once the conclave was over."

"The camerlengo doesn't have the authority to dismiss the commandant of the Swiss Guard. Only the secretary of state can do that. With the approval of the Holy Father, of course."

"The cardinal implied that he was going to be the next secretary of state. He seemed quite confident, actually."

"And did he tell you who was going to be the next pope as well?" Receiving no answer, Donati pointed toward the Arch of Bells. "Please, Colonel Metzler. Cardinal Francona is waiting for me."

"I'm sorry, Excellency. But I'm afraid I can't let you in."

"Why not?"

"Because Cardinal Albanese warned me that you would try to get into the restricted areas of the city-state tonight. He said heads would roll if you managed to get through. Or words to that effect."

"Ask yourself two questions, Colonel Metzler. How did he know I would be coming? And what is he so afraid of?"

Metzler exhaled heavily. "What time is Cardinal Francona expecting you?"

"Four minutes from now."

"Then you have two minutes to tell me exactly what's going on."

LIKE ALL THE CARDINAL-ELECTORS WHO entered the Casa Santa Marta that evening, Domenico Albanese had surrendered his phone to the dean of the Sacred College. He was not, however, without a mobile device. He had concealed one in his suite earlier that week. It was a cheap disposable model. A burner, he thought wickedly.

He was clutching the phone in his left hand. With his right he was parting the gauzy curtain in the sitting room window. As fortune would have it, it overlooked the small piazza at the front of the guesthouse, where Cardinal Angelo Francona was pacing the paving stones. Clearly, the dean was expecting someone. Someone, thought Albanese, who was no doubt trying to talk his way past the Swiss Guards at the Arch of Bells.

At 5:25 Francona checked his phone and then started toward the entrance of the guesthouse. He stopped suddenly when one of the Swiss Guards pointed toward the three men running across the piazza. One of the men was the sentry's commanding officer, Colonel Alois Metzler. He was accompanied by Gabriel Allon and Archbishop Luigi Donati.

Albanese released the curtain and dialed.

"Well?" asked Bishop Richter.

"He made it through."

The connection went dead. Instantly, two firm knocks shook Albanese's room. Startled, he slipped the phone into his pocket before opening the door. Standing in the corridor was Archbishop Thomas Kerrigan of Boston, the vice dean of the College of Cardinals.

"Is something wrong, Eminence?"

"The dean requests your presence in the chapel."

"For what reason?"

"He has invited Archbishop Donati to address the cardinal-electors."

"Why wasn't I told?"

Kerrigan smiled. "You just were."

DONATI FOLLOWED CARDINAL FRANCONA INTO the lobby. The first face he saw belonged to Kevin Brady of Los Angeles. Brady was a doctrinal soul mate. Still, he appeared stunned by Donati's presence. They exchanged a terse nod, then Donati looked down at the marble floor.

Francona seized his arm. "Excellency! I can't believe you brought that in here."

Donati hadn't realized his phone was ringing. He snatched it from the pocket of his cassock and checked the screen. The name on the caller ID shocked him.

Father Brunetti . . .

It was the pseudonym Donati had assigned to Veronica Marchese in his contacts. Under the rules of their relationship, she was forbidden to phone him. So why on earth was she calling now?

Donati tapped DECLINE.

Instantly, the phone rang again.

Father Brunetti . . .

"Turn it off, will you, Luigi?"

"Of course, Eminence."

Donati placed his thumb on the power button but hesitated.

He has two million reasons to keep his mouth shut.

Two million and one . . .

Donati accepted the call. Calmly, he asked, "What have you done to her?"

"Nothing yet," answered Father Markus Graf. "But if you

don't turn around and walk out of there, I'm going to kill her. Slowly, Excellency. With a great deal of pain."

DOMENICO ALBANESE WATCHED FROM ABOVE as Luigi Donati burst from the entrance of the Casa Santa Marta. His phone was in his hand, its screen aglow with the embers of Father Graf's call. Frantic, he seized Allon by the shoulders, as though begging for help. Then he swiveled around and searched the upper windows of the guesthouse. He knows, thought Albanese. But what would he do? Would he save the woman he once loved? Or would he save the Church?

Fifteen seconds passed. Then Albanese had his answer.

He tapped the screen of the burner phone.

Bishop Richter answered instantly.

"I'm afraid it's over, Excellency."

"We'll see about that."

The call died.

Albanese concealed the phone in the writing desk and went into the corridor. Like Luigi Donati five floors below, he was organizing his thoughts, separating lies from truth. His Holiness bore the weight of the Church on his shoulders, he reminded himself. But in death he was light as a feather.

51

VIA DELLA CONCILIAZIONE

"WHY DIDN'T YOU COME TO me in the beginning?" asked Alois Metzler.

"Would you have agreed to help us?"

"With a private investigation of the Holy Father's death? Not a chance."

Metzler was behind the wheel of an E-Class Mercedes with Vatican plates. He turned onto the Via della Conciliazione and raced toward the river, a rotating red light flashing on the roof.

"For the record," said Gabriel, "I only agreed to find Niklaus Janson."

"Were you the one who deleted his personnel file from our database?"

"No," answered Gabriel. "It was Andreas Estermann who did that."

"Estermann? The former BfV officer?"

"You know him?"

"He tried to convince me to join the Order of St. Helena a few years ago."

"You're not alone. Frankly, I'm disappointed he didn't ask me to join, too. By the way, he went to Canton Fribourg to see Stefani Hoffmann a few days after Niklaus disappeared."

"Was Janson a member of the Order?"

"More like a plaything."

Metzler drove dangerously fast across the Tiber. Gabriel checked his messages. Immediately after leaving the Casa Santa Marta, he had called Yuval Gershon at Unit 8200 and asked him to pinpoint the location of Father Graf's phone. As yet, there had been no reply.

"Where do you want me to go?" asked Metzler.

"The National Etruscan Museum. It's—"

"I know where it is, Allon. I live here, you know."

"I thought you Helvetians hated to leave your tidy little Swiss Quarter in Vatican City."

"We do." Metzler pointed out a pile of uncollected rubbish. "Look at this place, Allon. Rome is a mess."

"But the food is incredible."

"I prefer Swiss food. There's nothing better than a perfect raclette."

"Melted Emmentaler on boiled potatoes? That's your idea of cuisine?"

Metzler made a right turn onto the Viale delle Belle Arti. "Have you ever noticed that every time you come near the Vatican, something goes wrong?"

"I was supposed to be on vacation."

"Do you remember the papal visit to Jerusalem?"

"Like it was yesterday."

"The Holy Father really loved you, Allon. Not many people can say they were loved by a pope."

The Villa Giulia appeared on their right. Metzler turned into the small staff car park. Veronica's briefcase was lying on the paving stones. Her flashy Mercedes convertible was gone.

"He must have been waiting for her when she came out," said Metzler. "The question is, where did he take her?"

Gabriel's phone vibrated with an incoming message. It was from Yuval Gershon. "Not far, actually."

He retrieved Veronica's bag and climbed back into the car.

"Which way?" asked Metzler.

Gabriel pointed to the right. Metzler turned onto the boulevard and put his foot to the floor.

"Is it true what they say about her and Donati?" he asked.

"They're old friends. That's all."

"Priests aren't allowed to have friends who look like Veronica Marchese. They're trouble."

"So is Father Graf."

"Do you really think he'll kill her?"

"No," said Gabriel. "Not if I kill him first."

52

CASA SANTA MARTA

THE CHAPEL OF SANTA MARTA was squeezed into a tiny triangular plot of land between the southern flank of the guesthouse and the Vatican's khaki-colored outer wall. It was bright and modern and rather ordinary, with a polished floor that always reminded Donati of a backgammon board. Never before had he seen it so crowded. Though he could not be certain, it appeared that all 116 of the cardinal-electors were present. Each of the varnished wooden chairs had been claimed, leaving several other princes of the Church, including the cardinal camerlengo, a late arrival, no choice but to huddle like stranded airline passengers at the back.

Dean Francona had taken to the pulpit. From a single sheet of paper he was reading a series of announcements—housekeeping matters, issues related to security, the schedule for the shuttle buses between the Casa and the Sistina. The microphone was switched off. His voice was thin, his hands were shaking. Donati's were shaking, too.

I'm going to kill her. Slowly, Excellency. With a great deal of pain . . .

Was it real or a ruse? Was she still alive or already dead? Had he made the biggest mistake of his life by walking into this den of vipers and leaving her to her fate? Or did he make that mistake a long time ago, when he returned to the Church instead of marrying her? It was not too late, he thought. There was still time to abandon this sinking ship and run away with her. There would be a scandal, of course. His name would be dragged through the mud. They would have no choice but to go into seclusion. A Caribbean island, perhaps. Or a little villa in the hills near Perugia. Schubert's piano sonatas, a few paperbacks scattered on the bare tile floor, Veronica wearing nothing but his old Georgetown sweatshirt. For a few glorious months, she was entirely his.

Francona's voice dragged Donati from the past to the present. As yet, he had failed to explain Donati's presence in the Casa Santa Marta on the eve of the conclave. It was clear, however, that Francona's audience was thinking of nothing else. Forty-two of them had accepted the Order's money in exchange for their votes. It was a crime against a conclave, the sacred passing of the keys of St. Peter from one pope to the next. For now, at least, it was still a crime in progress.

Slowly, Excellency. With a great deal of pain . . .

They were not all hopelessly corrupt, thought Donati. In fact, many were good and decent men of prayer and reflection who were more than capable of leading the Church into the future. Cardinal Navarro, the favorite, would make a fine pope.

So would Gaubert or Duarte, the archbishop of Manila, though Donati was not convinced the Church was ready for an Asian pope.

It was, however, ready for an American. Kevin Brady of Los Angeles was the obvious choice. Youngish and telegenic, he was a fluent Spanish speaker with an Irishman's gift of the gab. He'd made mistakes with a couple of abusive priests, but for the most part he had emerged from the scandal cleaner than most. The worst thing Donati could do was tip his hand. It would be the kiss of death. He intended to bestow that on Cardinal Franz von Emmerich of Vienna.

Francona folded his paper in half, twice, as though it were a conclave ballot. Donati realized he still hadn't decided what he was going to say to these men assembled before him, these high priests of the Church. Admittedly, homilies were not his strong suit. He was a man of action rather than words, a priest of the streets and the barrios, a missionary.

A fighter of lost causes . . .

Francona noisily dislodged something from his throat. "And now a final piece of business. Archbishop Donati has requested permission to address you on a matter of the utmost urgency. After careful consideration, I have agreed—"

It was Domenico Albanese who objected, loudly. "Dean Francona, this is most unusual. As camerlengo, I must protest."

"The decision to let Archbishop Donati speak is entirely mine. Having said that, you are under no obligation to stay. If you intend to leave, please do so now. That goes for all of you."

No one moved, including Albanese. "Does this not constitute outside interference in the conclave, Dean Francona?"

"The conclave does not begin until tomorrow afternoon. As

for the question of interference, you would know better than I, Eminence."

Albanese seethed but said nothing more. Francona stepped away from the pulpit and with a nod invited Donati to take his place. He walked slowly toward the first row of chairs instead and stood directly in front of Cardinal Kevin Brady.

"Good evening, my brothers in Christ."

Not one voice returned his greeting.

53

VILLA BORGHESE

IN THE DARK, LONELY MONTHS after Luigi Donati's return to the priesthood, Veronica Marchese dreamed often of handsome young men dressed entirely in black. Occasionally, they came as lovers, but more often than not they subjected her to all manner of physical and emotional torment. Never once, though, did one lead her through the Borghese Gardens at the point of a gun. Father Markus Graf had exceeded all expectations.

She was in desperate need of a cigarette. Hers were in the handbag she had dropped in the car park of the museum, along with her phone, wallet, laptop computer, and nearly everything else one needed to survive in modern society. It was no matter; she would soon be dead. She supposed there were worse places to die than the Borghese Gardens. She only wished the priest walking next to her was Luigi Donati and not this neo-Nazi in clerical garb from the Order of St. Helena.

He was quite handsome, though. She would grant him that. Most priests from the Order were. She could only imagine how he had looked when he was a boy of thirteen or fourteen. According to the rumors, Bishop Richter used to invite novitiates to his rooms for private instruction. Somehow it had never come out. Even by Church standards, the Order was good at keeping secrets.

She walked on through the darkness. The umbrella pines lining the dusty footpath swayed in the cold evening wind. The gardens closed at sunset. There was not another living soul in sight.

"You wouldn't happen to have a cigarette, would you?"

"They're forbidden."

"And what about having sex with Swiss Guards in the Apostolic Palace? Is that forbidden, too?" Veronica glanced over her shoulder. "You weren't terribly discreet, Father Graf. I told the archbishop about you and Janson, but he didn't believe me."

"He would have been wise to listen to you."

"How did you kill him?"

"I shot him on a bridge in Florence. Three times. One for the Father, one for the Son, and the last for the Holy Spirit. Your boyfriend saw it all. He was with Allon and his wife. She's even more beautiful than you are."

"I was talking about the Holy Father."

"His Holiness died of a heart attack while his private secretary was in bed with his mistress."

"We're not lovers."

"How do you spend your evenings? Reading scripture? Or do you save that until the archbishop has had his fill?"

Veronica could scarcely believe such words had come from the mouth of an ordained priest. She decided to return the favor.

"And how do you spend your evenings, Father Graf? Does he still send for you? Or does he prefer—"

The blow to the back of her head was preceded by no warning and delivered with the butt of the pistol. The pain was otherworldly. It blinded her. With the tip of her finger she probed her scalp. It was warm and wet.

"I guess I touched a nerve."

"Keep talking. It will make it easier for me to kill you."

"If there was a God, he would let loose a plague upon the world that would kill only members of the Order of St. Helena."

"Your husband was one of us. Did you know that?"

"No. But it doesn't surprise me. Carlo always was a bit of a fascist. In retrospect, it was his most endearing trait."

They had arrived in the Piazza di Siena. Built in the late eighteenth century, it was named for the hometown of the Borghese clan. Veronica, on those rare occasions when she was inspired to take exercise, sometimes jogged a lap or two around the dusty oval before coming to her senses and lighting a cigarette. Like most Italians, she did not believe in the health benefits of regular physical exertion. Her daily routine generally consisted of a pleasant stroll to Doney for a cappuccino and a cornetto.

With a prod of the gun barrel, Father Graf directed her into the center of the esplanade. The cypress trees lining the perimeter were silhouettes. The stars were incandescent. Yes, she thought again. There were worse places to die than the Piazza di Siena in the Borghese Gardens. If only it were Luigi. *If only* . . .

Father Graf's phone tolled like an iron bell. The screen illuminated his face as he read the message.

"Have I been granted a reprieve?"

Wordlessly, he slipped the phone into his coat pocket.

Veronica lifted her gaze to the heavens. "I believe I'm having a vision."

"What do you see?"

"A man dressed in white."

"Who is he?"

"The one whom God has chosen to save that Church of yours."

"It's your Church, too."

"Not anymore," she said.

"When was your last confession?"

"Before you were born."

"Then perhaps you should tell me your sins."

"Why?"

"So I can grant you absolution before I kill you."

"I have a better idea, Father Graf."

"What's that?"

"Tell me yours."

54

CASA SANTA MARTA

PIETRO LUCCHESI ONCE GAVE DONATI a valuable piece of advice about public speaking. When in doubt, he said, begin with a quote from Jesus. The passage Donati chose to recite was from the nineteenth chapter of the Gospel of Matthew. *Again I tell you, it is easier for a camel to go through the eye of the needle than for someone who is rich to enter the kingdom of God.* The words were barely out of his mouth when Domenico Albanese once again objected.

"We are all familiar with the Gospels, Excellency. Perhaps you can come to the point."

"I'm wondering what Jesus would be thinking if he were here among us tonight."

"He *is* among us!" It was Tardini of Palermo, seventy-nine years old, a traditionalist relic who had been given his red hat by Wojtyla. He had accepted a million euros from the Order of St. Helena in exchange for his vote at the conclave. The money was in his account at the Vatican Bank. "But tell us, Excellency. What is Jesus thinking?"

"I believe Jesus does not recognize this Church. I believe he is appalled by the opulence of our palaces and the priceless art that hangs upon their walls. I believe he's tempted to turn over a table or two."

"Until recently, you yourself lived in a palace. So did your master."

"We did so because tradition demanded it. But we also lived quite simply." Donati looked at Cardinal Navarro. "Wouldn't you agree, Eminence?"

"I would, Excellency."

"And what about you, Cardinal Gaubert?"

Ever the diplomat, the former secretary of state nodded once but said nothing.

"And you?" Donati asked of Albanese. "How would you characterize the Holy Father's living arrangements in the Apostolic Palace?"

"Modest. Humble, even."

"And you should know. After all, you were the last visitor to the papal apartments the night my master died."

"I was," replied Albanese with appropriate solemnity.

"You were there twice that evening, were you not?"

"Only once, Excellency."

"Are you sure, Albanese?"

A murmur rose and then quickly died.

"It is not something I will ever forget," Albanese replied evenly.

"Because you were the one who found the body." Donati paused. "In the papal study."

"In the chapel."

"Yes, of course. It must have slipped my mind."

"That's understandable, Excellency. You weren't there that night. You were having dinner with an old friend. A woman, if I'm not mistaken. I omitted that from the *bollettino* so as not to embarrass you. Perhaps that was a mistake."

Duarte of Manila was suddenly on his feet, his face stricken. So was Lopes of Rio de Janeiro. Both were simultaneously appealing to Francona in their native languages to put an end to the bloodletting. Francona appeared paralyzed by indecision.

Donati raised his voice to be heard. "Since Cardinal Albanese has mentioned my whereabouts on the night of my master's death, I feel obliged to address the matter. Yes, I was having dinner with a friend. Her name is Veronica Marchese. I met her while I was struggling with my faith and preparing to leave the priesthood. I gave her up when I met Pietro Lucchesi and returned to the Church. We are good friends. Nothing more."

"She is the widow of Carlo Marchese," said Albanese. "And you, Excellency, are a Roman Catholic priest."

"My conscience is clear, Albanese. Is yours?"

Albanese appealed to Francona. "Do you hear the way he speaks to me?"

Francona looked at Donati. "Please continue, Excellency. Your time is running short."

"Thanks be to God," groaned Tardini.

Donati pondered his wristwatch. It was a gift from Veronica, the only object of value he owned. "It has come to my attention," he said after a moment, "that several of you are secret members of the Order of St. Helena." He looked at Cardinal Esteban Velázquez of Buenos Aires and in fluent Spanish asked, "Isn't that correct, Eminence?"

"I wouldn't know," replied Velázquez in the same language.

Donati turned to the archbishop of Mexico City. "What do you think, Montoya? How many secret members of the Order are with us tonight? Is it ten? A dozen?" Donati paused. "Or is it eighteen?"

"All of us, I'd say." It was Albanese again. "With the exception of Cardinal Brady, of course." He basked in a ripple of nervous laughter. "Belonging to the Order of St. Helena is not a sin, Excellency."

"But it would be a sin to accept money in exchange for, say, a vote at a conclave."

"A grievous sin," agreed Albanese. "Therefore, one should be extremely cautious before leveling such a charge. One should also bear in mind that proving such a case would be almost impossible."

"Not when the offense is blatant. As for caution, I don't have time for it. And so in my last remaining moments, I would like to tell you what I've learned, and what I intend to do if my demands are not met."

"Demands?" Tardini was incredulous. "Who are you to make demands? Your master is dead. You are a nothing man."

"I am the man," said Donati, "who holds your future in the palm of his hand. I know how much you received, when you received it, and where it is."

Tardini lumbered to his feet, his face the color of his biretta. "I won't stand for this!"

"Then please sit before you injure yourself. And hear the rest of what I have to say."

Tardini remained standing for a moment before lowering himself unsteadily into his chair with the help of Archbishop Colombo of Naples.

"For centuries," said Donati, "this Church of ours has seen enemies and threats everywhere it looked. Science, secularism, humanism, pluralism, relativism, socialism, Americanism." Donati paused, then added quietly, "The Jews. But the enemy, gentlemen, is much closer at hand. He is in this very room tonight. And he will be in the Sistina tomorrow afternoon when you cast your first ballot. Forty-two of you succumbed to temptation and accepted money from him in exchange for your vote. Twelve of you were so thoroughly corrupt, so brazen, you deposited that money in your accounts at the Vatican Bank." Donati smiled at Tardini. "Isn't that correct, Eminence?"

It was Colombo who blundered to Tardini's defense. "I demand that you withdraw your slanderous accusation at once!"

"I'd watch my step if I were you, Colombo. You accepted money, too, although your payment was considerably less than the one wily old Tardini received."

Albanese was now walking up the center aisle. "And what about you, Archbishop Donati? How much did you receive?"

"Two million euros." Donati waited for the pandemonium to subside before continuing. "In case any of you are wondering, I am not a member of the Order of St. Helena. In fact, the Order and I were on different sides when I was a missionary in the Morazán Province of El Salvador. They sided with the junta and the death squads. I worked with the poor and dispossessed.

Nor am I a voting-eligible cardinal. So the only explanation for the deposit in my account is that it was a pointless attempt to compromise me."

"You compromised yourself," said Albanese, "when you crawled into the bed of that whore!"

"Is that your phone I hear ringing, Albanese? You'd better answer it. I'm sure Bishop Richter is anxious to know what's happening in this chapel."

Albanese thundered a denial, which was drowned out by the tumult in the room. Most of the cardinals were now on their feet. Donati raised a placatory hand, to no effect. He had to shout to be heard.

"And to think how many poor people we could have clothed and fed with that money. Or how many children we might have vaccinated. Or how many schools we might have built. My God, I could have cared for my entire village for a year with that amount of money."

"Then perhaps you should give it away," suggested Albanese.

"Oh, I intend to. All of it." Donati looked at Tardini, who was trembling with rage. "How about you, Eminence? Will you do the same?"

Tardini swore a Sicilian blood threat.

"And you, Colombo? Will you join our pledge drive to help the poor and the sick? I expect you will. In fact, I anticipate a banner year for Catholic charities. That's because all of you are going to surrender the money you received from the Order. Every last penny. Otherwise, I will destroy each of you." His gaze settled coldly on Albanese. "Slowly. With pain."

"I was paid nothing."

"But you were there that night. You were the one who found the Holy Father's body." Donati paused. "In the study."

Cardinal Duarte appeared on the verge of tears. "Archbishop Donati, what are you saying?"

A silence descended over the room. It was like the silence, thought Donati, of the grotto beneath the altar of St. Peter's Basilica, where Pietro Lucchesi's body lay inside three coffins, a small puncture wound in his right thigh.

"What I am saying is that my master was taken from us too soon. There was much more work to be done. He was far from perfect, but he was a good and decent man of prayer and faith, a pastoral man, who did his best to lead the Church through turbulent times. And if you do not choose someone like him when you enter the conclave, someone who will excite Catholics in the first world and the third, someone who will lead the Church into the future rather than drag it into the past . . ." Donati lowered his voice. "I will destroy this temple. And when I am finished, not one stone will be left standing on another."

"The devil is among us," seethed Tardini.

"I don't disagree with you, Eminence. But you and your friends in the Order were the ones who opened the door to him."

"*You* are the one threatening to destroy the faith."

"Not the faith, Eminence. Only the Church. Rest assured, I would rather see her in ruins than leave her in the grubby hands of the Order of St. Helena."

"And then what?" asked Tardini. "What will we do when our Church is destroyed?"

"We'll start over, Eminence. We'll meet in homes and share

simple meals of bread and wine. We'll recite the Psalms and tell stories of Jesus' teaching and his death and resurrection. We'll build a new church. A church he would recognize." Donati looked at Cardinal Francona. "Thank you, Dean. I believe I've said quite enough."

55

VILLA BORGHESE

Veronica's car was parked haphazardly against the barricade at the end of the access road. The passenger-side door was slightly ajar. The keys were lying on the floor. Gabriel slipped them into his pocket and then drew the Beretta.

"Is there really no other way?" asked Metzler.

"What did you have in mind? A gentlemanly negotiation?"

"He's a priest."

"He killed the Holy Father. If I were you—"

"I'm not like you, Allon. I'll let my God be Father Graf's judge."

"He's my God, too. But that's probably a discussion for another time." Gabriel looked down at his phone. Father Graf's device was about two hundred meters to the east, in the center of the Piazza di Siena. "Stay here with the car. I won't be but a minute."

Gabriel set out through the shelter of the trees. After a few paces he came upon the Tudor facade of the Globe Theatre Roma, the reproduction of the legendary London playhouse where Shakespeare debuted many of his most beloved works. Surrounded by towering Roman umbrella pines, it looked sorely out of place, like an igloo in the Negev.

Adjacent to the theater was the Piazza di Siena. Gabriel could have painted it from memory, but in the darkness he could discern almost nothing. Somewhere out there were two people—a woman who was desperately in love with a priest, and a priest who had murdered a pope. And to think he was scarcely five hours removed from Jonas Wolf's Hitlerian shop of horrors in the Obersalzberg. He *was* a normal person, he assured himself.

All at once he remembered the oval track. The track he had to cross to reach the center of the piazza. It was a provable fact that it was not possible for a man, even a man of his build and agility, to walk upon gravel without making a sound. Gabriel reckoned that was why Father Graf had brought her here. Perhaps a gentlemanly negotiation was called for, after all. It wouldn't be difficult to establish contact. Gabriel had Graf's phone number.

The instant messaging application on Gabriel's Solaris allowed him to send texts anonymously. Carefully shielding his screen, he typed a brief message in colloquial Italian about dinner at La Carbonara in the Campo de' Fiori. Then he tapped the SEND icon. A few seconds later, light flared like a match in the center of the piazza. It was surprisingly bright—bright enough for Gabriel to determine their alignment and orientation. Father Graf held the phone in his left hand, the hand nearest Gabriel. He and Veronica were facing one another. Like the needle of a compass, the priest was pointed true north.

Gabriel moved in the opposite direction along an asphalt footpath. Then he crept eastward through a stand of umbrella pines until he was approximately level with Veronica and Father Graf.

He sent the priest another anonymous text.

Helllloooooo . . .

Once again light flared in the center of the piazza. Only Gabriel's position had changed. He was now directly behind Father Graf. They were separated by about thirty meters of grass and the dust-and-gravel oval track. The grass, Gabriel could cross with the silence of a house cat. The track, however, was a tripwire. It was too wide to traverse with a leap unless one were an Olympic-caliber athlete, which Gabriel most certainly was not. He was a man of advancing years who had recently fractured two vertebrae in his lower back.

He was still a damn good shot, though. Especially with a Beretta 92 FS. He only needed to illuminate the target with another text message. Then Father Markus Graf, murderer of a pope, would cease to exist. Perhaps he might find himself before a celestial tribunal where he would be sentenced for his crimes. If so, Gabriel hoped that God was in a foul mood when it was Father Graf's turn in the dock.

He composed another brief message—Where are you?—and fired it into the ether. This time, perhaps because of the wind direction, he heard the bell-like tolling of Father Graf's phone. Several seconds elapsed before a bloom of light illuminated the tableau at the center of the piazza. Unfortunately, the position of the two figures had changed. Both were now facing north.

Veronica was kneeling. Father Graf was holding a gun to the back of her head.

The priest turned when he heard the crunch of gravel beneath Gabriel's feet. Instantly, there was another burst of light in the center of the piazza. The light of a muzzle flash. The superheated round split the air a few inches from Gabriel's left shoulder. Nevertheless, he rushed headlong toward his target, the Beretta in his outstretched hand. There were worse places to die, he thought, than the Piazza di Siena. He only hoped that God was in a good mood when it was his turn in the dock.

DONATI WAITED UNTIL HE HAD left the Casa Santa Marta before switching on his phone. He had received no calls or text messages during his remarks to the cardinals. He tried Veronica's number. There was no answer. He started to dial Gabriel, but stopped himself. Now was not the time.

The two Swiss Guards at the entrance of the guesthouse were staring vacantly into the night, unaware of the pandemonium Donati had left in his wake. My God, what had he done? He had lit the match, he thought. It would be Cardinal Francona's task to preside over a conclave in flames. Only heaven knew what kind of pope it would produce. Donati didn't much care at this point, so long as the next pontiff wasn't a puppet of Bishop Hans Richter.

The southern facade of the basilica was awash in floodlight. Donati noticed that one of the side doors was ajar. Entering, he crossed the left transept to Bernini's soaring *baldacchino* and fell to his knees on the cold marble floor. In the grottos beneath him lay his master, a small puncture wound in his right thigh.

Eyes closed, Donati prayed with a fervor he had not felt in many years.

Kill him, he was thinking. Slowly and with a great deal of pain.

THE NIGHT WAS GABRIEL'S ALLY, for it rendered him all but invisible. Father Graf, however, betrayed his exact location with every undisciplined pull of his trigger. Gabriel took no evasive action, made no changes in heading. Instead, he advanced directly toward his target as quickly as his legs could carry him, the way Shamron had trained him in the autumn of 1972.

Eleven times, one for every Israeli killed at Munich . . .

He had lost count of how many shots Father Graf had fired. He was confident Father Graf had, too. The Beretta held fifteen 9mm rounds. Gabriel, however, required only one. The one he intended to put between the priest's eyes when he was certain he would not hit Veronica by mistake. She was still on her knees, her hands covering her ears. Her mouth was open, but Gabriel could hear no sound other than the gunshots. A trick of the piazza's acoustics made it seem as though they were coming from every direction at once.

Gabriel was now about twenty meters from Graf, close enough so he could see him clearly without the aid of the muzzle flashes. Which meant Graf could see Gabriel, too. He could wait no longer, approach no closer. A police officer might have stopped and turned slightly to one side to reduce his profile. But not an Office assassin who had been trained by the great Ari Shamron. He continued his relentless advance, as though he intended to beat his bullet to its target.

Finally, his arm swung up, and he placed the sight of the Beretta over Father Graf's face. But in the instant before Gabriel could place the required pressure on the trigger, a portion of the face was blown away. Father Graf then vanished from view, as though a hole in the earth had opened beneath him.

Gabriel stumbled to a stop, unsure of the direction from which the shot had come. After a moment Alois Metzler emerged from the darkness, a SIG Sauer 226 pistol in his outstretched hand.

He lowered the gun and looked at Veronica. "You'd better get her out of here before the Polizia arrive. I'll take care of it."

"I'd say you already have."

Metzler contemplated the dead priest. "Don't worry, Allon. His blood is on my hands."

56

VIA GREGORIANA, ROME

AT TEN FIFTEEN THE FOLLOWING morning, Gabriel was awakened by a quarrel in the street beneath his window. For a moment he could not recall the name of the street or its location. Nor did he have any memory of the circumstances under which he had reached his place of rest, a small and hideously uncomfortable couch.

It was the couch, he recalled with a sudden lucidity, in the sitting room of the old Office safe flat near the top of the Spanish Steps. Veronica Marchese had offered to sleep there. But in an ill-advised display of chivalry, Gabriel had insisted she take the bedroom instead. They had stayed up past two o'clock sharing a bottle of Tuscan red wine, which had left him with a dull headache. It paired nicely with the pain in his lower back.

His clothing lay on the floor next to the couch. Dressed, he went into the kitchen and poured bottled water into the electric kettle. After spooning coffee into the French press, he entered the spare bathroom to confront his reflection in the mirror. If only he were a painting, he could erase the damage. The best he could hope for was a minor improvement before Chiara's arrival. At Gabriel's suggestion, she and the children were coming to Rome for the start of the conclave. Donati had invited them to watch the opening ceremony live on television at the Jesuit Curia. He had asked Veronica to join them. It promised to be an interesting afternoon.

Gabriel filled the French press with water and read the Italian papers on his phone while waiting for the coffee to brew. The shocking events in Germany were of little interest to the editors in Rome and Milan. Only the conclave mattered. The *vaticanisti* remained convinced that the papacy was Navarro's to lose. One predicted Pietro Lucchesi would be the last Italian pope. In none of the papers was there any mention of a dead priest from a reactionary Catholic order, or a shooting in the Borghese Gardens involving a prominent Italian museum director. Somehow, Alois Metzler had managed to keep it quiet. At least for now.

Gabriel carried his coffee into the sitting room and switched on the television. Fifteen thousand Catholics, religious and lay, were crammed into St. Peter's Basilica for the *Pro Eligendo Romano Pontifice* pre-conclave Mass. Another two hundred thousand were watching on the jumbo screens outside in the square. Dean Angelo Francona was the celebrant. Arrayed before him in four semicircular rows of chairs was the entire College of Cardinals, including those cardinals who were too old to participate in the conclave that was now just hours away. Donati was seated directly behind them. In his choir dress, he looked every inch the Roman Catholic prelate. His expression was grave, determined. Gabriel would not have wanted to be on the receiving end of his stern gaze.

"What do you suppose he's thinking?"

Gabriel looked up and smiled at Veronica Marchese. She was wearing a pair of Chiara's old cotton pajamas. One hand was propped on her hip. The other was tugging at her right ear.

"I still can't hear anything."

"It was exposed to several gunshots with no protection. It's going to take a few days."

Her hand moved to the back of her head.

"How does it feel?"

"A bit of caffeine might help." She looked longingly at his coffee. "Is there enough for me?"

He went into the kitchen and poured her a cup. She took a sip and made a face.

"Is it that bad?"

"Perhaps we can walk to Caffè Greco later." She looked at the television. "They do know how to put on a show, don't they? You'd never know anything was amiss."

"It's better that way."

"I'm not so sure about that."

"Do you want the world to know what happened in the Piazza di Siena last night?"

"Is there anything in the papers?"

"Not a peep."

"How long will it remain a secret?"

"I suppose that depends on the identity of the next pope."

The camera settled on Donati again. "Luscious Luigi," said

Veronica. "He hated that article in *Vanity Fair*, but it made him a star inside the Church."

"You should have seen the waiters at Piperno."

"How lucky you are, Gabriel. Just once I'd like to share a lunch with him in public on a perfect Roman afternoon." She gave him a sideways glance. "Does he ever talk about me?"

"Incessantly."

"Really? And what does he say?"

"That you are a good friend."

"And do you believe that?"

"No," said Gabriel. "I believe you are desperately in love with him."

"Is it that obvious?" She smiled sadly. "And what about Luigi? How does he feel about me?"

"You would have to ask him."

"Ask him what, exactly? Are you still in love with me, Archbishop? Will you renounce your vows and marry me before it's too late?"

"You've never?"

She shook her head.

"Why not?"

"Because I'm afraid of what his answer might be. If he says no, I'll be heartbroken. And if he says yes . . ."

"You'll feel like the worst person in the world."

"You're very perceptive."

"Except when it comes to matters of the heart."

"You have a perfect marriage."

"I'm married to a perfect woman. Don't confuse the two."

"And if you were in my position?"

"I'd tell Luigi how I felt. Sooner rather than later."

"When?"

"How about later this afternoon?"

"At the Jesuit Curia? I can't think of a place I'd rather *not* be. All those priests," said Veronica. "And they'll all be gawking at me."

"Actually, I rather doubt that."

She made a show of thought. "What does one wear to a conclave party?"

"White, I believe."

"Yes," said Veronica. "I believe you're right."

AT THE CONCLUSION OF THE Mass, the cardinal-electors filed out of the basilica and returned to the Casa Santa Marta for lunch. Alois Metzler rang Gabriel from the noisy lobby. Father Graf, he said, was on ice in a Rome morgue. He would remain there until the conclusion of the conclave, when his body would be discovered in the hills outside Rome, an apparent suicide. Veronica's name would appear in none of the reports. Neither would Gabriel's.

"Not bad, Metzler."

"I'm a Swiss citizen who works for the Vatican. Hiding the truth comes naturally to me."

"Any word from Bishop Richter?"

"He left Rome last night on his private jet. Apparently, he's holed up at the Order's priory in Canton Zug."

"What's the mood like at the Casa Santa Marta?"

"If we get through the conclave without another dead body," said Metzler before ringing off, "it will be a miracle."

By then, it was nearly twelve thirty. Veronica's flashy convertible was parked in the street outside the apartment building.

Gabriel drove to her palazzo off the Via Veneto and waited downstairs while she showered and changed. When she reappeared, she was dressed in an elegant cream-colored pantsuit and a braided gold necklace.

"I was mistaken," said Gabriel. "Everyone at the Jesuit Curia will definitely be gawking at you."

She smiled. "We can't arrive empty-handed."

"Luigi asked us to bring some wine."

Veronica disappeared into the kitchen and returned with four bottles of chilled pinot grigio. It was a five-minute drive to Roma Termini. They were waiting outside in the traffic circle when Chiara and the children spilled from the station.

"You're right," said Veronica. "You're married to the perfect woman."

"Yes," agreed Gabriel. "How lucky I am."

57

JESUIT CURIA, ROME

THERE WERE TWO LARGE FLAT-PANEL televisions in the dining hall of the Jesuit Curia, one at either end of the room. Between them were a hundred or so priests in black cassocks and clerical suits, along with a group of students from the Pontifical Gregorian University. The male baritone din subsided briefly as a party of invited laity—two young children, two beautiful women, and the chief of Israel's secret intelligence service—entered the room.

Donati had changed out of his choir dress and was once again wearing the Vatican equivalent of business attire. He was locked in what appeared to be a serious conversation with a silver-haired man whom Veronica identified as the superior general of the Society of Jesus.

"The Black Pope," she added.

"That's what they used to call Donati."

"Only his enemies dared to call him that. Father Agular is the real Black Pope. He's Venezuelan, a political scientist by training and something of a leftist. A writer from a conservative American magazine once labeled him a Marxist, which Father Agular took to be a compliment. He's quite pro-Palestinian as well."

"How much does he know about you and Donati?"

"Luigi's file was purged of any reference to our affair after he became Lucchesi's private secretary. As far as the Jesuits are concerned, it never happened." Veronica nodded toward a table lined with soft drinks and bottles of red and white wine. "Would you mind? I'm not sure I can do this sober."

Gabriel added Veronica's four bottles of pinot grigio to the collection of wine. Then he poured three glasses from an open bottle of lukewarm Frascati while Chiara served the children pasta from the chafing dishes arranged along the neighboring buffet. They found an empty table near one of the televisions. The cardinal-electors had left the Casa Santa Marta and were gathered in the Pauline Chapel, the final stop before they entered the Sistina for the start of the conclave.

Veronica tentatively sipped her wine. "Is there anything worse than room-temperature Frascati?"

"I can think of a few things," answered Gabriel.

Donati and a smiling Father Agular approached the table. Rising, Gabriel offered the leader of the Jesuits his hand before introducing Chiara and the children. "And this is our dear friend Veronica Marchese." Gabriel's tone was uncharacteristically bright. "Dottora Marchese is the director of the Museo Nazionale Etrusco."

"An honor, Dottora." Father Agular looked at Gabriel. "I

follow events in the Middle East quite closely. I wonder if we might have a word before you leave."

"Of course, Father Agular."

The Jesuit contemplated the television. "Who do you think it will be?"

"They say it's Navarro."

"It's time for a Spanish-speaking pope, don't you think?"

"If only he were a Jesuit."

Laughing, Father Agular withdrew.

Donati pulled out a chair between Gabriel and Raphael and sat down. He scarcely acknowledged Veronica's presence. Beneath his breath he asked, "How is she doing?"

"As well as can be expected."

"I have to say, she looks wonderful."

"You should have seen her after Metzler killed Father Graf."

"He covered it up quite well. Even Alessandro Ricci is in the dark."

"How did you manage to convince him not to publish his story about the plot against the conclave?"

"By promising to give him everything he needs to write a blockbuster sequel to *The Order.*"

"Tell him to keep my name out of it."

"You deserve a little credit. After all, you saved the Catholic Church."

"Not yet," said Gabriel.

Donati looked up at the television. "We'll know by tomorrow night. Monday at the latest."

"Why not tonight?"

"This afternoon's vote is largely symbolic. Most of the cardinals will cast ballots for friends or benefactors. If we have a new pope tonight, it means that something extraordinary has taken place inside the Sistine Chapel." Donati looked at Raphael. "It's uncanny. If he had gray temples . . ."

"I know, I know."

"Can he paint?"

"Quite well, actually."

"And Irene?"

"A writer, I'm afraid."

Donati looked at Veronica, who was sharing a private joke with Chiara. "What do you suppose they're talking about?"

"You, I imagine."

Donati frowned. "You haven't been meddling in my personal life, have you?"

"A little." Gabriel lowered his voice. "She has something she wants to discuss with you."

"Really? And what's that?"

"She'd like to ask you a question before it's too late."

"It already is too late. Rome has spoken, my friend. The case is closed." Donati drank from Gabriel's wineglass and made a face. "Is there anything worse than room-temperature Frascati?"

SHORTLY AFTER THREE O'CLOCK, THE cardinal-electors processed into the Sistine Chapel. With the cameras watching, each placed a hand on the Gospel of Matthew and pledged, among other things, that he would not take part in any attempt by outside forces to intervene in the election of the Roman pontiff. Domenico Albanese repeated the oath with exaggerated solemnity, a sainted expression on his face. The television commentators praised his performance during the period of the interregnum. One went so far as to suggest he stood an outside chance of emerging from the conclave as the next pope.

"Heaven help us," murmured Donati.

It was nearly five o'clock when the last cardinal had sworn his oath. A moment later the Master of Pontifical Liturgical Ceremonies, a thin bespectacled Italian named Monsignor Guido Montini, stood before the microphone and declared softly, "Extra omnes." Fifty priests, prelates, and Vatican-connected laity filed out of the chapel, including Alois Metzler, who was wearing his Renaissance-era dress uniform and white-plumed helmet.

"Good thing he wasn't dressed like that last night," remarked Gabriel.

Donati smiled as Monsignor Montini closed the Sistine Chapel's double doors.

"What now?"

"We find a bottle of chilled wine," said Donati. "And we wait."

58

SISTINE CHAPEL

THE FIRST ORDER OF BUSINESS was the distribution of the ballots. Atop each were the words ELIGO IN SUMMUM PONTIFICEM: *I elect as supreme pontiff.* Next came a drawing to select the Scrutineers, the three cardinals who would tabulate the vote count. Three Revisers, who would scrutinize the work of the Scrutineers, were chosen next, followed by three *infirmarii*, who would collect the ballot of any cardinal too ill to leave his bed at the Casa Santa Marta. Cardinal Angelo Francona was relieved that none of the forty-two cardinals implicated by Luigi Donati were chosen for any of the nine positions. Though he was not a mathematician, he knew the odds of such an outcome were astronomical. Surely, he reasoned, the Holy Spirit had intervened to safeguard what little remained of the conclave's integrity.

The preliminaries complete, Francona approached the microphone and eyed the 115 men arrayed before him. "I know it's been a long day, but I suggest we vote."

If there was to be a breakdown, it would happen now. A single objection would require the conclave to adjourn for the night and the cardinals to return to the Casa Santa Marta. It would be interpreted by the rest of the world as a sign of intense rancor and division within the Church. In short, it would be a disaster.

Francona held his breath.

There was silence in the room.

"Very well. Please write the name of your chosen candidate on your ballot. And remember, if a vote cannot be deciphered, it cannot be counted."

Francona sat down in his assigned seat. The card lay before him, a pencil beside it. He had intended to follow conclave tradition and cast a complimentary vote on the first ballot. But that was no longer possible. Not after last night's fireworks in the Casa Santa Marta. Now was not the time to flatter an old friend or patron. The future of the Roman Catholic Church was hanging in the balance.

I elect as supreme pontiff . . .

Francona raised his eyes and contemplated the men seated around him. Who could it be? *Is it you, Navarro? Or you, Brady?* No, he thought suddenly. Francona believed with all his heart that there was only one man who could save the Church from itself.

He took up his pencil and placed the tip to the card. It was customary for cardinal-electors to disguise their handwriting, and thus their vote. Francona, however, wrote the name swiftly and with his easily identifiable flourishes. Then he folded the ballot in half, twice, and returned to the microphone.

"Does anyone require additional time? All right, then. Let us begin the balloting."

The procedure, like nearly everything else about a papal conclave, was designed to reduce the possibility of foul play. Voting was conducted in order of precedence. As dean of the Sacred College, Francona went first.

The Scrutineers were gathered on the altar, upon which stood an oversize gold chalice covered by a silver paten. Francona held up his ballot and recited aloud yet another oath.

"I call as my witness Christ the Lord, who will be my judge, that my vote is given to the one who before God I think should be elected."

He laid the ballot on the paten and, grasping the plate with both hands, tilted it a few degrees to the left. The ballot entered the chalice cleanly. It was another sign, thought Francona, that the Holy Spirit was indeed present.

He replaced the paten and returned to his seat.

THE PROCESS WAS DELIBERATELY CUMBERSOME and slow, especially when performed by largely sedentary men in their sixties and seventies, a few of whom walked with the aid of a cane. Even Kevin Brady, the energetic Angeleno, required thirty seconds to swear his oath and maneuver his ballot safely into the chalice. Emmerich took his sweet time about it, as did Majewski of Kraków. The swiftest was Albanese, who dumped his ballot into the chalice as though clearing bones from his dinner plate.

It was nearly half past six by the time the counting began.

With the paten in place, the first Scrutineer shook the chalice in order to mix the ballots. The third Scrutineer then counted the unread ballots to ensure there was one for each of the 116 electors. Much to Francona's relief, the numbers matched. If they hadn't, he would have been required to burn the ballots without tabulating them.

The ballots were now contained in a second, slightly smaller chalice. The Scrutineers placed it on a table before the altar and sat down. The arcane ritual that followed was nearly as old as the Church itself. The first Scrutineer drew a ballot and, after a moment's hesitation, made a small but significant amendment to the last page of the preprinted list of names before him. He then handed the ballot to the second Scrutineer, who did the same. The third Scrutineer could not hide his surprise when silently reading the name. A moment later, after piercing the ballot with a needle and red thread through the word *Eligo*, he read the name aloud into the microphone.

A low murmur moved through the conclave. The name surprised no one more than Angelo Francona, for it was the one he had written on his ballot. His candidate was unorthodox, to say the least. Surely it was his ballot that had been drawn first. He added the name to his own list and placed a check mark next to it.

The first Scrutineer drew another ballot. Startled, he shot an anxious glance toward Francona before handing it to the second Scrutineer. He placed a checkmark on his list of names and then handed the ballot to the third Scrutineer, who impaled it with his needle and thread. The name he read aloud into the microphone was the same name as the first ballot.

"Dear God," whispered Angelo Francona. Another murmur swept through the conclave, like the rumble of a passing aircraft. Someone else must have had the same idea.

THE SCRUTINEERS QUICKENED THEIR PACE, ten ballots in a span of just four minutes by Francona's watch. Three went for Navarro, one for Tardini, one for Gaubert, and five for Francona's dark-horse candidate. He had received seven out of the first twelve votes counted, an astonishing pace. It couldn't continue, thought Francona.

But it did. Indeed, Francona's dark horse received six of the next ten votes counted, and a shocking seven of the ten that followed. Francona marked each on his list. His candidate had received twenty of the first thirty-two votes counted, just shy of a two-thirds majority.

Eighty-four ballots remained uncounted. When Francona's candidate received half of the next twenty votes tabulated, Cardinal Tardini demanded that the first ballot be nullified.

"On what possible grounds, Eminence?" Francona was certain there were none. He looked at the three Scrutineers. "Draw the next ballot, please."

It went for Francona's candidate, as did fifteen of the next twenty. At which point the conclave erupted.

"Keep your voices down, brothers!" Francona's tone was scolding, a headmaster reproaching a roomful of unruly pupils. He glanced at the Scrutineers. "Next ballot."

It went for Albanese, of all people. Doubtless he had voted for himself. It was no matter; Francona's candidate captured seventeen of the next twenty ballots. He had received sixty-three of the ninety-four votes tabulated. Twenty-two ballots had yet to be counted. If the name of Francona's candidate appeared on fifteen of them, he would carry the conclave.

Four consecutive ballots went in his favor, along with six of the next ten, bringing his tally to seventy-three, five short of the seventy-eight required to be elected. The next ballot went for Navarro. After that, it was never in doubt. As the last votes were counted, there was pandemonium. This time Angelo Francona made no attempt to restore decorum, for he was gazing upward toward Michelangelo's depiction of the moment of creation.

"What have we done?" he whispered. "What in God's name have we done?"

THE SCRUTINEERS AND REVISERS COUNTED the ballots a second time and double-checked their tabulation. There was no mistake. The unthinkable had just happened. It was time to tell the rest of the world, not to mention the man who had just been chosen to be the spiritual leader of more than a billion Roman Catholics.

Francona loaded the ballots and the tabulation sheets into the older of the Sistine Chapel's two stoves and set them alight. Then he flipped a switch on the second stove, igniting five tissue-box-size charges containing a mixture of potassium chlorate, lactose, and pine resin. A few seconds later a roar arose from the thousands of pilgrims outside in St. Peter's Square. They had spotted the white smoke pouring from the chapel's chimney.

Francona walked over to the doors and knocked twice. They were opened instantly by Monsignor Guido Montini. It was obvious from his expression he had heard the reaction in the square.

"Bring me a phone," said Francona. "Quickly."

59

JESUIT CURIA, ROME

A T THAT SAME MOMENT, IN the dining hall of the Jesuit Curia, Archbishop Luigi Donati was watching the televised images of white smoke pouring from the chimney of the Sistine Chapel. His face was ashen. The speed of the decision suggested that the corrupt cardinals had ignored his warnings and voted for Emmerich. If that proved to be the case, Donati had every intention of following through with his threat. When he was finished, not one stone would be left standing on another. He would build a new church. A church Jesus would recognize.

Donati's fellow Jesuits, however, were electrified by the conclave's unusually swift selection of a new pope. Indeed, the commotion in the room was so loud that he could not make out what the commentators were saying. Nor, for that matter, could he hear his Nokia telephone, which was lying on the table next to Gabriel's. When he finally checked it, he was shocked to see he had five missed calls, all in the last two minutes.

"Dear God."

"What is it?" asked Gabriel.

"You'll never guess who's been frantically trying to reach me."

Donati dialed and raised the phone swiftly to his ear.

"It's about time," said Cardinal Angelo Francona.

"What is it, Dean?"

"Have you seen the smoke?"

"Yes, of course. Please tell me it isn't—"

"We've had an unexpected development."

"Obviously, Eminence. But what is it?"

"You'll know when you get here."

"Where?"

"There's a car waiting downstairs. I'll see you in a few minutes."

The call went dead. Donati lowered the phone and looked at Gabriel. "I could be mistaken, but I believe I've just been summoned to the Sistine Chapel."

"Why?"

"Francona wouldn't tell me, which means it can't be good. In fact, I'd feel better if you came with me."

"To the Sistine Chapel? You can't be serious."

"It's not as if you've never been there before."

"Not during a conclave." Gabriel tugged at the collar of his leather jacket. "Besides, I'm not really dressed for the occasion."

"What does one wear to a conclave?" asked Donati.

Gabriel looked at Veronica and smiled. "White, I believe."

To AVOID THE CROWDS IN St. Peter's Square, the car slipped into the Vatican through the motor entrance near the Palace of the Holy Office. From there it made its way around the back of the basilica to a small courtyard at the foot of the Sistine Chapel. Monsignor Guido Montini pounced on Donati's door like a hotel bellman. He seemed to be resisting an impulse to genuflect.

Montini had to raise his voice to be heard over the tolling of the basilica's bells. "Good evening, Excellency. I've been instructed to bring you upstairs." He looked at Gabriel. "But I'm afraid your friend Signore Allon will have to remain here."

"Why?"

Montini's eyes widened. "The conclave, Excellency."

"It's over, is it not?"

"That depends."

"On what?"

"Please, Excellency. The cardinals are waiting."

Donati gestured toward Gabriel. "Either he comes with me or I'm not going in."

"Yes, of course, Excellency. If that is what you wish."

Donati exchanged an apprehensive glance with Gabriel. Together they climbed a flight of narrow stairs to the Sala Regia, the glorious fresco-covered antechamber of the Sistine Chapel. A pair of Swiss Guards stood like bookends outside the entrance. Gabriel hesitated, then followed Donati inside.

THE CARDINALS WAITED AT THE base of the altar, dwarfed by Michelangelo's *Last Judgment*. After passing through the doorway of the *transenna*, Donati stopped abruptly and turned.

"Don't you see what's happening?"

"Yes," answered Gabriel. "I believe I do."

"No one in their right mind would want this. I've seen with my own eyes the toll it takes." Donati stretched out his hand. "Please grab hold of it. Drag me out of here before it's too late."

"It already is too late, Luigi. Rome has spoken."

Donati's hand was still suspended between them. He placed it on Gabriel's shoulder and squeezed with surprising force. "Try to remember me the way I was, old friend. Because in a moment, that person won't exist."

"Hurry, Luigi. You mustn't keep them waiting."

Donati glanced at the 116 men waiting at the altar.

"Not them, Luigi. The people in the square."

"What will I say to them? My God, I don't even have a name." Donati threw his arms around Gabriel's neck and clung to him as though he were drowning. "Tell her I'm sorry. Tell her I never meant for this to happen."

Donati drew away and squared his shoulders. Suddenly composed, he marched the length of the chapel and stopped directly in front of Cardinal Francona.

"I believe you have something you wish to ask me, Eminence."

Francona posed the question in Latin. "Acceptasne electionem de te canonice factam in Summum Pontificem?" *Do you accept your canonical election as supreme pontiff?*

"I accept," answered Donati without hesitation.

"*Quo nomine vis vocari?*" *By what name do you wish to be called?*

Donati stared at Michelangelo's ceiling, as if searching for inspiration. "To tell you the truth, I haven't a clue."

Laughter filled the Sistine Chapel. It was a good beginning.

60

SISTINE CHAPEL

IT WAS FITTING THAT DONATI'S first official act as pope was to affix his signature to a document that would reside permanently in the silence of the Vatican Secret Archives. Hastily prepared by Monsignor Montini, it formally recorded Donati's new name and his acceptance of the position of supreme pontiff. He signed the document at the table where the Scrutineers and Revisers had tabulated the votes. Eighty had gone to Donati on the first ballot, a shocking result. Not since the days of election by acclamation had a pope been elected so swiftly and by such an overwhelming margin.

Donati next withdrew to the Room of Tears, where a representative of the Gammarelli family, papal tailors since 1798, waited with three white linen cassocks and a selection of rochets, mozettas, stoles, and red silk slippers. Pietro Lucchesi had famously chosen the smallest of the three cassocks. Donati required the largest. He dispensed with the rochet, mozetta, and stole, and chose to wear his old silver-plated pectoral cross rather than the heavy gold cross offered to him. Nor did he select a pair of red slippers. His Italian loafers, which he had shined himself for his appearance before the cardinals at the Casa Santa Marta, were good enough.

Gabriel was not permitted to witness Donati's ritual rerobing. He remained in the Sistine Chapel, where the cardinals waited to greet the man to whom they had just handed the keys to the kingdom. The mood was electric but uncertain. The room's acoustics allowed Gabriel to eavesdrop on a few of the conversations. It was obvious that many of the cardinals had cast so-called complimentary votes for Donati, not realizing that an overwhelming majority of their colleagues intended to do the same. The general consensus was that the Holy Spirit, not Bishop Richter and the Order of St. Helena, had intervened.

Not everyone in the room was pleased by the outcome, especially Cardinals Albanese and Tardini. Only thirty-six had voted for another candidate, which meant a significant number of the forty-two conspirators had supported Donati's candidacy, perhaps with the misplaced hope he might overlook their financial transgressions and allow them to remain in their current jobs. Gabriel reckoned the College of Cardinals would soon see a rash of quiet resignations and reassignments. Long-overdue change was coming to the Catholic Church. No one knew how to operate the levers of Vatican power better than Luigi Donati. More important, he knew where the bodies were buried and where the dirty laundry was hidden. The Roman Curia, guardian of the status quo, had finally met its match.

At last, Donati emerged from the Room of Tears in his snow-white garment, a zucchetto upon his head. He was aglow, as though caught by his own private spotlight. So remarkable was the change in his appearance that even Gabriel scarcely recognized him. He was no longer Luigi Donati, he thought. He was the successor of St. Peter, Christ's representative on earth.

He was His Holiness.

In a few minutes he would be the most famous and recognizable man in the world. But first there was a last ritual, as old as the Church itself. One by one, in order of precedence, the cardinals filed forward to offer their congratulations and pledge their obedience, a reminder that the pope was not only a spiritual leader of a billion Catholics but one of the world's last remaining absolute monarchs as well. He chose to receive the cardinals while standing rather than seated on his throne. Most of the exchanges were warm, even boisterous. Several were frigid and tense. Tardini, defiant to the end, wagged his finger at the new pope, who wagged his finger in return. Domenico Albanese fell to his knees and begged for absolution. Donati told him to rise and then waved him away with the stain of a pontiff's murder still on his soul. There was a monastery in Albanese's future, thought Gabriel. Somewhere cold and isolated, with bad food. Poland, perhaps. Or better yet, Kansas.

There was one last precedent to be broken that evening. It came at 7:34 p.m., when Donati summoned Gabriel with a joyous wave of his long arm. The new pope seized him by the shoulders. Gabriel had never felt smaller.

"Congratulations, Holiness."

"Condolences, you mean." His confident smile made it clear

he was already becoming comfortable in the role. "You've just seen something only a handful of people have ever witnessed."

"I'm not sure I'll remember much of it."

"Nor will I." He lowered his voice. "You didn't tell anyone, did you?"

"Not a soul."

"In that case, our friends at the Jesuit Curia are about to get the surprise of their lives." He seemed to relish the thought. "Come with me to the balcony. It's not something you should miss."

He went into the Sala Regia and, followed by much of the conclave, set off along the Hall of Blessings toward the front of the basilica. Unlike his master, Pietro Lucchesi, he did not need to be shown the way. In the antechamber behind the balcony, he solemnly made the sign of the cross as the doors were opened. The roar of the multitude in the square was deafening. He smiled at Gabriel one final time as the senior cardinal deacon declared, "Habemus papam!" *We have a pope!* Then he stepped into a corona of blinding white light and was gone.

ALONE WITH THE CARDINALS, GABRIEL felt suddenly out of place. The man once known as Luigi Donati belonged to them now, not him. Unescorted, he made his way back to the Sistine Chapel. Then he headed downstairs to the Bronze Doors of the Apostolic Palace.

Outside, St. Peter's Square was ablaze with candles and mobile phones. It looked as though a galaxy of stars had fallen to earth. Gabriel tried Chiara's number, but there was not a cellular connection to be had. He picked his way through Bernini's Colonnade. The crowd was delirious. Donati's election was an earthquake.

Gabriel finally emerged from the Colonnade into the Piazza Papa Pio XII. To reach the Jesuit Curia, he had to somehow make his way to the other side. He soon gave up. A sea of humanity stretched from Donati's feet to the banks of the Tiber. There was nowhere for Gabriel to go.

He realized suddenly that Chiara and the children were calling his name. It took a moment to find them. Elated, the children were pointing toward the basilica, as though their father were unaware of the fact that his friend was standing on the balcony. Chiara's arms were wrapped around Veronica Marchese, who was weeping uncontrollably.

Gabriel tried to reach them, but it was no good. The crowd was impenetrable. Turning, he saw a man in white floating above a key-shaped carpet of golden light. It was a masterwork, he thought. *His Holiness*, oil on canvas, artist unknown . . .

PART FOUR

HABEMUS PAPAM

61

CANNAREGIO, VENICE

IT WAS CHIARA WHO SECRETLY informed the prime minister that her husband would not be at his desk at King Saul Boulevard on Monday morning. While purportedly on holiday, he had prevented a massive bombing in Cologne, dealt a severe blow to the ambitions of the European far right, and watched his close friend become the supreme pontiff of the Roman Catholic Church. He needed a few days to recuperate.

He spent the first three largely confined to the apartment overlooking the Rio della Misericordia, for God in his infinite wisdom had inflicted upon Venice a deluge of biblical magnitude. When combined with gale-force winds and an unusually high tide in the lagoon, the results were disastrous. All six of the city's historic *sestieri* suffered catastrophic flooding, including San Marco, where the crypt of the basilica flooded for only the sixth time in twelve centuries. In Cannaregio the water rose a historic six and a half feet in a span of just three hours. Particularly hard hit was the small island to which the city's Jews were confined in 1516 by the order of Venice's ruling council. The museum in the Campo di Ghetto Nuovo was inundated, as was the ground floor of the Casa Israelitica di Riposo. Waves lapped against the bas-relief Holocaust memorial, leaving the carabinieri no choice but to abandon their bulletproof kiosk.

Like nearly everyone else in the city, the Allon family huddled behind barricades and sandbags and made the best of it. Raphael and Irene looked upon their watery internment as a great adventure; Gabriel, as a blessing. For three waterlogged days, they read books aloud, played board games, undertook art projects, and watched every DVD in the apartment's modest library, most twice. It was a glimpse of their future. In retirement, Gabriel would be an expatriate again, a Diaspora Jew. He would work when it suited him and devote every spare minute to his children. The clock would slow, his many wounds would heal. This is where his story would end, in the sinking city of churches and paintings at the northern end of the Adriatic.

He checked in with Uzi Navot early each morning and late each afternoon. And, of course, he followed the news from Rome, where Donati wasted little time upsetting the curial applecart. For a start, there was his decision to reside not in the papal apartments of the Apostolic Palace but in an unadorned suite in the Casa Santa Marta. His first Angelus, delivered to an audience of some two hundred thousand pilgrims crammed into St. Peter's Square, left little doubt he intended to guide the Church in a new direction.

But who was this man who now occupied the throne of St.

Peter? And what were the circumstances of his shocking and historic election? The author of the *Vanity Fair* article hopscotched from network to network, describing the magnetic archbishop she had christened "Luscious Luigi." Several profiles explored his Jesuit roots and the period during which he served as a missionary in war-torn El Salvador. It was widely assumed, though never proven, that as a young priest he had been a supporter of the controversial doctrine known as liberation theology. This did not endear him to certain segments of the American political right. Indeed, one conservative referred to him as Pope Che Guevara. Another wondered whether the flooding in Venice, where he had worked for several years, might be a sign of God's displeasure in the conclave's choice.

Bound by their vows of secrecy, the cardinal-electors refused to discuss what had transpired inside the Sistine Chapel. Even Alessandro Ricci, the dogged investigative reporter from *La Repubblica*, appeared unable to penetrate the conclave's armor. Instead, he published a lengthy article on the links between the European far right and the Order of St. Helena, the reactionary Catholic fraternity about which he had written a best-selling book. Three of the figures implicated in the false-flag bombings in Germany—Jonas Wolf, Andreas Estermann, and Axel Brünner—were alleged to be secret members of the Order. So, too, were Austrian chancellor Jörg Kaufmann and Italian prime minister Giuseppe Saviano.

Kaufmann immediately denied the report. He was forced to issue a clarification when *La Repubblica* published a photograph from his wedding, which was officiated by the Order's superior general, Bishop Hans Richter. For his part, Saviano brazenly dismissed the story as "fake news" and called upon

Italian prosecutors to file charges of treason against its author. Informed that no such offense had been committed, he issued a tweet calling on his thuggish soccer-hooligan supporters to teach Ricci a lesson he would not soon forget. After receiving hundreds of death threats, the journalist fled his apartment in Trastevere and went into hiding.

Bishop Richter, secluded at the Order's medieval priory in Canton Zug, refused to comment on the story. Nor did he issue a statement when lawyers in New York filed a class action suit in federal court, accusing the Order of extorting money and valuables from desperate Jews during the late 1930s in exchange for promises of false baptismal certificates and protection from the Nazis. The lead plaintiff in the case was Isabel Feldman, the only surviving child of Samuel Feldman. In a sparsely attended news conference in Vienna, she unveiled a painting—a river landscape by the Dutch Old Master Jan van Goyen—that her father had turned over to the Order in 1938. The canvas, which had been removed from its stretcher, had been returned to her by the noted Holocaust investigator Eli Lavon, whose schedule did not permit him to attend the press briefing.

The exact circumstances of the painting's recovery were not made public, which gave rise to much unfounded speculation in the Austrian press. A website that regularly trafficked in false or misleading stories went so far as to accuse Lavon of being an Israeli agent. The story happened to be accurate, thus proving Rabbi Jacob Zolli's contention that the unimaginable can happen. Normally, Gabriel would not have bothered with a response. But given the current climate of anti-Semitism in Europe—and the ever-present threat of violence hanging over

Austria's tiny Jewish minority—he thought it best to issue a denial through the Israeli Embassy in Vienna.

He was less inclined, however, to repudiate a British tabloid report regarding his presence in the Sistine Chapel on the night of the historic conclave, if only to annoy the Russians and the Iranians, who were rightly paranoid about his capabilities and reach. But when the story jumped from publication to publication like a contagion, he reluctantly instructed the prime minister's irascible spokeswoman to dismiss it as "preposterous on its face." The statement was a classic example of a nondenial denial. And with good reason. Numerous Vatican insiders, including the new supreme pontiff and the 116 cardinals who elected him, knew the story to be true.

So, too, did Gabriel's children. For three blissful days, as the rains fell upon Venice without relent, he had them entirely to himself. Board games, art projects, old movies on DVD. Occasionally, when the combination of shadows and light was favorable, he lifted the flap of an envelope emblazoned with the armorial of His Holiness Pope Paul VII and removed the three sheets of rich stationery. The salutation was informal. First name only. There were no preliminaries or pleasantries.

While researching in the Vatican Secret Archives, I came upon a most remarkable book . . .

FINALLY, ON THE MORNING OF the fourth day, the clouds parted and the sun shone over the whole of the city. After breakfast, Gabriel and Chiara dressed the children in oilskin coats and Wellington boots and together they waded over to the Campo di Ghetto Nuovo to assist with the cleanup. Nothing had been spared, especially the museum's beautiful bookstore, which lost most of its inventory. The kitchen and common room of the Casa Israelitica di Riposo were in ruins, and both the Portuguese and Spanish synagogues suffered severe damage. Once again, thought Gabriel as he surveyed the destruction, calamity had befallen the Jews of Venice.

They worked until one and then took their lunch in a tiny restaurant hidden away on the Calle Masena. From there it was a short walk to the first of two apartments that Chiara, without bothering to inform Gabriel, had arranged for them to see that day. It was large and airy and, perhaps most important, dry as a bone. The kitchen was newly renovated, as were the three bathrooms. The price was high, but not unreasonable. Gabriel was confident he would be able to shoulder the additional financial burden without having to sell knockoff Gucci handbags to the tourists in San Marco.

"What do you think?" asked Chiara.

"Nice," said Gabriel noncommittally.

"But?"

"Why don't you show me the other apartment?"

It was located near the San Toma vaporetto stop on the Grand Canal, a fully refurbished *piano nobile* with a private roof terrace and a high-ceilinged, light-filled room that Gabriel could claim as his studio. There he would toil night and day on lucrative private commissions in order to pay for it all. He consoled himself with the knowledge that there were far worse ways for a man to spend the autumn of his years.

"If we sell Narkiss Street," said Chiara.

"We're not going to sell it."

"I know it's a stretch, Gabriel. But if we're going to live in Venice, wouldn't you prefer to live here?"

"Who wouldn't? But someone has to pay for it."

"Someone will."

"You?"

She smiled.

"I want to see his books."

"Where do you think we were going next?"

Francesco Tiepolo's office was on the Calle Larga XXII Marzo in San Marco. On the wall behind his desk were several framed photographs of his friend Pietro Lucchesi. In one was a youthful version of Lucchesi's successor.

"I suppose you had something to do with it."

"What's that?"

"The election of the first pope from outside the College of Cardinals since the thirteenth century."

"Fourteenth," said Gabriel. "And rest assured, it was the Holy Spirit who chose the new pope, not me."

"You've been spending too much time in Catholic churches, my friend."

"It's an occupational hazard."

Tiepolo's books were hardly immaculate, but they were in far better shape than Gabriel had feared. The firm had little debt, and the monthly overhead was low. Mainly, it consisted of the rent for the San Marco office and a warehouse on the mainland. At present, the firm had more work than it could handle, and several projects were in the pipeline. Two were scheduled to commence after the date of Gabriel's retirement, which meant Chiara would be able to hit the ground running. Tiepolo insisted they keep the firm's name and pay him a fifty percent share of the annual profit. Gabriel agreed to keep the name—he did not want his many enemies to know where he was living—but he balked at Tiepolo's demand for half of the company's profits, offering him twenty-five percent instead.

"How will I possibly live on such a paltry sum?"

"Somehow you'll manage."

Tiepolo looked at Chiara. "Which apartment did he choose?"

"The big one."

"I knew it!" Tiepolo clapped Gabriel on the back. "I always said you would return to Venice. And when you die, they'll bury you beneath a cypress tree on San Michele, in an enormous crypt befitting a man of your achievements."

"I'm not dead yet, Francesco."

"It happens to the best of us." Tiepolo gazed at the photographs on the wall. "Even to my dear friend Pietro Lucchesi."

"And now Donati is the pope."

"Are you sure you didn't have anything to do with it?"

"No," answered Gabriel distantly. "It was him."

"Who?" asked Tiepolo, perplexed.

Gabriel pointed toward the cloaked, sandaled figure walking past Tiepolo's window.

It was Father Joshua.

62

PIAZZA SAN MARCO

GABRIEL HURRIED INTO THE STREET. Like most in San Marco, it was covered in several inches of water. A few tourists were milling about in the dying twilight. None seemed to notice the man in a threadbare cloak and sandals.

"What are you looking at?"

Gabriel wheeled around to find Chiara and the children standing behind him. He pointed along the darkening street. "The man in the hooded cloak is Father Joshua. He's the one who gave us the first page of the Gospel of Pilate."

Chiara narrowed her eyes. "I don't see anyone in a cloak."

Neither did Gabriel. The priest had disappeared from view.

"Maybe you were mistaken," said Chiara. "Or maybe you just *thought* you saw him."

"A hallucination, you mean?"

Chiara said nothing.

"Wait here."

Gabriel set off along the street, searching for a destitute-looking clergyman amid the world's most exclusive storefronts. Eventually, he passed through an archway beneath the Museo Correr and emerged into the Piazza San Marco. Father Joshua was walking past Caffè Florian toward the campanile. The priest seemed to move across the floodwaters without disturbing the surface. He made no attempt to lift the hem of his garment.

Gabriel hastened after him. "Father Joshua?"

The priest stopped at the foot of the bell tower.

Gabriel addressed him in Italian, the language he had spoken in the Manuscript Depository of the Secret Archives. "Don't you remember me, Father Joshua? I'm the one who—"

"I know who you are." His smile was benevolent. "You're the one with the name of the archangel."

"How do you know my name?"

"There were recriminations after your visit to the Secret Archives. I overheard things."

"Do you work there?"

"Why would you ask such a question?"

"Your name doesn't appear on the staff directory. And unless I'm mistaken, you weren't wearing any identification that day."

"Why would someone like me require identification?"

"Who are you?"

"Who do *you* say that I am?"

His Italian was beautiful, but it was colored with an unmistakable accent.

"Do you speak Arabic?" asked Gabriel.

"Like you, I speak many languages."

"Where are you from?"

"The same place you are."

"Israel?"

"The Galilee."

"Why are you in Venice?"

"I came to see a friend." He noticed Gabriel looking at his hands. "I bear in my body the marks of the Lord Jesus," he explained.

Two women splashed past them. They stared at Gabriel apprehensively but seemed not to notice the man standing in ankle-deep water in sandals and a cloak.

"Were you ever able to find the rest of the gospel?" he asked.

"Not before it was destroyed."

"The Holy Father was afraid that would happen."

"Were you the one who gave it to him?"

"Of course."

"How were you able to open the door of the *collezione* without a key?"

He gave a sly smile. "It wasn't difficult."

"Did the Holy Father show the book to anyone else?"

"A Jesuit." Father Joshua frowned. "For some reason, my word wasn't good enough. The Jesuit agreed with me that the book was authentic."

"He's an American, this Jesuit?"

"Yes."

"Do you know his name?"

"The Holy Father refused to tell me. He said he was going to give the gospel to you when the Jesuit was finished with it."

"Finished with what?"

"His Holiness didn't say."

"Where were you when you had this conversation?"

"The papal study. But why do you ask?"

"The men who murdered the Holy Father were listening. They could hear his voice but not yours."

His expression darkened. "You must feel guilty."

"About what?"

"His death."

"Yes," admitted Gabriel. "Terribly guilty."

"Don't," said the priest. "It wasn't your fault."

He turned to leave.

"Father Joshua?"

The priest stopped.

"When did you remove the first page of the gospel?"

He raised a bandaged hand. "I'm afraid I must be on my way. May the peace of the Lord be with you always. And with your wife and children as well. Go to them, Gabriel. They're searching for you."

With that, he set off between the columns of St. Mark and St. Theodore. Gabriel quickly drew his phone and engaged the camera, but he could see no trace of the priest on the screen. He hurried over to the gondola station on the Riva degli Schiavoni and looked to the right and then the left.

Father Joshua was gone.

AT TWO P.M. THE FOLLOWING afternoon, Gabriel received a phone call from General Cesare Ferrari of the Art Squad. He claimed to have come to Venice on an unrelated matter and was hoping Gabriel might have a moment to answer a few questions before his return to Israel.

"Where?"

"Carabinieri regional headquarters."

Gabriel suggested Harry's Bar instead. He arrived a few minutes before four; the general, a few minutes after. They ordered Bellinis. Gabriel's immediately gave him a headache. He drank it nonetheless. It was irresistibly delicious. Besides, it was his last day of vacation.

"The perfect end to an imperfect day," said the general.

"What is it now?"

"Next year's budget."

"I thought fascists loved cultural patrimony."

"Only if there's enough tax revenue to pay for it."

"I guess bashing immigrants isn't good for the economy after all."

"Is it true they were responsible for the flooding here in Venice?"

"That's what I read on *Russia Today*."

"And did you happen to read Alessandro Ricci's article in *La Repubblica* this morning?" The general plucked an enormous green olive from the bowl in the center of the table. "The chattering classes think Saviano's coalition might not survive."

"What a shame."

"They say a private audience with the wildly popular new pope would do wonders for his position."

"I wouldn't hold my breath."

"His Holiness might want to reconsider in light of the fact that he was in Florence the night that Swiss Guard was killed. If memory serves, you were there, too. And then there's that missing priest from the Order of St. Helena. His name escapes me."

"Father Graf."

"You wouldn't happen to know where he is, would you?"

"Not a clue," answered Gabriel truthfully.

"Perhaps someday you'll tell me how all the pieces of this affair fit together." The general ordered two more Bellinis and surveyed the interior of Harry's Bar. "They did a remarkable job with the repairs. You wouldn't even know there was a flood." He gave Gabriel a sidelong glance. "I suppose you'll get used to it."

"You've obviously been talking to Francesco Tiepolo."

Ferrari smiled. "He tells me you're going to be working for your wife soon."

"She hasn't accepted my terms yet."

"Do you think she might allow me to borrow you from time to time?"

"For what?"

"I'm in the business of recovering stolen paintings. And you, my friend, are very good at finding things."

"Except for the Gospel of Pilate."

"Ah, yes. The gospel." The general removed a manila folder from his briefcase and laid it on the table. "That sheet of paper you gave me was produced by a mill near Bologna. A small operation. One man, in fact. Very high quality. We've found numerous examples of his work in other cases."

"What kind of cases?"

"Forgeries." Ferrari opened the folder and removed the first page of the gospel. It was still encased in protective plastic. "It looks like it was produced during the Renaissance. In truth, it was manufactured a few months ago. Which means the Gospel of Pilate, the book that led to the murder of His Holiness Pope Paul the Seventh, is a fraud."

"How were you able to date it so precisely?"

"The papermaker is on my payroll. I paid him a visit after my lab delivered its findings." Ferrari tapped the page. "It was part of a large order of reproduction Renaissance paper. Several hundred sheets, in fact. The size was appropriate for bookbinding. It cost the buyer a small fortune."

"Who was he?"

"A priest, actually."

"Does the priest have a name?"

"Father Robert Jordan."

63

VENICE—ASSISI

IT HAD BEEN GABRIEL'S INTENTION to return to Israel the following morning on the ten o'clock El Al flight from Venice's Marco Polo Airport. He instructed Travel to book four seats on the evening flight from Rome instead. The car, a Volkswagen Passat, he saw to himself. They departed Venice at half past seven, a full thirty minutes later than he had hoped, and arrived in Assisi a few minutes after noon. With Chiara and the children at his side, he rang the bell at the Abbey of St. Peter. Receiving no answer, he rang it again.

At length, Don Simon, the English Benedictine, answered. "Good afternoon. May I help you?"

"I'm here to see Father Jordan."

"Is he expecting you?"

"No."

"Your name?"

"Gabriel Allon. I was here with—"

"I remember you. But why do you wish to see Father Jordan again?"

Gabriel crossed his fingers. "I was sent by the Holy Father. I'm afraid it's a matter of some urgency."

There was a silence of several seconds. Then the lock snapped open.

Gabriel looked at Chiara and smiled. "Membership has its privileges."

THE MONK LED THEM TO the common room overlooking the abbey's green garden. Ten minutes elapsed before he returned with Father Jordan. The American Jesuit did not appear pleased to see the friend of the new Roman pontiff.

At length, he looked at Don Simon. "Perhaps you should give Signore Allon's wife and children a tour of the grounds. They're really quite beautiful."

Chiara glanced at Gabriel, who nodded once. A moment later he and Father Jordan had the room to themselves.

"Are you really here at the behest of the Holy Father?" asked the priest.

"No."

"I admire your honesty."

"I wish I could say the same."

Father Jordan moved to the window. "How much of the story have you managed to piece together?"

"I know that almost everything you told us was a lie, beginning with your name. I also know that you recently took delivery of a large order of reproduction Renaissance paper, which you used to produce a book called the Gospel of Pilate. The question is, was the gospel a fraud? Or was it a copy of the original?"

"Do you have an opinion?"

"I'm betting it was a copy."

Father Jordan beckoned for Gabriel to join him at the window. Together they watched Chiara and the children walking along a garden path at the side of the Benedictine monk.

"You have a beautiful family, Mr. Allon. Every time I see Jewish children, I think they are a miracle."

"And when you see a Jesuit pope?"

"I see your handiwork." Father Jordan gave him a conspiratorial smile. "Shouldn't you be in Israel?"

"We're on our way to the airport."

"When is your flight?"

"Six o'clock."

Father Jordan looked down at the two small children playing in the garden. "In that case, Mr. Allon, I believe you have just enough time for one last story."

HE BEGAN BY TAKING ISSUE with Gabriel on a small but not insignificant point. His legal name, he said, was in fact Robert Jordan. His mother and father had changed the family name shortly after they arrived in America in 1939 as refugees from Europe. They chose an anglicized version of their real surname, which was the Italian word for the river that flows from the Northern Galilee to the Dead Sea.

"Giordano," said Gabriel.

Father Robert Jordan nodded. "My father was the son of a wealthy Roman businessman named Emanuele Giordano. One of three sons," he added pointedly. "My mother was from an old family called Delvecchio. The name is quite common among Italian Jews. I must admit, I thought my own name was rather dull in comparison. I considered changing it many times, especially when I moved to Italy to teach at the Gregoriana."

"How on earth did the child of two Jews become a Catholic priest?"

"My parents were never very religious, even when they lived in Rome. When they came to America, they masqueraded as Catholics in order to blend in with their surroundings. It wasn't difficult for them. As Romans, they were used to the rituals of Catholicism. But I was the real thing. I was baptized and received my First Communion. I even served as an altar boy in our parish church. I can only imagine what my poor parents were thinking when they saw me up there in my little vestments."

"How did they react when you told them you wanted to become a priest?"

"My father could scarcely look at me in my cassock and Roman collar."

"Why didn't he tell you the truth?"

"Guilt, I suppose."

"At having forsaken his faith?"

"My father never abandoned his faith," said Father Jordan. "Even when he was pretending to be a Catholic. He was guilty because he and my mother had survived the war. They didn't want me to know that their relatives weren't so lucky. They were ensnared in the Rome roundup in October 1943 and sent to Auschwitz, where they were murdered. All without a word of protest from the Holy Father, despite the fact that it took place under his very windows."

"And you became a Catholic priest."

"Imagine that."

"When did you learn the truth?"

"It wasn't until November 1989, when I returned to Boston to attend my father's funeral. After the service, my mother gave me a letter he had written after I went off to the seminary. Obviously, it came as quite a shock. Not only was I Jewish, I was a surviving remnant of a family that had perished in the Holocaust."

"Did you ever consider renouncing your vows?"

"Of course."

"Why didn't you?"

"I decided I could be both a Christian and a Jew. After all, Jesus was a Jew. So were the twelve apostles whose statues stand guard over the portico of the basilica. Twelve apostles," he repeated. "One each for the twelve tribes of Israel. The original Christians didn't see themselves as founders of a new faith. They were Jews who were also Jesus followers. I saw myself in a similar light."

"Do you still believe in the divinity of Jesus?"

"I'm not sure I ever did. But neither did they. They believed Jesus was a man who had been exalted into heaven, not a supreme being who had been sent to earth. All that came much later, after the Gospels had been written and the early Church settled on Christianity's orthodoxy. That was when the great sibling rivalry began. The Church Fathers declared that the covenant between God and his chosen people had been broken, that the old law had been replaced by the new. God had sent his son to save the world, and the Jews had rejected him. Then, for good measure, they had cleverly maneuvered a gullible and blameless Roman prefect into nailing him to a cross. For such a people, the murderers of God himself, no punishment was too severe."

"They were your people," said Gabriel.

"Which is why I made it my life's work to heal the wounds between Judaism and Christianity."

"By finding the Gospel of Pilate?"

Father Jordan nodded.

"I assume your father's letter contained a reference to it."

"He wrote about it in considerable detail."

"And that story you told Donati and me the other day? The one about you wandering the length and breadth of Italy searching for the last copy of the Gospel of Pilate?"

"It was just that. A story. I knew that Father Schiller gave the book to Pius the Twelfth, and that Pius buried it deep in the Archives."

"How?"

"I confronted Father Schiller not long before he died. At first, he tried to deny the book's existence. But when I showed him my father's letter, he told me the truth."

"Did you tell him—"

"That I was the grandson of the wealthy Roman Jew who had given the book to the Order?" Father Jordan shook his head. "Much to my everlasting shame, I did not."

"Did you really try to find it? Or was that a story, too?"

"No," said Father Jordan. "I searched the Archives for more than twenty years. Because there's no reference to the gospel in the Index Rooms, it was a bit like looking for the proverbial needle in a haystack. About ten years ago, I forced myself to stop. That book was ruining my life."

"And then?"

"Someone gave it to the Holy Father. And the Holy Father decided to give it to you."

64

ABBEY OF ST. PETER, ASSISI

A T FIRST, HE THOUGHT IT was a practical joke. Yes, the voice on the phone sounded like the Holy Father's, but surely it couldn't really be him. He wanted Father Jordan to come to the papal apartments the following evening at half past nine. Father Jordan was to tell no one of the summons. Nor was he to arrive even a minute early.

"I assume it was a Thursday," said Gabriel.

"How did you know?"

Gabriel smiled and with a movement of his hand invited Father Jordan to continue. He arrived at the papal apartment, he said, at the stroke of nine thirty. A household nun escorted him to the private chapel. The Holy Father greeted him warmly, refusing to allow him to kiss the Ring of the Fisherman, and then showed him a most remarkable book.

"Did Lucchesi know of your personal connection to the gospel?"

"No," said Father Jordan. "And I never told him about it. It was my personal connection to Donati that was important. The Holy Father trusted me. It was just a stroke of dumb luck."

"I assume he allowed you to read it."

"Of course. That's why I was there. He wanted my opinion as to its authenticity."

"And?"

"The text was lucid, at times bureaucratic, and granular in its detail. It was not the work of a creative mind. It was an important historical document based on the written or spoken recollections of its nominal author."

"What happened next?"

"He invited me back the following Thursday. Once again, Donati was absent. Dinner with a friend, apparently. Outside the walls. That was when the Holy Father told me that he planned to give the book to you." He paused, then added, "Without informing the *prefetto* of the Vatican Secret Archives."

"Did he know Albanese was a secret member of the Order of St. Helena?"

"He suspected as much."

"Which is why Lucchesi asked you to make a copy of the book."

Father Jordan smiled. "Rather ingenious, don't you think?"

"Did you do the work yourself, or did you utilize the services of a professional?"

"A little of both. I was a rather talented illustrator and calligrapher when I was young. Not like you, of course. But I wasn't bad. The professional, who shall remain nameless, handled the artificial aging of the paper and the binding. It was an extraordinary piece of work. Cardinal Albanese would never have been able to tell the difference. Not unless he subjected the volume to sophisticated tests."

"But which version of the gospel did he remove from the papal apartments the night of the Holy Father's murder?"

"It was the copy," answered Father Jordan. "I have the original. The Holy Father gave it to me for safekeeping in case something happened to him."

"That book belongs to me now."

"It belonged to my grandfather before it was taken from him by the Order. Therefore, I am the rightful owner, just as Isabel Feldman was the rightful owner of that painting that magically resurfaced last weekend." Father Jordan scrutinized him for a moment. "I suppose you had something to do with that, too."

Gabriel made no reply.

"It never goes away, does it?"

"What's that?"

"The survivor's guilt. It gets passed down from generation to generation. Like those green eyes of yours."

"They were my mother's eyes."

"Was she in one of the camps?"

"Birkenau."

"Then you are a miracle, too." Father Jordan patted the back of Gabriel's hand. "I'm afraid there is a straight line between the teachings of the early Church and the gas chambers and crematoria of Auschwitz. To maintain otherwise is to engage in what Thomas Aquinas called an *ignorantia affectata*. A willful ignorance."

"Perhaps you should put it to rest once and for all."

"And how would I do that?"

"By giving me that book."

Father Jordan shook his head. "Making it public will accomplish nothing. In fact, given the current climate here in Europe and America, it might make matters worse."

"Are you forgetting that your former student is now the pope?"

"His Holiness has enough problems to deal with. The last thing he needs is a challenge to the core beliefs of Christianity."

"What does the book say?"

Father Jordan was silent.

"Please," said Gabriel. "I must know."

He contemplated his sunbaked hands. "One central element of the Passion narratives is undeniable. A Jew from the village of Nazareth named Jesus was put to death by the Roman prefect on or about the holiday of Passover, in perhaps the year 33 C.E. Much else of what was written in the four Gospels must be taken with a cartload of salt. The accounts are literary invention or, worse, a deliberate effort on the part of the evangelists and early Church to implicate the Jews in the death of Jesus while simultaneously exculpating the real culprits."

"Pontius Pilate and the Romans."

Father Jordan nodded.

"For example?"

"The trial before the Sanhedrin."

"Did it happen?"

"In the middle of the night during Passover?" Father Jordan shook his head. "Such a gathering would have been forbidden by the Laws of Moses. Only a Christian living in Rome could have concocted something so outlandish."

"Was Caiaphas involved in any way?"

"If he was, Pilate makes no mention of it."

"What about the tribunal?"

"If that's what you want to call it," said Father Jordan. "It was very brief. Pilate barely looked at him. In fact, he claimed not to be able to recall Jesus' physical appearance. He merely jotted a note for his files and waved his hand, and the soldiers got on with it. Many other good Jews were executed that day. As far as Pilate was concerned, it was business as usual."

"Was there a crowd present?"

"Heavens, no."

"What was the charge against Jesus?"

"The only crime punishable by crucifixion."

"Insurrection."

"Of course."

"Where did the incident take place?"

"The Royal Portico of the Temple."

"And the arrest?"

The bells of Assisi tolled two o'clock before Father Jordan could answer. "I've told you too much already. Besides, you and your family have a plane to catch." He rose and extended his hand. "God bless you, Mr. Allon. And safe travels."

There were footfalls outside in the corridor. A moment later Chiara and the children appeared in the doorway, accompanied by the Benedictine monk.

"Perfect timing," said Father Jordan. "Don Simon will show you out."

THE MONK SAW THEM INTO the street and then quickly closed the gate. Gabriel stood there for a moment afterward, his hand hovering over the intercom, until Irene finally tugged at his sleeve and looked up at him with the face of his mother.

"What's wrong, Abba? Why are you crying?"

"I was thinking about something sad, that's all."

"What?"

You, thought Gabriel. *I was thinking about you.*

He lifted the child into his arms and carried her through the Porta San Pietro to the parking garage where he had left the car. After buckling Raphael's seat belt, he searched the undercarriage more carefully than usual before finally climbing behind the wheel.

"Try starting the engine," said Chiara. "It helps."

Gabriel's hand shook as he pressed the button.

"Maybe I should drive."

"I'm fine."

"Are you sure about that?"

He reversed out of the space and followed the ramp to the surface. The only road out of the city took them past the Porta San Pietro. Framed by the archway, like a figure in a Bellini, was a white-haired priest, an old leather satchel in his hand.

Gabriel slammed on the brakes and climbed out. Father Jordan offered him the bag as though it contained a bomb. "Be careful, Mr. Allon. Everything is at stake."

Gabriel embraced the old priest and hurried back to the car. Chiara opened the satchel as they sped down the slopes of Monte Subasio. Inside was the last copy of the Gospel of Pilate.

"Can you read it?" he asked.

"I have a master's degree in the history of the Roman Empire. I think I can handle a few lines of Latin."

"What does it say?"

She read the first two sentences aloud. "Solus ego sum reus mortis ejus. Ego crimen oportet."

"Translate it."

"I alone am responsible for his death. I alone must bear the guilt." She looked up. "Shall I keep going?"

"No," he said. "That's enough."

Chiara returned the book to the satchel. "What do you suppose normal people do on vacation?"

"We are normal people." Gabriel laughed. "We just have interesting friends."

AUTHOR'S NOTE

THE ORDER IS A WORK of entertainment and should be read as nothing more. The names, characters, places, and incidents portrayed in the story are the product of the author's imagination or have been used fictitiously. Any resemblance to actual persons, living or dead, businesses, companies, events, or locales is entirely coincidental.

Visitors to Munich will search in vain for the headquarters of a German conglomerate known as the Wolf Group, for no such company exists. Nor will one find a restaurant and jazz bar in the Beethovenplatz called Café Adagio. Thankfully, there is no far-right German political party known as the National Democrats, but there are several like it, including the Alternative for Germany, now the third-largest party in Germany, with ninety-four seats in the Bundestag. BfV chief Hans-Georg Maassen faced calls for his resignation in 2018 over accusations that he harbored extremist political views himself and was quietly working to assist the Alternative for Germany's rise to power.

There is no restricted section of the Vatican Secret Archives known as the *collezione*, at least not one I uncovered during my research. Deepest apologies to the *prefetto* for shutting down his power supply and security system, but I'm afraid there was no other way for Gabriel and Luigi Donati to enter the Manuscript Depository undetected. They could not have been given the first page of the Gospel of Pilate, because such a book does not exist. The other apocryphal gospels mentioned in *The Order* are accurately depicted, as are the words of early Church figures such as Origen, Tertullian, and Justin Martyr.

It was Cardinal Tarcisio Bertone who undertook an ambitious renovation of two apartments in the Palazzo San Carlo to create a 6,500-square-foot luxury flat with a rooftop terrace. But Bertone's dwelling was a hovel compared to the palace in Limburg, Germany, that Bishop Franz-Peter Tebartz-van Elst, the so-called Bishop of Bling, renovated at a reported cost of $40 million. In May 2012, Ettore Gotti Tedeschi was removed as president of the Vatican Bank in connection with the sex-and-money scandal that became known as Vati-Leaks. An internal Vatican dossier on the rampant corruption of senior Church officials reportedly influenced the 2013 conclave that elected Pope Francis. The Vatican Secretariat of State condemned the media's pre-conclave reporting on the scandal as an attempt to interfere in the selection of the next supreme pontiff.

Former cardinal Theodore McCarrick of Washington, DC, reportedly funneled more than $600,000 from a little-known archdiocese account to friends and benefactors at the Vatican, including popes John Paul II and Benedict XVI. The *Washington*

Post found that several of the Vatican bureaucrats who received money were directly involved in assessing allegations of sexual misconduct leveled against McCarrick, which included accusations that he solicited sex while hearing confessions. An Episcopal Conference of Switzerland report released in July 2018 found a startling increase in *new* accusations of sexual abuse against Swiss priests. It is little wonder that Swiss Catholics, including my fictitious Christoph Bittel, have turned their backs on the Church in droves.

There is indeed a Catholic fraternity based in the Swiss village of Menzingen, but it is not the fictitious Order of St. Helena. It is the Society of St. Pius X, or SSPX, the reactionary, anti-Semitic order founded in 1970 by Bishop Marcel-François Lefebvre. Bishop Lefebvre was the son of a wealthy French factory owner who supported the restoration of France's monarchy. During World War II, then–Father Lefebvre was an unapologetic supporter of the Vichy regime of Marshal Philippe Pétain, which collaborated with the SS in the destruction of France's Jews. Paul Touvier, a senior officer in the notorious Vichy militia known as the Milice, found sanctuary at an SSPX priory in Nice after the war. Arrested in 1989, Touvier was the first Frenchman to be convicted of crimes against humanity.

Not surprisingly, Bishop Lefebvre also expressed support for Jean-Marie Le Pen, leader of France's far-right National Front and a convicted Holocaust denier. Monsieur Le Pen shared that distinction with Richard Williamson, one of four SSPX priests whom Lefebvre elevated to the rank of bishop in 1988 in defiance of a direct order from Pope John Paul II. Williamson, who is British, routinely referred to Jews as "the enemies of Christ" whose goal was world domination. While serving as rector of the SSPX's North American seminary in Winona, Minnesota, Williamson declared: "There was not one Jew killed in the gas chambers. It was all lies, lies, lies." He was expelled from the Society of St. Pius X in 2012, but not for his anti-Semitic views. The SSPX called his removal a "painful decision."

By the time of his death in 1991, Bishop Lefebvre was a doctrinal outcast and something of an embarrassment. But during the 1930s, as storm clouds gathered over Europe's Jews, a prelate who espoused views similar to Lefebvre's would have found himself largely in the Catholic mainstream. The Church's preference for monarchies and right-wing dictators over socialists or even liberal democrats has been painstakingly documented, along with the appalling anti-Semitism of many of the Vatican's leading spokesmen and policymakers. While few Catholic clerics supported the physical elimination of Jews from European society, the Vatican newspaper *L'Osservatore Romano* and the Jesuit journal *La Civiltà Cattolica* cheered laws—in Hungary, for example—that purged Jews from professions such as the law, medicine, banking, and journalism. When Benito Mussolini enacted similar restrictions in Italy in 1938, the men of the Vatican could muster scarcely a word of protest. "The terrible truth," wrote historian Susan Zuccotti in her remarkable study of the Holocaust in Italy, *Under His Very Windows*, "was that they wanted the Jews put in their place."

That was certainly true of Bishop Alois Hudal, rector of the Austrian-German church in Rome. It was Bishop Hudal, not my fictitious Father Schiller, who wrote a viciously anti-Semitic book in 1936 that tried to reconcile Catholicism and National Socialism. In the copy he sent to Adolf Hitler, Hudal penned an adulatory inscription: "To the architect of German greatness."

432

An Austrian national who was said to be obsessed with Jews, Bishop Hudal moved about Rome throughout the war in a chauffeured car that flew the flag of Greater Germany. Two and a half years after the Allied victory, he hosted a Christmas party attended by hundreds of Nazi war criminals living in Rome under his protection. With Hudal's help, many would find sanctuary in South America. Adolf Eichmann received assistance from Bishop Hudal, as did Franz Stangl, the commandant of the Treblinka extermination camp. All with the knowledge and tacit support of Pope Pius XII, who believed such monsters to be a valuable asset in the global fight against Soviet communism.

Pius's critics and apologists have engaged in a decades-long quarrel over his failure to explicitly condemn the Holocaust and warn Europe's Jews about the death camps. But his indefensible support of wanted Nazi mass murderers is perhaps the clearest evidence of his innate hostility toward Jews. Pius opposed the Nuremberg Trials, opposed the creation of a Jewish state, and opposed postwar attempts to reconcile Christianity with the faith from which it had sprung. He excommunicated every Communist on earth in 1949 but never took a similar step against members of the Nazi Party or the murderous SS. Nor did he ever explicitly express remorse over the death of six million Jews in the Holocaust.

The process of Jewish-Christian reconciliation would therefore have to wait until Pius's death in 1958. His successor, Pope John XXIII, took extraordinary steps to protect Jews during World War II while serving as papal nuncio in Istanbul, including issuing them lifesaving false passports. He was old when the Ring of the Fisherman was placed on his finger, and sadly his reign was brief. Not long before his death in 1963, he was asked whether there was anything to be done about the devastating portrayal of Pius XII in Rolf Hochhuth's searing play *The Deputy*. "Do against it?" the incredulous pope reportedly replied. "What does one do against the truth?"

The culmination of John XXIII's bid to repair relations between Catholics and Jews in the wake of the Holocaust was the milestone declaration of the Second Vatican Council known as *Nostra Aetate*. Opposed by many Church conservatives, it declared that Jews were not collectively responsible for the death of Jesus or eternally cursed by God. The great historical tragedy is that such a statement had to be issued in the first place. But for nearly two thousand years, the Church taught that Jews as a people were guilty of deicide, the very murder of God. "The blood of Jesus," wrote Origen, "falls not only on the Jews of that time, but on all generations of Jews up to the end of the world." Pope Innocent III wholeheartedly agreed. "Their words— 'May his blood be on us and our children'—have brought inherited guilt upon the entire nation, which follows them as a curse where they live and work, when they are born and when they die." Were such words spoken today, they would rightly be branded as hate speech.

The ancient Christian charge of deicide is universally regarded by scholars as the foundation of anti-Semitism. And yet the Second Vatican Council, when issuing its historic repudiation, could not resist including the following seventeen words: "True, authorities of the Jews and those who followed their lead pressed for the death of Christ." But what source did the bishops use to justify such an unequivocal declaration about an event that took place in a remote corner of the Roman Empire nearly two thousand years earlier? The answer, of course, was that they relied on the accounts of Jesus' death contained in the four Gospels of the New Testament—the very source of the vicious slander they were at long last disavowing.

Needless to say, the Second Vatican Council did not suggest excising the inflammatory passages from the Christian canon. But *Nostra Aetate* nevertheless set in motion a scholarly reappraisal of the canonical Gospels that is reflected in the pages of *The Order*. Christians who believe in biblical inerrancy will no doubt take issue with my description of who the evangelists were and how their Gospels came to be written. Most biblical scholars would not.

No original draft of any of the four canonical Gospels survives, only fragments of later copies. It is widely accepted by scholars that none of the Gospels, with the possible exception of Luke, were written by the men for whom they are named. It was the Apostolic Father Papias of Hierapolis who in the second century provided the earliest extant account of their authorship. And it was Irenaeus, the heresy-hunting leader of the early Church in France, who declared that only four of the many gospels then in circulation were authentic. "And this is obviously true," he wrote, "because there are four corners of the universe and there are four principal winds." Paul Johnson, in his monumental history of Christianity, asserted that Irenaeus "knew no more about the origins of the Gospels than we do; rather less, in fact."

Johnson went on to describe the Gospels as "literary documents" that bear evidence of later tampering, editing, rewriting, and interpolation and backdating of theological concepts. Bart D. Ehrman, the distinguished professor of religious studies at the University of North Carolina, contends they are riddled with "discrepancies, embellishments, made-up stories, and historical problems" that mean "they cannot be taken at face value as giving us historically accurate accounts of what really happened." The Gospels' depiction of Jesus' arrest and execution, says Ehrman, "must be taken with a pound of salt."

Numerous critical biblical scholars and contemporary historians have concluded that the evangelists and their editors in the early Church consciously shifted the blame for Jesus' death from the Romans to the Jews in order to make Christianity more appealing to gentiles living under Roman rule and less threatening to the Romans themselves. The two primary elements utilized by the Gospel writers to blame Jews for the death of Jesus are the trial before the Sanhedrin and, of course, the tribunal before Pontius Pilate.

The four canonical Gospels each give a slightly different account of the encounter, but it is perhaps most illuminative to compare Mark's version to Matthew's. In Mark, Pilate reluctantly sentences Jesus to death at the urging of a Jewish crowd. But in Matthew the crowd has suddenly become "the whole people." Pilate washes his hands in front of them and declares himself innocent of Jesus' blood. To which "the whole people" reply, "Let his blood be on us and our children!"

So which version is accurate? Did "the whole people" really shout such an outlandish line without a single dissenting voice, or not? And what about Pilate washing his hands? Did it happen? After all, it is no small detail. Obviously, both accounts cannot be correct. If one is right, the other is necessarily *wrong*. Some might argue that Matthew is simply *more* right than Mark, but this is an evasion. A reporter who made such a mistake would surely have been reprimanded by his editor, if not fired on the spot.

The most plausible explanation is that the entire scene is a literary invention. The same is likely the case for the Gospels' inflammatory accounts of Jesus' appearance before the Sanhedrin. Religious scholar Reza Aslan, in his riveting biography of Jesus titled *Zealot*, asserts that the problems with the Gospels' accounts of a Sanhedrin trial "are too numerous to count." The late Raymond Brown, a Catholic priest who was widely regarded as the greatest New Testament scholar of the late twentieth century, found twenty-seven discrepancies between the Gospels' accounts of the trial and rabbinic law. Boston University professor Paula Fredriksen, in her landmark *Jesus of Nazareth, King of the Jews*, likewise questions the veracity of the Sanhedrin trial. "Between their duties at the Temple and their festive meals at home, these men would have put in a long day already; and besides, what need?" Fredriksen is equally skeptical that there was a tribunal before the Roman prefect. "Perhaps Jesus was interrogated briefly by Pilate, though this, too, is unlikely. There was no point." Aslan is more definitive on the question of an appearance before Pilate. "No trial was held. No trial was necessary."

There is perhaps no more compelling voice on this subject than John Dominic Crossan, the professor emeritus of religious studies at DePaul University and a former ordained priest. In *Who Killed Jesus?*, he asks whether the Gospels' incendiary depiction of the tribunal before Pilate was "a scene of Roman history" or "Christian propaganda." He answered the question, in part, with the following passage: "However explicable its origins, defensible its invectives, and understandable its motives among Christians fighting for survival, its repetition has now become the longest lie, and, for our own integrity, we Christians must at last name it as such."

But why revisit the tortured history of Christianity's relationship with Judaism? Because the longest hatred—the hatred born of the Gospels' depiction of the Crucifixion—has risen again, violently. So, too, has a brand of racially based political extremism that apologists refer to as "populism." The two phenomena are undeniably linked. For proof, look no further than the 2017 Unite the Right rally in Charlottesville, Virginia, where white nationalists protesting the removal of a Confederate memorial chanted "Jews will not replace us!" as they marched by torchlight and snapped off stiff-armed Nazi salutes. Or the Tree of Life Synagogue in the Squirrel Hill neighborhood of Pittsburgh, where a white nationalist angry over Hispanic immigration murdered eleven Jews and wounded six more. Why did the gunman target Jews? Could it be that he was gripped by an irrational hatred even more powerful than his resentment of brown-skinned migrants looking for a better life in America?

The brilliant economist Paul Krugman of the *New York Times* made the connection between the simultaneous rise of anti-Semitism and race-based populism in the same column that produced the quotation that appears in the epigraph of this work. "Most of us, I think, know that whenever bigotry runs free, we're likely to be among its victims." Unfortunately, the outbreak of a global pandemic, coupled with a sharp economic downturn, is likely to make matters worse. In the darkest corners of the Internet, Jews are being blamed for the pandemic, just as they were blamed for the Black Death in the fourteenth century.

"Never forget," Rabbi Jacob Zolli tells Gabriel during the opening scenes of *The Order*, "the unimaginable can happen." The outbreak of a global pandemic would seem to bear that out. But even before the Covid-19 crisis, anti-Semitism in Europe had risen to a level not seen since the middle of the last century. To their credit, Western European political leaders have roundly condemned the resurgence of anti-Semitism. So, too, has Pope Francis. He has also questioned the morality of unfettered capitalism, called for action on climate change, defended the rights of immigrants, and warned of the dangers posed by the rise of the European far right, which regards him as a mortal enemy. If only a prelate like Francis had been wearing the Ring of the Fisherman in 1939. The history of the Jews, and the Roman Catholic Church, might well have been written differently.

ACKNOWLEDGMENTS

I AM ETERNALLY GRATEFUL TO MY wife, Jamie Gangel, who served as my sounding board while I worked out the details and structure of a complex plot involving the murder of a pope, the discovery of a long-suppressed gospel, and a conspiracy by the European far right to seize control of the Roman Catholic Church. When I finished my first draft, she made three crucial suggestions and then skillfully edited my final typescript, all while covering the impeachment of a president for CNN and caring for our family during a global pandemic. I share many traits with my protagonist, Gabriel Allon, including the fact we are both married to perfect women. My debt to Jamie is immeasurable, as is my love.

I had hoped to finish *The Order* in Rome but was forced to cancel my travel plans when the coronavirus ravaged Italy. Having written two previous Vatican thrillers, and several others with scenes set in or around the Vatican, I have formed many cherished friendships with men and women who work behind the walls of the world's smallest country. I have stood in the lobby of the Swiss Guard barracks, shopped in the Vatican pharmacy and supermarket, visited the conservation labs of the Vatican Museums, opened the door of the stove in the Sistine Chapel, and attended a Mass celebrated by the Holy Father. I wish to express my gratitude to Father Mark Haydu, who was an invaluable resource throughout the writing process, and to the matchless John L. Allen, who literally wrote the book on how a conclave works. For the record, neither influenced my depiction of the anti-Jewish nature of the Gospel accounts of Jesus' death.

I am forever indebted to David Bull and Patrick Matthiesen for their advice on restoration and art history, and for their friendship. Louis Toscano, my dear friend and longtime editor, made countless improvements to the novel, as did Kathy Crosby, my eagle-eyed personal copy editor. Any typographical errors that slipped through their formidable gauntlet are my responsibility, not theirs.

I consulted hundreds of newspaper and magazine articles while writing *The Order*, along with dozens of books. I would be remiss if I did not mention the following: Ann Wroe, *Pontius Pilate*; James Carroll, *Constantine's Sword: The Church and the Jews*; Paul Johnson, *A History of Christianity*; Paula Fredriksen, *Jesus of Nazareth, King of the Jews: A Jewish Life and the Emergence of Christianity* and *From Jesus to Christ: The Origins of the New Testament Images of Jesus*; John Dominic Crossan, *Who Killed Jesus?: Exposing the Roots of Anti-Semitism in the Gospel Story of the Death of Jesus*; Reza Aslan, *Zealot: The Life and Times of Jesus of Nazareth*; Bart D. Ehrman, *How Jesus Became God: The*

Exaltation of a Jewish Preacher from Galilee; Bart D. Ehrman and Zlatko Pleše, *The Apocryphal Gospels: Text and Translations*; Robert S. Wistrich, *Antisemitism: The Longest Hatred*; Daniel Jonah Goldhagen, *A Moral Reckoning: The Role of the Catholic Church in the Holocaust and Its Unfulfilled Duty of Repair* and *Hitler's Willing Executioners: Ordinary Germans and the Holocaust*; John Cornwell, *Hitler's Pope: The Secret History of Pius XII* and *A Thief in the Night: Life and Death in the Vatican*; Michael Phayer, *The Catholic Church and the Holocaust, 1930–1965* and *Pius XII, the Holocaust, and the Cold War*; Susan Zuccotti, *Under His Very Windows: The Vatican and the Holocaust in Italy*; David I. Kertzer, *The Popes Against the Jews: The Vatican's Role in the Rise of Modern Anti-Semitism*; Uki Goñi, *The Real Odessa: Smuggling the Nazis to Perón's Argentina*; John Follain, *City of Secrets: The Truth Behind the Murders at the Vatican*; Carl Bernstein and Marco Politi, *His Holiness: John Paul II and the History of Our Time*; John L. Allen Jr., *Conclave: The Politics, Personalities, and Process of the Next Papal Election*; Thomas J. Reese, *Inside the Vatican: The Politics and Organization of the Catholic Church*; Frederic J. Baumgartner, *Behind Locked Doors: A History of Papal Elections*; and Gianluigi Nuzzi, *Merchants in the Temple: Inside Pope Francis's Secret Battle Against Corruption in the Vatican*.

We are blessed with family and friends who fill our lives with love and laughter at critical times during the writing year, especially Jeff Zucker, Phil Griffin, Andrew Lack, Noah Oppenheim, Susan St. James and Dick Ebersol, Elsa Walsh and Bob Woodward, Michael Gendler, Ron Meyer, Jane and Burt Bacharach, Stacey and Henry Winkler, Kitty Pilgrim and Maurice Tempelsman, Donna and Michael Bass, Virginia Moseley and Tom Nides, Nancy Dubuc and Michael Kizilbash, Susanna Aaron and Gary Ginsburg, Cindi and Mitchell Berger, Andy Lassner, Marie Brennan and Ernie Pomerantz, and Peggy Noonan.

A heartfelt thanks to the remarkable team at HarperCollins, who managed to publish a book under circumstances no thriller writer could have imagined. I am especially indebted to Brian Murray, Jonathan Burnham, Jennifer Barth, Doug Jones, Leah Wasielewski, Mark Ferguson, Leslie Cohen, Robin Bilardello, Milan Bozic, Frank Albanese, Josh Marwell, David Koral, Leah Carlson-Stanisic, Carolyn Bodkin, Chantal Restivo-Alessi, Julianna Wojcik, Mark Meneses, Sarah Ried, Beth Silfin, Lisa Erickson, and Amy Baker.

Lastly, the outbreak of the deadly coronavirus required my children, Lily and Nicholas, to once again live under the same roof with me as I struggled to complete this novel before its deadline. For that, I am grateful, though I'm not sure they would say the same. Like many young American professionals, they teleworked from their childhood rooms during the lockdown. I enjoyed occasionally dropping in unannounced on their video conference calls. Their presence was a source of great comfort, joy, and inspiration. They, too, are miracles, in more ways than one.

ABOUT THE AUTHOR

Daniel Silva is the award-winning, #1 *New York Times* best-selling author of *The Unlikely Spy, The Mark of the Assassin, The Marching Season, The Kill Artist, The English Assassin, The Confessor, A Death in Vienna, Prince of Fire, The Messenger, The Secret Servant, Moscow Rules, The Defector, The Rembrandt Affair, Portrait of a Spy, The Fallen Angel, The English Girl, The Heist, The English Spy, The Black Widow, House of Spies, The Other Woman,* and *The New Girl.* He is best known for his long-running thriller series starring spy and art restorer Gabriel Allon. Silva's books are critically acclaimed bestsellers around the world and have been translated into more than thirty languages. He resides in Florida with his wife, television journalist Jamie Gangel, and their twins, Lily and Nicholas. For more information, visit www.danielsilvabooks.com.